THE COMPLETE DARKNESS COLLECTION

REFUGE INC., BOOK 1-3

Leslie Lee Sanders

LLS BOOKS
QUEEN CREEK, ARIZONA

Leslie Lee Sanders/LLS Books
Queen Creek, Arizona
www.leslieleesanders.com

Publisher's Note: This is a work of fiction. Names, characters, places, and incidents are a product of the author's imagination. Locales and public names are sometimes used for atmospheric purposes. Any resemblance to actual people, living or dead, or to businesses, companies, events, institutions, or locales is completely coincidental.

Book Layout ©2013 BookDesignTemplates.com

Cover Design: Mina Carter

The Complete Darkness Collection/ Leslie Lee Sanders. -- 1st edition.
ISBN-13: 978-0615873961 (LLS Books)
ISBN-10: 0615873960

Dedicated to those struggling with their very own darkness.

"I would hurl words into this darkness and wait for an echo, and if an echo sounded, no matter how faintly, I would send other words to tell, to march, to fight, to create a sense of the hunger for life that gnaws in us all."

—RICHARD WRIGHT

Table of Contents

Before the Darkness i

Companions 1

Escaping Reality 13

The Journey 33

Denial 49

Search for Refuge 57

Back on Track 73

Close Encounters 81

Dust to Dust 97

Refuge or Rescue 101

Now or Never 113

Death's Landfill 123

Lying for Gain 131

Between the Lines 141

Amid the Darkness 149

Prologue 151

Adjusting to Insanity 155

Revisiting Trust 167

Rekindling the Flame 177

Contradicting Emotions 187
The Plan 197
Moving Up 207
Stumbling Upon Truth 217
Revelations 227
The Truth 237
Keycard 247
Confronting the Truth 259
Hide and Seek 267
On the Run 279
Playing it Safe 289
Into the Night 299
Beyond the Darkness 311
Prologue 313
Expressions 315
On the Road Again 325
Encounters 331
On a Quest 339
A Helping Hand 345
Upon Approach 355
Breaking and Entering 365
Cleansing 373
Down Below 389
Surprises 399

Answers....405
A Losing Battle....415
Separation....427
Letting Go....437
Epilogue....449
Darkness Eternal....455

ABOUT THE AUTHOR....457

BEFORE THE
DARKNESS

REFUGE INC., BOOK 1

Leslie Lee Sanders

LLS BOOKS
QUEEN CREEK, ARIZONA

CHAPTER ONE

Companions

Damn the sun's heat, damn the sour taste of blood in Elliot's mouth and damn the asteroid that rudely interrupted his perfect life.

The sun beat down on him hotter than he knew was possible, like Satan's tongue licking at his neck. He never expected to live to see the sun or to feel its blazing heat. However, two days passed since impact and here he was, drained from intense dry heat and little food. Despite the devastation, he had survived—was possibly the only one.

Walking for the past twelve hours had helped him keep his mind off of the deep-rooted feeling of doom. Were there other earthquake survivors? He had no idea, but his optimism had been high following the last unexpected quake that had violently shaken the city. His city. If he lived by merely hiding in the basement of his house, then there had to be others out there alive as well. He just had to find them.

Glass and metal fragments from the surrounding neighborhood homes and offices crunched beneath his feet with every sluggish step. His pace had slowed over the past twelve hours considerably, however he pushed himself to keep moving, searching no matter how drained he felt. He must continue. No excuses.

There had to be other people, someone who could give him the relief he so desperately sought. What he would give for a little communication, affection, assurance; just some of the human necessities he needed to gather his strength. After twelve hours of listening to nothing but the strong wind, the crunch of debris beneath his feet and his own pained voice, it wouldn't be too long before he started going crazy. Perhaps he feared that the most.

A mound of twisted metal, splintered wood and shattered concrete blocks beckoned him to rest. Hell, it could've been a roaring mountain of fire instead. He'd still stop there and rest a while. It had to be thirst and dehydration that were slowing him down. His body craved liquid refreshment. His tongue stuck to the top of his mouth and his busted lip as he tried to lick at the irritated cut to moisten it. He took an invigorating sip of water from his twenty ounce bottle, the one he found sealed during his trek. Only about eight ounces of water remained which was another problem he would soon need to address. He chuckled as he looked across the mangled Arizona desert.

"Where the hell am I going?" He had no idea where his trek had led him or where he would end up, but he grinned like a maniac and peered as far west as his eyes would allow. His hand went up to shield his eyes from the slowly setting sun while memories flooded his head of what used to stand tall and proud but now were toppled over and in ruins thanks to Mother Nature. For some unknown reason, this tickled him somewhere deep inside. He laughed involuntarily maybe out of sheer desperation; chest heaving as he chuckled like a fool who'd just heard the funniest joke ever told. Laughing seemed odd ... yet reasonable. What else would a madman do?

White smoke billowed from piles of rubble where small fires had once been. Far in the distance, what appeared to be a lone brown dog limped away in the opposite direction. Some of the abandoned vehicles that littered the deserted street were crushed under the weight of massive dislocated palm trees that were once snuggly planted for beautiful landscaped scenery. Even with all the destruction surrounding him, he continued to laugh.

"The beginning of insanity, huh?" He shook his head, still with a smile on his swollen lips. "No, the beginning was the first time I started talking to myself."

He took another sip and sighed, allowing the warm water to coat his lips and tongue with a welcomed layer of moisture that seemed to evaporate seconds after contact.

Suddenly, his breath escaped him in a huff. The horrible sight before him triggered panic to grip him in the pit of the stomach. A small, lifeless body, probably of a child, lay pinned halfway beneath a wide wooden panel in a rubble pile. The long, curly blonde hair that stuck out from beneath the panel led him to suspect the body was that of a little girl. Gulping didn't stop his heart from nearly beating out of his chest, it only added to the weird drumming in his veins. He had no urge to investigate. She was dead. He knew that from the amount of dried, rusty-colored blood soaked in her hair and the gravel around her. She was...dead.

He moved his palm across his chest and let it hover over the insane pounding. Seeing the little girl reminded him how alone he was in a ruined world. However, he couldn't dwell on it. Doing so would just cause him to panic. He continued walking west guided by the setting sun. He tried to remain strong and determined, but he could feel that power slowly slipping away. During his entire twelve-hour hike, he had not seen one dead body and hoped he wouldn't. In all truth, the thought of seeing the dead never crossed his mind. He knew most of his neighbors evacuated the city a couple days before the impact.

Also knowing the Texas-sized asteroid was supposed to impact somewhere near the west coast had given him hope that his family in Georgia was safe. He guessed the asteroid touched down probably overseas. If it would've hit the west coast as everyone feared, wouldn't Arizona be completely obliterated? Either way, hope for his family's wellbeing dissipated when those six massive earthquakes rolled through one after the other. The last quake was so powerful it destroyed his beloved neighborhood and all that he'd grown familiar with. There was no doubt, wherever the asteroid hit, Earth was reacting to the sting.

Because of the asteroid, his perfect life was now shattered. Perfect may have been a stretch since it consisted of him losing his job and breaking up with Jeff all in the same week. The sudden news that an asteroid was headed his way to fuck up life even further didn't discourage him much. Hell, it could've been God's will to finally finish him off. But ever since coming to in the basement of his ruined home damn near unscathed, he figured that wasn't God's will after all. After crawling out of the rubble, he'd been fixated on walking nonstop for twelve exhausting hours in the unrelenting Arizona heat.

The easy way out wasn't an option anymore. He wanted to fight, to survive.

Looking over his shoulder back east, he noticed an eerie dark grey color looming on the horizon. That strange darkness wasn't there several hours ago. Could it possibly be smoke coming from an enormous fire? Speculating on the darkness made him panicky and he didn't function well on panicky. This was true from experience. Besides, several hours ago had been early morning and the sun hadn't peeked over the horizon then. What did he know of asteroids and earthquakes anyway? All he knew was that they could kill and he didn't want to think about death right now.

That poor, blonde little girl.

No more looking back east. He wouldn't look up at the sky again, for that matter. Not if he valued his sanity and mental strength or what was left of it. He gave the eerie darkness one last glance and continued walking west. Though, something caught his eye. He paused and pivoted to see what looked like a young man walking along the road far in the distance. Adrenaline raced through his body. Was he seeing correctly? The man walked head down as if he carried more than the world's burden's on his shoulders and had already given in.

"Hey!" Elliot called out. *Please be real. Please be real.*

The man looked up, stopped in his tracks and even from the distance between them he knew the man was excited to see him too. The man began jogging toward him and he jogged in the man's direction. His heart pitter-pattered with excitement and pure relief. He was *not* alone.

When the tall, fit man approached, he ran up to him with a huge, bright smile and arms outstretched. Elliot hugged him as if he were hugging a dear friend. And the feeling wasn't off. His relief resembled that of seeing a good old buddy again after so many years, and just in the nick of time. At the exact moment he needed him.

"My God." The man squeezed tighter, nearly collapsing under Elliot's embrace. "Thought I was the only one alive. So happy to see *you*."

"You have no idea how happy I am to see you." He separated their bodies. "I've been dragging my feet for hours looking for someone else to keep me sane."

The man chuckled. Even with the devastation around them Elliot managed to make the poor guy chuckle. He didn't want to take credit yet, they both seemed immensely happy to not be the last person alive.

"Adam." He placed a calming hand on Elliot's shoulder.

He sighed. Instant comfort. "I'm Elliot."

"Elliot." Adam huffed, catching his breath. "Been walking forever and have no idea where I'm going."

"Yeah, I'm just as lost. Phoenix doesn't look much like Phoenix anymore, huh?"

Adam nodded again and sighed. "Just knew I was out here alone. But *now* it should be easier to get out of this mess. Right?"

This mess? This *disaster* was more like it. Elliot attempted to smile.

"Two heads are better than one." Adam's breath seemed to return to normal.

Elliot lifted his bottle. "You need some? It's water."

"No, thanks." The small pack on Adam's back bounced slightly as he turned. He slid it off his shoulders and took out the water bottle he had tucked in there, along with some granola bars still in their individual packages. Elliot hadn't eaten since he began his trek, maybe even a couple hours before then and those bars looked appetizing.

"Do you mind?" He pointed to the bars. "It's been a long while."

"Oh, sure, sure." Adam handed him a bar and took one for himself. "Eat up."

The package contained two crunchy granola bars but they both were crumbled within the wrapper. Elliot didn't mind. He already felt some energy returning to his exhausted body.

Adam bit into his bar and watched him eat with bright green eyes and a tiny grin on his dry lips. Even with a layer of dust and dirt coating Adam from head to toe, Elliot could easily make out his handsomeness. He was fascinated by the way Adam talked too. With the start of every sentence he never said *I* or *you.* It sounded a little funny at first, almost as if he didn't want to waste time with unnecessary words no matter how small. However, Elliot could understand wanting to get to the point quickly.

Elliot was covered in a layer of dirt and dust as well. He briefly looked down over himself. He must've looked crazy wearing a pair of camouflage cargo shorts and his black *Made with Pride* T-shirt with rainbow-colored letters.

"See that dark color on the horizon?" Adam pointed to the east, suddenly looking somber. "That's a wall of smoke, ash, dust and who knows what else, and it's coming our way."

"What? What do you mean?" A bit of panic began to stir in his stomach like a bowl of his mother's spicy and overly greasy chili. He'd thought the worst was over.

"Ever heard of impact winter?" Adam's green eyes pierced his and neither moved. "What's headed for us isn't good. We're gonna have to take shelter somewhere and fast before it blocks out all light and it gets so dark we won't be able to tell which way is up. Can't run from it either," he added, as if predicting Elliot's next question. "Been watching it for a couple hours now and it's moving pretty fast."

"What do you mean it's going to get dark?" He knew he looked like a wide-eyed idiot, but he didn't care much about his appearance at the moment.

"Let me put it this way. Once the sun sets we're not gonna see it rise for quite some time. That wall of soot headed our way is so thick it will block out the sun. It will take months, maybe years, for all the crap to fall down."

"Are you sure?" He dipped his eyebrows suspiciously. "How do you know all this?"

"When those assholes finally told us that an asteroid might hit, I went looking for info about anything to do with asteroids hitting Earth and that's what I found out. We need to find some shelter."

Elliot looked at the dark grey horizon. Indeed, the cloud of unnerving darkness grew bigger, wider, closer. His heart dropped, it sank in the pit of his stomach like a ton of concrete rubble. "We're not going to make it, huh?" He gulped, suddenly feeling defeated. Panic. "What's the point in finding shelter when we're not gonna live to see the sun again?"

Adam grabbed his hand, gave it a gentle squeeze and let it loose before Elliot realized it had happened. The friendly squeeze hadn't been part of his imagination. A look of sincerity and concern painted Adam's handsome face. "I was beginning to think the same thing and then I saw you. Like I said, two heads are better than one."

That gloomy horizon spelled doom. Knowing it was coming from the east coast hit him hard. That meant Jeff in New York, and his mother, father and brother in Georgia probably didn't survive. If somehow they did survive, the darkness surrounded them like a swarm of angry bees and they probably wouldn't live for long. Who knew what the dark cloud brought with it; falling ash, fire, unbearable heat? The massive earthquakes he had experienced—the ones that left Phoenix an unrecognizable landfill—probably did as much damage or worse to places experiencing the same violent quakes. And what of the place that experienced the actual impact?

Adam continued walking west and Elliot followed close on his heels. He hadn't known tears were dripping down his cheeks until Adam looked back at him with sadness in his eyes. Then he felt the warm wetness on his dirt-caked cheeks and wiped them away with the back of his hand. For so long he'd been wishing for someone to talk to, someone to accompany him in his search for hope, someone to keep him strong and determined. He couldn't just break down now. His prayers had been answered with the presence of Adam. Now he had a reason to move on.

Again, promising himself not to look back east, he sped up to walk alongside his newfound companion. Maybe engaging in conversation would take his mind off of doom. "Why didn't you get out of here when everyone else did?"

Adam stared at the ground as he walked. His hand combed through his dirty, short, blond hair. "Can't escape it. So why run, you know?"

"Yeah, I know."

Adam quickly glanced over at him. "That's why you stayed?"

"Yeah. I didn't think I was going to make it too far. So I said my peace and was in my basement when the last quake hit. Could you believe I woke up with my house in ruins on top of me? It took me forever to crawl out. How did you, you know, make it?"

"Was in my car in the garage." He shrugged. "Had packed a few things, got in my car, locked the door and put the key in the ignition. I knew I wouldn't be able to drive anywhere because of all the cars on the roads and freeways. Didn't really wanna go anywhere. I knew no matter where I went, I couldn't escape it." He huffed, looking as if he'd rather leave it behind him. "So I got out and started walking. Only after I crawled out of what was left of my garage. We're lucky to walk away from it, you know?" Adam patted his back and smiled briefly.

"I saw a little girl back there." Elliot threw back his thumb, gesturing behind him without turning, without facing what had now vividly burned into his memory. "She's dead." Why did that image pop in his mind at that time and why did he decide to tell Adam? He guessed hearing about how lucky he was reminded him of how unlucky the little girl had been. Maybe he could shake some of his guilt by telling someone about her. Or would it have been better to force himself to forget her?

"I've seen some crazy stuff too." Adam sighed, avoiding eye contact. "We'll be alright though. See that building up there that looks like it won't fall over at any minute?"

He looked ahead about a quarter mile at what used to be Nice Smile Dental, a small, standard single story dental office. It looked unaffected except for a few broken windows. "I see it."

"That's where we're going." Adam suddenly picked up speed, damn near leaving him in the wind. Adam must've been excited to see a nearly undamaged building they could use as shelter. Elliot sure was, even more excited now that he had someone he could call a companion. They were both in the same predicament and they both wanted the same thing...to survive.

He struggled to keep up. Walking so fast over loose rubble made it difficult for him to keep his balance, and in his haste he slipped. His leg slid against a piece of twisted, jagged metal before he landed on his ass. "Shit!" Bright red blood oozed from his wound as he sat on the dusty pile of rubble. How in the hell did he lose his balance?

Adam quickly rushed to his side. "Shit," he echoed. "Put some pressure on it."

He obeyed and placed his hand over the three-inch gash on his shin and squeezed, grimacing in pain as blood trickled through his fingers. "I need something to wrap around it. My hand's not gonna stop it from bleeding."

Adam pulled his shirt over his head and took off the white tank he had on under it, ripping it down the middle to make it one long piece of fabric. Elliot took in Adam's waxed, muscular torso and strong arms that bulged with every tug and tear of his shirt. Then pain immediately took his attention away from the six-pack abs and directed it back to his throbbing leg.

"Here, let me wrap this around it." Adam knelt down and gingerly tended his wound. As soon as he tied the last knot, he placed his T-shirt in his pack, swung the pack over his shoulder and offered his hand. Elliot grabbed it and allowed him to pull him to his feet. Without a second lost, Adam placed an arm around Elliot's waist and together they continued their trek toward the dental office.

"Where's your family?" Elliot asked as they made their way past huge chunks of cement blocks that were rocked and shaken from the nearby houses and small buildings.

"Probably dead," he said, nonchalantly. When Elliot looked at him with raised eyebrows, Adam ignored his questioning stare and said nothing else about it. Instead he gestured with his eyes. "Watch your step here."

"Sorry about your family." Elliot carefully stepped over a small pile of debris.

"No need for that." Adam paused and looked into his eyes. A stern look. An honest look. "I think we're the only lucky ones."

They walked slowly, cautiously as they approached the dental office. The small parking lot was littered with trash, papers and other garbage they had to maneuver around and over to get to the door.

"Were you living alone?" He glanced at Adam's hard, bare chest and quickly looked away. Something about his physique helped him take his mind off of impending doom. He wasn't quite sure if that was a good thing or not.

"Just me and my fiancée." He scoffed, shaking his head. "She ran like everyone else. Took off toward Denver with her family as soon as she got news of the asteroid. I'm sure if those assholes gave us a year's warning instead of a couple days she would've left a year ago. Either way, look how far running's got her."

"Well, you don't know." Elliot shrugged, being extra cautious with his step. "Maybe there're tons of people still alive in Denver and—" He didn't bring attention to Adam's second scoff. Clearly, speaking about his fiancée and the possibility of her being alive was a touchy subject. He guessed it would be since she left him in Hell to fend for himself.

"I know you're trying to stay positive, Elliot, but like I said, we're the only lucky ones."

CHAPTER TWO

Escaping Reality

Arriving at the abandoned dental office, Adam led Elliot to a plastic chair in the corner of what looked like the front lobby. Elliot placed his nearly empty bottle of water on the floor beside him and took a seat. His chest rose and fell rapidly as he took in a few deep breaths, forcing himself to relax.

The office looked like a closet of junk. It didn't look any different than the littered lot outside. Tables, chairs and even computers were scattered around as if a massive whirlwind tried to carry them away and failed. The dimness made it difficult to make out the largest of objects in the darkened corners due to the power outage that extinguished all electricity since the first quake but, nonetheless, they had shelter. Where was that okay we're safe feeling?

Adam sat his backpack on the floor and began to move furniture around the room. "I'm gonna try to clear some space and block some of these broken windows."

Elliot sat silently, watching Adam move about the room. Adam was an attractive man with exceptional features. He seemed young, probably in his mid to late twenties like Elliot. He looked tall, fit and strong. He gauged Adam's strength from the way he effortlessly lifted a huge potted tree and placed it in front of a broken window to hold up some drywall he had placed against it. Even the way Adam spoke interested him. Not all of his sentences were brief and to the point, but those that were urged Elliot to listen regardless.

He had so many questions for Adam but didn't know which to ask first. "How long were you and your fiancée together?" Good start to engage in friendly conversation, nothing too personal right off the bat.

Adam continued to move around the room, eyes diligently searching the cluttered floor. "Four years." He picked up and threw some empty, crushed boxes aside.

Elliot raised an eyebrow. "Were you happy?"

"As happy as a person could be." He kicked a pile of papers into a corner, the rustling sound bounced off of the walls for a few seconds. "How about you? Were you living alone?"

Elliot grimaced at his injured, bloody leg. He assumed Adam didn't directly ask about his marital status because he shamelessly exhibited his favorite Made with Pride T-shirt. Thank goodness same sex marriage wasn't legal in Arizona. He'd regretted many dumb things he'd done and getting married to Jeff would've been one of them. He's always been so impulsive when it came to Jeff. He knew he would've married Jeff without thinking twice about it. All Jeff had to do was ask. Pathetic. Anyhow, Adam's question seemed to be an attempt to change the subject. As happy as a person could be. Adam sure didn't behave like a happily involved man. And judging by his fiancée's eagerness to leave him, she wasn't happily involved either.

"Yeah, I lived alone for the past week or so." He glanced at Adam, anticipating his response. "I was staying with my boyfriend until we broke up last week."

Adam paused and looked back over his bare shoulder at him. "Sorry to hear that."

"He accused me of taking him for granted." He scoffed and wiped his eye with a knuckle.

"Sorry about that too." Adam chewed his bottom lip and stood motionless for a few seconds. What could he possibly be thinking about? He then continued to move furniture around the room. "You know that saying that goes something like, be thankful for every day because you don't know what the future holds?"

Elliot nodded, rolling his eyes. "Yeah, I've heard people say that plenty of times."

Adam paused, looking ahead with a vacant stare. "I really get the meaning now."

"Yeah, crazy how it takes an asteroid nearly killing you to make you understand things."

Elliot watched Adam clear a path and made his way back to his side. He knelt down and pulled back a piece of the fabric around Elliot's leg. "So, did you?"

He squint his eyes, confused. "Did I what?"

Adam looked up, locking eyes with him. "Did you take him for granted?"

He stared back into those enticing, bright green eyes. Even without the sun shining directly into them, they still shined like emeralds. "Relationships are complicated and it takes two to make it work. I didn't take him for granted. He just didn't want to put in the effort to make it successful."

Adam grinned slightly. "You don't like to be wrong, am I right?"

"You're wrong." He looked away sheepishly.

"Of course." A slight grin lingered on Adam's lips. "How does your leg feel?"

"Hurts like hell."

"We need to find something clean to wrap around it so it can start healing." Adam stood then made his way down the hall to one of the back rooms. From Elliot's angle he couldn't see anything back there but he heard the crash and bang as Adam threw things around. He waited and Adam returned with a small bottle of antiseptic and gauze still in its sterile package. "You need to come see this." Adam paused, wide-eyed.

Panic hit him in his chest like a sledgehammer. "What is it?" Another body? Several dead bodies?

"Calm down." Adam put his hands out before him. "A broken water main out back. It's like a geyser out there. Come on." He placed an arm around Elliot's waist again and helped him up from his chair. Slowly they made their way down the hall—where two rooms were located adjacent to each other—and out the back exit.

There it was, a beautiful jet of clear, fresh water shooting up about twelve feet in the air from a huge crack in the side of the road near a water hydrant. It rained down in huge drops on the hot, littered street around them. Elliot smiled when a breeze brushed some water droplets against his hot, dry face. So refreshing.

"I'm going for it." Adam unbuttoned and unzipped his dark blue jeans.

Elliot couldn't help but stare, watching Adam's fingers slide unintentionally slowly and sensually down the length of his fly. "What are you doing?"

"I'm gonna take advantage of this while I can." Adam pulled off his socks and shoes and slid his pants off. He threw them both down by the exit door. Standing in a pair of dark blue boxer-briefs that hugged his narrow hips and firm ass in a way that made Elliot's breath catch, Adam pointed to Elliot's Cargo shorts. "Need help out of those?" When he didn't answer, Adam lifted an eyebrow and added, "You might not experience this again."

Suddenly Elliot had an intense urge to look back east, but he fought it with everything he had and lifted his T-shirt over his head instead. "You're right. I might not experience this again." As soon as he stripped himself of his socks, shoes and shorts, he carefully limped toward the spouting water.

Adam, in all his excitement, ran directly toward the jet. Arms outstretched, he stood under the falling water and savored it as it fell over his taut body.

Elliot slowly limped his way over. Cold water fell over his almost naked body and he gasped as the first drops hit his thirsty skin. It was more refreshing than he could ever imagine. He replayed Adam's words in his head, over and over. *You might not experience this again.* So he tilted his head back and soaked up the freshness, remembering how each cooling drop felt on his aching body. He opened his mouth wide and allowed the water to fill it before swallowing, tasting. Amazing. He listened to the plop, plop of water splashing and collecting into the puddles around him. Damn near bliss.

"I'll go get our water bottles so we can fill them up." Adam jogged back to the office. The sun hit the water droplets on his skin at the perfect angle, causing light to reflect off of his fit body and his smooth back muscles to glisten. Once he disappeared inside, Elliot closed his eyes and allowed the rays of the sun to heat his skin.

You might not experience this again.

Before long, Adam was back under the stream, filling their bottles to the brim with the pure, cool, refreshing goodness. "That darkness is moving in. Maybe we should go back inside and I'll take a look at that leg." When the bottles were filled, he wrapped his free arm around Elliot's waist to assist him in his walk back to the office.

Elliot quickly turned in his arms. For a second that felt like hours, they stared into each other's eyes. In that moment, which felt like an eternity, a sense of hope trickled over him. The intense sense of promise guided him as he brought his lips to Adam's. The water streamed down over their bodies as he closed his eyes and gently sucked Adam's bottom lip. Adam's lips relaxed and a rush of warm, granola-scented breath brushed the cool, wet skin of his upper lip.

Then Adam bowed his head, breaking the kiss. He still had an arm embracing Elliot while he effortlessly cradled the two water bottles in the other arm.

"I'm sorry," Adam said in a soft and low voice.

Before he could say anything else, Elliot reminded him, "We might not experience this again." He looked into Adam's eyes, seeing what he couldn't fully see before but always knew lay hidden under a thin layer of dust that was no longer there ... a gorgeous man. Adam possessed such beautiful golden skin, flawless complexion and the most beautiful blushed lips he'd ever seen on a man. He placed his hand on Adam's chin and lifted his head slightly to kiss his blushed lips again.

After another innocent, electrifying peck, Adam turned away again. "Let me look at that leg, alright?" He kindly turned Elliot down. However, Elliot needed comfort and affection, something to take his mind off of the people and the luxuries he no longer had. For a while that mesmerizing kiss seemed to work. Unfortunately, it hadn't worked for long.

Adam kept an arm around his waist and guided him toward the office, while glancing over his shoulder. "I think that dark cloud is gonna make it here sooner than I thought."

"Aren't you scared?" Elliot kept his gaze down and as far away from the east as possible.

"The scary part's over." Adam looked toward the east. "The asteroid already struck. Our job now is to stay clear-headed and to do what we have to do to stay safe."

Suddenly a deep snarl came from behind them, stunning and stopping them in their tracks. Quickly, Elliot peered over his shoulder and was confronted with what resembled a large, angry pit bull. It wouldn't have frightened Elliot as much if he wasn't injured, enabling him to run or defend himself. "What do we do?" He stared unblinking at the big, brown dog as it stared back at him and bared its fangs.

"Just move toward the door slowly." Adam tugged him a little in the direction of the office, arm still around his waist. "No sudden movements."

The dog's growl rattled the hairs on the back of his neck. He imagined being maimed by the roaring beast at any second. He slowly limped to the door but fear made him constantly look over his shoulder at the animal.

Adam peered back too. "It's hurt on its left side. Don't worry. It's probably scared of us more than we are of it."

He glanced back again. Blood covered most of the dog's left side. On the same side, it tucked his hind leg under its belly as if it were injured too. That confirmed his suspicions. It was the same dog he'd seen earlier, limping away from him. He grabbed the door handle just as they reached the office and quickly hopped inside. Adam followed, but before closing the door fully they waited to watch the dog through the small crack.

The dog watched them too for a few seconds and then turned to a nearby puddle of water to drink from it. After having enough to drink, it lay down on the wet asphalt beside the puddle, content.

Adam laughed softly. "It was just thirsty. Poor mutt." He looked to Elliot. "You okay?"

Elliot nodded while his heart raced, threatening to burst from his chest.

Carefully, they entered one of the dental rooms. Dental instruments and broken glass lay scattered around the dusty carpet. The table drawers were opened, some broken with all of their contents on the floor. Adam turned over a heavy-looking, metal patient chair, sat it upright and helped him onto it. The chair had a thick layer of smooth, black leather on top where the patient would sit comfortably. Elliot waited as Adam grabbed some antiseptic and sterile gauze still in the foil packaging and sat beside him in what was probably the doctor's chair.

"It's not bleeding much. That's good." Adam untied the torn, wet shirt from his leg. "I'm just gonna clean it up and dress it better, alright?" He avoided eye contact as his talked, but Elliot nodded anyway.

"Thanks for taking care of me. You're like...my hero." He shifted in the chair, getting more comfortable. "Did you go to school for this or something? A doctor, maybe?"

"Nah, I'm no doctor." Adam kept his eyes on his working hands, cleaning around the outside of the wound with the sterile gauze. "I worked for the Maricopa County Police Department. I took basic first aid training."

"So you're a cop?" Fear still tunneled through his veins but he was impressed and forced a smile anyway.

Adam nodded, keeping his focus on Elliot's wound. "Yep, a police officer."

"So, you *are* a hero then. Phoenix's hero. Not just my hero." Elliot smiled genuinely. "I'm just a cashier, was a cashier at Food Plus. But was fired last week."

"Fired?" Adam finally looked up at him.

"Apparently, I didn't care enough about customer service because I didn't service the customers well enough." He shook his head and rolled his eyes. "That's what the big guy said. His exact words. My job was to ring them up and that's what I did. I guess he wanted me to smile constantly and pressure them into buying a bunch of junk they didn't want or need. Honestly, who wants to smile when you feel so miserable?" Adam dropped his gaze back to his working hands and Elliot shrugged. "But that doesn't matter anymore, huh?"

After a couple of minutes of silence, Elliot prevented hot tears from welling up in his eyes. "I'm sorry for kissing you. I didn't want to make you feel...awkward or anything. I'm just so excited to run into you. I was caught in the moment, you know?"

Adam put his hand on Elliot's bare shoulder, comforting. "Don't worry about it. As long as we stick together we'll make it through this mess."

He had said that before and before it had comforted Elliot, but hearing it again didn't have much of an effect on him.

"I'm so lost. I miss my family, my boyfriend, my house. It feels like I'm dreaming or something. Like this isn't really happening." Elliot sat forward, placing a hand on each of Adam's shoulders. "Am I dreaming? Or worse, I'm dead. We're dead, aren't we? Or maybe...maybe I've already gone insane and you're just part of my imagination. Am I right? I'm imagining you helping me?"

Adam moved forward, damn near pressing his forehead to Elliot's. "If you imagined me then you have a great imagination, because I'm not the hero you think I am. I'm just like you, a survivor, nothing more and definitely nothing supernatural."

Elliot shook his head. Confused. "Then why are you here with me, helping *me*?"

"I'm sure you would stay and help me if I were hurt. Anyway, two heads are better than one, remember?"

He nodded, agreeing.

Adam shifted in his seat but continued to tend to the wound with a smile. Attractive, shallow laugh lines framed his red lips in little parenthesis. But before his smile had a chance to fade, the building started to rumble and shake, rattling everything that wasn't secured to the floor.

Elliot gasped. "Another quake!" The roaring sound of objects smashing and crashing around them startled him. He allowed Adam to quickly help him up from the dental chair and they huddled in a corner of the room. The shaking grew worse as the seconds went by. The wall adjacent to them began to crack and weaken. Pieces of drywall crumbled from the damaged spots and from the ceiling directly above them.

"We need to take cover." Adam's voice rose above the powerful sound of destruction. "Looks like the roof's about to cave in."

Elliot's eyes scanned the room while he thought of a plan. The only thing that could possibly protect them from falling debris was the large, metal dentist chair he had just been sitting on. He pointed to it and swiftly Adam left the corner to get ahold of the chair and drag it back to their corner of the room. He kicked it over, it tumbled to the side, he heaved it over once more and they both crouched under the heavy, leather-protected metal.

Just a mere second after taking cover, a support beam came crashing down in the hallway just outside of the room while the quake went on violently shaking the world around them. The thunderous sound of objects crashing, breaking, splitting and shattering simultaneously drummed throughout the cramped office. It seemed like forever had passed before the thundering finally stopped. Elliot and Adam stayed motionless for minutes after, panting desperately to catch their breaths.

Adam gripped Elliot's shoulder as they knelt beside the chair. "You all right?"

"I'm scared shitless." He looked to Adam with huge, frightened eyes. "We're not going to make it. I can't live like this, without a sun, with just us. What do we do? How could we live without the sun?" The same sun he'd damned earlier. Just his luck to curse the very thing he couldn't live without the most. "It's all over. It's too late now."

"Elliot, calm down." Adam wrapped a strong arm around him and ran his fingers through Elliot's damp, dark hair. If Adam's intent was too comfort him it definitely worked.

Elliot mimicked him by tangling his fingers in Adam's dirty blonds. He felt the panic gently subside. Elliot needed confirmation. His voice was low, melancholy. "We're going to die, aren't we?"

"No, we're not." Adam's voice grew strong and confident.

Despite Adam's confidence, Elliot couldn't shake the achiness in his chest. "We are. I can feel it." The churning of his innards sent a burning sensation to the pit of his gut.

"No...we're not." Adam gently pulled Elliot into him, embracing him, surrounding him with a warm pair of arms, protection.

Soft, puckered lips brushed Elliot's and he couldn't help but to open his mouth, allowing Adam's tongue to tease at his own. They licked and tasted one another's tongue, alternating between soft pecks on the lips and slick tangles of wet muscle.

Elliot tried to suppress his groan but failed. Should he feel so safe in a stranger's arms so soon? Is indulging in a kiss really .... "Ahh..." Adam's kiss pulled him in deeper than any kiss he'd ever experienced before. Fueled by adrenaline and fear and transitioning into passion and desire, the kiss was more than what Elliot craved. He absolutely needed it. His tense, achy body continued to relax against Adam's and Adam lured him in; holding, pulling, and gripping one another with what felt like an unspoken intention of never letting go.

The weight of Adam's body pressed Elliot back against the dusty carpeted floor, and as Adam rested on top of him, Elliot cradled him between bent knees. Adam supported most of his weight on his forearms by placing them on both sides of Elliot's head. Their kiss grew deeper, rougher and more intense. Their tongues licked harder. Their faint, sweet-smelling granola breath mingled. Pain pricked the small cut on his lip, however, the pleasure he received quickly overpowered any pain.

He raised his hands to Adam's biceps and squeezed while he thrust his hips slightly, careful to keep his wounded leg out of the way. His erection pressed against Adam's through the fabric of their wet boxers. The addictive wave of pleasure raced through his body causing him to instinctively thrust his hips faster, harder. Adam must have took his cue because he ground his pelvis against Elliot's too, pressing and grinding their hard-ons together.

A breathy moan brushed past Adam's lips, making Elliot shudder in anticipation. He reached below and quickly pushed Adam's boxer-briefs down over his ass. He did the same to his own boxers, freeing his erection and crushing it against Adam's. Their warm, slick pre-come mixed, providing lubricant as their cocks glided alongside one another's and ground into the other's lower abdomen.

He explored Adam's body with his hands, squeezing and gripping his solid shoulders, his firm ass. Adam's smooth, hard body gave him all that he needed; distraction, comfort and pleasure all at the same time. He couldn't ask for more at the moment. The muscles in his pelvis clenched and his balls drew up toward his body as an intense orgasm threatened to tear through him.

"I'm close," Elliot warned in a breathy whisper.

"Me too." Their lips still grazed one another's as they spoke and the sultry bass in Adam's voice nearly sent Elliot over the edge. He missed the sound of another's voice, especially the deep rumble of a man in pleasure. *So that's what being alive felt like.*

To quickly relieve the tension, Elliot reached between their hot, sweaty bodies to grasp both of their cocks in a firm grip. He began a rhythmic tug and pull with his hand, watching the pained-pleasured look sweep across Adam's handsome face.

Adam winced, biting down on his bottom lip. He groaned and his body shuddered just as Elliot felt the first shot of warm semen escape Adam's cock and trickle down over his hand and wrist. Elliot continued to pump his fist, collecting the semen as extra lubricant. In no time, he came too, breathing heavily and crying out in absolute pleasure and relief. The room spun, this time from the shock to his senses instead of a quake.

It took a couple minutes to whine down. But finally Adam stood, immediately pulled up his underwear and put his hand out to Elliot. He allowed Adam to assist him to stand. He stood, balancing, positioning most of his weight on his uninjured leg and pulled his boxers up over his hips. Their torsos were wet and sticky with a mixture of semen and sweat. Elliot used some leftover gauze to clean himself the best he could and passed some to Adam to do the same. "Thanks."

Adam focused his emerald eyes on him as he continued to wipe at his chest. "For what?"

"For putting up with me." He stared back, unsure of Adam's feelings toward him. "I don't mean to act like a whiny little bitch or something, but...well, I'm fucking scared, you know?" When Adam smiled warmly a heavy weight lifted from Elliot's heart.

"I was on the verge of giving up before I met you." Adam moved closer, bringing their bodies millimeters from each other. "I should be thanking *you.*"

Elliot went for it. He threw all his inhibitions aside and pulled Adam to him by his waist. He pressed his lips to Adam's blushed red lips. Adam held Elliot's elbows in his hands and kissed him back, even sliding his tongue between Elliot's bruised lips.

Elliot broke the kiss. He kept his eyes closed and lowered his forehead to Adam's shoulder. "I'm really scared."

"I know. I'm scared too." Adam's gentle voice was soothing. "But there's no room for huddling in a corner and giving up. It's not over yet."

He looked up into Adam's eyes, reading his expression. "I know. You're right."

Adam looked stern, serious. "You have to stop thinking about what we don't have and start thinking about how to keep going. We gotta prepare for tomorrow."

"Tomorrow isn't coming." Elliot felt the heat of anger on his temple.

Adam placed his hands on Elliot's shoulders. "Then we gotta live for today."

Elliot nodded. "You're right." He cleared his throat, straightened his shoulders and forced a smile. "You're right. I can't believe I'm letting this asteroid get to me like this."

"You hear what you just said? It's normal to be scared after what we lived through. The way to push through it is by not letting your fear take over. Now, let's go wash off in the water out back." He wrapped an arm around Elliot's naked waist and helped him around the mess in the room to the hall. They carefully made their way around the fallen beam and to the back exit.

When he opened the door, Elliot expected to see the refreshing jet of water spraying into the air and into the street. Instead, a sinkhole as big as an average backyard pool marked where the water had once jetted from the crack in the side of the street. The water, even the hydrant was gone, possibly sucked down into the dark abyss.

Elliot stared wide-eyed from the doorway. "Shit, what happened?"

Adam moved forward, cautiously inching closer to the wide, gaping hole. "Maybe the earthquake did it somehow." He moved closer, looking down into it.

"What's in there?" Elliot called from the doorway, his grip tightened on the doorframe in anticipation.

"A ... muddy hole."

Suddenly, a ball of fire streaked through the sky, catching Elliot's attention back to the east. The fireball swept across the frightening scene of blackened clouds that resembled death in its misty form. Against the fast approaching darkness, the fireball appeared rather small and a tail of fire followed it like a serpent from Hell announcing its presence.

"Look." Elliot pointed to it as it arched in the distance toward the dark horizon.

Adam looked up just in time to see it disappear behind the rim of the horizon. "Jesus." He huffed, shaking his head.

Back west the sun slowly set behind big purple mountains illuminating the western sky in fiery orange and red hues. The dark cloud back east moved so fast, Elliot knew it would cover them in a matter of hours.

Adam made his way back from the sinkhole. "I'm glad we used the water when we did. You okay?"

Elliot nodded even though he could barely breathe. Adam's face was flushed and his eyes somber, but Elliot pretended not to see it. Adam's eyes told him things he didn't want to know.

And just when Elliot thought his troubles were nearly over, he heard a vicious growl and a bark. Adam jolted and turned just as the injured pit bull came out of nowhere and leapt toward him. Adam stumbled and fell back onto the gravel with a thud and the dog slowly limped toward him, showing off his bloody canine teeth.

Elliot froze but he knew had to do something other than stand there. The instinct to protect himself by closing the office door—ensuring a barrier between him and the vicious dog—crossed his mind, but then the image of the unfortunate blonde haired girl popped in, replacing it. She wasn't able to fight off what had killed her but Elliot had the ability to fight off what threatened Adam's life. He couldn't let his fear control him. Courage rushed him like a mad bull in the form of adrenaline and he sped toward the bleeding dog. What was his next move? He wasn't sure, but was relieved when the dog whimpered and turned away, looking back as he slowly retreated.

"Get!" Elliot yelled and kicked a pile of gravel in the dog's direction.

The injured canine tucked its wounded leg up near its belly as it disappeared behind an enormous pile of rubble.

"Are you hurt?" Elliot grabbed Adam's hand in a firm grip and helped him to his feet.

"Just a little scratched up. That's all." He dusted off his ass and his bruised shoulder.

Elliot limped back to the door. "Let's get in before it comes back."

They went back into the room where they had just been intimate, kissing and writhing against each other. Adam sat in the same corner behind the overturned dentist chair, and he stared blankly, solemnly at the dirty floor before him. "I'm a liar."

"Huh?" Elliot sat beside him, placing a gentle hand on Adam's knee. "What did you lie about?"

"Everything." Adam ran both hands through his hair and huffed. "I'm not the hero you think I am. I worked as a dancer at a nightclub. I was working the night before they decided to share the excellent news about the asteroid." He scoffed at his sarcasm. "My job was to take off my clothes and dance for horny women. Jena—well, my fiancée made me take a first aide class with her when she went for a medical assistant job. That's why I knew how to take care of your leg."

Elliot dipped his eyebrows. "So you're not a cop?"

Adam slowly shook his head, a guilty expression in his eyes. "I impersonated one. I wore a police costume as part of my act. Velcro pants, Aviators and all."

That explained Adam's fit, waxed body. Elliot looked down at the same spot on the floor that Adam stared at, feeling gullible. "Why'd you lie?"

"You ever wanted to be somebody else? Meeting you was my chance to reinvent myself. Be the man I always wanted to be." Adam finally looked up at Elliot. "Who wants to introduce themselves as a stripper?"

"Look, Adam, I don't care." Elliot shrugged. "I don't care if you're a cop or just impersonate one on a stage. Does it matter? It doesn't change anything. But—"

Adam turned, meeting Elliot's gaze. "But?"

"You're gay, right?" Elliot dipped his eyebrows, secretly hoping that Adam had lied about being engaged or maybe even been unhappy in love and yearned for male companionship. "I mean, you mentioned your fiancée and told me that you were happy, but...never mind. It doesn't matter." Elliot scoffed. "It's not like what we did meant anything. It was spontaneous and we were scared. Hell, the inevitable happened, right? Stuff like this make people do all sorts of things they normally wouldn't do, huh?"

Was the uncomfortable pitter-patter in his chest and the huge lump in his throat an effect of the jealousy he harbored because of Adam's presumed devotion to his fiancée? He didn't know Adam at all. Hell, half of what he knew had been a lie. Yet, he felt a connection that he wanted—no, needed—to hold on to. Yes, already an emotional link between them had been established, Elliot was sure of it.

Adam nodded. "You weren't the first guy I've messed around with. Back in high school, me and a Drama kid used to fuck around a little. I've never told anybody—not my fiancée, my friends, nobody. You're the only other person who knows."

"So you never came out?"

"It's not like that. I fell in love with my fiancée and never had a second thought about it. Whatever thoughts I had about men didn't faze me. But when you kissed me..." A crimson hue tinted his cheeks. "That kiss brought back a lot of feelings I thought were left back in high school. Your eyes, they...they kind of sucked me in."

Elliot grinned, the lump in his throat dissolved. "Your confession made up for any lie you could have told. Knowing the truth somehow makes hiding out at the dentist not so bad."

"That's not all I lied about." Adam sheepishly looked away as he spoke. "We're probably not gonna make it through this."

"No, you're just scared like me." Elliot squeezed Adam's knee. "Be scared. It's okay. An asteroid hit. It's okay to panic."

"No, listen." Adam removed Elliot's hand from his knee and turned to face him. "I know why there are so many crazy earthquakes. That fireball we saw in the sky. That's probably not the only one."

Elliot's eyes narrowed. "What are you saying?"

"I saw one of the stories on the news before it hit. Pieces of the asteroid and loose pieces of earth go into the atmosphere and get stuck in orbit. Then they fall back to Earth over a few days...all over Earth."

Elliot smacked his lips. "Some scared news reporter on TV told you this?"

"Yeah." Adam nodded, staring unblinking. A serious look in his eye. "That darkness, those clouds, they're proof that the worst is yet to come."

Elliot stared, absorbing Adam's words. "You believe that?"

Adam slowly nodded. "Sorry."

"You said we were gonna get through this so that's what we're gonna do." Elliot grabbed Adam's hand and interlocked their fingers. "Fuck whatever the TV said. That information isn't always right."

Adam's head hung low and he pulled his hand away from Elliot's grip. "Aren't you the courageous one." Sarcasm lingered on his words.

Elliot glared, insulted by Adam's unexpected mockery. "I've just decided I'm tired of running around like a scared and hurt girl, reacting to trauma. I'm ready to do what we have to do to keep going."

Elliot, angered by Adam's sudden coldness, pulled Adam toward him and kissed him hard and rough. His tongue licked eagerly, his grip tightening with every other beat of his heart as if he were reaching or searching. He wasn't reaching for comfort or searching for pleasure. No, he was proving his strength in his kiss; his physical and emotional strength, something Adam needed to know existed. He broke the kiss and they both sat silently, shoulder to shoulder in the corner of the darkening room. He still felt lucky to run into Adam. Knowing Adam had fooled around with another man before meeting his fiancée made the connection he felt even stronger. Elliot was curious about his relationship, since earlier Adam seemed to shun it.

"Aren't you worried about your fiancée?"

Adam stared ahead, a dazed look frozen on his face. "She's gone. She left me to find her family in Colorado. Doubt she made it."

Elliot wondered if Adam's nonchalant demeanor was his way of coping. Elliot stared at the eerie shadows on the walls surrounding them. They seemed to creep across the wall waiting to engulf them in their blackness. "I tried calling Jeff, my ex-boyfriend, when the news about the asteroid broke. The phones wouldn't work for some reason. Not cell phones or the landlines. Watching everyone panic in the streets outside of my house made me want to crawl into a corner and just die already."

"Like we're doing now?" Adam's eye caught Elliot's as he glanced over at him. Elliot was sure he saw him roll his eyes.

"I figured the people who had newer, stronger homes would live through this before I did. And here I am damn near flawless while Jeff is back in New York probably suffering."

"Sorry to tell you this, but Jeff is probably dead."

Elliot's head sprang up. He was surprised at Adam's lack of tact. "What's with the asshole routine, huh? What's going on?"

"Be realistic."

They stared at each other. Elliot wondered how Adam could transform from a caring hero to a complete douche. The way Adam stared at him was as if he were waiting for his next words. There had to be a reason why he would act like a prick in a situation like this. Especially since a few seconds ago he shared himself so intimately and willingly.

Elliot wouldn't question it. He dare not do anything to loosen their bond now. Instead of lingering on the subject, Elliot changed it. He looked away first. "So, what's the plan?"

Adam stood and drug his feet across the room to stand before the broken widow. He peered out, arms crossed over his broad bare chest. "The plan? Get our water and stuff, then get the hell out of here."

"You want to leave?"

"Can't trust this place. It's not proper shelter anymore. No point in staying."

CHAPTER THREE

The Journey

Adam observed Elliot as they dressed outside on the small porch in the back of the dental office. Elliot's eyelids would occasionally flutter, causing his eyelashes to beat rapidly against the tops of his cheeks like tiny black butterflies. He'd never seen a person blink that way before. Elliot seemed unaware of his odd blinking. Or maybe he was used to it and chose to ignore it. Maybe it was some sort of involuntary tic he was forced to live with. Strangely, Adam found it attractive.

The poor guy was going through a lot and Adam felt guilty for taking out his frustrations on him. But talking about his life, more specifically, his fiancée was taking a toll on him. How could he damn near have sex with someone—a stranger, another man—so soon after meeting, while she's out there in need? Elliot had said people do all sorts of things they normally wouldn't do in these kinds of situations.

Adam watched Elliot as he slid his water bottle in the back pocket of his shorts and stood with his back toward the east. Adam snorted, disguising his grin. As strong and confident as Elliot tried to be, his body language screamed fear. He could see it in his reluctance to look behind him at the blackened sky. Adam wouldn't mention it. Hell, he was scared too.

He offered a hand, testing. "Ready?"

"Let's do it." Elliot nodded, refusing his assistance.

Adam threw his backpack over his shoulder and started walking west, guided by the distinct peak of dark purple mountains over the orange backdrop of sky far ahead of them. The huge sinkhole resembled a pitch black opening to hell as they carefully made their way around it.

Silence swamped them for a steady fifteen minutes. Only the sound of gravel echoed around them with every hastened step. The tainted smell of smoke, rotten eggs and a mixture of ammonia wisped passed Adam's nostrils. The smell arrived a couple hours ago just before the sky overhead darkened from both the dreary dark cloud and the sun setting over the horizon. It was faint then but more noticeable now. He had no idea what caused the foul smell.

A light thump on Adam's backpack drew his attention over his shoulder to his frazzled friend. "Do you have a flashlight in there?" Elliot cleared his throat, probably to shake off the urgency in his voice. "We should use it soon. I don't even know what I'm walking on."

Adam took off his pack and blindly searched inside for his flashlight. When his fingers glided over the smooth, long, metal handle he pulled it out and handed it to Elliot.

"This is heavy." Elliot switched it on. The beam shined on his shirt, lighting up the elaborate rainbow letters. He grunted, flinched and turned the light around toward the ground. "This is a handful."

"It was one of my stage props." Adam pulled a granola bar out of his pack and offered one to Elliot. He took it.

"Finally you speak. You've been quiet since we left."

"Don't have much to say, I guess." Adam took a bite of the bar and savored the taste of salty peanuts and sweet honey baked oats on his taste buds.

"How about telling me where we're going."

Adam shrugged. "Gonna keep walking until we find somewhere safe to rest." When Elliot didn't add another question he glanced down at his dressed wound. "How's the leg?"

"It's alright. The more I walk on it, the less pain I feel."

He nodded, taking note of the way Elliot stood with most of his weight on his good leg and his back to the east. He finished his bar in one big bite and swung his pack over his shoulder again. "Ready?"

Elliot nibbled his bar and continued walking. Adam followed in close proximity. "Why don't you tell me something?" Elliot said.

Adam shrugged. "Something like what?"

"I don't know. Something about you." Elliot glanced up at him then looked back down at the patch of light he swept over the littered ground before them. "What kind of car do you have?"

Adam wasn't sure why the car he owned would be an interesting topic, but he rolled with it. "A Mazda I bought on the side of the road for five hundred and me and a friend fixed up."

"Nice!" Elliot sounded too enthusiastic for a piece of junk that was pretty useless to them now. "Did you and your friend pimp your ride? Bling it up?"

"No, we rebuilt the engine. It was shot. Didn't run when I bought it."

"Oh, I thought you meant you *fixed* it up, you know?"

Adam could barely make out the nervous chuckle that snorted from Elliot. "I danced for a living. How would I afford to pimp my ride if I could barely afford to pay my rent?"

Elliot shook his head. "I don't know. I watch too much MTV."

Then it hit him. Elliot was trying to cheer him up. His attitude did go sour after they messed around and mentioned Jena, maybe Elliot noticed. There was the guilt again. He was being a complete asshole, but he couldn't help but feel uneasy. He felt exposed and it gnawed at him. He wasn't an emotional type of guy. He hated talking about his feelings and his failures, and he'd resorted to doing just that right after his much needed orgasm. How pathetic. He hated that part of himself and tried desperately to keep all of his hang-ups deep inside where they belonged. But he didn't want to alienate Elliot; his only friend.

He inhaled and attempted to rekindle the conversation. "Tell me something about *you*."

"Me?" Elliot didn't take his eyes from the flashlight beam. "Hmm, well, my mom, dad and brother live in Atlanta. I haven't talked to them in months."

"That's a long time."

"True. But what would you do if you lived twenty minutes away from your parents, made a surprise visit to see them at their house, and walked in on a huge party? My brother and family I haven't seen in forever were there, at my parents' house, living it up without me."

Adam frowned, thinking. "They didn't invite you?"

"No. But everyone else sure was invited." Steam seemed to blow from Elliot's ears as he spoke. "And I know what you're thinking. It's not because I'm gay. No, they didn't invite me because I was content without them. I'm not their baby. I didn't need them like Sammy needed them, to help pay his rent and stock his fridge with food for a house they paid rent for. He's such a moocher, younger than me by only two years yet they still baby him."

He had no idea how to respond to that. "That's fucked."

"Damn right it's fucked." Elliot glared at the flashlight as he hobbled faster, rage seemed to fuel him and take his mind off of any pain he might have had. "I would speak up and tell my mom how her babying him would make him dependent for the rest of his life, but she didn't want to hear it. She didn't like hearing the truth. My dad, he just went along with whatever, dishing out money here and there for him."

Adam could hear the strain in Elliot's voice as he spoke. He sounded like he would burst into tears at any moment.

"They stop inviting me over. I thought it was just that one time, but Sammy was kind enough to let me know there were plenty of parties I wasn't a part of. That was just the only one I happen to walk in on. God, I felt so betrayed." Elliot's voice softened. "I didn't need them like Sammy did. I had my own life so they just forgot about me. And you wanna know the worst part about it?"

Adam nodded. "Hmm?"

"Even after they abandoned me, I still waited, hoping the next time I would get an invitation. Later, when Sammy was helping me and Jeff pack our stuff to move to Phoenix, I found out there were other parties."

"That's—"

"Fucked. I know. And yet, I wish I never would've left." Elliot turned his head and met Adam's gaze. "I wonder if they missed me as much as I missed them."

Adam didn't know what to say. He dropped his gaze. How upsetting that must have been to have a family that excluded him and made him feel like he didn't matter, like he wasn't important to them, to betray him, as Elliot put it. Somewhere inside, his heartache for Elliot was briefly eclipsed by the awe he had for him to stand up for himself. Even if Elliot felt his brother was the favored son, Elliot had spoken up about the unfairness between them regardless of the consequences. If only Adam was brave enough to confront his own demons. He sighed as an invisible vise clenched and churned his innards. The least he could do was share *something* about himself. But he wouldn't go too deep. He wasn't ready to go too deep.

"I don't have any brothers or sisters." Adam said. "My father died at fifty when I was still a kid, lung cancer. My mom was young, her early thirties when he died. Still young and stupid she got into drugs and ran off with a boyfriend a few years later. I ended up living alone until I finally graduated high school. Then later, at twenty-one, I took a job at The Rodeo as a bartender." There, that should do it. He inhaled and tasted dust, exhaled and felt relief. That wasn't too bad. He didn't go deep at all.

"You were a bartender too? Where did you learn to tend bar?"

"Learned on the job. They only hired me 'cause the club manager wanted some 'hunky guys' out front to bring in the ladies and the bucks. They hired me only because I promised to be a dancer for them when I learned a thing or two. I met Jena there the year I started bartending. She and her girlfriend were regulars. Less than a couple weeks later we were dating and about a year after that I started dancing."

"Did you like dancing?" An innocent smile curled Elliot's bruised lip.

The thought of helping Elliot's bruise heal with a soft, wet kiss made Adam lick his own dry lips. Then he looked away, tearing the image from his mind. "It was okay."

Over the next few minutes of silence, Adam's mind wandered, remembering the feel of Elliot's hard body on his wet skin. The way they moved in unison, rubbing their hard, slick cocks together. Allowing the power of their orgasm to pull them from their harsh realities and transport them into heavenly bliss. If only for a brief moment, it felt so . . . good.

"Do you hear that?" Elliot paused. "I heard footsteps."

Adam paused and listened, looking in the direction of the flashlight beam.

A shadow ran by. Elliot swept the light across the dusty trail, following the shadow and lighting up a fallen concrete wall that used to serve as a divider between homes. Then the bark gave it away.

"Damn dog is back," Adam whispered. "Hand me the light." If the damned thing decided to attack he would use the long, heavy, metal flashlight as a weapon. Elliot gave him the flashlight and the dog growled, peeking out from behind the collapsed concrete divider.

Adam braced himself. "Get somewhere safe," he said, while keeping the light glued to the dog.

"Where am I supposed to go?" Elliot said quietly.

But before Adam could answer, the dog came rushing forward. He lifted the flashlight, ready to strike, but the dog stopped a few feet ahead of him. Adam shined the light on it again. "Get!" he yelled but the bleeding dog didn't budge. He stepped forward and the dog moved backward. "Go on. Get going!" The dog whimpered, turned as if it was gonna leave but made a full circle and cocked his head and stared at Elliot. Then he sat down and licked at the wound on its hind leg.

"It's scared." Adam said, relaxing. "It doesn't want to hurt us, it's just being defensive." He looked to Elliot, seeing a half-eaten granola bar in his hand. "Try giving it a piece of that."

Elliot raised his hand, staring at the bar. "I forgot I even had this." He broke off a piece and threw it in the dog's direction where it landed on the ground near it. The dog stood, sniffed at the granola bar and devoured it.

"Knew it. He's harmless," Adam said.

Elliot broke the rest of his bar into bite sized pieces and tossed them beside the dog. "Let's go."

They continued walking along the isolated path, carefully making their way over and through rubble, abandoned vehicles and fallen trees guided by the flashlight. Adam glanced over his shoulder at the rustling behind them. The dog followed them closely. Its head hung low and its dark eyes looked up at them like a hopeless, begging child in need. It was pathetic how much the mutt tugged at his heartstrings. He was pathetic to allow it. "The damn thing's following us."

Elliot turned to look behind him and then swiveled to look ahead again. "It probably wants some more food."

"Too bad." Adam pivoted, flashing the light on the dog and lighting up its dirty brown coat of fur. "Get, dog." He stomped his foot.

"Get the hell outta here." It whined and scurried away behind what was left of someone's home. They barely had enough food for themselves, they had to ration it the best they could. He sure didn't have enough granola bars to feed three mouths let alone his and Elliot's.

He sighed at the realization. "We're gonna need more food and water."

Elliot pointed toward the south. "Food Plus is that way."

Adam could only make out the silhouettes of buildings far in the distance. They were nothing more than dark, odd shaped remnants of structures that used to be twice their size, and lit up with streetlights and glowing signs.

"Do you remember if there's one that way?" He didn't want to stray from the plan, walking west. He wasn't sure where he was going but it seemed to be the logical thing to do. If angry, menacing darkness was approaching from the east, escape them by traveling west. It made sense.

"There's a gas station up here." Elliot nodded excitedly, and then shook his head. "No wait, that's on Roosevelt and Main. Damn it."

Adam paused, thinking. "If we head to Food Plus it'll take us another thirty minutes or so to get there."

"We could do it. Don't worry about my bum leg."

"It's not your leg I'm worried about. We'd have to climb over and through all this junk and who knows how long that'll take. It'll take forever to get back on track." Adam looked around, pointing the light as far as it would go to the west.

"Let's go to Food Plus and stock up on food and water. Who knows, maybe we can take shelter there too."

"I wanna stay on track. We walk west until we run into...something."

"Something?" Elliot dipped his brows. "You mean someone. You really don't think everyone's dead, huh?" The way Elliot looked at him, scrutinizing with his eyes, doubting, and judging made Adam a bit defensive. An uneasy energy surged between them. Elliot was onto him, he knew he was playing a role; the role of a macho man that everyone, including his fiancée expected him to be.

Instead of answering, Adam ignored the question. "Let's just keep walking."

"No, answer me." Elliot tugged his shoulder, forcing Adam to turn and stare at him. Challenging him to come clean. "You don't really believe everyone's dead, do you?"

"What does it matter what I think?" His voice raised an octave, stunning Elliot and making him take a step back.

"I'm using both of our heads to make the best decisions. You're the one who saw a news report about this stuff. I trusted you. If you think there are people still alive maybe we should find them."

Of course, everyone always counted on Adam to know what's best, and when he failed they blamed him. "*I'm* the one using both of our heads. You asked me what the plan was and I told you. I didn't ask you to trust me. I'm looking out for myself and you should do the same."

Elliot backed down, voice lowering. "I thought we were in this together. Two heads are better than one."

"Look, I'm doing the best I can. I told you, I'm not the hero you think I am." Adam had to stop there. He couldn't go too deep. He shrugged, looking into Elliot's hurt brown eyes. His stomach ached. He wished he had the balls to cradle Elliot's face in his palms and brush apologetic kisses from one corner of his lips to the other, but he had to think about his survival and consider his fiancée. Lusting after Elliot was doing him no good. It was making him take a step back, back to a place he didn't want to be. "Look, I—"

"What was that?" Elliot stood still, looking around with his big brown eyes.

"Huh?"

"Did you feel that?"

At that exact moment the earth beneath Adam's feet began to shake. "An earthquake."

"Another one? Shit."

The vacant vehicles on the littered road began to sway as the rocking got stronger. Chunks of concrete and brick fell from what was left of some of the buildings, and far in the distance the screeching sound of heavy, hot steel twisting and bending cut through the air. Then like a bomb detonating, the sound of a building collapsing tore through the night behind them. Then unexpectedly, like a thief caught red-handed, the trembling stopped.

"What was that?" Elliot asked. "You think it was an aftershock."

"Maybe, let's keep moving."

A pained yelp cut through the silence, sending a cold chill down Adam's spine. He turned around facing where the sound was coming from. Again, an agonizing howl tore through the silence.

Elliot brought his hand up to his wide mouth. "Oh, no. Something's happened to that dog."

They stood silently, listening for proof that the dog was in trouble. When the squealing cry sounded again, Adam hastily made his way to the crying where whining and whimpering noises came from under a pile of wood and rubble. "It's trapped in there." He sat his pack and the flashlight down, angling the light to illuminate the massive heap of concrete ruins, and then he began lifting and throwing huge blocks off of the pile. Elliot joined him, picking up and clearing away as much debris as they could.

They cleared as much as they could manage. The only thing left standing in their way was a big, solid slab of concrete. When Adam lifted one end of the heavy slab it teetered. The back end lowered allowing him to lift his end only about a foot high.

"Crawl in there and tell me if you see it," he said through clenched teeth as he bore the immense weight of the slab.

Elliot grabbed the flashlight and shined it in the space under the debris. "I don't see anything. Hold on."

Adam heard the heavy clunking as Elliot moved away some more blocks. "This is really heavy," he warned, hoping Elliot would hurry. He couldn't hold it for long.

Elliot crawled nearly halfway inside. "Oh, I see it!"

"Grab it."

"I can't. I think it's stuck."

"Let me take a look," Adam said, the weight of the slab tiring his arm muscles. Just as Elliot crawled out Adam dropped the slab and took a few deep breathes. "Can you lift that?"

"I can try." They exchanged positions and Elliot lifted the hefty slab, testing. "I can't hold it for long."

Adam took his cue and grabbed the flashlight. He crawled into the hole and shined it in the direction of the whimpering. The dog's head stuck out from a smaller pile of crumbled concrete blocks. Adam crawled closer and carefully dislodged a block, freeing the dog, except it didn't come out of the rubble as he expected it to.

"Think it's really hurt." He called out to Elliot. "I'm gonna pull it out."

"Just hurry. This thing is heavy."

Adam crawled forward, breathing in dust and dirt as his face grazed the ground. He reached into the smaller crevice and carefully took hold of the scruff on the back of the dog's neck. He gently yet quickly pulled the dog out of the narrow opening and into the cavity with him. He tried to back up out of the hole and pull the dog with him, but there wasn't enough room and he didn't have a tight grip. His heart raced as he felt the concrete slab slowly weigh down on the back of his thighs, pinning him to the dusty ground.

"What are you doing? You're gonna crush me."

Elliot grunted. "Hurry. Too heavy."

"Elliot, don't drop that on me." As he talked he managed to wiggle and squirm, slowly backing up out of the hole; one hand gripping the flashlight, the other pulling the injured dog. The slab of heavy, ragged concrete scraped the back of his thighs and ass.

"Hurry," Elliot cried. He grunted again, sounding like a muscle man lifting three hundred pounds. "Damn it, Adam. Hurry!"

The slab rose, allowing Adam to better slide out with the dog. As soon as they were clear, Elliot dropped the slab. It teetered, the back end lifted rapidly as the front end crashed to the ground. Dirt and dust pillared up around them. The sound of rocks settling on the pile rushed around them for a few seconds.

Elliot slumped forward, hands on his knees as he breathed heavily in an attempt to catch his breath.

"You were close to dropping that on me." Adam shined the light on the rubble pile, imaging the dire consequences if that very thing had happened.

Elliot inhaled sharply. "No. I was *not* gonna drop it. Not until you were out of there." He coughed. "I swear."

The sincere look in his quick blinking eyes told Adam he was telling the truth. That and the fact that he hadn't dropped it. He looked down at his feet where the dog lay. It rested on its side motionless, looking up at him with blinking, sorrowful dark eyes. Adam saw that the dog was male and most likely a cross breed. His brick-like head, thick muscled neck, stocky body and tapered tail suggest that it was a Pit Bull Terrier.

He kneeled beside the dog. Blood seeped from a filthy two inch tear in his left hind leg. Instinctively Adam glanced at Elliot's leg. The similarities in their injuries were uncanny. "I think he was crushed." He shook his head, ran his hand through his own dusty hair and sighed. "He's dying."

Elliot frowned. "So we just leave him here?"

"Or put him out of his misery." He met Elliot's eyes with a questioning look.

Elliot's eyes widened. "I can't do that."

Adam huffed. "I'll do it." He knew since he brought it up he would have to be the one to carry it out. He sat the flashlight down, angling it to light the area as best as possible. He picked up a cinder block from the pile he just crawled out of, and while standing over the dog, he lifted the hefty block above his head.

"I can't watch this." Elliot closed his eyes and turned around.

Adam's heart pounded so fast and hard he felt it in his thumbs as he gripped the cinder block. He looked down at the dog. The dog looked up at him and let out a hoarse bark as if to protest. Adam's bottom lip trembled and his grip tightened. Sweat trickled down the back of his neck and the environment suddenly grew deathly quiet. For a second he thought he had gone deaf. He bit his bottom lip to keep it from quivering, and the muscles in his arms began to ache from the weight of the cinder block in his hands. He closed his eyes, trying to calm himself when a pair of strong yet soft hands overlapped his own, removing the cinder block from his grip.

"Don't do it." Elliot whispered in his ear.

He felt the warmth of Elliot's body as he pressed against his back. Elliot gently sat the block down on the ground and Adam dropped his hands to his side, thankful that Elliot had stopped him from doing what would've been on his conscience for days and maybe weeks to come.

"You went through all that hell to save him and now you're just gonna turn around and kill him? No, I won't let you do that to yourself or him."

Adam stared at the dog, too ashamed to look at Elliot. "Thank you."

Elliot chuckled. "Why are you thanking me? You're the hero. I knew you were."

"You helped." Adam said, finally looking up. He smiled slightly, already feeling guilt mixed with a bit of relief.

"I did," Elliot said proudly. "So that makes me your sidekick, huh? What should our names be?" Adam sat down beside the dog, watching as Elliot thought, admiring how he could take a devastating moment and turn it into something comforting, relaxing. "I know," Elliot continued. "You can be Midnight Man. In the darkness or the mid of night, Midnight Man prowls the destruction, with double M's on his sexy chest, to rescue anyone and any dog in need."

Adam blushed at his *sexy chest* reference and was glad Elliot couldn't see his red cheeks in the poor lighting.

Elliot grinned. "And his sidekick Dark Lad, with the ability to lift anything no matter the size—"

"Dark Lad?" Adam snorted.

"Yeah, you know, Midnight? Dark?" He gestured at the ominous dark sky above them. "Dark Lad stays true to the word sidekick by never leaving Midnight Man's side no matter what."

Heat gathered in Adam's chest. "Thanks."

"No need to thank me." Elliot reached down and placed a hand on Adam's shoulder. "You'd do the same for me, huh?"

They stared at each other silently for a moment. Adam focused on the soft outline of Elliot's jaw and the fullness of his pouty bottom lip. His stomach hurt from the knots that gathered in the pit of it. He swallowed, his mouth salivating at the thought of tasting the tongue of the sensual-looking man who stared back at him.

The dog's panting took their attention away from each other and brought Adam back to reality. Elliot knelt beside the dog and patted its head. "Maybe he's thirsty and hungry."

Without a second thought, Adam grabbed his pack and dug inside for his bottle of water and a granola bar. He drizzled the water into the dog's mouth, watching as it lapped at the stream frantically. The dog lifted its head from the ground in an attempt to get more water.

"Easy. Easy." Adam caressed the head and then opened the granola package. He held a piece of the bar in his palm and offered it. The dog sniffed at it, and then suddenly gulped it down once he realized it was food. Adam fed it the rest of the package and watched as the dog struggled to stand. It shook its body, shaking off a layer of dirt, and sat. It stretched its injured hind leg and licked at the bloody wound.

"He looks better already." Elliot smiled widely. His smile lightened the mood. "Let's clean up the leg like you did mine. You have some more gauze and antiseptic?"

Adam grabbed some sterile gauze and the bottle of antiseptic from his pack. He'd taken some from the dental office for Elliot's wound, so he had plenty to spare for the dog. Elliot helped hold the dog still as Adam cleaned, covered and wrapped the hurt leg. Once finished, the dog stood and sniffed around in his backpack, probably for more granola.

Adam yawned. "Let's rest here a while." He cleared the area of litter with his feet. "We can use some of this trash and stuff to build a fire for light."

Elliot huffed, frowning. "Like camping, but not really."

"Come on, Dark Lad." Adam tapped Elliot's shoulder. "If the superhero doesn't complain, the sidekick doesn't either."

Elliot scoffed, rolling his eyes. "I never said you were a *super*hero." He helped gather some wood pieces. "But you're not far from it."

CHAPTER FOUR

Denial

Elliot watched the flames dance around in the makeshift stone-walled pit, and the dog limp about sniffing at the litter around them. Elliot stretched his legs out on the ground near the fire. "I think he's still hungry."

"He's had three bars already." Adam reclined back against the slanted slab that rested on the pile of concrete blocks he had crawled under. "Be completely out of bars before you know it. Might have to make a trip to that Food Plus."

Their campfire illuminated the area around them enough for Elliot to make out Adam's handsome features. Everything else outside of their close circle was cloaked in blackness. He couldn't make out anything beyond ten feet, which he didn't mind. The limited light source made him feel protected. He imagined relaxing inside a small bubble that included Adam and their new four legged friend, safe from the deteriorating world outside the bubble.

The dog limped over and lay down on the ground next to Elliot. "Look, he likes me."

"I see that." Adam smiled, causing the parenthesis lines around his mouth to deepen.

"Since he's gonna stick with us, maybe we should name him." He ran his hand along the dog's short, dark brown coat. Something caught his eye. The hairs around the dog's neck lay flat in a uniform ring as if he once wore a collar. Also the dog's ears were cropped. "Looks like he's had a name before."

"Huh?"

"He used to wear a collar, and someone took good care of him. His nails are trimmed and he seems pretty healthy other than the leg. What do you think his name is?"

"Don't know."

"Come on, guess."

"Uh, Spot, Max, Titan?"

Elliot called to the dog, "Titan. Titan?" When the dog didn't respond he frowned. "No, it's not Titan."

Adam shrugged. "Just make up a name."

Elliot stared at the dog, thinking. "Titan sounds pretty good."

Titan was a good name. It signified strength, importance, and power. Kind of like Adam. Elliot watched Adam relax, rocking his head back against the slab. There was no denying he was a good-looking man. It took everything Elliot had to keep from jumping him like a sex-starved maniac. He admired his self-discipline. Thinking of discipline, he realized he hadn't looked back east since they left the dental office. He was stronger now, ready to do whatever he had to do to survive. But although the darkness completely blanketed them, he just couldn't commit to looking above at the murky clouds. So he settled on staring at Adam.

Dirty thoughts of hot, wet sex entered his mind. He knew his thoughts were mostly out of desperation; desperation to escape reality, but they were welcomed.

Seconds of silence slowly rolled by. In the midst of the calm, Elliot encouraged his fantasies by studying Adam as he leaned his head back and exposed his long neck, his jaw tightened and relaxed repeatedly. He imagined licking and nibbling the tight muscle on the side of Adam's neck, tasting the saltiness of his sweat. He remembered the image of him standing nearly naked under the jet from the broken water main while water fell over his muscled body, and the sun rays bounced off of his tanned skin. Watching him now—legs stretched out on the ground in front of him and crossed at the ankles, hands resting on his lap, the great cock that hid beneath his jeans— made him excited. He could feel his heart race and his own cock swell from the imagery.

Then Adam opened his eyes, lifted his head and met his gaze with a questioning stare. "You watching me?" His eyes narrowed and his cheeks reddened just as they did earlier when Elliot had mentioned his sexy chest.

Elliot smirked. "I'm actually doing more than that."

Adam looked flattered for a split second, a glint of appreciation in his eye, and then he looked away. No problem. Elliot knew exactly how to get his attention back, and he needed his attention. If Adam wasn't up for a little reality vacation to a place of bliss he just might panic. He had to be stronger than that. No, he *was* stronger than that.

He crawled over and sat next to Adam who seemed a little shocked at first. Was he not expecting him to be so forward, so needy? Surely Adam knew what he was thinking.

They stared into each other's eyes. Elliot missed the stunning green in Adam's already. He would probably never see that unique color in his eyes again especially in the poor, dim light of the campfire. Another reason to be thankful for the sunshine when they had it.

Adam's demeanor was a mixture of anticipation and trepidation, as if he wanted Elliot to make a move but was unsure about it at the same time. His eyes said *touch me*, but his body language said *too close.* Elliot didn't want to do anything drastic. He didn't want to give Adam a reason to be unsure about him. However, he couldn't stop his gaze from traveling to Adam's lips. God, what he would give to have those lips on his lips, on his body, on his cock. When he looked back up into his eyes Adam was looking at his lips too, probably thinking the same thing.

Elliot's cock ached. It throbbed with the beat of his heart, rapid, steady and with full force. He moved his lips closer toward Adam's and stopped just millimeters away, unbuttoned and unzipped his cargo shorts and slipped his hand inside to grip his own hard cock. He licked his lips slowly, watching the mesmerized look on Adam's face. "I can suck you," Elliot whispered.

Adam inhaled sharply at those words. He liked it. Elliot liked the thought too. He took Adam's hand and stuffed it in his shorts to replace his own. A sigh escaped Elliot's lips and he closed his eyes when Adam palmed his cock and began a pleasurable game of tug and pull. The pleasure intensified as the seconds progressed. Elliot's toes curled and he brought his lips to Adam's. Their kiss was tender, all lips but rapidly evolving. Their tongues eagerly licked one another's, gliding, tasting. He moaned when Adam's thumb brushed the head of his cock, slathering pre-come liberally on and around the tip. Adam's moan followed, mimicking Elliot's cry of pleasure.

"I wanna suck you." Elliot reached for the bulge in Adam's jeans and massaged the hardness against Adam's firm thigh. "I wanna suck you off and taste every last bit of it on my tongue."

"Yes," Adam hissed, kissing him harder, deeper. His hand twisted around Elliot's cock, milking pent up pleasure from his aching body.

"Oh, fuck. Don't stop." He felt the warmth of the copious lubricant ooze out of his rigid cock, maintaining an easy glide. Elliot was about to come any minute. "You're so perfect. So fucking perfect."

"Sshh." Adam kissed him, probably to quiet him. But he couldn't think of one reason Adam would want to keep him quiet. He didn't want to think. All that was on his mind was his impending orgasm.

"Don't stop. I'm close," Elliot breathed as Adam's hand moved faster, tug and pull, tug and pull. Elliot grunted, feeling his eyelashes flutter as his eyes rolled to the back of his head. "Ooh, God." Before Elliot could stifle his cry of pleasure he was coming. Rope after rope of warm semen pulsed from his stiff cock and drizzled down over

Adam's knuckles. He panted rapidly and took a minute to fully catch his breath and center himself in a world that seemed to spin forever. Once the fireworks cleared his bleary vision, he fumbled with the button on Adam's jeans. "Now I can taste you." He popped the button and peeled back the jean flaps. "And I can suck you *all* night." He grinned flirtatiously and dipped his head to Adam's lap, a great way to escape a disastrous reality.

Adam grabbed his shoulders, stopping him. "You don't have to do that."

"I want to." Elliot caught a glimpse of that unsure look in his eyes. "Trust me, I wanted to do this to you all day." He brushed a soft kiss across Adam's lips and whispered, "Since I laid eyes on you."

Adam shook his head. "I just...I can't let you do that." He turned his gaze away, staring blankly at the darkness in the distance over Elliot's shoulder.

"You don't want to get off?" By the way Adam fisted Elliot's cock earlier he would've never guessed. He seemed to enjoy it more than Elliot, jacking him like he was going to orgasm from it himself. Now why would Adam torture himself by denying a generous offer, a perfect chance to get something good out of the demolished existence they were suddenly forced to live in?

"This isn't me." Adam shook his head. "I can't keep doing these things."

Elliot tried to hide his scowl as he buttoned and zipped his shorts. "This isn't you? What are you trying to say?"

Adam shrugged, rubbing dirt in his palms to remove the stickiness from his hands. "I don't do this—these things." His voice rose faintly. "Not anymore. Not since Jena."

"Jena's gone." Elliot glared, refusing to hide his anger and frustration. "She left you, remember? Plus, you said no one was alive so who cares what you do—"

"Oh, come on, Elliot." Adam buttoned his jeans. "Use your head for once."

Elliot's mouth dropped opened. Stunned, he wondered how Adam could talk to him like a cheap, dimwitted whore, especially after their intimacy. But mostly, what caused his shock was the sudden familiar feeling of betrayal. "So you do think there are other survivors. You asshole."

"I'm an asshole? It figures." Adam slid over a foot, making room between them.

Elliot chose to ignore the gesture or at least not bring attention to it. "You told me there were no more lies, but here you are lying about other survivors."

"I don't know if there are other people out here or not, but if we're alive anything's possible." Adam's defensive tone and angry eyes mirrored Elliot's.

"So you think your fiancée is still alive?" Elliot heard his voice rising but allowed it. It felt good, therapeutic, and necessary. "You're planning to see her again, to get back with her and forget that she left you behind when you needed her most?"

Adam's handsome facial features twisted into a menacing glare. "What's it to you? You're not my wife. You're not my fiancée. You're not my boyfriend. You're nothing to me. Hell, we haven't even fucked."

Elliot's chest filled with painful heat. "Damn near."

"Never."

That word hit him like a pile of stones to the gut, but he refused to react to the sting. "So why did you tell me everybody's probably dead?"

"Because I wanted you to stop whining and face reality. Grow a backbone, damn it."

"What the hell's gotten into you?" Elliot wished he could put a finger on Adam's sudden resentment. "You damn near fuck me in that dental office, you give me these flirty looks, you jack me off and now you don't even want to sit by me? We're supposed to look out for each other, make some damn progress, but all we're doing is going backwards."

Adam ran both hands through his hair, anxiously. "You're trying to turn me into something I'm not."

"What, gay?" Elliot shook his head, a detached smile on his face. "You said yourself that you and some kid used to fuck around in high school. Or was that a lie too?"

"I'm not that kid anymore."

"No, you're not. But I know exactly who you are. You're a lying prick who's in denial."

Adam laughed quietly, hanging his head down between his bent knees. "Lying? Denial? I'm not the one parading around like everything's okay. Like all of a sudden I'm strong, confident and fearless but still won't grow the balls to look east."

"Fuck you." Elliot sneered, taking his comment to the gut. "Who's the big, tough, manly man who's too pussy to admit his fiancée doesn't love him and he loves dick?"

Adam's snapped his head toward him. "You don't know Jena or me."

"I know you well enough." Elliot felt a tickle on his cheek and quickly swiped away the tear with his hand. He'd be damned if he would cry, especially in front of Adam.

Adam slowly nodded, staring at the dimming fire. "So now we know where we stand."

He wasn't sure what that meant but to hear those words and the nonchalant way Adam said them worried him. He didn't want to be a dick, but he was hurt. Adam cut him deeper in ten minutes than his exes had in years. His insides felt hollow, gutted from Adam's blasé attitude. But before he could let it sink in and linger, a gust of wind blew by, kicking up dirt and dust and making their fire roar. Elliot stood when Titan did, watching him whimper and bark at nothing in particular.

"Now that we know where we stand," he said sarcastically, "maybe now is a good time to keep moving."

Adam stood, got his pack and swung it over his shoulder to loosely hang. "Ready?"

"As ready as I'm gonna be." He made sure his lack of enthusiasm came through in his words. "What's the plan?"

Adam looked back at him and shrugged. "Gonna visit Food Plus, stock up on some supplies, and then look for other people." His gaze dropped and a flash of what looked like sadness swept across his face. "Look, Elliot. I'm sorry."

"Save it." Elliot stopped his words with a dismissive wave of his hand. "I don't need your apology."

"I didn't mean to be so harsh." He kicked dirt over the dying embers of their campfire.

"If you didn't mean to then you shouldn't have." Elliot started walking toward the direction of Food Plus. "Come on, Titan." The dog stood motionless, panting. "Titan?" He whistled and Titan trotted to him, following. "You're gonna have to learn your new name." Elliot patted his head and continued walking, hearing that familiar sound of heavy footsteps follow closely behind.

CHAPTER FIVE

Search for Refuge

The building was nearly a pile of bricks when they arrived, no signs of life or electricity. The once lighted and erect Food Plus sign now lay on the ground surrounded in slivers of glass. Only the large F and P were still intact. One corner of the grocery store was still standing, and aisles of what was left of putrid food and other supplies lay crushed under pieces of the roof that had caved in. Pink fiberglass insulation and glass shards from the windows and light bulbs covered the entire lot.

"Careful," Adam warned as he made his way to the shelves that were still upright. It must've been the bakery section because all he could reach were various assortments of stale breads and pastries. He stocked up on as many packaged cookies and dried fruit as he could fit into his pack.

In the darkness, Elliot crawled over debris to a nearby case of bottled juice that looked unblemished. He took a bottle of what was probably warm orange juice and downed it entirely in seconds.

Adam shined the flashlight around the lot and saw small orange papers lying around. At first he thought they were store coupons. At closer look he determined they were flyers. The bold black letters read: Refuge Inc., A Secure Future. Encircled around the center of the R was a silver ring or halo and below that was a local phone number and website address. It was odd. He couldn't recall what company it was or why there were hundreds of their flyers lying around the Food Plus lot. It was probably nothing. He was looking too much into it. It may very well be nothing more than a housing development or some sort of school or something. Anything with the word *refuge* on it perked his interest so he stuffed the flyer in his pants pocket. He would ask Elliot about the flyer to see what he knew of it. In the meantime he continued rummaging, peaking over his shoulder at Titan whose head was in a bag of chips he'd ripped open, eating the contents.

"I don't see any water. But I got these." Elliot limped toward him carrying several sealed bags of beef jerky and bottles of orange juice. He cradled everything in one arm and pulled a pack of condoms out of his pocket, unblemished and still enclosed in the foil wrapper. "Found these too." He shrugged, not making eye contact as he stuffed them back in his pocket.

"Bag's full. Can you carry all that in a grocery bag?" Adam knew Elliot was making sure he knew about the condoms. Even so, Adam didn't want to acknowledge them. What was he supposed to say anyway? Whatever he said would've made the moment more awkward.

Elliot found a grocery bag and stuffed the jerky and the rest of the orange juice inside.

"Ready?" Adam asked.

"Come on, Titan." Elliot called and whistled. The dog followed.

Although he had turned down Elliot's sexual advances, he could see Elliot trying to move on from that incident. During the walk from the campfire to the grocery store he'd tried to apologize but Elliot wouldn't hear it. He knew he'd made a mistake the moment he opened his mouth and said *no*. The mistake was in hurting Elliot. He'd tried for so long to let go of that part of his life. Being that guy had done more harm to him than it did any good. His relationship with Jena had been affected and he would never live it down.

Surviving the impact was Adam's second chance to be the man he truly was, not some weak, man-loving failure. But he didn't want to think of his failures, he didn't want to go that deep. He hated reliving those painful memories. He wouldn't go back to that place. However, the knowledge that they now had condoms caused his stomach to quiver nervously. Butterflies?

Adam wasn't sure where they were headed. At times it was difficult to tell what direction they were going in. His sense of direction was skewed especially since structures and landmarks had collapsed in huge mounds of unrecognizable fragments. Even the stars were concealed by the darkness. In all of the chaos it never occurred to him to tuck a compass in his pack.

As they walked silently in the dark, cool air, Elliot broke the silence first.

"What time do you think it is?"

Adam shrugged. "Doesn't really matter now. Time doesn't mean much." He took off his pack and pulled out a wristwatch. "It's about ten."

"How long were we walking?"

"Four hours?"

"I wish I had my cell phone." Elliot sighed. "I miss my cell phone. And hot dogs and marshmallows too. The campfire reminded me of those."

The campfire. Images of stuffing his hand in Elliot's shorts came to mind. Then the condoms replaced that picture. Adam shook his head, shaking the images away. "You're right, you know," he said.

Elliot frowned. "About?"

Adam gulped, building the courage. "I'm a liar. I lied all my life."

"About being gay?" Elliot nodded and huffed. "Yeah, I know."

Adam shrugged, head hanging low. "It's hard for me to let it go. You know?"

"Let what go?" Elliot threw his hands in the air. "Why don't you tell me what's going on with you?"

"I can't go too deep."

Elliot stopped walking, anger in his rapidly blinking brown eyes. "What the hell does that mean? First you're on, then you're off. You're warm, then cold. You want me, then you don't. Why are you afraid to leave the closet? It's just you and me now, Adam. I accept you."

Adam exhaled, his control slipping through his fingers. "It's not that."

Elliot crossed his arms across his strong chest, glaring. "Then what is it?"

He shook his head. "Coming out always meant suicide to me."

"Oh, get over it." Elliot smacked his lips in annoyance. "I came out years ago and I'm still alive. Not even a fucking asteroid can get rid of me."

"You're stronger than I am." In terms of being out, proud and self-confident, Elliot proved to be much tougher than he.

"I'm so sick of gay guys acting straight because they're pussies. It's always people like me who get hurt! Since you're so bad at being straight, man up and be *you* already."

Adam sighed, bowing his head. He would have to go there, to that deep, hollowed out cave within his chest cavity. He'd have to return to those dark memories and confront them again. "Jena found proof of...sessions I had online with other men. Explicit sessions. She called me a liar, a cheat ... a fag. She said my nasty behavior was what prevented us from getting pregnant. We've been trying for months. Finally, when the news came out about the asteroid, she just left me. She thought I was too weak to keep her safe. She didn't even want me to go with her. So I stayed." He sniffed and cleared his throat. After a few silent seconds he added, "I loved her. I still love her."

Elliot huffed. "That's pathetic."

Adam's head popped up. "What?"

"You still love her after what she did to you?" He rolled his eyes.

"It's not so easy to just switch it off after so many years. Plus, look what I've done to her. I deserved it."

"You deserve to be called names and be walked out on? She left you in the middle of a fucking crisis. What would that make you if you'd done that to her? A total asshole." He shook his head and continued walking, leaving Adam.

It occurred to Adam that Elliot could be right. However, uneasiness crept inside him from seeing Elliot turn his back on him. He followed. "I opened up to you. I told you things I've never told anyone, and you walk away from me?"

"I'm still by your side." Elliot glanced over his shoulder at him. "And even though you're in your own personal crisis, I'm not Jena. I'm not gonna leave you. Sidekick, remember?"

Adam's eyebrows pulled together and he put his hand on Elliot's shoulder, stopping him. "So you forgive me for earlier, then?" He stared, pleading with his eyes. The last thing he wanted to do was cause a rift between him and the only friend he had.

Elliot looked over to him and could barely keep eye contact. "I've been rejected before. I'm a big boy, I'll live." He kept walking.

Adam was more than impressed by Elliot's strength, he was a bit envious of his courage to come out and be himself. He wished he was as courageous. Either way, Elliot was right about everything. Adam owed him more than a handful of lies, because he hadn't left him. Pathetic, he was still in love with someone who had.

He continued following Elliot, shining the light as far ahead of them as it would go. Then he saw it, a huge car insurance ad plastered on a billboard which had toppled over and now lay on the side of the road. What caught his eye was the R with a circle around the center that was spray painted on the billboard with black spray paint. He quickly pulled the crumpled flyer out of his pocket.

"Elliot," he called out, adrenaline rushed through his veins at the possibility. "Look at this."

Elliot took the orange flyer out of his hand. "Yeah? So?"

"Look." He pointed the light to the downed sign. "It's Refuge Inc. Heard of that? A secure future?"

"No." Elliot's frowned, examining the flyer. "What is it?"

Could it be refuge, shelter, and other people? "Not sure. I found that at Food Plus."

"Yeah, I saw them too. Millions of them everywhere." He handed it back to Adam, and stared at the fallen billboard. "I thought they were just trash and just ignored them."

Adam stared too and noticed a spray painted arrow on the corner pointing in the direction they were going. "Look at the arrow. Let's follow it." He took the lead, his steps hastened as his adrenaline surged. "Don't know what this means. Maybe it's a gathering place for survivors?"

"You think?" Elliot eyes widened in excitement, that Adam heard in his voice.

When were the flyers placed at the store? No one would have printed them and scattered them around an abandoned and destroyed grocery store for potential survivors, or would they? Or worse, someone placed those flyers in the store long before the impact. But that would mean they knew about the asteroid much longer than when news finally broke. Was it possible? Of course it was. NASA could detect a threat from space a decade in advance or more. Probably. If so why didn't they give everyone adequate warning? What use would it have done if they couldn't prevent the worst from happening anyway? But something else occurred to him. The thought of some elaborate government cover-up troubled him, but government cover-ups and conspiracies were the last thing he wanted on his mind right now.

The streets were littered with abandoned cars, trucks and even bright yellow school busses. The sidewalk was riddled with cracks and in some places the sidewalk was completely severed, which Adam figured was dangerous, so they stuck to the street, weaving in and out of the cars. Titan followed closely behind, panting with every limp.

Elliot laughed softly. "If we find other people I'm gonna fall down in tears, I'm warning you."

Adam chuckled, feeling his eyes grow narrow and the dimples around his mouth crease with his smile. They were actually laughing. Adam hadn't laughed in a very long time.

They walked and walked. Nearly an hour passed since they cut through a community of crushed homes, looking for more Refuge Inc. signs to lead them in the right direction but instead found nothing.

"Look!" Elliot pointed ahead at a dark one story house. "You see that?"

Adam swept the light ahead, looking for more black painted R's but didn't see any. "What is it?"

Elliot rushed toward what could have been the backyard of a house where a massive covered wooden box sat. On closer look, Adam knew exactly what he was looking at.

"It's a hot tub," Elliot said excitedly.

Adam grinned at Elliot's enthusiasm. "I doubt it's hot."

"But it might have water in it." Elliot examined the outside of the wooden cube. "It looks good. No damage. Now help me open it."

Together they unhinged the corner locks and removed the lid. The smell of chlorine permeated the dank air. It looked brand new inside with an oval shaped fiberglass tub and crystal clear water.

Elliot dipped his hand in. "It's freezing but we can still use it to clean up."

Adam nodded. "We'll make camp here and try to get some rest."

He shined the light at the dark, empty house which reminded him of something from a horror movie the way the windows were broken and the back door swung lazily on its hinges. The side and front of the house was caved in, which made for poor shelter. But he made a mental note of searching it for anything useful before they left.

The fire was crisp and bright. It lit up Titan as he limped off to explore the empty shell of the house. The light of the fire also glowed around the hot tub enough for Elliot to see as he hopped in and washed off the dirt and dust that had collected on their bodies. Adam was courteous enough to turn his back while Elliot bathed, awaiting his turn in the freezing water.

"Adam, what's your last name?"

He poked at the fire with a stick. "Weber."

"Adam Weber, hmm." Elliot chuckled. "Nice."

"And yours?" The heat of the fire increased a bit, scorching the fine hairs on his knuckles.

"Stewart. Elliot Stewart."

"Common."

"Yeah, so is Weber." The sound of splashing water resounded through the night.

Adam took the moment to clear up what had been nagging at him since leaving their last resting place. "Look, I feel bad for how I acted earlier."

"I was just getting over it." The water splashed as Elliot climbed out of the tub behind him. "We don't have to bring it up."

"It's not fair to you. To lead you on. To lie. But I'm so used to it. Lying to keep people from questioning me. Lying to keep the people around me happy."

"The whole 'I'm gay but afraid to admit it' thing is pretty pitiful." Elliot snorted. "Too many guys use that as an excuse not to get permanently involved or fall in love."

"It's real." He glanced over his shoulder at Elliot, and then quickly turned back to the crackling fire. "Sorry my problems are too cliché for you. But it's real. It exists. Messing around with men caused me too much trouble."

"Then it's time to get over it. What do you have to lose now anyway? Jena's already gone." Elliot sat down on a patch of grass if front of the warm, glowing fire. He was naked, wet and covering his pelvic area with his dusty shorts. "Jena's gone," he repeated as he looked into Adam's eyes. The sadness conveyed in his frown.

As much as he hated to believe it, again Elliot was right. Jena remained forever gone. And somehow the blow was more intense when he heard it from Elliot's mouth instead of his own. Was he really trying to fool himself into thinking Jena still loved him? He always thought actions spoke louder than words. Her actions told him plenty.

The gauze on Elliot's leg sagged and dripped with water. "Let me get that." Adam grabbed his pack and took out the supplies he needed to change Elliot's dressings. While placing fresh, dry gauze on Elliot's leg he thought aloud, "I wonder if she really loved me at all."

Staring at his bandaged leg, Elliot's eyebrows pulled together. "I wonder if you really were in love with her or if you were just using her as your cover."

Adam stared into Elliot's eyes, proving his sincerity. "I loved Jena. As pathetic as it may be, I loved her. I wanted a kid with her, I wanted to marry her, and I needed her."

"Not as much as I need you." Elliot looked away guiltily. "Look at us. We're both blaming each other for our problems when we're making the problems. It doesn't have to be this way. If you let me, I can take care of you the way you take care of me. Better than anyone ever has." The look in his eyes was genuine. Adam knew Elliot needed him. He didn't want to admit it but he needed Elliot just the same. After such a disaster, life wouldn't be the same. It made sense. Adam understood how two lonely fools would need one another as part of their survival.

"Your turn." Elliot nodded in the direction of the hot tub.

Adam walked over and removed his clothes, fully aware that Elliot's eyes were on him, drinking him in like a dried up sponge. He stepped into the tub, submerging everything below his waist in the cold water. Slowly he brought water to his chest with a cupped hand. He looked over his shoulder at Elliot who watched him bathe with an aroused glint in his eyes.

"You have a bruise on your hip," Elliot said, standing.

Adam ran his palms over his wet cheeks. "Crawling into that hole to get Titan."

"I did that, huh?" Elliot's voice was closer, right behind him. "When the concrete slab got too heavy and it grazed the back of your ... thigh." A hand caressed his shoulder. "I wasn't gonna drop it. Sorry for the bruise." Elliot's low and husky voice had the sound of sexual arousal lingering on every word.

Adam turned slowly to face Elliot. He was naked, no longer hiding behind his shorts, and his erection dark, stiff and pointed straight out in front of him.

"Sorry, I can't help it." Elliot's hands traveled down over Adam's chest and down over his abs. "You're just so...tempting."

Heat rushed Adam so fast his skin burned despite the freezing water he stood in. Adam swallowed hard enough for Elliot to hear. He could feel his cock hardening from Elliot's soft, sensual caresses. He stared at the bruise on Elliot's lip and for a split second he imaged his cock between them. Elliot's cock grew firmer by the second. He knew because he couldn't keep from eyeing it, watching it lengthen and rise. The deep contours on the sides of Elliot's lower abdomen cut straight to his groin and turned Adam on more than he knew was possible. Elliot's tight, flat stomach with a fine patch of dark hair below his navel made Adam's blood race through his body.

Elliot cupped his hand and applied water over Adam's sensitive skin. "You're so perfect."

Adam bowed his head. "Far from it."

"You're so damn beautiful."

Adam looked up, seeing the lust in Elliot's eyes and wondered if it matched his own. He climbed out of the tub, brushed his thumb across the bruise on Elliot's lip and planted a kiss there. "I—I want to but—"

"Don't say anything." Elliot grinned flirtatiously. "You still want to get off, right? Well, I still want to suck you all night."

Adam answered by licking Elliot's lip. Elliot moaned and opened his mouth. His tongue teasingly slid out to lick Adam's. Suddenly they were licking each other's tongues and sucking one another's lips, deeply, sensually, passionately. Their bodies pressed together, crushing their stiff cocks against the other's abdomen. Elliot dropped to his knees on the grass and left a trail of wet kisses up and down Adam's muscled thighs. He wrapped his fingers around Adam's thick, heavy cock and guided it into his warm mouth. His tongue swirled around the engorged tip and Adam huffed, rolling his head back and closing his eyes. He leaned back against the hot tub and a pleasing groan escaped his lips. He'd had an indescribable pent up need for sexual release that nagged at him like an annoying insect ever since the campfire incident, and finally the relief hit him strong.

Elliot's warm, wet, tantalizing licks traveled from the tip of his cock, down the thick vein underneath, and further down to his heavy balls. He shuddered as Elliot sucked his balls into his mouth, alternating between one and the other. He could hear Jena's angry voice yelling obscenities in his ear and he grimaced. The things she said, the names she called him, the heartbreak was all there, resurfacing. Again, second thoughts.

"Elliot, wait."

Elliot looked up, eyes low with desire, panting like a deep sea diver who finally came up for air. "It's okay," he murmured, the muffled words vibrated against his balls. "You can come on me. I like it."

With that, Adam couldn't muster the words to stop him, to interrupt the desire that suddenly surged through him. "You like it?" His chest rose and fell rapidly with the thought of seeing his milky stickiness on Elliot's moist lips.

Elliot nodded. "You can do anything you want to me. I'll love it." He dipped his head again, teasing his balls with quick flicks of his tongue.

Adam ran his fingers through Elliot's dark, damp hair. Part of him wanted to pull his head away from his body and tell him *no.* But the other part got exactly what he wanted; Elliot took his cock deep down his throat. He gently pulled Elliot's head back, looking down at long beating eyelashes. With his free hand Adam grabbed his cock and traced Elliot's bottom lip with the tip, coating his blushed lips with a thin layer of pre-come.

"You like that?" The words Adam fantasized saying to hot hungry men so many times.

"Uh huh." Elliot nodded, licking at the flared head.

"Open up." The fantasy played out the way Adam had always envisioned.

Elliot opened his mouth, tongue out. Adam placed his throbbing cock onto the tip and slowly thrust his hips, sliding it in to the base. He felt the tightening around the head where his cock met Elliot's throat and he moaned as Elliot swallowed around it.

Elliot bobbed his head, taking him in deeper and slowly pulled back allowing his cock to nearly slide out completely. Elliot made a slurping sound as his cheeks hollowed from the intense suck, and then went forward again until his mouth touched Adam's pelvis and his cock couldn't go any further.

An intense urge to thrust and fuck Elliot's mouth struck him, but he gripped Elliot's hair in his fist instead, trying to find his self-control. "Jesus, Elliot," he breathed, panting like an athlete after a game.

Elliot finally pulled back and began a rhythmic bob of his head, sucking, licking, slurping and lapping hungrily at his swollen cock. Adam hissed, unable to control his responses. His toes curled when Elliot's sexual groans and moans penetrated his ear. It amazed him how Elliot could be so aroused by pleasuring someone else...him. He looked down, watching an attractive man with gorgeous, full, wet lips wrapped around his cock. He breathed so hard he thought he might pass out.

His cock unexpectedly popped from Elliot's damp lips and Elliot licked his own finger liberally, the same way he'd just licked Adam. The same hand grazed his balls as he reached behind them to tease Adam's hole with his wet finger. The tip breached the outside and Adam gasped.

Elliot grinned. "You never—"

"No, never."

Elliot stood, licking Adam's abs and nibbling his nipple along the way up. "I can be your first."

Adam sheepishly looked away. "I don't think I'm ready for that."

Elliot kissed him hard, pressing their lips together passionately, tongues wrestling. He whispered against Adam's lips, "You can do me. You can do anything you want to me."

Adam bit his own lip to stifle his groan and to retain his self-control. "You're too much." He couldn't help but realize Elliot must really trust him.

"I'll lead you through it." Elliot's lips still so close to his own.

"What about lube?" Was he actually considering it?

"We'll use saliva." With that, Elliot grabbed a condom from the pocket of his shorts, he tore the wrapper and gently rolled the condom down the length of Adam's cock. He knelt down and took Adam in his mouth again. This time when he stood, Adam's cock was nearly dripping with saliva. "I'm clean. Aren't you?" He turned, pressing his back to Adam's chest, and aiming Adam's cock to his warm, tight spot. "Still, I've been thinking about using those condoms since I found them."

Instead of answering or saying anything, Adam grabbed Elliot's hips and thrust forward slightly. Elliot grunted as the tip of Adam's cock popped inside.

Adam halted. "God, you're so tight."

"But it feels good, huh?" His voice was low and guttural. "Go all the way in. It feels better that way."

Adam took the lead and pulled Elliot back by his hips as he thrust forward, then pulling back to allow the wetness to distribute properly. When he thrust again, he went in all the way. Elliot's ass cheeks rested in the curve of his pelvis, and Adam breathed against his ear. "Yes, this feels good."

Hands grabbed Adam's arms and wrapped them around Elliot's body. "Hold me."

Adam licked Elliot's ear, feeling the urge to nibble, moan and buck his hips. His cock throbbed at the thought, from the need. He was buried deep inside a man, Elliot, for the first time and it felt absolutely amazing, naughty even, but that only made the experience better.

Elliot's muscles tightened around Adam's cock and they both groaned. The intense pleasure and dirty thoughts made adrenaline race throughout Adam's body. He felt his cock shoot out a copious amount of pre-come. "I'm so horny. I was never this horny in my life."

Elliot rested his head back against Adam's shoulder, allowing Adam to be his anchor. "You wanna fuck me now?"

"Yes," he whispered, breathing rapidly as his cock pulsed.

"Touch me first." Elliot licked his lips and again Adam felt his cock ache and throb.

He ran his hands down over Elliot's hard chest and abs. The warmth on his palms mimicked fire from the hotness he felt. He continued down to the short, coarse curls that surrounded Elliot's rigid cock and fisted his hardness, which was also wet with pre-come. He gently jerked it and Elliot moved forward, pulling off of Adam's cock and causing his eyes to roll back in his head. Elliot quickly sat back, slamming Adam back inside his tight hole. Adam shuddered. He couldn't control his hips any longer and they began to rock on their own, fucking Elliot rhythmically.

"Not yet," Elliot whispered, bringing their sexual dance to a halt. "Kiss me first."

The teasing frustrated Adam but aroused him even more. "It feels too good."

"I know." Elliot turned his head and they shared a passionate kiss. Adam pulled him tight against his body and moaned into the kiss. Elliot whispered, "Now fuck me."

Adam didn't hesitate. He pressed his hips against Elliot's ass and swiveled them slightly until his cock slid out several inches just to thrust back inside. "Fuck," he growled and thrust forward.

Elliot's pleasurable cries soon echoed through the empty streets and Adam pressed on, thrusting and bucking so hard Elliot slumped over and supported himself by holding on to the edge of the hot tub. He moved along with Adam's motions, pulling all of Adam's self-control out through his cock.

Suddenly Adam pulled out. "Come here," he growled.

Elliot turned and dropped to his knees in front of him. Adam pulled off the condom and tossed it aside—no worries, he was also clean—he jerked his cock a few times and suddenly ropes of semen splashed over Elliot's lips and chin. Adam let out a harsh grunt as the last of it spurted from his stiff cock, dripping down over his knuckles. Euphoria rapidly hit him, making him light headed and weak. He panted, leaning against the hot tub while Elliot continued to lick at his sensitive balls.

He looked down in time to see Elliot stroke himself, his fingers moving rapidly over the tip of his engorged cock. Elliot's hot breath hit his balls in short, hasty pants and almost immediately he felt the warm splash of semen graze his thigh. Elliot groaned and sat back on his heels. His head rested on the inside of Adam's thigh. They were spent and it was bliss.

CHAPTER SIX

Back on Track

Elliot woke up on top of his clothes he had spread out on the lawn. Adam was fully dressed, crouched by the dying fire and poking it with a long stick. Titan drank from a plastic bowl near the hot tub.

"Morning." Adam grinned.

"Morning?" He looked up at the pitched black sky. "Doesn't feel like morning."

"It's nine o'clock." Adam threw him what was left of a bottle of orange juice. "You slept for about nine hours. I just woke up about thirty minutes ago."

Elliot drank the rest of the juice and got up to dress. He noticed out of the corner of his eye that Adam looked away. He turned to him. "What's wrong?"

Adam finally looked back at him and shook his head with a forced smile on his face. He could tell the smile was forced because Adam's eyes didn't narrow much like they did when he smiled genuinely.

He sighed. "Don't tell me you're having second thoughts."

"No." The smile turned genuine. His eyelids narrowed and the laugh lines around his mouth deepened. "Was trying to hold back my smile."

"Why, does my dick look funny?"

Adam chuckled and threw the stick into what was left of the fire. "I had a great time last night."

It felt weird to hear those words come from Adam for two reasons. First, their lovemaking he referred to felt like it happened all in the same night since it was difficult to gauge time. Second, the last two times they were intimate Adam had treated him differently afterward.

"No regrets?" Elliot looked into his green eyes, questioning.

"There were a few times Jena tried to lay a guilt trip on me but I told her to go fuck herself."

Elliot laughed. It felt good to laugh. "It's nice tearing ourselves away from...this." He looked around at the destruction that surrounded them.

Adam frowned and dropped his gaze to the simmering fire. "Gotta admit. Still love her though."

Elliot nodded, heart suddenly beating faster, harder, aching. "I figured that much."

"She was my best friend for so many years. Actually envisioned having a little guy running around the house. It felt... right."

Elliot smiled warmly, walked to Adam and brought their foreheads together. "I'll never leave you. I promise." Maybe Adam needed to hear those words. Maybe then he would allow Elliot to be the one he fantasized about instead of Jena.

Adam looked into his eyes as if deeply searching for a connection. "I believe you. We're in this together." Elliot slowly pressed his lips to Adam's to indulge in an innocent kiss. However, instead of indulging, Adam pecked the corner of his mouth and quickly separated their bodies.

Elliot observed Adam's forced smile, this time choosing to not bring attention to it. "Ready?" Elliot read Adam's body language like words written on his face. He was pretending that everything was okay, lying even, if Elliot wished to look at it that way. Why was it so hard for Adam to accept who he really was? Elliot wished he could grab him by the arms and shake some sense into him. He knew how difficult it was to deal when your world suddenly changes because you feel you're becoming someone else. He'd been there, done that...when he was fifteen. Adam had to be seeing thirty soon and he beat himself up constantly because of his feelings. Poor guy. He must be torn apart from confusion. Elliot wouldn't bring it up. He wanted Adam to trust him, not run away and stay hidden behind a facade. He wanted to protect him from himself and be the comfort he needed. He could do that much for the man who did the same for him. "The plan?" Elliot asked.

"We're gonna find out what and where Refuge Inc. is."

The dark continued to envelope them for the next two hours of nonstop walking. Adam really didn't feel like they were making much progress until he saw another R with a halo around it spray painted on the outer wall of a freeway overpass. He languidly strode across the fractured concrete bridge, looking behind him occasionally at Elliot whose pace seemed to be much slower.

The dog, however, appeared to have a surge of energy running through him. He moved much faster than either of them, trotting ahead to sniff at a ragged car tire on the side of the freeway bridge.

Once at the spray painted area of the bridge near the freeway ramp, Adam stopped to rest and wait for Elliot to catch up.

Elliot took his water out of his pocket. "I need a minute. I don't feel good." He took a swig.

Adam's light shined against the wall and ran his hand over the chipping black paint. "What's the matter?"

"My head's killing me, my leg fucking hurts and that damn rotten smell is making me nauseous."

He noticed the putrid smell too and how it grew stronger as time went on. "Sit down and rest," he suggested.

Elliot slid down the wall and laid his head back against the dusty concrete, and the bag of beef jerky and what was left of the bottles of orange juice on the floor beside him. "Sit with me."

Adam shook his head and scoffed. "If I sit down I might not get back up. Just warning you."

"You know, I've been thinking." Elliot chuckled. "I wonder what the hell Refuge Inc. is and if we're just wasting our time looking for it."

"What else are we gonna do with our time?" He shined the light around at what looked like a car parked next to the outer wall on the other side of the wide bridge. "The place might have other people. That's what we're looking for, isn't it? It might be some sort of shelter or medical center."

Titan trotted back from his leisurely stroll up the bridge, sat down next to Elliot and licked his face, making him smile. "You're a good dog. And to think I was so scared of you."

"I was scared of you too, Elliot."

"Me? Why me?"

"I really thought there was no one else alive, and was ready to say my peace with everything. Then I saw you and realized I had a second chance and that scared the hell out of me. I didn't want a second chance. Wanted to bury all my issues and move on to whatever was next for me. Seeing you meant I had to be ... well, conscious of myself. I didn't want you to know the real me or my fuck-ups. And I didn't want to believe that other people could be alive to know me and my fuck-ups either."

Elliot looked up at him, meeting his eyes. "But now you know you don't have to hide anymore, right?"

Adam nodded. That was easier to say for Elliot. He didn't have a bag of bones he'd rather leave buried in a closet somewhere. It was better to change the subject than to add to the question. "And you? Were you afraid?"

"I was hysterical. Who wouldn't be?" Elliot answered with wide eyes. "I tried to hold it together the best way I could, because I know how I tend to get. Me and Jeff had a little argument once. He accused me of using him to get from Georgia to here. He thought now that I had moved, I didn't need him anymore. Which was not true. The argument got heated and he left me that night. I panicked. It was the second night in a new, unknown place and he left me. I wanted to call him to tell him I was sorry, but I had dropped my phone in the dish water earlier that day." Elliot paused and massaged his temples with his fingertips. "I had no way of getting ahold of him. I didn't want to bother my neighbors late at night and ask to borrow their phone, so I just panicked. I don't function well in panic mode and I lost it. I lay in bed feeling miserable until Jeff came back. It was pathetic. I was on the verge of that fear again until I saw you." He looked up at Adam with an uncomfortable look in his eye. "I probably did panic a little back at the dental office."

"It's okay."

"Okay? Look what I've done to you. I pretty much forced you to admit you're gay at the most difficult time ever. I should've known what that can do to a person. To have to deal with multiple crises at the same time. How fucked up and selfish am I?" He shook his head.

"It's okay." Adam stepped closer, wanting desperately to rest his hand on Elliot's shoulder to calm him, but held back in fear of disturbing him more instead.

"No, I had to admit I was gay once too, you know?" Elliot's hands gestured and flailed about as he spoke. His frustration visible. "At fifteen it was fucking hard. Every day was torture emotionally, mentally and physically. And my lover once left me too. That was devastating. And now I can officially say I experienced a worldwide catastrophe. Fucking insane. And you're going through all three of those disasters at the same time. Unbelievable!"

"It's not your fault." Adam reached out to touch the skin on Elliot's arm, to soothe him—

"I could have lessened the blow a bit by keeping my hands to myself," Elliot muttered.

Adam's hand stopped inches from Elliot's arm and he turned in silence, placing his back and his suddenly sagging shoulders to Elliot. "We're headed in the right direction so let's keep walking." Everything Elliot said was true, but admitting he was dealing with an internal crisis wasn't going to make anything better. Acknowledging the fact that his internal crisis now included the odd, emotional feelings he harbored for Elliot was torture enough.

Elliot didn't say another word. The breeze on the dusty street was all that sounded around them, reminiscent of tiny pebbles rolling around atop a hard surface. And once again they were on their way.

The rotten smell of ammonia and death suddenly became more apparent. The stench reminded Adam of a septic tank full of waste and harsh chemicals. He desperately tried to ignore it. "Why did you leave Georgia?" The thought had been on his mind since hearing the dreadful details of Elliot's argument with his boyfriend.

Elliot's pace was slower than usual and his cough interrupted the brief silence before he answered. "I wanted to get far away from my family. I figured I could make new friends with people who really cared about me instead of staying and constantly getting disappointed."

"You were that miserable?"

"Yeah, I started to hate everything. My brother, my parents, my house, my life. I hated how they treated me. Like the odd-ball since I was a teenager. I had to get away. I needed new scenery."

They treated Elliot like an odd-ball since he was a teenager? A fifteen year old teenager who'd just come out? Adam was curious but didn't want to disappoint Elliot by asking about his coming out. He already guessed it was a painful time for him. "Was it easy? Leaving them behind, I mean."

"Yeah, it was easy. I was happy to leave. I couldn't wait to leave. But—" A series of hacking coughs followed, reminding Adam of an elderly man that had one too many cigarettes over the years. "But—" More coughs.

"You okay?" He gently rubbed a hand over Elliot's back to help ease the cough.

Elliot shook his head and cleared his throat. "I feel like shit. I'm all achy and nauseous. Isn't it hard to breathe? I need to rest."

Adam looked around, thinking. The rotten smell in the air was bothering him too but not as much as it seemed to bother Elliot. Or was it something else that had Elliot feeling so awful?

"Let me take a look at your leg." Adam handed the flashlight to Elliot as he slid down the freeway median to sit on the asphalt. "Shine this on your leg while I take a look." He carefully unwrapped a few layers of gauze and found that the bleeding had slowed considerably, since it hadn't saturated past the first couple layers. But as he continued to unravel the layers, he also noticed a yellowish discharge coming from the wound itself and the gash looked red and puffy. It didn't look good at all and it definitely didn't look like it was going to get any better. He cleaned and redressed the wound and sat beside Elliot against the freeway median.

"I can feel my heartbeat throbbing in my leg," Elliot said groggily. "It wasn't like that before."

"You need some antibiotics." Adam rubbed his forehead with the tips of his fingers. "I wouldn't mind some aspirin for my headache either."

Elliot huffed, shaking his head. "My leg's infected, huh?"

"Don't know for sure, but it looks like it."

"Shit." He slammed his fist down on his knee. "This is the last thing we need right now."

"Right. We need to get to a hospital." Adam glanced around at the surrounding darkness. "Where's the closest one?"

"I doubt there will be doctors there. Everyone left, you know."

"I know, but there has to be medicine still. Plus, don't hospitals have an emergency power supply?"

"A backup generator, yeah." Elliot hacked out a few cackling coughs. "Let's hope we find a hospital that's still standing."

"Come on." Adam stood and held out his hand. "If we turn around and go in the opposite direction we should run into Arrowhead Hospital."

Elliot grabbed his hand and stood with Adam's assistance. "Thank you." He smiled. "I would be a mess if it wasn't for you."

Adam flashed a brief smile and wrapped his arm around Elliot's waist. "Let's keep moving."

CHAPTER SEVEN

Close Encounters

By the time they approached the parking lot of Arrowhead Hospital hours had passed and Elliot's ill health worsened. He was tired and at times felt as if he had blacked out for the majority of their journey because he couldn't remember most of the trek.

Many of the hospital windows were broken and the top two floors of the five story building looked damaged or collapsed. Elliot couldn't determine the extent of the damage from where they were outside, but besides the structure of the hospital he saw a few lights illuminating several rooms of the building.

There was power, but it wasn't reliable.

They had followed the dimly glowing lights for miles. Every time he had opened his eyes, off in the distance he would see light coming from the windows of the hospital growing bigger and getting closer. The light reminded him of the flame of a burning candle by how it flickered, off and on it went.

He coughed then chuckled. "It'll be great if there's a doctor or two on duty."

Adam scoffed. "I'm keeping my fingers crossed."

It was instinctive to enter the hospital through the emergency room entrance. Elliot expected, or prayed, that a doctor *would* see Adam struggling to get them both through the jammed and cracked automated glass doors and run to their rescue. That didn't happen.

Titan squeezed through a twisted part of the entrance almost effortlessly. He stood on the other side, watching and panting with his mouth gapped and tongue hanging out like a mocking grin on his canine face. He watched Elliot and Adam struggle to maneuver through the doors as if he were taunting them.

Once inside, a creepy chill came over him. There was something quite eerie about the quietness, the lack of noise and people, and the long halls with wheelchairs in the middle of the floor as if everyone suddenly evaporated into thin air in the middle of their everyday actions. Some of the halls were lighted with long florescent lights, while the others were dark and grimy looking, reminding him of a scene out of a horror movie.

He met Adam's glance in an unspoken mutual understanding. "I think this is why some people are afraid of hospitals."

Adam kept his arm around Elliot's waist as they moved further into the hospital, past the front desk and to the first room they could find. It was part of several rooms combined into one massive one and each space was separated by a long white curtain that ran around a twin sized hospital bed. And all of the beds looked comfortable and welcoming. He allowed Adam to help him onto the nearest bed and immediately he closed his eyes. Even if it were for a second he needed to close his eyes.

"You'll be fine here while I look around?" Adam's voice penetrated the silence and instead of opening his eyes Elliot envisioned Adam looking down over him.

"I'm not gonna move. It feels too nice."

Even though Elliot's eyes were closed Adam nodded. Now where do they keep medicine in the hospital? The pharmacy. He needed to find the pharmacy and get Elliot some antibiotics and pain killers so his condition wouldn't worsen. The entire walk from the freeway to the hospital he damn near had to drag Elliot along, making the walk take longer than it would otherwise. Elliot kept dragging his feet and mumbling nonsense at times. It scared him. He had to do whatever he could do to get Elliot's health back to one hundred percent again.

They had even passed by another spray painted R that pointed in the opposite direction of where they were headed, but he knew if he didn't get Elliot some meds quickly he would regret it.

What was Refuge Inc. anyway? He had no idea. It could be some sort of safe haven for survivors equipped with medical personnel and all the necessities they needed. It could turn out to be a complete waste of time. He couldn't risk Elliot's wellbeing in order to find out. As soon as Elliot was better they would continue to investigate the spray painted R's. In the meantime, he needed the pharmacy.

The panel on the wall said the pharmacy was located on the ground level, which he was on. He would follow the signs until he found it.

He read the sign at the end of a hall after he turned down another hall, and then another. It read: Outpatient Pharmacy & Gift Shop.

Before entering he realized by looking through the glass windows of the gift shop that it had been ransacked. It looked like anything that would have been important and useful was gone. All that was left were wilting flowers in vases, spilt chocolates and the heart shaped boxes they came from, greeting cards, balloons and various other useless items. He entered and carefully made his way through the litter to the register. On the wall behind the register were a few individual packages of generic aspirin and cough lozenges. He opened a pack of aspirin and swallowed the two white pills whole. Then stuck what was left in his backpack. He needed to visit the real pharmacy to find some antibiotics.

He continued to look around the hospital for the main pharmacy. Once he found it—security door off of its hinges, and ransacked worse than the gift shop—his heart sank. There were very few bottles, vials and syringes still left in the small room but he had no idea where to start. He walked into the room with shelves knocked to their sides and plastic containers laying everywhere, and picked up a bottle containing a clear liquid. He read the label and shook his head in frustration. What was Terbutaline? He had no idea if he held a miracle in his hand or a disease, much less how to administer it and the dosage. He was lost. He added the bottle to his growing collection of medicine in his backpack. He picked up a few other bottles and packaged prefilled syringes, and after reading the label he stuffed them in his pack too.

He looked for a word ending in 'cillin, but had no luck. Even if he did hit the jackpot and found some penicillin he wouldn't know how to use it to help Elliot, afraid he would end up hurting him instead. Maybe the medicine he collected would come in handy later somehow, maybe not. Either way he knew medicine was too precious in situations like these to just leave it behind.

He made it back to Elliot who slept on the hospital bed. Titan had found a spot to curl up in towards the corner of the massive room and lay there silently as if respecting Elliot's slumber. Despite the way Elliot's leg looked, he seemed rather peaceful, comfortable and relaxed. Adam wanted to give him some of the aspirin he'd found but he didn't want to interrupt his sleep. Instead he stood beside the bed and slowly, gingerly swept the back of his fingertips over Elliot's eyebrow then again across the bruise on his lip. Taking on the caretaker role was natural to Adam and it felt good. Especially when he knew the person he was taking care of would do the same for him. Realizing that having someone by his side during a terrible life changing tragedy was all that it took for him to honor his role. And looking down at Elliot, while he relaxed in a welcomed slumber, not only brought memories of Jena to mind but to heart.

Elliot was everything Jena was not; supportive, open minded, tender and most importantly Elliot was still by his side. It made a huge difference in Adam's outlook knowing he was not alone. And maybe that was all Elliot needed too. He was thankful to have found Elliot.

He brushed his finger across Elliot's temple, physically appreciating the man by his side. That's when Elliot opened his eyes. First the lids fluttered like two dark moths but then they slowly opened.

Elliot smiled. "That feels nice."

Adam nodded and dropped his hand. "Still feel like shit?"

"Tell me you found some morphine," he said, sitting up on the bed. "I feel a little better. I think I was really exhausted and just needed to get away from that stink out there and get some more sleep. But my leg is still killing me."

"Aspirin should help." Adam gave him two pills and his bottle of water. "Couldn't find much medicine. Looks like someone got to it long before me."

"This hospital is huge." Elliot glanced at his bummed leg. "There's got to be medicine somewhere."

"There's medicine I just don't know what to do with it."

"Can't we look for some medical books or something to tell us what to use and how to use it?"

"We don't even know if your leg is really infected or not. We're not doctors. What if we make things worse?"

Elliot bashfully diverted eye contact and his face reddened slightly. "It's nice to know you care about me."

Funny, Adam felt the same way. "I'll go see what I can find. You rest, alright?" He squeezed Elliot's shoulder and headed down a different hall.

He stopped in the lobby where four elevators were located. He contemplated entering one and investigating the upper floors, but knowing the top two floors were possibly damaged and not knowing for sure if it was worse than what it looked like from the outside, not to mention the intermittent power, he decided to take the stairs. No sense in doing something stupid and possibly getting stuck in the elevator or something similarly unfortunate.

Upon entering the second floor, ultra-bright light flooded him. The halls were too quiet and an ominous feeling crept over him. He didn't like the thought of being in a hospital alone. And to add to the weird feeling, in the distance he heard the repetitive beeping of a monitor.

He followed the hall down until he saw a brown rectangular sign hanging from the ceiling that read: Intensive Care Unit. Beyond the sign all the lights were dim, causing the possibly once comfortable ambience to take on a menacing aura.

He looked around what he considered was the intensive care unit receptionist desk—a huge horseshoe shaped counter—he searched for anything of interest. He found some wooden Popsicle stick things, some small alcohol pads still in the foil, Band-Aids and—

The lights flickered; on, off, on and finally they went out. He noticed the hallow sound of the room as the air conditioner shut down and the distant methodical beeping suddenly stop. He had left the flash light downstairs with Elliot. So he was left standing in an utterly dark room alone, feeling exposed. But before the dark began to seep in and take hold of his flight or fight instinct, the lights blinked back on. The beeping continued and the sound of the air conditioner kicking back on swirled around him. He let out a slow exhale and—

A dark shape wisped by from of the corner of his eye. It was fast enough for Adam not to fully make out what it was when he abruptly turned to catch it. He didn't hear anything other than the faint sound of that damn monitor beeping in the distance.

"Hey!" he called out. Backing away from the desk and moving slowly in the direction of the shadowy wisp. "Anyone there? Elliot, is that you?"

He moved slowly, quietly trying to engage all of his senses at once. He struggled to hear footsteps or something to give him the idea he wasn't going out of his mind and seeing things. Then he began rummaging through the possibilities. Titan couldn't have followed him, the doors were closed. Could other stray dogs or animals get inside the hospital somehow? Or ... were there people still inside?

His internal questions were answered as soon as he turned a corner and saw a person, an elderly woman, sitting on the hospital bed in one of the darkened rooms. The monitor beside her bed glowed with green words, numbers and lines jumping around the screen and changing as the seconds went by. The woman herself looked pale, frail and a little uneasy.

Adam put his hands up as if he'd just been caught by a police officer doing something illegal. "Don't be scared. I'm just looking for medicine for my friend. He's downstairs. He's hurt. And... I didn't think I would find anybody here. Didn't think anybody else was alive." He chuckled nervously. "You okay? You need help?"

When the woman didn't answer he added, "Me and my friend thought we were the only ones alive. This is great!" The woman just stared, unmoving. "Are...are you okay? Are you...alive?"

"Of course I'm alive, you idiot. Who are you?" The woman's deep voice and no nonsense tone startled him for a moment. He wasn't expecting to hear a ragged and authoritative voice come from such a little old lady.

"My name's Adam. Me and my friend Elliot are looking—"

"So you're not here to rescue me?" She glared, narrowing her beady eyes.

"Well... sure. But I'm not who you think I am. I'm just a guy who happened to make it out of this mess."

She shook her head. "Put your arms down," the lady demanded. "You look like a fool. Of course you're not here to rescue me. Look at you. Look like Death has already snapped you up." She coughed and wheezed. "So you're looking for medicine for your friend? Where is he?"

"Downstairs in the emergency room area. He hurt his leg pretty bad. Are you okay? Have you been left here alone?"

"No, I wanted to stay. I wanted to stay with my husband."

Adam glanced around the room where he saw an older man crouched in the corner.

"That's Harold," the woman said. "He's the one you were calling out to a few minutes ago. Poor bastard. He wouldn't be able to hear you if you were screaming through a loud horn."

The elderly man stood, holding on to the wall as his weak looking knees knocked together attempting to bare the weight of his delicate frame. "That's not true, Edna. I can hear just fine." The wrinkles around his mouth deepened in what looked like a scowl. "I didn't want to speak up, that's all."

"Anyway," the woman continued. "You don't happen to have a cigarette, do you?"

"Uh, no. Sorry." Adam shook his head.

"No cigarette? Well, not much medicine here, so looks like we're both shit out of luck."

Harold chuckled as he slowly made his way to her bed to sit on the edge. "She's been hankering for a cigarette since the folks here up and left. I told her if she wanted a cigarette she first had to get somewhere safe. It's not safe here. Backup lights and such keep going on and off. One of these times they're not coming back on."

"I wasn't leaving my husband no matter what the damn lights are doing, you dumb fool." She reached behind her and threw a pillow at Harold.

Adam's eyebrows pulled together. "I thought *he* was your husband," he said, referring to Harold.

"This poor fool? He's not my husband. My husband's over there. Across the hall. I didn't dare leave him behind, and Harold wouldn't leave me."

Harold smacked his lips together, wetting the shriveled skin. "Someone had to take care of you, Edna."

Adam sensed some sort of love triangle but didn't question it. Instead he explained, "We were looking for other people. If we find refuge you all have to come with us."

"There's no one out there?" Harold asked.

"Everyone's gone. But I think there might be a refuge of people and we're walking around looking for them. We'll find them and you can come with us."

"I couldn't go with you if I wanted to, and neither can they. Diabetes took my leg, Harold has a bad hip and my husband's in a coma."

Harold put his bony hand up to interrupt. "You said *refuge* like Refuge Inc.?"

"Yes!" Adam's eyes widened as hot adrenaline pumped through his veins from the excitement. "Refuge Inc. You know what that is?"

"Heard some fella on the radio saying some nonsense about Refuge Inc. in the valley."

"Yeah, did he say where this place is?" Adam asked.

"Just in the valley. Uh, what was that saying, Edna?" Harold turned to the lady.

"What are you talking about some Refuge Inc.?" Edna said, looking annoyed.

Adam pulled the orange flyer out of his pocket and presented it to Edna. "This is Refuge Inc. Someone spray painted billboards and walls with arrows and I think the arrows are pointing to where this place is, but it's hard trying to guess where the next sign will be. Is the guy still on the radio?"

"What is it?" Edna asked, pointing to the flyer.

"Think it's a place for survivors to go. There's probably lots of people, doctors, water, food and medicine. It's probably the place we need to go to be safe," Adam said.

"Or it's probably a scam," Harold added. "The radio is busted. Batteries went dead. But the old kook on the radio talked about predicting this for years. The last we heard from him was a few days ago, the old nut. It's a scam, I'll tell you that much and I wouldn't trust it."

"That's ... possible." Adam sighed, thinking. The guy on the radio predicted this? *This* as in the asteroid, the devastation? What exactly was Adam searching for? And if he found it, what would he be getting himself into? "Where's the radio? Can I take a look at it?"

"It's over in that corner." Harold pointed. "The right contribution for a secure future. Uh huh, that's the slogan."

Adam retrieved the small black radio and quickly examined it. Inserts for cassette tapes were on the front of the worn radio and on the back no power cord existed, the battery compartment was opened and the batteries were missing. It required two C batteries to operate and he didn't have any.

"The right contribution for a secure future?" Adam thought aloud. "Sounds like some sort of investment firm."

"I tell you this much," Harold said. "Nowadays everybody wants your money. It's a scam."

"I need to go tell my friend about you guys." Adam sat the radio down in the corner. "Give me a few minutes and I'll be right back."

Edna shooed him off as he quickly made his way out the door.

Elliot was still lying on the bed when Adam made it downstairs. Adam's excitement about finding other survivors nearly made him burst from his skin. He needed desperately to share the news with Elliot, but he didn't want to disturb his sleep.

Maybe it was his enthusiasm or his sudden sense of hope that made him brush the tips of his fingers across the bruise on Elliot's lip again. Elliot's eyes opened, staring back at him with half-closed lids. How did Adam know he would awaken? Possibly because the last time he touched Elliot he had wakened him. Then, he had aspirin. Now, he had nothing but good news.

"They're people here." He was sure his eyes enlarged as the words flowed from his lips.

Elliot quickly sat up in bed. "You mean alive?"

Adam chuckled. "Yes, alive."

Elliot's eyes lit up too. "Are they doctors? Do they have medicine?"

"It's a couple of old folks. Well, there're three actually, but one is in a coma. Some kind of love triangle going on I think, anyway they're stuck here waiting for help."

"But we're not alone?" Elliot tugged Adam's arm, pulling him closer, eyes bright with enthusiasm. "So that means... there are probably more people alive out there somewhere."

Adam quickly nodded. "Right. This Refuge Inc. might be the right place to go, after all. The old man, uh, Harold said he heard something about it on the radio. Not much, but he said they're somewhere in the valley."

"Right, we know that much from all the spray paintings." Elliot held onto to Adam's hand with both of his, a subtle gesture of hope.

Adam relaxed his hand, allowing hope to settle. "He also said he thinks it's some sort of scam. But who would run a scam in the days right after a disaster?"

Elliot nodded and stared at the bright white linoleum floor. "Isn't that the best time to run a scam when people are desperate and helpless?"

"But for what, money?" Adam dipped his head to look into Elliot's eyes, in the hopes of recapturing his gaze. "Money doesn't matter right now. We can't just go and buy a bunch of stuff. Everything's destroyed, right? If anything, we should be collecting bottle caps or some crap. A bottle cap seems more valuable than a dollar right now."

"That's what I was thinking." Elliot looked up, locking their stare. "What's money gonna do for anybody?"

"So it might not be a scam. It's probably the one place we should be looking for."

Elliot looked down again and sighed. "What else did he say?"

"He said their slogan is, 'The right contribution for a secure future.' I'm not sure what that means, but it might just be some fancy jargon they use."

"Contribution? That just seems weird." Elliot let go of Adam's hand, withdrawing, regressing, the hope in his eyes dwindling. "Why would they use fancy jargon if they're trying to help survivors? Wouldn't 'Find us for help' be better?"

"I don't know." Adam huffed, frustrated. "I don't know, but we gotta find out. This could be what we need."

"I don't know either." Elliot stared at Titan who slept in his snuggly looking corner. "Why don't we sleep on it and figure it out later."

Adam frowned. "It feels like we don't have enough time."

"We have enough time to sleep at least." Elliot rubbed his head.

"You feel alright?" Adam patted his shoulder gingerly.

"Just tired." Elliot yawned. "I think I need some more rest. My body's begging for it."

"Well, lie down and relax."

"What are you gonna do?"

"Don't know." He shrugged, scratching at his temple. "Guess I can go and see what else the old couple knows."

Elliot slid over in the bed, making room. "Why don't you come rest for a second."

Adam stared at the empty space of bed. It was no more than a foot or two of space for him, yet the plush bed was enticing and to sit so close to Elliot was tempting. He sat down. "Never thought something like this would happen in my lifetime. Thought I would see a chupacabra before an asteroid."

Elliot snorted. "Hell, me too. Kind of scary, huh?"

"More than scary, it's reality. You know those what-ifs games people play? Like what would you do if an asteroid was on course to hit Earth?"

Elliot nodded. "Yeah. I used to do that all the time." He stared at Adam's lips while he talked.

"Someone asked me that once. When I was a kid."

"What was your answer?"

"I would fly to the moon and live there to avoid it." He chuckled. "Dumb kid. Never thought that in a couple days after the asteroid hit I would actually become close enough to a stranger to care about him more than I care about myself."

They locked eyes for a brief second, but it was enough to cause Adam's heart to skip a beat. Was it nervousness for being so revealing, something he wasn't used to doing? Or was it that odd something else?

Elliot's smile was warm and inviting. "Maybe some people are surprised by the things they allow themselves to feel at times like these. I never felt closer to anyone in my life. I trust you."

Adam smiled, surprised. "You trust me?"

Elliot didn't blink or move his eyes from Adam's. "I do. I really do. What if we never found each other? Do you know how different things would be?"

Adam shrugged. "I don't know."

"Come on. Think about it." Elliot rubbed Adam's thigh casually. "What if? What if we both kept walking and never ran into each other? You think we would have made it this far?"

"Anything's possible." Adam gulped at the sudden heat that rushed his groin. "But I know I probably wouldn't have tried so hard. Probably would have given up."

Elliot nodded. "God, I'm so glad you're here." His hand rubbed Adam's thigh slowly, sensually kneading the muscle. "So I don't have to die alone."

Adam smiled, trying to keep a lighthearted energy. "You're not gonna die. I won't let it happen."

"But what if?" Elliot turned slightly to face him. "What if I died? What if I went to sleep right now and never woke up?"

Adam stared back into Elliot's worried eyes, which were two dark orbs that resembled the eyes of a lost puppy. "That's not gonna happen."

Elliot tangled his fingers into the bottom of Adam's shirt and pulled him closer. "At least I would die a happy man, huh?" Adam felt the light stubble on his own cheek as Elliot's lips grazed it, kissing it softly. He moved his lips to Adam's where he left a wet peck on his bottom lip. "Make love to me."

Adam could hear his heart thump, thump, thump in his ears and his cock hardened as Elliot's palm slid under his shirt and caressed his chest. He whispered Elliot's name but hadn't realized it until he heard it echo in his ears.

Elliot licked Adam's lips and moved to sit on top of him, pushing Adam back against the mattress at the same time. "Please, Adam," he whispered in a deep, husky voice. "Love me. Just for tonight."

Adam slid his palms over Elliot's firm chest. For the first time without hesitation he said, "Yes," and took Elliot's mouth in a deep, wet kiss. He felt a tug of energy pulling him farther from what he was afraid of and closer to what he truly wanted; to be loved too ... even if it were just for a night.

They kissed and simultaneously removed their clothes, their own and each other's, only breaking the kiss once to pull their shirts over their heads. The minute they were completely naked, Adam carefully rolled them over on the bed so he lay on top of Elliot, mindful of Elliot's injury. Instantly, the memory hit him like a sack of bricks; the first time they were intimate in the dentist office, this time felt the same but different. It was the same position, the same sensations, but something else was there. Something that felt so right.

Elliot's thick erection dug into Adam's lower abdomen, familiar, welcomed. He kissed Elliot harder, rougher, licking deep into his mouth, primal urges taking over. He repositioned himself so Elliot cradled him between his thighs and their stiff cocks pressed against one another's. He moaned and began to rock, the pleasure taking over him. Elliot too, moved with him in unison, while he separated their lips to nibble Adam's ear.

"I don't want to think about what happened," Elliot whispered in his ear. "Make me forget."

Adam paused and looked down into Elliot's fluttering, scared eyes. It must've been the devastation, their fight for survival, the feeling of hopelessness that he wanted to forget. Elliot looked so attractive when his eyelids fluttered, like two dancing moths. Elliot lifted a condom in his hand, one that he must've had on standby. Adam took the condom and quickly slipped it on. He cautiously, instinctively lifted Elliot's leg and hooked it over his shoulder. Once secured, he moistened his fingers with saliva and applied the moistness, which made it easier for him to slowly penetrate Elliot's tightness.

Elliot grunted as Adam pressed inside. "That's it. Love me." His grip on Adam's hips tightened with the first thrust. Heat traveled Adam's body in waves as he rocked and buried himself deeper and deeper into Elliot's warm body. He tucked his face in the dip of Elliot's neck, panting and grunting with each thrust. Elliot's hands caressed his shoulders, his back and ass. They were rubbing, gripping and scratching at his flesh making him tingle with pleasure. Adam breathed in Elliot's scent. The smell of a hot, aroused man turned him on more than ever. His thrusts began to change from short and rhythmic to long and hard, and it all felt amazing.

He nibbled Elliot's skin and a warm wetness brushed the side of his face, stealing his attention. He lifted his head to once again look down into Elliot's eyes. Tears ran down the sides of Elliot's face to puddle in his ears. Elliot stared back at him. Neither said a word. Adam thoughtlessly kissed the tears away.

CHAPTER EIGHT

Dust to Dust

Elliot awoke to a dank smell that suddenly caught in his throat as he breathed. He coughed, struggling to catch his breath. Even Titan, who lay in the corner of the room, hid his nose under his paw from the harsh smell.

"What is that?" Elliot sat up in bed and looked through the splintered glass of the broken sliding doors and saw brownish dust blowing into the room through the small opening.

"No idea what that is." Adam got up from the bed and wiped the sleep from his eyes as he and Elliot quickly got dressed. He went to the broken door, picked up a handful of the dust and pressed it in his fist. They both were surprised to see the fine, smelly, dry material mold together under the pressure of his grip like a batch of clay. Adam shined the flashlight outside into the darkness. Elliot could see tiny flakes of the material falling from the sky and shimmer in the beam of light like snow. "What's going on?" Was this it? Was this Death itself creeping upon them?

Adam looked at the residue on his hand. "This stuff is dry and loose but sticky at the same time. If we breathe this in—"

"We just won't go out there." Elliot blinked, shaking his head.

Adam mimicked him by shaking his head too. "We can't just stay here. No one's looking for us. No one knows that we even exist, let alone that we need help. We need to find Refuge Inc."

"What if there's no Refuge Inc.?" Elliot threw his hands up. "Has that crossed your mind? Then what?"

"There has to be." Adam scoffed. "Who would put all the effort into printing and passing out flyers and painting billboards all over Phoenix? Who would do that?"

"Maybe the question you should ask is, '*why* would someone do that?'" Elliot's fingers drummed against the sides of his thighs. "What if Refuge Inc. *is* some sort of sick hoax like the old man said, put on by sick people that want to send you on a wild goose chase for nothing? What if they were a refuge and meant well but are now doing no better than us? What if it's just another hospital somewhere were there's no medicine and it's filled with people like us waiting around for help that's never coming? Or worse, waiting to die."

Adam picked up his pack and dug inside. "Guess there's only one way to find out."

Elliot grimaced at the back pack. "What are you doing?"

"I'm leaving some food with you so I can go look for help. It's not much."

"What are you talking about? You're gonna leave me here?"

"I can move faster and get farther by myself. Plus, you can watch over Edna and Harold until I get back." Adam handed Elliot a handful of broken granola bars in their individual packages. "That's all I got. I'll keep the dried fruit." Titan didn't provide adequate help carrying the grocery bag full of packaged beef jerky while Adam assisted Elliot in their trek to the hospital, so he left it and the orange juice behind.

Elliot pushed his hand away and scowled. "No. You're not leaving. You want to die, is that what you want? 'Cause that's what you're gonna get if you go out there."

"No, that's what's gonna happened to all of us if we stay here and do nothing." Adam moved forward with the bars in his hand. "Now, take these."

Elliot backed away. "I said no. No!"

"Fuck, Elliot. I'm doing this for us, don't you get it?" He threw the handful of granola bars onto the empty bed.

"And I'm trying to protect you. The best thing for us to do is stay put. We're safer here. We're safe from everything out there."

"No, we're not. Soon the dust will get in here and we'll be breathing that stuff in. We'll run out of food and water. Your leg will get worse. The backup electricity will go out for good. Hell, we'll probably be forced to eat Titan or turn to cannibalism just to stay alive, who knows." His jaw tightened with tension.

"Don't say that." Elliot refused to hide his disgust. He let it hover in his voice. "That's not funny."

"It's not a joke." Adam gave him serious eyes, a no nonsense look. "We're gonna have to do all we can to survive and that starts with me finding this Refuge Inc. and getting us all some help." He stared at Elliot unblinking. "You understand?"

"I understand that I will never see you again, if that's what you mean."

"Jesus." Visibly annoyed, Adam shook his head, gave Elliot a quick peck on the cheek, threw his pack over his shoulder and made his way to the door.

"Fine," Elliot cried out. He balled his fists and dug his fingernails into his palm, straining to hold back tears in response to the kiss that felt like nothing more than the goodbye it was. "Go save the world, Midnight Man. Go find refuge and medicine and make it all better for us poor, suffering folks. I bet that magical place has all we need; all the medicine known to man, all the hot food we can eat, showers too—no, hot tubs, tons of them for you to fuck in. Everything we ever wanted."

Adam didn't turn around. He didn't do anything but attempt to make the opening to the door a bit wider so he could squeeze through comfortably, pulling and tugging on the warped metal frame that held the splintered glass.

"Maybe that's a sign," Elliot said angrily. "Maybe that's a sign telling you to stay here."

"I'm leaving, Elliot," Adam said, still trying to pull open the doors wider. "I'll be back with help. I promise."

"No, you won't." Elliot felt it in his heart, in his bones, in the air. Adam wasn't coming back. Before he could say another word he saw his own hands on Adam's shoulders forcefully pulling him away from the door and its twisted metal frame. It was as if he were watching a projection of himself acting out—taking hold of Adam's back pack, and pulling, yanking with all his might—but had no control over it.

Adam squirmed, trying to free himself from Elliot's grip. Calmly he demanded, "Let me go."

"No, you're not going out there." Elliot tugged and jerked, grunting through clenched teeth and wheezing in the struggle. Titan's quick barks echoed throughout the room as they scuffled.

"No, I'm leaving. Now let me go, Elliot!" Adam shrugged, turned and lurched forward, pushing Elliot back. Elliot stumbled and fell to the floor on his ass, twisting his injured leg in the process.

"Fuck." Elliot grimaced in pain. "My fucking leg."

"Sorry." Adam rushed to his side along with Titan who immediately began licking Elliot's face. "Here, take my hand. I didn't mean to—"

"You asshole!" Elliot quickly stood and swung his fist, connecting it to Adam's right temple. Adam grunted and spun around with the force of the punch. He kept his back to Elliot and brought his hand to the side of his face. Elliot sniffed. He swore he heard Adam sniff too. "Leave. Go on, leave. Just like everyone else who betrayed me and gave up on me. Just leave."

Adam adjusted the pack on his back, switched on the flashlight, pulled the collar of his shirt over his nose and mouth, and without even a glimpse over his shoulder he slipped out of the door and into the darkness. Elliot was more than sure he wouldn't see him again. The darkness had already taken him.

CHAPTER NINE

Refuge or Rescue

The dust wasn't as bad as Adam initially thought. It fell slowly, sporadically, and there was less of it than he originally believed. The clumps near the hospital door must have collected there over time and the crevices made it difficult for it to blow away. He had realized he didn't need to shield his face so he let go of the collar of his shirt a while ago.

Heading in the direction they came from and shining the flashlight at any and all debris that he passed, he looked for more painted R's. Maybe he had missed some on the way to the hospital. Stepping over gravel and litter and hearing only the soft echo of the crunch made him realize how lonely he was. His first instinct was to look back over his shoulder at the hospital where he'd left Elliot, Titan and the elderly couple. Some of the hospital windows shone with a dim yellow light. He felt better instantly.

Bringing Titan along would have been a good idea. Even though he would be without a back and forth conversation, he would've still had someone to talk to. Titan wouldn't want to come along anyway, the way the dog had barked at him during his and Elliot's little scuffle told him who the dog sided with. Even though there were no sides, just two scared men reacting to trauma. Besides, initially he had attempted to put the dog out of his misery. If it wasn't for Elliot, he might've gone through with it and would've regretted it as well.

Maybe Titan remembered that incident too and had picked Elliot's side then, long before their scuffle. Either way, Titan never meant any harm. He knew that now and was pleased Elliot had intervened.

Approaching the place he had seen the last R, he slowed his pace. He had walked about a mile from Arrowhead Hospital and although the arrow pointed the direction he was going, it drew him further from the hospital, Elliot, and the old couple. How long would he have to walk until he found this place? And as Elliot had put it, what would he do if this place didn't exist? But Refuge Inc. had to be something important. Who would put themselves through so much for a prank, and at a time when lives were at stake? It was inevitable he'd find *something.*

The rotten smell lingered in the air and threatened to induce vomiting on several occasions, forcing him to eat some dried fruit before he ended up dry heaving all night.

The dust continued to fall from above at a steady pace; not changing much since he'd left the hospital. The sheer existence of the dust made him believe that he was probably right about the dark clouds and what it brought with it. It troubled him to think of being surrounded by trickling particles of asteroid and the strange filth it produced upon impact.

He looked back toward the tiny pixel of light far in the distance. Nearly an hour passed and he hadn't found a thing, not a painted R, a flyer, nothing whatsoever. He was on the verge of walking in a totally different direction. Maybe he'd missed some signs.

Maybe—

The ground beneath his feet began to tremble. Adam anchored himself between a wall and a large metal dumpster that he assumed was once in some grimy alley. Maybe he *was* in a grimy alley and hadn't realized it. The dumpster rumbled like a drum as it rattled and bounced around. The noise was overwhelming, reverberating in his ears. And before he knew it, the quaking stopped. Were these quakes some sort of aftershock? They had started out strong and in close proximity to one another, but then they became less intense and less frequent. How many more would there be until the quakes ceased for good?

Adam looked in every direction, using what ruined landmarks he could make out as guides. He wasn't sure which way he wanted to continue walking in. He couldn't determine which direction made better sense to follow. However, something caught his eye. When looking back toward the hospital, he couldn't find that soft pixel of light anymore. He strained his eyes looking for the shining light that glowed from the hospital windows, a flicker, something. Instead he found nothing but darkness encircling him from all sides. He switched off the flashlight, allowing the darkness to swamp his eyes so he could easily find the tiniest pinprick of light out there in the night.

Nothing.

Had the backup lights finally gone out for good? Suddenly he knew what direction he needed to go in ...back to the hospital.

He flicked the switch to turn the flashlight back on, but it didn't come back on. "Damn it." He hit the handle against his sweaty palm repeatedly until the light came on but immediately it went out again. "Damn batteries." He quickly took his pack off and blindly searched inside for the extra batteries he had thrown in there. Once he found them he worked hastily, removing the flashlight head, feeling for the little metal nub at the end of each battery to determine the correct way to place them inside the handle.

Being subjected to the pitch black had a way of making him feel completely vulnerable. He imagined dark, blood-sucking creatures making their way to him under the cover of the darkness. Even as he replaced the flashlight batteries he felt as if he were quickly trying to load a gun with bullets to defend himself from the half dead and hungry creature waiting to sink its sharp teeth into his flesh.

The light came on and he quickly swung the flashlight around, looking over his shoulder at the environment as goose bumps covered his arms. He chuckled. "Creatures of the night," he mumbled. "I must be crazy."

He hoisted his pack on his shoulder and began the tedious walk back to the hospital. The only thing that bothered him as much as not finding Refuge Inc. was the scuffle between him and Elliot. Thinking about the punch that landed on his temple made the side of his face throb, but he didn't want to give the fight that kind of power over him. Naturally when he stopped thinking about it the throbbing ceased. He didn't want to acknowledge the fight at all. Harboring harsh feelings toward someone who only wished to help him and keep him safe wasn't part of his character.

He just chalked it off as a misunderstanding, a stress related mishap that wouldn't happen again.

There were much more important things to worry about in their shattered world.

The trek did a number on his leg and thigh muscles, but he finally made it back to the unlit hospital. He expected Elliot and Titan to greet him, but found nothing in the room where he'd left them, only dark corners and unrecognizable silhouettes instead.

"Elliot!" he called out. He ran to the stairs and rushed up the staircase to the second floor ICU. Edna and Harold were sitting on the bed with a small candle. "You guys alright?"

"We're just fine." Edna nodded. She held the outer glass shell of the small red candle on her lap. "So he found you?"

Adam stood in the wide doorway, shaking his head. "Who?"

"Your friend," Harold said and pointed a bony finger Adam could barely make out in the dim red glow of the candle. "Uh, what's his name again?"

"Elliot," Edna finished. "He went out some odd hours ago looking for you."

"He left?" Adam felt his eyes widen and his palms start to sweat from the intense feeling of dread that quickly hit him. "It's dangerous out there. He doesn't even have the things he needs and his leg—"

"He told us about that dust falling out there, and I tried to talk some sense into him," Edna said in her matter-of-fact tone. "He said he needed to find you and bring you back here. He took that dog and left."

"I gotta go get him." Adam rushed down the hall.

"Hey, wait," Harold called out. "Did you find the refuge?"

Before Adam hit the stairs he answered, "Not yet. But when I do I'll send help for you. I promise." He promptly made his way down the stairs, out of the hospital and back into the gloom.

Why would Elliot do something as stupid as leave the hospital, and when did he muster up the courage to suddenly do so? Adam walked the same trail he took the first time he went out. He didn't know which direction to go or which direction Elliot would take. His strategy was to backtrack toward the freeway overpass where Elliot first felt weakened. If Elliot were looking for him, he would look where they both had seen the last sign. That spray painted sign was on the concrete wall at the start of the freeway overpass. Adam swept the light across the dark, dirtied path, looking for footprints or other signs that Elliot's had walked the same path.

Still, nothing.

Why hadn't he crossed paths with him on his return?

After a slow, tiring hour of dragging his feet, Adam sat on the edge of the sidewalk and yawned. He'd depleted his energy. Surrounding him were nothing but the frightening darkness and the soft taps of ash hitting a crinkled piece of newspaper on the ground next to him. As he looked around his blackened environment, he hoped to hear Elliot or Titan's footsteps. Elliot wouldn't have gone out without some sort of light, how else would he expect to find him. However, Adam didn't see light for miles in every direction.

"Elliot!" he yelled into the night. "Elliot, you there? Can you hear me?"

He waited, listening for anything in return and again got nothing.

He rested for a few minutes before going farther towards the freeway. Long, slow minutes dragged on. His light was strong enough to light up a space fifteen feet ahead, where finally he saw a line of abandoned vehicles and the painted R where the two of them had rested before making their detour to the hospital.

The road he was on lead him straight onto the freeway overpass. The road was divided into six lanes with a narrow concrete median. A few cars on his side of the median were parked parallel to each other on all three lanes, cars that were once attempting to leave the city going south toward Tucson. But where had the occupants gone? Surely they didn't have enough time to walk out of the city before the earthquakes begun. Could they have gotten another ride? The cars were crammed in around themselves as if they were involved in some sort of collision. And he hadn't seen any dead bodies other than the one's he'd seen crowding the inside of his neighborhood church when he first began his trek.

There had been about a couple dozen bodies in that church, some slumped over in the pews, other's gathered around the full size plastered image of Christ, holding onto each other like children grasping their father's coattail when he'd threatened to leave them behind. The empty Styrofoam cups were crushed in their deathly grips or lying amongst their bodies like trash. Adam knew better than to assume the cups where just trash. The things people resorted to. The horrors he witnessed and wished he hadn't seen.

Though, the abandoned vehicles made him wonder. Who had abandoned them and where were these people? Could they have followed the painted signs to Refuge Inc.?

Adam walked past the painted R and farther down the freeway overpass, carefully weaving in between cars and their wreckage as he made his way down the bridge. The arrow near the R pointed south, now he could continue to go in the direction he had intended to go before Elliot had gotten sick, and they had to make the detour to the hospital. If Elliot wandered this direction he would have made it much farther than the overpass by now. But there was no way to know for sure which way Elliot had gone. So Adam kept walking. He'd run into Elliot or refuge either way.

Almost to the middle of the bridge, Adam stopped and shined his light on another R painted on the outer concrete wall. This particular R pointed up, which indicated he needed to turn west at that exact moment. But the sign in the center of the bridge pointed in a direction that was impossible for him to go unless he jumped off the bridge.

Adam scratched his head. He leaned over the outer wall of the bridge, which was nearly chest height, and shined his flashlight down onto the dust and trash littered freeway about twenty feet beneath him. A lone white minivan was parked on the freeway, and spray painted on the hood was another R that pointed west.

Bizarre. The minivan was the only vehicle on the freeway beneath him and it couldn't have been on the lane for more than a few days. Adam stepped back, dumbfounded. What was going on? That question repeated in his head like the reverberation of a ringing bell when he felt a cold wetness on his shirt. He looked down, surprised to see his shirt sticky with black wet paint. He examined the painted R on the wall in front of him and couldn't believe his eyes.

The paint was fresh. Someone had just painted the wall.

"Hey," he called out to nothingness. "Hey, anybody there? I need help. We need help. Anybody?"

Adrenaline kicked in and excitement rushed through him making him fidgety. His chest rose and fell rapidly as he tried to catch his breath. He didn't know what to do but follow the direction the arrow pointed. He shined the light down the side of the road he was on. He stood in the middle of the bridge, debating. It seemed like a complete waste of time to walk to one end of the long bridge or the other just to find his way down a ramp to the freeway below, and walk all the way back up the freeway lanes to where the minivan was parked. The ramps at both ends of the bridge had what looked like a fifteen foot wall running along the sides of the ramp, preventing him from making a swift trip out of it.

He shined the light over the center median and across to the other three lanes of the bridge to a car that was nestled in a broken part of the exterior wall toward the end of the bridge near the ramp. The car must have hit the wall at an unbelievably high speed because a five foot gash in the concrete trailed behind the wrecked car. The crash had broken a huge chunk of concrete from the wall completely, and the car nestled slightly over the edge.

Adam quickly made his way over the center median to the other side of the bridge. Once at the gash in the wall, he noticed thick metal support rods sticking out from the broken concrete like one inch thick claws on the hand of a giant robotic beast. He peered over the side and realized he was closer to the gravel covered slope underneath the bridge. Climbing down would be much quicker and easier than going all the way around. He shined the light down onto the slope of dirt and pebbles the city used to landscape the sides of the freeways and ramps. He determined it was about a twelve to fourteen foot jump. He could either jump down and get to the minivan in less than five minutes, or waste another hour climbing over walls, maneuvering around cars and walking through junk just to get to the same place.

He warily made his way around the mangled car that rested between the car and what was left of the broken wall. The smell of burnt oil hit his nostrils. At closer examination it occurred to him the whole car had been on fire. The interior of the car excluded a body which he'd expected to see, but was blackened and charred, smelling of burnt leather. The side and front of the car must have hit the exterior wall because it had smashed and dented in the metal like an old and used soda can. One of the rear tires hung over the broken wall and some of the strengthening rods were somehow coiled around the rear bumper, holding the car firmly in place as it leaned slightly over the edge of the bridge.

Adam secured his pack on his back and slid the glowing flashlight into the mesh pocket on the side. Light illuminated from the flashlight right below his armpit. It was enough to light a few feet of space around him and help him see as he climbed down. He scaled the wall with one hefty jump, sat on top and swung his legs over. The thought of jumping from that height was unnerving. Maybe if he lowered himself down near the broken edge of the wall and hung over the side his feet would be closer to the slope and would close the gap between him and the slope by about six to eight feet.

Slowly, he climbed down between the burnt car and the broken wall. He felt some of the steel rods prod his hip as he squeezed through the hole. Even in the poor light, he figured all he had to do was back out of the space and grab onto the ledge to climb to the lower part of the broken wall. But before he did anything else, he nudged the car with his foot just to be sure. If it weren't secure it would have budged. It didn't.

Content, he stuck his bottom out over the edge of the bridge and simultaneously grabbed on to the lower ledge. Instantly, his feet gave way and he found himself dangling over the side of the freeway overpass. It had been his intent to do just that but as he hung there, legs flailing like a ragdoll in the wind, he began to have second thoughts.

He looked down at the street below him. It was difficult to make out how far the jump was since the flashlight in his pack lit up his body better than it did anything else, blinding his view of the world beneath him.

His fingers ached and he realized he had to jump soon or gravity would pull him down in a nasty fall when he least expected. Knowing this he still didn't feel comfortable letting go. That spot directly beneath him seemed too far for him to jump and land safely. He reached out to his right, feeling for a secure place along the ledge to grab onto. The more he slid to the right, the farther from the car he'd be and the closer he'd be to the slope beneath him, further lessening the gap between him and the ground.

He reached, grabbing a piece of the concrete wall. Confident, he prepared to let go with his other hand in order to slide over again, but the concrete gave way in his hand. Dangling off the side of the bridge with one hand, he almost yelled out for help but remembered he was alone. He reached up and grabbed the ledge again and with both hands he tried desperately to climb back up onto the bridge where he knew he would be safe. He made a note to scold himself for making a senseless decision once he climbed to safety, but at the moment he needed to focus on the climb.

As he reached up with one hand, blindly pulling at a support rod to hoist himself up, he thought how stupid he had been to ever think jumping off of a bridge was a good idea. In his panic and haste, he grabbed the rod with his other hand as well.

The rod must have been weakened, damaged, or just a sorry excuse for support, because it bent with his weight.

It could have been merely seconds but time seemed to move slowly. Adam felt the rod curve in his grip and heat up his palm as it gradually gave way. Glimpses of Elliot and Jena popped into mind. His body felt weightless, but time moved so slowly he was able to sort out his thoughts and realize the sensation was nothing other than free fall.

He hit the ground with a loud thud. He landed on his back yet he was still moving, no, sliding. His backpack had absorbed most of the impact but the impact still knocked the wind out of him. And as he slowly slid down the gravel covered slope he tried to catch his breath, realizing he probably underestimated the height of the drop.

Finally, the sliding stopped and he came to rest atop sharp chunks of gravel. Breathing returned along with a painful burning in his chest. His ears popped, but instead of ringing he heard a loud whining or … a creaking. He quickly removed his pack and grabbed the flashlight. Pointing the light up toward the sound, he realized where the noise was coming from but it was already too late. The car directly above him—the car with the blackened and charred interior, the car with the rear tire that hung over the bridge, the car in which the robotic beast-like claws held onto its bumper securely—was in a free fall of its own, moving closer and closer.

CHAPTER TEN

Now or Never

Elliot couldn't pinpoint what had gotten into him to cause him to go ballistic and hurt Adam. All he could think about was getting Adam back to where it was safe, the hospital. Refuge Inc. was not a guarantee.

He thought himself lucky to have found an extra flashlight in one of the drawers in the hospital room. He was looking for more pain killers—Adam had forgot to throw him some of those when he unloaded the granola bars on him—instead of pain pills he found a flashlight. It was smaller than the one Adam carried but it got the job done. Finding the flashlight had been the push he needed to go back out into the darkness and find his friend.

The last few hours of walking felt like days to him and probably Titan too. He made sure to walk south, back in the direction where they came. Adam had mentioned seeing a spray painted sign on their way to the hospital. Instead of looking for that particular sign, he'd just go back to the last sign they'd seen on the freeway bridge. It made sense so that was the plan.

But already he had been walking for hours and hadn't seen one sign or the freeway. He had questioned himself earlier but now he really needed to think about it; was he going the wrong way?

It was possible that he started out in the right direction and accidentally made a detour somewhere along the way. The difficulty was determining what way he was walking without the assistance of a compass or landmarks. He had been following the smaller streets but some of the streets twisted and turned and others led to dead ends, leaving him cutting across house lawns and building lots.

He looked down to Titan. "Where are we going?"

Titan let out a soft bark in response, wagging his tapered tail.

Elliot looked around him, trying to get his bearings. Large pieces of dust that sometimes resembled ash or a mixture of the two fell down over him. The wound on his leg ached.

He continued his slow but determined trek. Titan followed alongside him.

"You make a good sidekick, Titan." He chuckled. "I wonder why I never got a dog instead of a boyfriend. Talk about being loyal. At least you won't ever leave me, huh?"

Titan shook his body, shaking off a layer of dirt and picked up the pace.

"Maybe I spoke too soon." Elliot hastened his steps to keep up. "Or maybe my problem is putting my heart out there for other people to crush it so easily. Maybe I love too easily, too hard and that's why I get hurt so bad."

He swept the light toward the side of the deserted road where a square metal sign announced: I-10 Ahead.

Not only was I-10 a landmark, allowing him to get his bearings, it was the freeway he was looking for. Now finding the overpass with the R painted on it would be that much easier.

"If I didn't love so damn hard I wouldn't have someone to risk my life for," he said, with a skip in his step.

The laptop snapped shut just as Jena walked into the room wearing her Hello Kitty maternity pajamas—a matching black polyester pant set with

the face of the dotted eyed cat stamped all over it. The shirt hit mid-thigh in the front and higher up on her bottom in the back.

She glanced at him and rolled her eyes, pulling her hair up into a messy bun. "It's because there's more fabric in the front to accommodate a growing belly. And to get a growing belly—or to make getting pregnant easier at least—I'm gonna wear maternity clothes any chance I get." She giggled.

Her crazy superstitions and her giggle always made Adam laugh, but this time he didn't. This time he wanted to vomit. He could feel the unpleasant churning in his stomach.

She sat down beside him on the bed and took the laptop from his lap to place it on her own. "You ready to be a daddy?"

His head hurt just thinking of what that question entailed. A baby, a wife, a lie he'd be living for the remainder of his life. The headache was almost enough to get his troubled mind off of the laptop.

And then she lifted the screen.

"Jena, wait!" His head throbbed, his stomach turned, and sweat moistened his palms. "Jena!" He struggled to breathe. "Jena, I'm sorry." His chest, his ribs, his arm ached.

He opened his eyes to blackness and a sudden intense pain in his right arm and along his right side. Turning his head slightly, he could see the roof of the charred car as it rested on its side and on top of his arm, pinning him to the gravel slope. The pain in his arm rushed him tenfold. "Jena!" he called out. "Jena, get help."

He blinked, realizing Jena wasn't there. He must have been dreaming. Reliving an agonizing memory he'd rather forget. The person he should have been calling out for was Elliot, but he wasn't there either.

He lay there, allowing light flakes of dust to feather across his face. Steadying his breathing, he tried to move. Stuck and in a panic he kicked his feet and tried desperately to free his arm which was trapped under the car from his shoulder. The pain was unbearable, excruciating even though his fingers were numb. How long had he been lying there with a car halfway on top of him? He had no idea how much time had passed or if Elliot was in a similar unfortunate predicament. Hell, had Elliot done what *he'd* set out to do and found Refuge Inc.?

The thought quickly escaped him when the pain increased. He cried out like a wild animal clutched in the painful grip of a bear claw trap. He lay still, motionless, and the pain lessened. He could see the mangled car easily, and even make out the wall next to him, the wall that held the car up on its side, preventing it from falling over and off of him. Light suddenly illuminated around him and he remembered his flashlight. He moved his head, looking around at his surroundings, searching for the flashlight with limited mobility. The flashlight rolled a little down the slope and rested too far away for him to grab it.

Nausea unexpectedly hit him and his stomached clenched. He heaved but nothing came out. Was Elliot okay? Was he lost or seriously injured? Would Elliot forgive him for pushing him down, for hurting him, for leaving him?

Elliot had said that they would never see each other again if he left. Had he fulfilled that prophecy? What more could he do if he was stuck under the car forever but die? He would die without telling Elliot how sorry he was, how stupid he was, how much he cared for him.

The pain returned. Adam bit his lower lip and groaned through his nose. He knew better than to do something as stupid as jump off of a freeway overpass. Even at the last minute when he had a change of heart and tried to climb back up, he knew how crazy the idea was. What was he thinking? He knew the dangers and chose to ignore them. Now look at him. Some hero.

A warm relief grew between his legs and he hadn't known he was urinating until the liquid ran over his groin and soaked his jeans. Even knowing what was happening he couldn't stop it. Suddenly the feeling of helplessness sunk in. Humiliation and shame washed over him. Even though he was the one who left the hospital, he felt abandoned and worthless. The urge to see a familiar face, to hear the voice of another human being, to feel a human presence overwhelmed him. The urge quickly turned into more than a necessity. He felt hollow, like an empty shell, like nothing. And he understood that feeling to be death. The death he dreaded and had escaped by denying who he was, who he was always meant to be.

Finally, he experienced the inevitable ... his tortuous suicide.

Maybe he *was* dying. Maybe he was bleeding out from somewhere, maybe the warm sensation between his legs was blood. He lifted his head to take a look, but couldn't hold his head up long enough to inspect. With every move the pain in his arm increased. Besides, it was too dark down there to make out the presence of blood anyway.

He used to wonder what it felt like to have death on your heels. And now he knew. Every path they took and every detour was an attempt to escape death, but it had finally caught up with him. The Adam he was familiar with had perished and was simultaneously going to die halfway pinned under a burnt and twisted heap of metal.

Now he was worse off than having an asteroid fall out of the sky hurling down toward him. At least with the asteroid he had a chance. Pinned under a car, in pain and no one around to help him was much worse. "What a way to go," he mumbled through clenched teeth.

A strange noise echoed in the distance, pulling him from his grim thoughts. He struggled to hear where the sound came from. Pain sliced through his arm and shoulder like a sharp, heated blade. His eyelids closed and all went peaceful.

Calm seized him. Adam heard the faint sound of a voice. Someone was calling his name. He opened his eyes to an intense bright light. Was this the end? Was this that infamous white light at the end of the tunnel guiding him to whatever came after? Then he heard the sound of lapping as a wide, wet tongue licked his face.

"Adam!" Elliot knelt beside him and placed his hand on Adam's chest, putting the flashlight down near them. "Oh, shit. Shit! Adam? What happened? You okay? Can you move? Can you hear me?"

"One question at a time." Adam grimaced, his arm ached and throbbed. "I climbed down and it fell and—" He pushed the slurping dog away.

Elliot gasped. "You climbed down from up there?" He shined his light up at the bridge with a puzzled looked on his face. "Why?"

"I saw another R," Adam murmured.

"Thank God I saw your flashlight shining." Elliot scoffed, shaking his head. "How do I get you out of this? Here, grab my arm. I'll pull you out."

"No, no. It'll hurt like hell." Adam wondered if Elliot understood what he just said about the R or just chose to ignore it for now.

"It'll hurt?" Elliot shook his head again, a breathy urgency in his voice. The sound of him trying to keep his composure but finding it difficult. "Wouldn't it hurt less if I pulled you out? Maybe I can lift it." Before Adam could protest he stood and limped to the front of the car, out of Adam's sight. Titan followed and must've got in the way, causing Elliot to demand, "Sit and stay. Okay, Adam," he said, getting Adam's full attention. "I'll count to three. On three you slide out, okay?"

"Elliot, no."

"Yes, yes. I gotta try something!"

"You can't—"

"You trust me?"

Adam wanted to remind Elliot of his own wound on his leg and tell him he didn't have the strength to lift a car, but the thought of Dark Lad—with the ability to lift anything no matter the size—coming to his rescue, fueled his optimism. He crossed his fingers.

"Okay, on three." Adam braced himself. He listened as Elliot prepared himself too, and finally the sound of gravel beneath Elliot's feet quieted.

"Okay, one, two, three." Elliot grunted.

Adam knew he was trying desperately to lift the car but the car wouldn't budge. After a second, the car slightly rocked toward him, sending a bolt of sharp pain up his shoulder and down his side. "Stop!" Adam cried. "Just stop." He panted and groaned, trying to control the pain.

Elliot returned to his side, panting and fidgeting. "It's too heavy and I think if I keep messing around with it I might tip it over on top of you. Fuck." Elliot turned his head, looking around their environment, probably trying to come up with a better idea.

"Someone *just* painted an arrow on the bridge, pointing to that van over there." Adam gestured with his uninjured arm. However, doing so drained him of energy. "I climbed down to get to it."

"Did you see who painted it? Do you think they're still around here?" Elliot's eyes glistened with wetness, tears he kept at bay. "Maybe they can help, huh?"

Adam's luck had run out. There was no one out there who could help him. "Maybe."

"Help!" Elliot called out, his pained voice echoing in the isolated streets. "Somebody help us!"

"Elliot." Adam sighed, his voice lowered as his words slurred. "I'm fucked."

"No, you're not. All we have to do is—"

"I feel ... strange. Like, almost like ... I'm dying."

"What are you talking about?" Elliot dipped his head to look into his eyes while he gingerly placed his hand on Adam's chest. "It's just your arm. People live ... without an arm all the time. And I don't even see blood. It's not that bad."

"I didn't climb down," Adam admitted, eyes blinking slowly, speech slowing. "I fell. I could be bleeding inside."

It was silent.

Adam closed his eyes for a welcomed moment and opened them to an angry glare on Elliot's face.

Elliot's voice was low, guttural and full of anger. "You asshole. You're just gonna lay here and give up? You gonna give me some pussy excuse to give up on me?"

"Elliot, there's nothing we can do." Adam pleaded with his eyes for understanding. "I'm fucked. Look at me. I'm fucked!"

Elliot waved a dismissive hand. "Wanna know the plan? Well here it is. I'm gonna find whoever is spray painting this goddamned place and drag their ass back here to help me get you outta here. That's the plan."

"I feel it. Inside of me. It's a hollow feeling. It's over." Adam went on as his body slowly weakened.

"And you're gonna hang tight until I get back."

"What if I'm gone when you get back?" Adam said, forcing Elliot to acknowledge the possibility. "What if this is it?"

Elliot plopped down next to Adam and stared ahead at nothing. He swallowed repeatedly, his Adam's apple rising and falling again and again. Adam knew he was trying to keep calm and control his emotions. "The 'what if' game, huh? I hate that damned game."

"Yeah," Adam whispered.

The silence, the stillness, the need to emotionally release lingered in the air. The unnerving sensation twisted in the hallow pit of Adam's gut. His arm went numb again and the urge to close his eyes beckoned him. "Always wondered something about you, but never asked."

"What is it?" Elliot hugged his knees to his chest and fidgeted with his hands as he stared off in the distance.

"The way you blink—"

"I'm surprised you didn't ask earlier." Elliot wiped at his eyes with the back of his hand. "It's blepharospasms. A condition I had as a kid. It only happens when I'm stressed, or don't get enough sleep, or the light's poor, or—"

"I think it's sexy," Adam interrupted, confessing. He rested his head back and finally closed his eyes. A smile twisted his lip.

Elliot sniffed. "When I hit you, did it hurt?"

Adam forced his eyes opened and turned his head to look at his friend, his companion, his lover. "It hurt but not on my face." It was silent for a few seconds, seconds that felt like hours during which he silently appreciated why his heart ached worse than his injury.

Then Elliot spoke, breaching the stillness. "Sorry for hitting you." He gulped. "You know, there was something I wanted to ask you too."

"Now or never."

Elliot cleared his throat. "Why didn't you ever marry ... her? You were with her long enough to do it."

Adam huffed. This was his chance to fully come clean. He owed Elliot that much. "Was stalling."

"You admit that you wanted a baby and wanted to get married because you were trying hard to be straight?"

"Don't know." Would it be so terrible to admit that now, at a time like this? Did he want to end it knowing Elliot was right about Jena and his engagement? Would admitting it mean he was a bad person?

"You're in denial," Elliot said in a matter-of-fact tone.

Adam lay still, ensuring that the pain in his arm wouldn't come back. "Your family ignored you 'cause they wanted you to believe you didn't matter to them. That you were worthless to them. Being gay had a lot to do with your family not inviting you over, but you're so happy in your skin that you don't see it or didn't want to see it. Maybe *you're* in denial." Adam kept his eyes on Elliot. "You admit that?"

Elliot bit his bottom lip, refusing to look in Adam's direction. Adam felt tickles of tears run down the side of his face. He didn't try to stop them. There was no reason to.

Elliot cleared his throat, gulping so hard Adam felt his discomfort. "Maybe you're right. Maybe they were intentionally assholes to me because I'm gay. But no matter how much denial we're in, there's one thing I know for sure. I know I can't live without you." He turned his head and finally looked to Adam. His eyes were red and puffy even without the presence of tears. "You know that too." He coughed. "I'm gonna get you outta there," he said, standing. "You just hang tight." He dusted his bottom off, picked up his flashlight, whistled at Titan and he and the dog went limping down the street toward the minivan.

Adam finally lowered his eyelids.

CHAPTER ELEVEN

Death's Landfill

The R and the arrow were spray painted on the hood of the minivan. Elliot ran his hand over the paint. He was expecting it to smear but the only thing that smeared was the light layer of dust that collected there. The paint was as dry as the other signs he'd run into. But Adam had mentioned a spray painted sign on the bridge that had been wet. He even saw traces of black paint on Adam's shirt. So the person responsible had to be around somewhere in the proximity.

Finding the person would be hell. It was hell finding Adam. But he had to do something other than leave Adam stuck under a car while he skipped off to find paradise. He swore to himself, whenever he found the person responsible for sending them on such a wild goose chase and putting their lives in jeopardy, he was gonna take out his frustration on him.

Hastily, he checked the inside of the van for anything useful including the car keys. With no luck, he followed the direction of the arrow. Walking and walking down the lonely freeway with Titan by his side.

After what felt like an hour of walking, stopping a couple times to rest and give him and Titan a drink and a bite, he came upon a pile of crushed vehicles jumbled together in a mass of metal. Peeking into a few of the cars, he was astonished to find several bodies thrown about inside as if a whirlwind of its own pick them up and flailed them around to their deaths. There must've been similar deaths all around Phoenix. Was he lucky not to have seen too many scenarios of tragic accidents and dismantled bodies? Instantly, nausea rushed him and he lurched forward, spewing his stomach contents.

Broken glass lay around the street like tiny crystals coated in dried, rusty-colored, coagulated blood. So much for trying not to think of death. The image of Adam pinned halfway under that burnt car popped into mind. He must be in immense pain, holding on for Elliot to somehow come to his rescue. Standing around looking at the grim sight before him, thinking of the possibility of a tarnished future without Adam, had his mind reeling.

The smell of smoke and a hissing sound caught his attention. Titan must've heard and smelled it too, because he shot off up the ramp into the darkness.

"Titan!" Elliot followed the dog up the long ascending ramp, listening to the soft pads of Titan's paws as they pitter-pattered against the asphalt, and followed the intense smell of smoke.

Once at the top of the ramp, he shined his light at the corner gas station which smoldered from what looked like an intense fire induced by a major car accident. Black smoke billowed from under the hood of several collided cars. Three of the individual self-service fueling stations lay crushed and in pieces around the small lot, burned nearly beyond recognition.

As Elliot carefully made his way closer to the convenience store directly next door, the charred wood paneling around the front entrance cracked and chipped, and inside looked as if it has been looted of its most valuable contents. Seeing no sense in standing around wasting precious time, Elliot continued walking toward the descending ramp across the street continuing his search for more freshly painted R's and the person accountable for them.

Titan had another mission in mind. The dog stopped, turned and stared at the convenience store.

"Come on, Titan." Elliot whistled. Titan trotted to Elliot, turned back around as if quickly changing his mind and stood to stare at the store. Suddenly the sound of an old, empty metal soup can rattled behind the store. Titan let out a threatening growl, still staring, unmoving. The image of another dog, a mutt much more threatening than Titan, popped into Elliot's mind. Damn, how would he defend himself from a menacing, hungry beast?

Then something else occurred to him. The rattling also sounded familiarly similar to that of a can of spray paint when you shake it. Titan continued to bark, each bark resonating throughout the streets.

"Anybody there?" Elliot shined the flashlight on the darkened corner that led to the back of the store where the sound had come from. Titan stopped barking and cocked his head when a face peeked around the corner and stared back at them.

A small bright light shined back at him. Elliot shielded his eyes with his hand, preventing the light from blinding him. "Hello? Who's there?"

"I'm Tami," a woman's voice called out. "Who the hell are *you?*"

Titan barked repeatedly.

"My name's Elliot," he said over the barking and lowered his light, hoping the woman would do the same. "I'm looking for someone to help me and my friend. He's pinned under a car and I can't pull him out by myself. Can you help?" Titan continued to bark and Elliot nudged him with his leg. "Quiet, Titan! Go, go over there." Elliot pointed shooing the dog away. Titan trotted further behind him, stopping to look back over his shoulder several times.

The woman finally lowered her light and came from behind the corner. She stood tall and thin with light brown hair pulled into a ponytail behind her head. On her shoulder was a dirty, pink beach bag. Behind the wall another woman emerged, a black woman, shorter, and voluptuous with wide hips. Her hair was wrapped in some sort of fancy colorful dressing. She too carried a bag, a large, beige cloth-looking one.

"I don't think there's much we can do to help you," Tami said as she came nearer, the other woman trailing her closely. As the women gradually approached, Titan backed away into the darkness, but Elliot didn't move. Instead he studied them, making out more of their features. Even though the women were coated in a thin layer of dirt and looked as tired as he felt, they were young—about his age—and healthy looking, very capable of assisting him with Adam.

Elliot shook his head. "We've been walking for hours, days even, searching for other survivors, and as soon as I find you, you refuse to help me?"

"We're on a mission of our own, guy," the dark-skinned woman said as they continued to slowly move forward, almost cautiously. "Like my friend said, there's not much we can do. Sorry."

"My name's Elliot." He reminded her with a bit of spunk in his tone. "My friend is dying. It's probably just an hour of your time and I promise after he's safe I'll leave you to your mission."

The women paused several feet away from him and looked at each other as if considering if they should help or not. Tami shrugged and stared at the woman accompanying her. "Maybe he could help us."

"Help you do what?" Elliot interrupted. "Spray paint everything out here? I'll do whatever you need me to do. Just help me first."

"I'm looking for my daughter," Tami said, interrupting his pleading with a questioning stare.

"I only met an old couple in Arrowhead Hospital who's still there." Elliot put his right hand up as if to swear on the bible in court.

"But I *promise* I will help you find your daughter if you help me first." The urgency in his voice should've clued them in to the importance of their cooperation.

While the women talked quietly amongst themselves, Elliot tried desperately to be patient so they could make their decision. He pointed his light at them when his patience ran out. "What do you say? We gotta hurry."

"Can you get the light out of my face?" Tami shot daggers with her makeup smeared eyes.

Titan emerged from behind Elliot and suddenly began to bark, pant and wag his tail. Before Elliot could figure out what had got him so excited, Titan ran forward and playfully jumped up on Tami, pressing his paws onto her thighs.

"Hey, guy. Get your dog!" the other woman demanded, in a shaky, uneasy voice.

"Titan!" Elliot whistled. "Come here. Titan."

"Charlie!" Tami screamed. "Oh, my God, Anita. This is Charlie." She looked to Elliot with the happiest smile, rolls of pearly white teeth gleaming in the dimness. "Where did you find him? This is my daughter's dog. I thought he looked familiar. What happened to his leg? He looks so different."

"Oh, I picked him up a day ago or so." Elliot dipped his brows, thinking. "Time is really strange—"

"You gotta tell me where you found him." Tami's voice drenched in emotion that her eyes conveyed with tears. She scratched the dog's head, which he seemed to like a great deal. "He was with my daughter when she ran away from the compound and they never left each other's side. We should look for her in the area you found him."

"Sure. Sure," Elliot nodded. He couldn't help but wonder, "Is the compound part of Refuge Inc.?"

"Did you leave the compound too?" Tami sniffed, wiped at her stray tears and petted the dog lovingly.

"No, no. But you're talking about Refuge Inc., right? Is it a place for survivors?"

"If you don't know what it is then how do you know the name?" The woman who Tami referred to as Anita stared fixedly, waiting for his response.

"My friend, Adam, has a flyer he found. It has the same symbol on it that you're painting all over the place. He thinks it's for survivors." She didn't say anything so Elliot asked, "Well, is it?"

"It has everything you'll ever need to survive," Anita said, a hint of disdain in her voice. She didn't look up. Instead she watched the dog lick her friend's face.

Elliot nodded, not sure how he felt about her claim. There would definitely be more questions that needed answers, but Adam couldn't wait much longer. "Follow me. We gotta help my friend and we gotta be quick."

Tami glared, unmoving. "My daughter is out here alone. She needs me. I can't just leave her to fend for herself."

"We don't even know you," Anita added with the same look of disregard in her dark eyes that painted her face when she mentioned Refuge Inc.

Elliot clasped his hands together before him. "Look, you need my help and I need yours."

"I need to find my daughter, okay," Tami interrupted. "She's only eleven. She's been missing for a couple days now without food or water. It's my fault she left the compound." She turned to her friend. "I should've never mentioned Gabriel. I should've never told her he wasn't coming back. He was everything to her."

"I know. I know." Her friend placed a hand on Tami's back to console her. "Most dads are to their little girls."

"But the way I said it," Tami went on, tears running down her face. "I just came out and told her not to bother curling her hair for him, because he'll never see it. What kind of person am I?" She balled on her friend's shoulder. "I deserve to just die already."

"You were scared, Tami," Anita said, speaking softly, tenderly. "I'm sure she'll forgive you. She loves you."

"Please, help me," Elliot interjected. He pressed his palms together, eyes begging, pleading. "We don't have a lot of time and ..." He paused, rewound their conversation in his head and realized the ultimate tragedy. "You said your daughter had curly hair?"

"Yeah?" Tami said, sniffing.

"Was it really long and blonde, kinda like yours but lighter?"

"Yeah. Yeah. Did you see her? Where is she?" Tami's eyes lit up with hope. Elliot's heart sank. He saw the girl, but her body lay under a mound of debris drenched in a pool of dried blood. She was the first dead body he'd laid eyes on hours after he started his trek. That poor little blonde girl.

CHAPTER TWELVE

Lying for Gain

The walk back to Adam was tedious. The entire time Elliot refused to make eye contact with the women, staying considerably ahead of them so they wouldn't want to engage in conversation. He knew once they learned the truth, that Tami's daughter was likely dead instead of locked safe inside of a home, they would be infuriated. More lies upon lies would do too much harm so he tried his best to avoid saying anything at all, using his haste to convey his urgency.

He hated lying about such serious things, but Adam was in critical need. If he didn't tell the women that lie and encourage them to help him save Adam in exchange for details on where the girl was, Adam wouldn't have a chance at all. Elliot felt like an evil manipulator, like a deceitful prick preying on two poor women for his own gain. But the girl was dead. There wasn't a life or death issue with her, even if her mother didn't know that yet. Maybe they would understand and have pity on him when he did tell them the truth.

When they finally reached Adam he was unresponsive. His flashlight was still illuminating the area, showing the burned car resting on its side and on top of Adam's arm.

"Oh, my God!" the women said in unison as they came around the car to where Adam lay.

He was motionless on the slope underneath the bridge and in an awkward position. It was as if he'd been struggling to free himself while Elliot was gone. Elliot knelt down beside him. It seemed as if Titan knew Adam was hurt and somehow tried to soothe the pain with licks to Adam's face, but Elliot pushed the dog aside. "Adam?" He quickly tapped the side of his face with his fingertips. "Adam, wake up."

Adam groaned, opening his eyes. "Did you find it?" he murmured.

Did he mean the wet painted R, the people who painted them or Refuge Inc.? Elliot didn't ask for clarification, instead he said, "I found some help. You're gonna be okay."

Anita handed her oversized bag to Tami and went to Adam's side. "I'm Anita. Don't worry. We're gonna get you out of here." She stood and walked around the car, examining it.

Tami and Titan stood off to the side as if waiting for the right moment to step in. Tami kept both of her hands clasped over her mouth, watching.

Elliot caressed Adam's sweaty forehead. "You okay?"

"I'm tired," Adam mumbled, with eyes closed.

Elliot wiped the dust and dirt from Adam's cheek, seeing a red and slightly swollen bruise on his temple where he had punched him earlier. He leaned down and planted a kiss on the exact spot. He sat back just in time to see a smile curl Adam's lip.

"Okay." Anita came around the darkened corner from behind the rear of the overturned car. "Looks like most of the weight of the car is against the wall. That's what's holding it up. All we have to do is lift it just enough for one of us to pull him from under it."

"Good." Elliot stood, readying himself.

"But—" Anita started.

Elliot raised an eyebrow. "But?"

"But we're on a slope with all this loose gravel, so the slightest movement might cause the car to slide either down the slope, or on its roof or both. Not good."

"We just gotta be careful and quick." Elliot nodded, happy with his decision.

"How did this happen?" Tami whispered, probably talking to herself rather than directing the question to anyone in particular. "Poor guy." She had tears in her eyes, probably from the fears of losing her daughter and watching Adam in so much pain. It had to put a huge amount of stress on anyone in that predicament.

"It was an accident," Elliot frowned, dusting his hands on his shorts. With a firm look he pointed to Tami, seeing the absolute terror in her eyes and for a split moment he felt her anxiety in his gut. "You grab ahold of his good arm and you pull as fast and as hard as you can when I say so, okay?"

Tami nodded and cautiously went to Adam's side. Adam's eyes were still closed and he looked as exhausted as a sprinter who had ran several laps. She leaned over and wrapped her dainty hands around his wrist while Elliot and Anita went to the front of the car.

"Alright," Elliot continued passing out orders, even though he felt guilt trying to stop him and force him to come clean about her missing daughter. "Anita, on the count of three we'll lift the front of the car as high as we can. Tami, you grip his arm tighter and pull him with everything you got as far away from the car as possible just in case it wants to fall or slide."

"Right," Tami said and rearranged her arm, hooking her and Adam's elbows for a better grip.

"Okay," Elliot knelt down and slid his fingers in a crevice under the front of the car near the tire. Anita did the same but on the underside of the front bumper. He looked at the woman beside him who looked as ready as he was. "Lift with your legs not your back, okay?" Something he learned while stocking boxes of goods at Food Plus. "You ready?" Anita nodded, but he couldn't count. It was on the tip of his tongue. *One, two, three.* But instead of counting he stood.

"I'm sorry." He looked down at Tami, staring at the dried bloodstain soaked on the knee of her pants.

"Why?" Her bottom lip trembled.

"I saw your daughter a few miles from my neighborhood." Elliot refused to make eye contact no matter how hard he tried. No, he didn't refuse, his body just wouldn't let him. "She was buried halfway under rubble. Sorry."

Anita gasped. "What?"

"She's dead." He clarified. "I'm sorry. I'm so sorry."

"You said you passed her taking shelter in an abandoned house." Tami stood from beside Adam and stepped forward, eyes wide as a maniac ready to strike. She pointed her narrow finger like a loaded gun. "You lied to me, you bastard. You used us."

"No, no." Elliot tried pleading with his eyes. "I need your help and I feel bad for lying to get you here but...I need you. That's why I'm telling you now. I couldn't live with myself if I didn't..." The anger in Tami's eyes showed through her tears and suddenly replaced any trace of heartache on her face, even though he knew the pain was still there. "Please understand why I lied." His voice caught as he pleaded, palms pressed together before him, eyelids heavy from threatening tears. He swallowed and looked down at Adam, knowing time was slipping away. "Please."

"We're already here." Anita took her place in front of the side turned car and squatted, ready to lift. "On the count of three."

Tami sniffed and wiped her wet eyes with the back of her dirty hand. Even so, tears flowed from them and anger shown through them. She knelt beside Adam and locked her arm around his. "On three."

Elliot slid his finger back in the crevice and positioned himself. "One, two, three."

They moved together like a fluid choreographed dance. He felt his thigh muscles burn, the wound on his leg ached something fierce, and his fingers did the same—but the car slowly lifted.

Adam let out an agonizing howl above Tami's demands. "Keep lifting," she shouted. "Go, go, go!"

The shouts and cries that echoed through the streets rattled in Elliot's ears. Before the last echo faded, Tami had pulled Adam and his limp arm several feet away from the car.

"Now," Elliot grunted through clenched teeth and he and Anita let the car fall back down to the earth. He was lightheaded. He must have been holding his breath. Even so, he quickly rushed toward Adam and his agonized whimpering. In his haste he slipped on the gravel beneath his feet and fell on his ass once, stumbling twice after. He dropped to his knees, feeling the small rocks dig into his skin as he crawled over Adam, straddling his body.

"Adam." Elliot planted a chaste kiss on his cheek. "I'm so happy," and another kiss, "you're okay," and another. Awkward behavior? Who cared? As soon as he felt Adam's hand on the small of his back, he couldn't care if another asteroid hit then. He had Adam in his arms. That's all that mattered.

Adam brought his trembling hand to Elliot's face. "Now who's the hero?"

Elliot snorted. "I'm not the hero because that would make you the sidekick."

"The problem?"

"The problem is you make a shitty sidekick." Elliot looked down into Adam's tired eyes. "You don't know how to stay by my side."

"Never again." Adam pulled Elliot forward and delivered a brief kiss to his forehead. "I'll never leave you again. That's a promise."

Elliot overflowed with the sudden euphoric feeling of relief. Everything would be okay. It all would be okay.

Then Tami's voice shattered his relief. "Now tell me where my daughter is."

When Elliot glanced back at her, she held her and Anita's bags on her shoulder, and an impatient look in her eye.

He stood and gently pulled Adam up to sit. Adam's swollen arm dangled beside him. It looked broken with a huge purple bruise over the length of it. The skin on it had cuts and bloody punctures where small stones had dug into it. Adam grimaced and groaned in pain. "I need something to use as a sling."

Elliot gathered up Adam's backpack and flashlight near the car.

"Where is my daughter?" Tami's voice was loud and demanding.

"Uh, she's ..." Elliot unzipped the pack, overturned it and emptied most of its contents onto the floor. There's was nothing that could double as a sling. He dropped the bag. "You can use my shirt."

"No, use my headscarf," Anita said, stepping forward. She unraveled it from her head, revealing long, thick, dark curly locks of her own. She moved forward to hand it to Elliot when Tami stopped her.

"Don't give him anything until he tells me where Jess is."

Elliot shook his head, trying to organize his thoughts. "Her body was a few miles from my neighborhood."

"And where exactly is that?"

Anita placed her arm on Tami's. "Just because he saw a girl's body with that description doesn't mean it's Jess."

"That's right." Tami's eyes widened at the possibility. "But we have to go see for ourselves just to be sure." She turned to Elliot. "So where is she?"

Adam slouched over, reaching for a bottle of water next to his empty backpack. "Who are you guys? What girl?"

Elliot picked up the water bottle and opened it, and then handed it to Adam. "They're the ones spray painting the R's."

"Refuge Inc.?" Adam seemed to sober up, a hint of excitement in his eyes. "Take us there."

"You don't deserve to be there," Tami growled. "He told us my daughter was alive to get us to help you, but he lied to us. Using us. So don't ask for my help anymore."

"That's not fair." Elliot shook his head. "I told you the truth before you helped. I was trying to do the right thing. I feel bad for everything that's happened but you guys weren't gonna help me. I had to do something. You still decided to help me and I appreciate that but—"

"It's alright. We'll just follow the signs," Adam said, wincing in pain. "You don't have to take us."

"The signs are for my daughter." Tami glowered, tucking stray light brown strands of hair behind her ear. "We painted them to help her find her way back. That's all we could do. No one else wanted to help. Everyone is looking for their own loved ones, or looking for food or supplies, or are sick. It's chaos. But me and Anita had to do something for ourselves. Us. We don't have time to worry about everyone else."

"So Refuge Inc. is a place for survivors?" Elliot asked. "There are other people there?"

"Lots of people," Anita said with somber eyes. "But not more than there are dead. I never saw so many dead bodies in my life. In homes, cars, building, churches—"

"And my daughter might be one of them." Tami shook her head, already she was balling. "Tell me where my daughter is, and I will tell you how to get to the compound. That's all I'm willing to do for you."

He had no issue telling her where he'd seen the girl. Yet, the way they all stared at each other silently raised red flags. Elliot could see in their faces that they were all wondering the same thing. Would there be more lies for personal gain? They didn't trust him.

Anita crouched down near Adam and assisted him in making a sling with her long, colorful head wrap. "Please do the right thing." She peered into Adam's eyes with such a sorrowful gaze Elliot's heart ached … for all of them and their pain and losses. Elliot was gonna to the right thing, no doubt, but were they? Where would they lead him and Adam? They were too badly injured to continue roaming Phoenix in search of painting Rs.

He watched as Anita handled Adam with care. Titan sniffed at the dried fruit on the ground beside them. Elliot owed them more than he could give, but he knew they were exaggerating about Refuge Inc., making it seem like the place with the solution, with "all they would ever need" as Anita said earlier with sarcasm. If that was so, why weren't they there? Why would the daughter run away from such a great place after a disaster? Why wouldn't anyone else help them in their search? They were lying to him to get back at him for telling his own lies, and to get the information they needed. However, if they were lying about this place, why would they direct the beloved daughter back there?

He could see the deceit in Tami's eyes. He always intended to tell her the truth about her daughter, and even give her the location where he saw the body. However, for Adam's sake—for Adam's steadfast belief in Refuge Inc. and all of its magnificence—he couldn't mention his skepticism. He'd rather roam the dark, haunted streets all night, looking for a phantom utopia than confront the women and their lies. As long as he was by Adam's side, he was content.

"Back east. Near Nice Smile Dental in the surrounding neighborhood." Elliot glanced down at Adam's exhausted smile. "Now how do we get to Refuge?"

Anita stood and pointed. "Follow this freeway down to Seventh Street, turn south and you'll see a blinking red light in the distance on South Mountain. That light is the radio antenna for the compound. You can't miss it." Anita had spoken, however, she wouldn't lift her gaze to meet Elliot's, or rather *couldn't.*

Tami turned to leave when Anita stopped her. "Let's give him some pain meds. We can't leave him like this."

They looked to Adam and the pain written on his face with a grimace. Elliot went to sit beside him, not much he could do but offer him another drink of water.

Tami eyed the mess of contents that lay beside them next to Adam's backpack, illuminated by the dim light of the flashlight which lay beside the burnt car. "Give me your flashlight for some pain meds."

"Our flashlight?" Elliot shook his head. "We need that."

"You have two, you only need one." Tami unknowingly smeared more of the dark makeup around her eyes with the back of her hand. "Come on. Hand it over."

Adam grunted, swallowing a mouthful of water. "We already have pain killers, we don't need yours. Keep 'em for yourselves."

That was right. Elliot had forgotten about the aspirin Adam had found in the hospital. Maybe Adam had forgotten about it too until now. Not much it could have done if they remembered it earlier anyway.

"I have Vicodin." Tami dug in her bag to produce a small brown prescription bottle. "It's pretty strong stuff."

Adam nodded.

"And I want those batteries too," Tami added, "and you can have this whole bottle. There're four pills in here. It should last you a long time. And I want some of that dried fruit too."

"Tami!" Anita whispered. "That's enough."

"Enough?" Tami shouted. "They're lucky I'm even offering pain meds." She gave Elliot a dirty look and tossed the bottle of pills to him. Then she gathered the flashlight, a bag of dried fruit and all of the extra batteries in the spewed contents on the ground.

Before he could say *thank you,* they quickly headed down the street and out of sight. Titan followed behind the girls, trotting along briefly. Before they got too far he paused and watched the women as they continued to walk, then he turned around to hobble right back to Adam and Elliot's side.

Adam sighed, a slight grin on his lips. "We're gonna be okay."

CHAPTER THIRTEEN

Between the Lines

Adam knew there were other survivors. The proof was in the two pair they'd encountered on their unbelievable journey. He thought back to hours ago when Anita talked about seeing so many dead bodies. He'd only seen the few in his neighborhood church, Elliot only saw the body of the little girl. Either way, he knew there were more dead out there, probably hundreds, thousands, millions more. He felt fortunate enough not to have encountered them although he mourned for them.

They'd been walking, following Tami's directions, for what felt like hours. They only stopped once to rest. They had fallen asleep for several hours underneath an overpass which was miles from the one he had grown so familiar with.

Adam popped the last few painkillers in his mouth, swallowing the white oval pills. His arm hurt and throbbed worse than ever, but the thought of reaching shelter and getting medical attention, real food and fresh water fueled him. His legs felt weak and his muscles sore, especially while walking after so many hours of rest.

"Thank you," Adam murmured, as they approached Seventh Street. "For saving my life. Now that's a true hero."

"You do what you have to do for the people you ... care about." Elliot slid a glance at him. "Right?"

"Right." Adam nodded, delving deeper. "You surprised me. I came back to the hospital and you were gone. Didn't think you would leave."

He heard Elliot gulp while his eyes followed the sway of the steadily weakening flashlight beam as they walked. "I thought the same about you."

"Sorry for that."

"Don't apologize. I get it," Elliot said, "You were doing what you thought you had to do to help. I left for the same reason. I should've stayed. I know that now."

"*I* should've stayed." Adam glanced to Elliot's sad eyes. "I know that now."

Adam stopped to catch his breath and rest his aching legs. Instead, Elliot surprised him with a short, sweet kiss. Elliot's lips remained pressed against his and Adam's indulged, allowing his tongue to lick alongside Elliot's for a brief moment. The heated kiss, that very moment, made him feel well restored even if it only lasted a few seconds. They broke the kiss and stared into each other's eyes. They were surrounded by much that was wrong—devastation, darkness, silence and mysterious ash that fell from the sky—but the emotion that burrowed into Adam's heart felt so right.

Titan squeezed between the two of them and Elliot swept the small light along the furry mass at their feet. Pain returned to Adam's arm. He was about to express his anticipation of receiving more powerful medicine at Refuge Inc. when Elliot pointed ahead.

"Look, there's the red light." The light blinked as small as a pin nail far in the distance "That has to be it."

Time seemed to move extremely slowly as foot after foot stepped one in front of the other. They had stopped looking at the wristwatch long ago; knowing time didn't matter much as long as they made progress. An hour, possibly hours, passed behind them and before they knew it their destination was right before their very eyes.

Approaching the desert edge of South Mountain, bright white flood lights shined as bright as the sun, illuminating an area surrounded by a cluster of large mountains, saguaro cacti and dried up bushes. The flat desert region was cleared of debris and occupied by dozens of people. Some people were dressed in white jumpsuits with a single zipper running from the collar down to the waist, with face masks and a collection of dust on their shoulders like a pad of snow. Others were dressed in plain clothes; jeans or nicely detailed work suits, but all the people were occupied. A few people were placing long, plain foldout tables near two big white medical field tents with the words Refuge Inc. marked on them in bold printed script. An image of a silver ring encircled the R of the word Refuge, and a line of about a half dozen injured people waited, possibly to be treated.

Elliot laughed quietly. "I didn't think it was real. I didn't think we would find it, but we're here." His smile grew wide, genuine. "Look. You were right."

Most of the people in the white uniforms had face masks covering their noses and mouths, probably to keep the scarcely falling dust or the rotten smell from entering their lungs. Far in the distance, about twenty yards away, a chain linked fence with coils of barbed wire on top surrounded what looked like the official entrance into the side of the nearest mountain; a wide metal archway which lead deeper inside the immense rock. The dark archway lit up with several rolls of lights on inside walls.

Near the big white medical tent a man in a similar white uniform raised a bottle of water in his hand and waved them over. Adam took Elliot's hand in his and interlocked their fingers, ignoring the pain in his other arm and the uneasy feeling in his gut. "Ready?"

Elliot nodded excitedly and they moved toward the tent.

A speaker sounded in the distance near the metal archway. The words it repeated echoed off the surrounding mountains in a casual male voice. "Your contribution is essential to a promising future. We cherish your support. Your involvement is a vital asset for a better tomorrow. We cherish your support." And on and on it went, repeating the same sentences.

They quickly walked hand in hand toward the waving man in the white uniform. Upon approach, the man handed Elliot the bottle of water and pointed to Titan as the dog panted, its tongue dangling out the side of its mouth.

"The dog won't be allowed to go inside the compound." The words were barely recognizable, muffled by the white facial mask covering the man's nose and mouth. "They have a special place for pets to go." He placed his hand on Adam's shoulder and quickly led them inside the medical tent, Titan on their heels. "Names?"

"I'm Elliot and this is Adam." Elliot helped Adam along as they closely followed the man to a small black laptop computer that sat on a small metal desk in the corner of the tent. "He tried to look past the mask at the man beneath it but all he could make out were dark eyes; dirty, pale skin; short, well groomed hair, and the blue latex gloves on the man's hands.

The man leaned over the computer and quickly pecked the keyboard with both index fingers. "Elliot what?" His voice rushed and muffled.

At first Elliot had no idea what the man was asking, but then his mind clicked into gear. "Uh, Stewart. Elliot Stewart."

The man continued a steady peck at the keys. Once finished his eyes shot to their interlocked hands and his eyebrows dipped when he looked back up at them. "And your friend?" He jerked his head toward Adam, hands hovering millimeters above the keyboard.

"Adam Weber." Elliot answered. He glanced around inside the tent. It was spacious, clean and empty. No people being treated as he expected. "Are you medical? Do you work for the government or something? He really needs some help and quick. A car—"

"All your questions will be answered inside the compound." The man stopped typing, again his fingers rested in midair. "Occupation?"

Adam cleared his throat. "Do you really need this information right now? Can you get us some help first?"

"Yes, I need this information before we can treat you." He rolled his eyes and shook his head as the look of impatience took over his body language. "Occupation?"

"I work ... I *used* to work as a customer service rep." Elliot's words rushed together as he rapidly spoke. "At Food Plus, I didn't—"

"Occupation?" the man interrupted, looking to Adam.

Elliot didn't mind that the man cut him off. Maybe he had other people he needed to help too. It was the way the man looked at him that made him uneasy.

Adam cleared his throat again, his eyes low and bloodshot. "I worked as a ... as a ..." he cut his eye to Elliot. "A police officer for Phoenix."

The man continued to slowly click at the keys. Elliot took the moment to give Adam a questioning glance, but Adam looked like he was in too much pain to care what Elliot thought about him lying anyway.

"Don't have any way to pay for this," Adam added. "That recording is talking about a contribution—"

"Sure you have a way to pay for this," the man said. He turned his head slightly toward them, eyes locked on to Adam's. "Everyone does."

Adam and Elliot exchanged an awkward look. Elliot spoke first. "What do you mean?"

The man stopped typing and stood erect. He sighed. "Why do you think I need all this information before we can treat you? You provide what you can offer and we give accordingly. Simple as that. Now hand me the bag."

Elliot brought his hand to the strap around his shoulder. "Wait, this is our stuff. We need this."

"We have more stuff inside," the man said. "Plenty of stuff. If you don't want to cooperate stop wasting my time and go back to where you came from. If you want our help," he held out his hand, "give me the bag."

Elliot looked to Adam as he slipped the backpack from his shoulder. "What is this place exactly?"

"Your salvation." The man snatched the bag from Elliot's grip then reached across the small desk to unlock a little black box. Once unlocked and opened he pulled out a plastic cartridge. "Your hand?"

Elliot held out his hand. "What is this?"

"You sure do ask a lot of questions." The man turned his hand over and stamped the word *Pod 4* onto the back of his hand with what looked like black ink from the cartridge. He did the same to Adam, except Adam's hand read *Pod 6*. "Go through that archway there and they will treat you inside. Just show them the stamp on your hand. I'll have someone take the dog to the vet inside." He snapped his fingers and another person in a white mechanical suit, face mask and blue latex gloves appeared behind them with a collar and leash. "In the meantime, it'll be in the canine nursery with other dogs."

Adam and Elliot's first and last names were written on a dog collar in black marker that was placed around Titan's neck. As soon as the leash was attached, the mysterious person led the dog out the backside of the tent.

The man glanced behind them, picked up a bottle of water from a box of bottles on the floor and raised it in the air, waving with his other hand simultaneously. Pivoting, Elliot saw a group of three people covered in dust approaching the tent.

"I got work to do." The man mumbled, shooing them away with his hand. "Go inside and they'll help you."

Elliot and Adam followed a newly paved road toward the metal archway. Upon approach, the tall and abundant flood lights which gave light to the surrounding area heated the paved road beneath their feet. The smell of hot tar mingled with the overpowering rotten smell Elliot had gotten used to. As far as Elliot knew, the paved road led deeper inside of the huge, dark tunnel with thick metal walls. What lay beyond the tunnel? He didn't know. Although the uncertainty of what lay ahead rattled his nerves, it fueled him as well. It seemed to fuel Adam too as his pace quickened with his determination.

"We did it." Adam gripped his injured arm to his body with his stamped hand. "I admit, the past few days . . . crazy. If we never found each other things would've been different. I'd probably be dead if it wasn't for you."

Elliot placed a comforting hand on the small of Adam's back. "I couldn't do any of this alone." Nearly inside the tunnel, large round lights alongside the walls of the passageway lighted their way in the darkness. "Feels like we're crossing into a new beginning for us, huh?"

"Something like that." Adam held out his hand and Elliot took it. "Yeah, a new beginning."

THE END

AMID THE DARKNESS

REFUGE INC., BOOK 2

Leslie Lee Sanders

LLS BOOKS
QUEEN CREEK, ARIZONA

Prologue

When the heavy, rusted metal door to the compound closed, Adam knew it would be closed for good, trapping him and a couple hundred people underground and away from the devastation on the other side.

The word *trapped* came to mind only because it perfectly described the claustrophobic feeling that overwhelmed him. He'd thought he'd gotten used to being in such close quarters with so many injured and frightened people. He was wrong. For nearly a month, it never really felt like the salvation he heard on so many people's tongues.

He made his way through a crowd of people who stood crying, praying and staring at the thick latched door as if they were attending a funeral, mourning the loss of their previous lives. For many, that was exactly what was happening. For others—the women and men in fine clothing who looked as if they harbored every necessity they could ever need—Adam was sure it was the beginning of a new life. The glass half full concept.

The skin on Adam's arm itched under its cast, but he distracted himself by touching the cold metal door with his good hand, a silent goodbye to the hellish world beyond the barrier, a world so familiar yet altered.

A warm hand on his shoulder stole Adam's attention. He pivoted to stare into worried brown eyes with eyelashes that fluttered uncontrollability like a small winged insect. He smirked.

"What are you doing?" Elliot glanced over his shoulder repeatedly, paranoid. "These people are gonna go nuts any minute and try to knock that door down all at once. You're asking to be trampled. Come on."

He allowed Elliot to grab his hand and pull him to the back of the crowd and down the hall which led to Pod 4. The long metal corridor echoed with the sound of their footsteps as they made their way to the large shell shaped area at the end.

"The speakers said we'll have to get used to our own pods and—"

"I know what the speakers said." Out of the six rooms in the pod, Elliot pulled Adam to the first room on the left and pushed the metal door open. It creaked and whined on its hinges, and echoed back through the corridor. "I'd like to know who's behind all of these stupid messages before I start obeying them."

"They're just trying to help ease the panic by answering questions and keeping order." Adam walked into the small chamber and instinctively looked up at the lone rectangular sound speaker that hung from the corner of the cramped room. There were two twin beds in the room, each with a mattress and a box spring on squeaking metal frames with wheels. Just like his room. Adam sat on a bed, looking around at the boxes piled in a corner. "Are you ever going to go through your stuff, get organized?"

"Get organized?" Elliot glared. "Look at us. We're wearing hospital scrubs in an underground bunker that's just been sealed off from us ever leaving, and, and you're thinking about being organized?"

"They're not scrubs."

"We look like mental patients." Elliot stood and paced the narrow space between the two beds. "I don't like this. Not at all."

"Who likes it?" Adam scoffed. "We're not supposed to like it. We're surviving and it's not easy to do."

"It'll be easier if they let us wear our own clothes at least." Elliot continued to pace.

He was right. Adam didn't understand why they took their personal items and gave them boxes of necessities from Refuge Inc.'s own supplies. Toilet tissue, toothpastes, even on the left breast pocket of the scrubs they wore was all labeled with a blood red R and a shiny silver halo around it.

Static broke over the small speaker in the corner of the room, and then a monotone male voice broke the white noise.

"Thanks for your cooperation. The compound door has been closed and will remain as so until the dust clears out of the valley and all of the Phoenix area. This is for our protection and for a secure future. We ask that you all report to your assigned pods for proper organization of your duties. Thank you for your cooperation."

Elliot shook his head. "Who is that?"

"Whoever it is they're trying to get us all organized." Adam stood. "Sounds like we all have duties assigned to us.

CHAPTER ONE

Adjusting to Insanity

Elliot didn't want to blurt out the obvious, but things didn't seem to be going too well. Maybe it was the fact that they had closed the one and only door that led to the outside that scared him most. Knowing he was trapped inside, terrified him more than what was outside.

Still, the atmosphere of the underground compound felt ominous. There were dark, dank rusted metal and concrete corridors with huge rusted bolts holding the seams of metal together. The musty smell of moisture and body odor overpowered his senses. The sticky humidity he felt in certain areas, especially the large main room where the people were gathered saying their last goodbyes to the outside world was too much to bear. What hadn't escaped everyone's thoughts was the hostile world outside the compound that grew more and more dark and angry as the days carried on. The world they were being protected from.

He reached down and scratched the scar on his shin. The gash had healed but the flesh under the scar itched at times. Remembering his wound made him think of Titan. He hadn't seen his four-legged companion since they first stumbled upon the compound. The last time he'd seen the dog, men in breathing masks had led Titan off on a leash with a collar they had written his and Adam's last names onto with a permanent black marker.

They had promised to take good care of him. Maybe he was doing much better than Elliot at the moment. Maybe his wound had healed amazingly and he was playing around with other mutts without a care in the world, eating great dog food instead of the granola bars he and Adam were feeding him, drinking gallons of fresh water, and playing with hundreds of dog toys. Maybe Elliot didn't have anything to worry about after all.

He did worry about the old couple they had run into at Arrowhead hospital during their trek to find Refuge Inc.

He'd made sure to tell some of the men in white coveralls and breathing masks about Harold and Edna, and was assured that a search party would be sent to rescue them. However, he hadn't heard anything since. And every time he asked about the couple and Edna's comatose husband no one had any definite answers.

"Go check the medical station," they said. "If they're here and they're sickly as you say, then they would be in the medical station especially if they require meds."

Every week he had checked the medical station and every week ... nothing.

There were likely a couple hundred people living in the compound all with different worries and undertakings. Maybe one day soon he would see the old couple and know they had made it.

Elliot had to get out of his tiny, stuffy room. He would like to explore the compound more but guards in their dark blue uniforms kept a watchful eye on the stairwell to the floors and pods below. He had only explored the cafeteria and medical station at the end of the main hall on his own floor, and had no idea what lied below. He imagined it was the same hustle and bustle of people coming and going or sitting around with no task at all.

Elliot left his room and went to the main room near the metal door they just closed and locked. Dozens upon dozens of people gathered near a long white fold-out table with six stacks of paper on them. Most of the people silently sat on long wooden benches that were placed against the two main walls opposite each other to read the paper in their grasp. Others glanced at the fading ink on the backs of their hands and chose a sheet from a selected pile.

Elliot tripped over a crack in the concrete floor, which stemmed from uneven ground, as he made his way to the table where the six large stacks of paper were placed. Each stack had a different pod number printed on it from one through six in black ink. Elliot quickly took one paper from each stack and leaned against the wall to read them next to a man in a deep blue blazer and dark dress pants who leaned against the dusty, rusted corner of the wall. Odd. Mostly everyone was wearing thin, flimsy hospital gowns or scrub-like uniforms that were terrible at keeping heat in. Elliot had assumed no one had access to their personal items except a handful of people he'd seen here and there.

The man looked at ease which was also weird. Where did he come from and why was he the only one looking so casual and comfortable. The man seemed so out of place.

"Hey, I'm Elliot." He put out his hand for the man to take it.

The man hesitantly grabbed his hand and shook. "Mason," he said, staring off into the distance as he casually wiped his hand on the leg of his pants.

Elliot frowned. What was that about? Was he too dirty to get eye contact, a decent handshake and conversation from this guy? Unsure, he glimpsed down into his own hand to make sure nothing was on it. "Nice suit. You come here with that on?"

"Do you want something from me?" Mason glared, looking annoyed and insulted.

Elliot shrugged, adopting Mason's facial expression, glaring back. "Just asking about your suit."

"And asking about my suit's gonna lead to another question, and another until you finally get the answer you really want." He wiped his mouth with the back of his fist and stood erect, looking down at Elliot. "So what do you want?"

Elliot looked up at the guy, strengthening his backbone to stand taller, tensing his shoulders. "I just asked about your damn suit." He shook his head and continued walking down the corridor. Turning the corner, a quick moving mass plowed into him and nearly knocked him down.

"Watch it!" The woman looked up at him. "Well, I'll be damned."

He remembered the long blonde hair on the woman—the hair that resembled the poor blonde girl who haunted his dreams—and instantly recognized her. "Tami?"

She glared and shook her head. "Well, well, well. Looks like you found your way after all. I'd hope you'd gotten lost."

And just like his memory, her friend Anita appeared behind her, walking down the long dimly lit hall that echoed with her footsteps. Her dark mocha skin and dark brown eyes made her look more radiant than she did outside the compound.

The awkward tension between the girls and him was evident. The hollow noise reverberating from the metal walls seem to suddenly go quiet. Anita moved closer and paused beside Tami. Her head was wrapped in another colorful wrap that resembled the one she had given him weeks ago to wrap around Adam's injured arm as a sling.

"You look alright. Better than we last saw you." Anita pursed her lips and crossed her arms under her small breasts. "Where's your other half? Is he doing good also?" Before he could answer, she rolled her eyes and continued. "That's good to know."

Elliot crinkled the papers in his fist, guessing her snarky attitude resonated from their last encounter outside the compound. "You guys look good too." Without the makeup smears on Tami's face she looked less frantic and manic than she looked the last time he saw her. But the anger was still there, he saw it in her scrunched eyebrows and the tightness of her jaw.

"Well, my life would be better if I never ran into you again. Nice day." Tami smiled, it dropped and she rolled her eyes, brushing past him.

Anita put her hands on her thick hips. "We found her, you know." The blonde girl? Tami's daughter? The girl they spray painted Phoenix with the Refuge Inc. symbol for? "Maybe you'd like to know, the body you sent us to was Jess. We spent hours burying her and saying goodbye. And now we all must go on as if it never happened." She was about to walk off, brush by him as her friend had done, but he put his hand on her shoulder, gently stopping her in her tracks.

"I swear I didn't mean to make this worse for you guys." He swallowed, looking directly into her dark brown eyes. "I hate that I ever saw some of the shit I've seen. But please understand, if I never lied and told you she was alive you would've never helped me and my friend. Adam would still be pinned under that car right now or worse if it weren't for you guys. He could've died."

"At least there's been one death only half of us have to live with. Good luck and goodbye." She walked off down another hall before Elliot could tell her little Jess had been on his mind too, always and probably forever. Would it have changed anything if he let them know? Probably not. They may have thought he deserved the pain and guilt. He probably did.

He continued to his room and sat on the thin pad of a mattress atop his bed. Out of habit he glanced up at the speaker in the corner, not knowing who was behind the messages and when they would be heard kind of made him on edge. The stupid announcements had a way of sounding out of nowhere. How would he be able to effectively adjust to the changes when so many things were odd and out of place? It didn't feel natural to live in such cramped spaces with so many others. He felt like an animal sometimes rather than a human being. His room was always cold and plan. No family pictures and obviously no wide-paned windows on the concrete wall. There was nothing to look at or rarely anything entertaining to do. He always stared at the off-white ceiling, looking for the spider that spun the web in one of the darkened corners while thinking of nothing in particular.

Instead of staring at the blank walls and spider webs he shuffled through the stack of papers he'd gathered and read from the sheet titled *Pod 4.* His pod. It was a description of the duties enlisted to all the people in Pod 4. Such things as; food handling, cooking, food storing, inventory, meal planning and serving. He frowned and flipped to the sheet labeled *Pod 6* which were the quarters Adam had been assigned to. The duties read; law enforcement, pod patrol, surveillance, guarding and escorting, peacemaking, emergency assistance, etc.

If Adam would've told the truth about his occupational experience and told them he was a male dancer would he be handling food or something similar to Elliot's duties? Hell, maybe Elliot should've lied about where he used to work too. Who knew what he'd been assigned to do.

Elliot quickly flipped through the other sheets, reading: Pod 1, maintenance; Pod 2, cleaning; Pod 3, hygiene; and Pod 5, medical. Everyone definitely had duties assigned.

Nearly an hour had passed when Adam pushed the door open to Elliot's room. His head hung low as he entered and sat on the empty bed, paper in hand. "I'm not ready for this."

Shirtless, Elliot sat up from his reclined position on the opposite bed. His abdominal muscles on his narrow waist flexed with the lift. His brown eyes searched Adam's face and his short, dark hair was attractively mussed atop his head. "Yeah, I'm not ready either."

"Law enforcement? Wonder if I can do something else." Adam crumpled the sheet of paper, the toned muscle in his forearm bulged slightly. He tossed the wad on the bed beside him and groaned.

"Do something else like what?" Elliot pointed to his sheet on the floor beside him and scoffed. "Food handler?"

"Have to contribute somehow." Adam sighed, rubbing the well-formed muscles of his neck and shoulder, trying hard to keep his gaze from the toned ripples of Elliot's torso. "We all gotta make this work. We're all part of keeping this place afloat. What we put into this determines what we get out of it. That's what 'the right contribution for a secure future' means."

Elliot nodded. "And what if we don't want to contribute but stay in bed all day instead? What are they gonna do, throw us out? I guess that would be your job, huh?"

Adam continued to massage his neck, eyes diverted to the cold, chipped concrete floor. "I'm sure if they want us to uphold the law there's some kind of punishment for those who break it." Finally he looked up at Elliot, their eyes meeting, a silent worried exchange.

"What a life, huh?" Elliot stood, his drawstring pants loosely hung from his narrow hips, exposing the deep lines on his lower abdomen that sliced deeper below the rim of his pants. Elliot glanced at the speaker perched in the corner of his room like some intruder. "I ran into Tami and Anita a while ago."

Adam shook his head, confused. "Who?"

"The girls who helped us out there? The ones who were looking for their missing daughter?"

Of course. Where would he be without their help. "Did you thank them for me?"

"Could barely get a word in through all the bitter words they had for me." Elliot huffed, and mimicked Adam by rubbing his neck and shoulders. "They hate me. They'll always hate me no matter how much I thank them or apologize." He began to pace. "I just wish everything could go back to the way it used to be. To me having my family, my boyfriend—" he paused. "Sorry, I really didn't mean that. Not like that, I mean. Like ... what I meant was—"

"I get it, Elliot." Adam nodded, while images of his fiancée flashed before his eyes in her Hello Kitty maternity pajamas she wore, believing it'll help them conceive. "Wish things were the way they were too. Hard to adjust to change sometimes. Thinking of your family, your ex love, and how life used to be isn't strange. It's comfort. It's familiar. It's normal."

Elliot sat beside him, their thighs touched and suddenly butterflies began to flutter in the pit of Adam's stomach. Nerves? Arousal? A little bit of both maybe. Elliot gazed into his eyes, tracing an invisible line from Adam's eyes, nose and lips. "You still think about her, huh?"

Adam blinked. "Think about who?"

Elliot dropped his gaze, a look of sadness flashed across his face. "You know who."

Adam wanted to be honest, but since they found refuge his and Elliot's intimacy had been scarce. Ever since finding a community of frightened, desperate people all trying to coexist, their intimacy had been reduced to a few sessions of making out here and there when the chaos was the least present. And quick pecks on the cheek—that stood as a gesture of their undying companionship—when times were hectic. How could he tell Elliot that Jena was still on his mind after seeing their closeness dwindle over the last month?

Adam didn't want to lie so he chose not to answer. Instead he placed his hand on Elliot's thigh and ducked to look into his eyes. His heart pounded rapidly against his ribcage as he examined the little flecks of gold amongst the prominent brown of Elliot's irises.

What had happened to them was easy to understand. There was no longer a desperate time for escapism or a need for sex as an emotional release. What they needed now was the closeness and the bond of a trusting nonsexual but intimate relationship that one or the other always felt compelled to acknowledge with an intimate look, touch or kiss. At least he sensed that was what Elliot wanted.

He tested his theory by leaning forward, gently squeezing Elliot's thigh. His eyes lowered and he brushed his bottom lip along Elliot's, beckoning him. Elliot lifted his head ever so slightly and finally their lips pressed together in a full-on kiss. The heat from Elliot's breath sent a bolt of pleasure to Adam's loins and back up his spine. As much as they could benefit from a nonsexual friendship, keeping sex out of the equation to protect their feelings and judgment, it was very difficult to enforce when Elliot was so close to him. He enjoyed their closeness. He needed it. Too bad the kiss was brief and chaste, prematurely broken by Elliot.

"I need to apologize." Elliot stayed close, millimeters away from Adam's lips.

"For?"

"For forcing you to come out."

"Elliot—" Adam huffed and pulled away.

"Adam, wait. Please, let me finish." Elliot dropped his gaze to his feet again, taking on a rather bashful demeanor Adam wasn't used to. "I should've been more understanding. As a gay man myself, I know how important it is for you to come to terms with your homosexuality. By making you come out I was really being selfish and needy. And look what that's done to us."

"What did it do?" Adam shook his head, eyebrows dipped.

"It made us more distant than bring us closer. We never mention it. We just walk around, going on with our lives like everything's okay."

"It's not okay." Adam stared at the cast on his arm, trying to distract himself from the awkward situation. "Things out there are not okay. And that's the problem. Not us." *Where was Elliot going with this conversation?*

"Even kissing you is weird." Elliot sighed. How he looked so distraught. "Can't you feel it? You feel it, right? Like it's forced or something? You're not ready for a relationship with a man, especially now that we've been thrown back into a life with other people. We're used to living again instead of fighting for our lives and being led by our emotions."

Kissing was weird? He'd never felt that way. Adam couldn't even make eye contact with him, embarrassment keeping him from attempting. He cleared his throat, realizing what was happening. Elliot didn't feel connected anymore and wanted space. What a blow. "I'm not ready for a serious relationship at all." He looked up into Elliot's fluttering brown eyes. Space between them would probably be for the best, especially since things change so drastically between them. It must've affected Elliot more than he thought. "You're my only friend. The only person I trust. But—"

Elliot scoffed. "You trust me?"

"Yes, I trust you. And I know you got my back so I respect you for that. I'll always have yours. Always, but ... you're right. Things changed."

Elliot stared at him for a while, probably processing the information and what it meant for them. Then he slowly nodded, understanding. A few awkward seconds ticked by without anyone making a sound. They both avoided eye contact. And odd energy lingered in the atmosphere. Finally, Elliot cleared his throat. "How's the arm?"

"Itchy. I hate this damn thing. The splintered bone should've healed by now. Can't wait to take this cast off." Adam pushed a finger under the cast to try and satisfy the itch, somewhat thankful for the sudden change of subject.

Elliot stood, scooping up his paper from the floor and his shirt from his bed. "Well, I'm gonna go check out the cafeteria. See how I'm gonna *contribute*." He made a face and walked to the door.

Adam's heart ached. "Elliot?"

He turned. "Yeah?"

"You ... okay?"

Elliot huffed, chest rising and falling quickly. "It's not the worse that's happened." He chuckled and shrugged. "I'll live." He attempted a crooked smile and left the room.

CHAPTER TWO

Revisiting Trust

To protect and serve. Adam could do that. First day on the job and all seemed to go rather smoothly. What's the worst that could happen anyway? He rested against the wall and peered at the dozen or so people in the main room near the rusted metal door.

The room was dim with just one large center light shining from the ceiling. And smaller lights above the entrances to the six halls that fanned out from the main room. Even the halls had dim lit lights shining from the metal beams placed above strategically every six feet or so. No matter how many lights were on they still managed to cast shadows and dark corners, making the environment feel a bit ominous at times.

Some of the dozen people in the main room had just returned from eating their afternoon meal in the cafeteria. Others hung around reading white pamphlets with the infamous red R on the cover. So far, standing around people-watching wasn't so bad.

Several heavy footsteps suddenly echoed down the hall, marching in unison, making their way closer to where Adam stood keeping watch, or rather trying to look important in his dark blue, two piece uniform that was no different than the scrub-like clothes he wore just the day before. The only difference was the dark blue color and the word *Guard* embroidered over the left breast.

Four men in the same dark blue uniform appeared around the corner. Their faces void of expression, their body language on guard and serious. In the center of them marched a trim, clean-shaven older man, his salt and pepper hair noticeable. He kept both arms locked behind his back, lengthening his spine and improving his posture. He nodded to the men and women as he passed them. Most watched him, nodding back and others didn't seem to care.

Adam couldn't help but notice the old man's demeanor; proud, authoritative, reassured. His clothing weren't anything special, a large white tunic over dark grey pants. But it was his jewelry that stood out. The silver cross hanging around his neck, embellished with dozens of tiny sparkling diamonds was unusual.

Everyone had all their unnecessary belongings taken away. A price to pay for the medical treatment, food, and supplies given to them when first arriving. But this man was adorned with a beautiful piece of unnecessary jewelry.

Adam couldn't eyeball it for long because out of the corner of his eye he saw a dark mass moving quickly across the crowded room. Before he could focus on it, a large black object went flying through the air, striking the adorned man on his temple. The man kneeled, bringing his arms up around his head as defense, while the men surrounding him left him alone to capture the assailant before he could escape. During their struggle with the assailant, Adam got a better look at the guy. He was a tall, light skinned man, wearing a dark suit and missing a fancy dress shoe. The man yelled above the sounds of the guards demanding him to get on the floor. "He's a fraud. A fucking fraud. One hundred and sixty thousand. You asshole." The men finally pinned him down, binding the man's hands behind his back with a thick plastic zip tie.

Suddenly a thin, dark haired woman wielding a serrated steak knife appeared behind the adorned man. She let out a high pitched howl as she raised the blade above her head. Adam hadn't realized he was already in action until he grabbed the woman's wrist and gave it a sharp twist making her drop the knife. Then half of the guards took over and tackled her to the ground as well.

"Jesus, man, you saved me." The man's eyes were wide as he looked back and forth between the jagged blade on the rough, uneven concrete floor and Adam.

Adam backed away, palms opened and raised before him, shaking his head. He didn't want to get involved especially in something like assault and attempted murder and a man's accusation of fraud. It all sounded too heavy in the weeks immediately after a catastrophe, but the man was about to be stabbed. He couldn't just stand there and hope for the best.

The people nearby rushed away while others came from the halls to take a closer look at the sudden commotion, packing the corridor.

Among the chaos, the cross wearing man called out to him, "What's your name, man? Tell me your name."

Adam turned, rushing down the hall to Pod 4, squeezing through the bodies of nosy people and trying to ignore their curious stares. He quickly tapped on Elliot's room door, whispering Elliot's name in an urgent whisper. With no response he pushed the door opened. Elliot was gone. Adam quickly made his way back down the hall through the crowd of people. All eyes were on him as he made his way back to the main room that connected all the halls. He needed to get to the cafeteria. Elliot could help ... somehow.

"Stop right there!" A hand on his shoulder stopped him in his tracks. He turned to greet one of the guards. "The prophet wants to talk to you."

The prophet? Was that who the cross wearing man was? Adam looked around the room. Three of the six guards were escorting the shoe-throwing man toward the door that led to the stairs. Where were they taking him? The woman too was being escorted by a guard right behind the man. Were there holding cells below? "What does he want?"

"Discuss it will him. Let's go." The guard grabbed Adam's cast and Adam yanked his arm away.

He glared. "I can walk on my own."

The guard trotted alongside him as they followed the prophet to the staircase. It felt like he too would be punished for stopping that knife-wielding woman.

Two men in dark blue uniforms guarded the entrance to the staircase. When they approached the two guards stepped aside and allowed them through, then quickly took their places at the door again once they entered.

Inside the square shaped stairwell hundreds of stairs ran along the four walls and led down further than Adam could see. Round dimly lit lights were embedded into the concrete of each wall, barely lighting up the dark stairwell. Down below were more rows of lights that disappear deeper below. Half of the guards continued down the staircase pulling and pushing the two assailants further down as they went, leaving Adam, the prophet and a couple other guards on the top landing.

"I didn't mean to get involved." Adam stared into the prophet's steel blue eyes. "It's none of my business, and I shouldn't have jumped in the middle of it."

The prophet scoffed. "You're wearing a blue uniform. You're supposed to jump in. That's your duty, your contribution to the compound." He crossed his arms and cocked his head. "Are you telling me you just wanted to stand there like everybody else and watch me go down?"

Adam shook his head. "No."

"Who would run this place if I went down?" He dipped an eyebrow.

Adam scratched his temple. "That's not what I meant. I—"

"You do possess the skills necessary to do your tasks, right? Or should I send you to deal with disposal?"

"Look, I'm sorry." Adam shrugged. His forehead felt damp with sweat. "I don't want any trouble. I don't want to get involved. I have enough on my mind as we all do and I just want—"

"You know what I want?" The prophet pointed a finger at him.

He shrugged. "I—I don't—"

"I want everyone here to relax, cooperate, contribute and make the most out of a dreadful situation. I want some appreciation from you and from everyone else whose lives I saved. Is that too much to ask? No, right? Tell me *no*."

Adam looked at the few guards and their no-nonsense facial expressions to read whether this was a serious discussion or not. He cleared his throat. "No?"

"Good. See, that's not too bad, right?" He smiled, displaying two perfect rows of white teeth. "Now, what's your name?"

"It's not important."

"Cooperation, man. You have no idea what I've done for you, because if you had you would cooperate with me instead of—"

"Adam. My name is Adam." Annoyed that giving the man what he wanted still wouldn't result in him shutting up.

"Adam?" The man waited.

"Weber."

"What got you this task in law enforcement, Adam?"

He shrugged. "I was assigned to Pod 6 and the task sheet said this was my job."

"Don't play stupid, Adam." The man moved closer, a mere inch between the tips of their noses. "What occupation did you have before our little asteroid came to visit?"

Adam glared, remembering the stage, the lights and all of the screaming aroused women in the audience. "Police officer."

"So you know how to protect and serve, don't you?" After a few seconds of silence, he cleared his throat. "Well, don't ya?"

"Sure." Adam could smell the tobacco on his breath as he was being scolded like a little child. A smoker with pearly whites?

"You did the right thing by intervening and stopping that woman." He stepped back. "Oh, boy, did you do the right thing." He rubbed his temple and sighed. And almost as swift as a flying insect, the man swung his opened hand back and slapped the guard next to him across his face. Nearly all the guards standing in the small stairwell gasped. "You should've been watching my ass! What kind of contribution was that, huh? I should take all your little goodies away. You want that?"

The guard rubbed his red cheek. "No, sir."

"That's right." The tendon on the prophet's neck tightened and he gritted his teeth. He looked to Adam. "I appreciate your help today, Adam. Today, you've done more than these guys ever did."

Adam nodded and turned, exiting the stairwell and entering the main floor where a dozen people watched as he stepped over the black dress shoe on the floor and turn down the hallway to Pod 4.

The massive dimly lit kitchen held many sizes of pots and pans in the center of the ceiling, hanging from an elaborate mechanical device that consisted of some sort of metal cage and pulley system. Elliot had just finished digging through the cabinets and drawers along with a dozen other cooks and food handlers, trying to familiarize himself with all the cooking utensils.

Out of the corner of his eye, begging for his attention was the bright multicolored head wrap in Anita's hands as she rewrapped her long, curly hair with it. She must've felt him staring because she glanced his way and did and double take. "You gotta be kidding me." She stared at his white cook's uniform just as he noticed hers.

"You're a cook too?" Elliot closed the drawer he had opened, dumbfounded. He would be working alongside her every day?

"Food handler." She shook her head as she twisted and tucked the end of her headscarf at the back of her head, somehow keeping the brightly colored dressing tightly in place. "You know anything about cooking or handling food, for that matter?" Her bad attitude carried over in her voice. She didn't even bother to look his way while she spoke to him.

"I was a cashier at Food Plus." He shrugged. "I rang up people's stuff. Sometimes I would stock food—"

"So that's a *no* then." She rearranged the butcher block on the counter in front of her, while a half dozen others in white uniforms and aprons rushed into the kitchen.

"So what's for dinner?" one of the guys asked. "I say we make the compound's signature dish; baloney soup with caramelized onions and white rice. Mm, mm, mm. I can taste it already."

Elliot recognized the guy. He was the same sarcastic douche who's been serving the upper level's food since they arrived along with the five guys behind him. He never asked his name, was never interested to know it, but whoever he was he had a way of taking control and making himself the leader of the kitchen. After giving everyone orders, including instructing Elliot and Anita to cut and sauté a massive amount of onions, the guy relaxed enough to tend to the rice.

Elliot glanced at Anita who was in her zone, cutting, peeling and dicing onions like a pro, throwing them in a huge metal stock pot by the handful. "Where'd you learn to cook?"

She rolled her eyes. "Do you really care? Or are you trying to make conversation?"

"What's wrong with either?"

"There's nothing wrong. Only I have no interest in talking to you."

"How many times do I have to tell you I'm sorry?"

"No more. Please, stop. If I hear 'sorry' again I just might bash my head into a wall."

"Well, what else am I supposed to do?"

"How about show it. Anybody could say how sorry they are, but it's actions that speak louder than words."

Other than the sound of the guy ordering people around it was quiet. Finally Elliot broke the silence between them. "Why did you guys come back?"

"What?" Anita stopped cutting onions and wiped her forehead with the back of her gloved hand. "What are you talking about?"

"When I first met you guys and asked you if Refuge Inc. was a place for survivors, you said sarcastically, 'It has everything you'll ever need to survive." So if that was sarcasm and this place didn't have everything you need, why did you bother coming back?"

Anita glared, leaned toward him and whispered angrily, "You think this place is all it's made out to be? Yeah, they might have everything you'll ever need but for a cost. What do you think this whole contribution crap is about? It's ridiculous. They just hand us job titles without knowing if we're even capable of actually doing the job or not. They just go on what we tell them our skills are?" She shook her head.

"Well we all gotta do stuff around here to keep this place running smoothly, right?" Elliot wasn't sure if he were trying to look for confirmation or convince himself.

She shrugged. "What exactly are we running? All we're doing is handling food while the person on the P.A. system is really running things. I never even heard of Refuge Inc. until Tami mentioned it when the asteroid news went out. Right when we heard about it, and everyone started to panic, she became convinced. She dug up some papers her husband had sent her from Afghanistan where he was stationed and dragged me, Jess and their dog Charlie to this place that same day.

"It was strange. There were people everywhere, waiting to get inside, chaos everywhere you turned, and confused people in white Refuge Inc. suits frantically trying to organize everything. I had so many questions but she couldn't answer them, she had more questions than I did. All I kept thinking was, wow this place was set up for survivors super quick. It had to have been built long before we even heard of an asteroid in our solar system. So they must've known, right? It couldn't be a coincidence. They must've known something in order to build this place." Her concerned, sorrowful eyes pleaded with him for an answer, for understanding. "And don't you say a damn man had visions or something. A prophet my ass."

Elliot slowly nodded, eyes fixated on hers. The flyers they found outside scattered over the parking lot of Food Plus came to mind. The flyers that initially lead him and Adam on the hunt for Refuge Inc.

She mimicked his nod. They were in agreement. "The first time coming here we didn't stay long, because Jess ran away looking for her dad and we left to go find her. I was never looking forward to coming back. But to answer your question, I knew we didn't have a chance out there." She glanced back over her shoulder then lowered her voice. "I always felt that something's not right here."

Elliot nodded. "Yeah, I get that feeling too."

"Especially when they wouldn't let animals inside."

"Like Titan, er, I mean Charlie." Elliot shook his head. "I named him Titan before I knew he was you guys' dog."

"Yeah, Charlie was Jess's best friend. That dog never left her side. Her mom, Tami, didn't like him much, but I did. It brightened my day to see the dog make Jess so happy. The dog pretty much replaced her dad who's she barely got to see." She moved closer, eyes widened and voice low. "They took him to the vet with the other dogs, huh?" The way she said it made Elliot a bit uneasy.

He narrowed his eyes, listening closely. "Yeah."

"Have you seen him since?"

"Actually, no."

"I don't think you ever will." She dropped her gaze to her hand where she peeled the outer layers off of the onion. "First they were making all kinds of excuses to not allow the pets in. Some people were told different things. They told us that pets needed to be checked out and treated before allowing them inside. They said they would bring them inside to the internal vet once everything cleared. There's a rumor going around. Some pet owners are saying they closed the compound door without bringing the animals in first. Salvation my ass."

CHAPTER THREE

Rekindling the Flame

When the shift was over and handed off to the next shift, Elliot couldn't stop thinking about going back to his room and getting off of his feet for a few minutes. When he opened the room door, Adam was sitting on his bed and greeted him with a brief flash of a smile, his emerald green eyes dazzling in the light.

"I got a new roommate." Adam gestured to the empty, twin-sized bed in front of him. "A bitter man. Probably in his late fifties and never stops talking about how unfair his stint in law enforcement was. Name's Joe. You got a roommate yet?"

Elliot shook his head and sat on the empty bed. Everyone in his pod had a place to sleep so there was no need to move people around. "No roommate. Do I smell like onions?" He lifted his shirt collar to his own nose and sniffed.

Adam chuckled. "I don't smell anything."

"Lucky you, cause I sure do." He pulled his shirt over his head and threw it aside. "So what's going on?" He lied back on the bed, hands folded over his navel.

"Something's going on?" Adam rested his elbows on his knees, narrowed his eyes, and subconsciously bit his lower lip.

Elliot couldn't tear his eyes away. "I come back from peeling and cutting onions and you're in my room, waiting for me. What's going on?" He caught a look of worry in Adam's face, and the delay in his answer told him something serious had happened. He sat up on the edge of the bed. "You can tell me if you want."

Adam cleared his throat. "I met the guy who runs this place."

Elliot sat up straighter, eyebrows raised. "Really? What's he like?"

"Strange, really. Salt and pepper hair. Fit man. Wears a cross around his neck encrusted with diamonds and... I stopped a woman from trying to stab him."

Elliot's eyes widened. "What? She was trying to kill him? Where? When? Why?"

"A few hours ago, and I don't know why. They ended up taking her and some guy who was probably working with her below probably to stay in jail cells or something."

Elliot brought his hand to his forehead. "Are you okay?"

"I'm fine except ... he brought me to the stairwell and yelled at me like a little kid. Then thanked me for helping him. It was weird. Really weird."

"First day on the job and you prevent a murder." Unbelievable. Elliot didn't know where to go with that news. "I'm glad you're all right."

"Thanks." Adam took a deep breath and sighed, chest rising and falling rapidly. "So how was your job?"

"Onions, nothing special." Elliot shrugged. "Except, Anita—the one with the colorful head wrap—she's a cook too. I could've sworn she hated me, but we started talking and she told me about a rumor going around about the pets. She thinks the pets were locked outside when they closed the compound door."

Adam grimaced. "So Titan's still out there?"

"They call him Charlie. And he's probably stuck out there with a dozen other pets." Poor dog. He and Adam saved his life just so he could end up suffering in the end? If he was out there he was without water, food or shelter.

"I feel so bad for making them think that little girl was still alive when I knew she wasn't..." God, did the remorse brutally kick his ass. He felt his chest tighten up with just the thought of what he did. "And I'm gonna find Charlie for Anita. I'm gonna take her advice and *show* her how sorry I am. This is the only thing I know to do. I gotta try to make it up to them." His head hung low between his knees and his breath caught. All the sleepless nights he had, waking up from nightmares about that little girl. When he could've been dreaming of the beauty of Adam's body instead.

"You did what you had to do to get me out from under that car." Adam's voice was soft and comforting. "I'll help you, okay? I'll do everything I can to get you some answers, alright?"

"Thank you, Adam."

They stood simultaneously and embraced. Adam snaked his good arm snug around Elliot's waist, pulling him close. His other heavy casted arm rested on Elliot's hip. Prickles on Elliot's skin lingered where Adam touched him. He tucked his forehead inside the curve of Adam's neck, running his palms down the small of his back, feeling the familiar .strength of his toned body. Elliot inhaled the scent of warm, sweet hazelnut on the surface of Adam's skin. He exhaled into the crook of his neck. Warmth rushed him, nearly melting him into Adam and his comforting embrace. Adam turned his head and left a gentle peck on Elliot's cheek, lips lingering for more than a few seconds. Then Adam backed away, head bowed and eyes diverted. "Sorry, that was just ... a habit."

"Don't apologize. It's okay." He patted Adam's shoulder, hating that the embrace ended so soon. "It's not a big deal. I know it doesn't mean anything." Saying that aloud made his chest heat up with an undying flame. The pain was severe but he ignored it, and reminded himself they weren't ready for a relationship and its complications.

"Gonna get going." Adam finally looked up into Elliot's eyes. He stared back, watching Adam's alluring green eyes search his face. Adam's gaze traveled from his eyes, down his nose and to his lips. Then the corner of Adam's mouth twitched from a smile threatening to form. "You have freckles." Astonishment carried in his tone. "Never knew you had freckles."

Maybe he never really looked. Excitement filled Elliot's chest. What was it that made Adam see them now? In time, maybe Adam would see more of who Elliot really was. Maybe there would be a time where they could focus on building a real relationship instead of of that stemmed from fear and confusion. Maybe Adam would give him another chance, a chance to start over and do things the right way, a chance to redeem himself. He smiled. Adam smiled too before leaving the room.

How strange that hugging and kissing Elliot had become second nature. Leaving Elliot's room with an appreciation of the man's beauty had his head spinning. However awkward the moment was, his heart couldn't slow its pace and might not for a long time.

Elliot was definitely something special. For Elliot to try so hard to repair his broken relationship with not only him by taking a step back and allowing him to heal without an intimate relationship to interfere, but also fix the relationship he created with a couple of complete strangers, showed a lot of character. And no matter how much Elliot had prodded and pushed for him to come out back then, Adam knew he was a good man with good intentions. If being intimate with Elliot would eventually lead to an uneasy relationship especially if they didn't let it evolve naturally, the least he could do was show his appreciation for Elliot's efforts by finding out where the pets had gone.

Adam made his way down a corridor leading to the nurse's station. The last time he'd visited the place was when they first found the compound. Then, it was chaotic. There were injured people everywhere and not enough staff to treat them. Some had to be treated in the halls due to the overcrowding of wounded people. It was an absolute mess.

But now, the halls were quiet and nearly empty, possibly due to the fact that everyone had healed and now had duties to attend to around the clock. His duty wasn't quite over since he was on-call constantly. At least he didn't have to stand guard anymore, until tomorrow at least.

Adam pushed the door opened. Inside, the large room echoed with his footsteps as he made his way to the long counter containing a double basin sink and faucet which lined one of the walls. There were filing cabinets and desks placed evenly in the room. Also a couple examination beds behind privacy curtains that were hung open. It was the only room he'd seen that had concrete floors that weren't cracked or chipped, but the green tint on it made the room take on an unsanitary look. He grimaced.

"Can I help you?"

The voice came from behind, but he couldn't turn around. The light, at eased tone and clearly pronounced words stunned him with their familiarity. He turned, exhaled and looked right into the eyes of his long lost fiancée. "Jena!"

"Oh, my God. Adam?" Her eyes welled up instantly and she ran forward, jumping into his arms.

He lifted her in his arms and twirled, smiling so hard it hurt, forgetting about the cast on his arm. "So glad you're okay." He put her down and caressed her cheek. "Let me look at you."

She looked up at him with glistening brown eyes. Her auburn hair hung from a messy ponytail with a couple inches of her much darker roots visible. A pair of light green scrubs hung off of her tiny frame. Around her neck she wore a Hello Kitty trinket on a silver chain.

"Are you okay?" She caressed the cast on his arm. "What happened?"

"It was crushed under a car, but I'm fine. Don't worry about me. How have you been?"

"Crushed? My God."

"Trust me, it's better now. Everything's better now. Now, how are you?"

"I'm doing alright. I missed you so much."

"I missed you too. So much." He tucked a loose strand of auburn hair behind her ear as she lifted herself up on her tip toes to press her soft, moist lips to his. She kissed him with soft, wet pecks. Immediately thoughts of embracing Elliot just moments ago came to mind. Following that thought was the memory of Jena opening his laptop which contained explicit text and pictures he shared with anonymous gay men. The laptop she took from his lap, his life hasn't been the same since.

He pressed his forehead to hers. "Look, I—"

"Before you say anything, let me tell you how sorry I am." As she spoke he watched her lips move, while he mindlessly fingered the trinket that dangled from her neck. "I was angry. I was stupid. I shouldn't have left you. I don't know what the hell I was thinking. I love you."

"I love you too, Jena, but I have to be honest." He inhaled and sighed.

"You love me. I love you. That's all that matters now." Jena kissed him again. "That's all that should've mattered. Here, sit down. Let me look at your arm."

Adam sat in a flimsy foldout chair near an old, rusty, metal desk. Most of the green paint chipped from the edges and corners. The light reflected from her necklace, stealing his attention. "Where'd you get that necklace from?"

She avoided eye contact. "Oh, this old thing? My uncle Tom gave it to me."

"Wealthy Tom? The uncle that didn't want us together and wouldn't help you financially as long as we were together? The uncle that said I'd never amount to anything or be able to take care of you? He didn't want anything to do with you as long as you were with 'that male stripper.' And now you're wearing a necklace he gave you? When did he give it to you?"

"It doesn't matter." She tucked the necklace in the front of her shirt. "Your arm looks good. Let me see if they got a file on you." She left, opening a drawer on the file cabinet against the far wall. It squeaked and whined as she pulled out the drawer, took out a manila folder and slid the drawer back in. She opened the folder and made her way back. "Yeah, you got the cast nearly six weeks ago. And it says here that they suspected small hairline fractures. That should be healed by now. You want me to remove the cast?" She finally looked at him.

"How long you been here?"

She looked away, hesitating. After a few seconds she finally met his stare. "Since the last time we saw each other."

He stood, rubbing his temple. "You mean you left me and came here? How did you even know about this place?"

"My uncle. I left to be with him and he brought me here. I only started working in the station since we all got our duties. They needed more medical staff."

He'd spare her the details about what he'd been through to find the compound. However, he wanted to be honest. Had to be honest. "I'm here to find out where the vet is. Thought medical staff would know where wounded animals are kept."

She shrugged. "I don't know. Actually, I haven't heard anything about animals or veterinarians here."

"Who should know?"

"I don't know. The people running this place?" The adorned man he'd spoken to earlier, the prophet would probably be the person to ask. "Why are you looking for a vet?"

"It's for my friend, Elliot. I met him while walking all over the city looking for help before finding this place. He's a really special guy."

"Special?"

"Yeah, special." Adam stared at Jena, sending the hint with his stare. She got it completely. He could see the exact moment she got it when her jaw dropped.

She rubbed the back of her neck. "So what are you trying to say, Adam?"

"He made me confront my demons and made me realize the truth about myself."

"What, that your queer?" Jena quickly sat. "You really think you're queer?"

"Jena—"

I know you, Adam. You were just curious and experimenting online. I know that now. If you were queer you wouldn't have loved me for so long and you sure as hell wouldn't have gotten me pregnant."

"What?" Adam shook his head, leaning forward. Did he hear her correctly? "You were pregnant? But we were trying for so long without any luck."

"Not *were.* Am. I *am* pregnant." She smiled. "I'm pregnant with your kid. We did it."

He glanced at her belly looking for the hump. "But, how?"

"I know you don't need me to explain the birds and the bees. See? I knew we could make it happen. It must've happened a few weeks before we lost each other because I'm about three months already." They had "lost" each other? He didn't remember it that way. He remembered her leaving him to fend for himself. The smile on her face was forced. He could see it. She was unsure about him.

"So we're gonna have a kid?"

She nodded. "You see?" She kissed his lips. "We can be the family we always wanted to be."

CHAPTER FOUR

Contradicting Emotions

Elliot paced back and forth in his room. One arm tucked behind his back, the other rubbing the stubble on his chin. He needed to speak to someone who knew where the pets would be taken inside the compound. Someone with authority. Hastily he left the room and hustled down the hall toward the main room where two men were guarding the stairwell.

"I need to find where the pets are being held."

The guard on the right shook head and pointed down the hall Elliot just emerged from. "No, you don't. No one uses this stairwell unless he's the prophet."

Elliot scoffed. "Well, do you know anything about the people's pets and where they are? Did they leave them out there?" He nodded toward the metal door on the other side of the room.

"I can't help you." The guard's stiff shoulders framed his slightly puffed out chest and bulky upper body. He was a large stocky built man but his brute didn't intimidate Elliot.

Elliot couldn't help glaring. "Well, do you know who can?"

"I said I can't help you, now move away from this door." He stepped forward, fists clenched at his sides and eyes glued to Elliot's. Elliot didn't move, he didn't even blink. The guard looked down at him. "Someone tried to stab the prophet earlier and you think I'm just gonna let you go in there? We got orders to keep everyone out of the stairwell and on their own floors for everyone's safety, and that's what we're doing."

The other man reached out and quickly tapped the guard's shoulder. "Don't you think we should keep that to ourselves? I mean ... you know?"

"Yeah, yeah. I'm not getting enough for that." The guard pointed down the hall again, and Elliot turned to leave. But instead of going back to his room he went down the hall to Pod 6. There were a few men in dark blue uniforms that resembled Adam's but no Adam anywhere.

Elliot looked around the spacious shell shaped room at the few men. "Did anybody come here with a pet?" No response. "Hello? Anybody?"

"What's it to ya?" One man stood from the corner bench and began a slow trek toward him. Suddenly all eyes were on them.

"I'm trying to find out where they're keeping the pets or even if they're here?"

"I don't know nothing about no pets." The man shrugged.

A quick cough came from behind. "They didn't bring them in." Elliot turned to face a tall, fit man wearing the same dark blue uniform as everyone else. He coughed again, clearing his throat. "They're still out there in that God forsaken hell storm."

"How do you know?" Elliot moved closer.

"Never saw any damn animals come in this damn place, that's how."

"Are you sure?"

"Do I look sure?" The no-nonsense look he projected said enough.

It was hard to come to terms with the possibility of people's pets, including Titan—the companion he had grown to love—being left out in a hostile environment with no one to care for them. Without food, water, or shelter they were likely to die out there. Not to mention he would be letting Tami and Anita down again this time by killing their little girl's dog.

"Thanks." He left the pod and walked lazily down the hall. What was he to do now? What possibly could he do or say at this point? Then something occurred to him. Maybe the guy was wrong. Just because he didn't see any animals come in didn't mean that they hadn't.

He had to find a way to get to the other parts of the compound. He had to find answers.

Adam dunked his head in the basin of cold water, eyes closed he didn't come up for air until his lungs felt like they would burst. Water sheeted off of his face as he emerged and stared at his reflection in the clouded mirror. The single restroom light shown dimly, reminding him of the Intensive Care Unit at Arrowhead hospital where he'd met Edna and Harold, the first of many survivors.

How were they doing? Were they holding up still waiting for rescue? Had they made it out of there somehow? Overlapping his thoughts were other concerns, forcing their way into his jumbled mind. He was going to be a daddy? Jena still loved him? What was he supposed to do now? Forget about Elliot completely and continue his life with a fiancée and a kid? Were they still considered engaged?

In the same basin of water he submerged his bare arms. Using one hand to wash his arm the best he could, switching between the two. His skin felt tingly where the cast once been, but refreshing to finally be able to clean it and let air hit it.

A nice, hot shower would have been ideal to help cleanse him of all the dirt and muck that clouded his head worse than the mirror before him clouded his view of himself. However, the only shower they had was nothing but a room he couldn't even stretch his arms out in completely. It had a rusty pipe in the center of the ceiling that drizzled water out, and mostly used for filling large pots or buckets when needed. It was in dire need of maintenance and a cleaning itself.

He'd been doing what mostly everyone else was doing, washing off in the restroom basins using a washcloth and the bottle of soap Refuge Inc. provided them. Cleaning after yourself was pretty simple especially when you only messed up the makeshift metal sink on a concrete pedestal that shared space in a room with a toilet and a mirror.

A knock on the restroom door interrupted his thoughts. "Babe, you okay in there?"

Hearing Jena call him *Babe* after what they've recently been through made him shudder. She sounded as if she wanted to continue right where they left off, forgetting everything that happened in between. Should he just be thankful that she and their unborn baby were alive and safe and forget about the rest? If so, it was difficult to do.

"Are you okay?" Jena's voice penetrated effortlessly through the thin, compressed cardboard-like material of the door.

"Give me a second." He grimaced, dropping his head and pinching the bridge of his nose. Habits die hard. "Be out in a second." He could hear her footsteps disappear as she backed away from the door.

He inhaled and sighed. Elliot wouldn't take the news of a baby lightly. Hell, knowing that Jena's back in the picture would surely piss him off. Especially after all they have been through trying to get him to come to terms with his sexuality and the fact that Jena had abandoned him.

He respected Elliot. Elliot was the reason he had a breath to breathe. Because of Elliot he realized a lot about himself that he would've never known otherwise. Just because they didn't indulge in a full-on emotional and physical relationship while trying to make it in the compound didn't mean they never would. Elliot was special.

Elliot knew him like no one else, not even Jena. Elliot deserved more than what he was giving him.

Even now, Elliot wanted to right his wrongs, apologizing for not understanding Adam's sexuality issues and issues with Jena, insisting for the time being they should only be friends. Elliot was on a mission to show his sincerity and find Titan to reunite the dog with his owners. He would always be grateful to Elliot for stopping him from mercy killing the canine, for walking miles on a bummed leg to find help when he was pinned under the car, and for being a true sidekick and companion.

Elliot deserved so much more than he was giving him.

"People of the compound, brace yourselves for the news," the speakers sounded in the medical station, quickly Adam stepped out of the restroom to listen. *"Impact winter is fully among us. It will be years before Phoenix or the world will be habitable again ... if ever. But don't be alarmed, I see a bright new day ahead with plenty of smiles and lots to be happy for. Your children will see this day, as will your children's children. So be grateful. Thank you for your cooperation. Let's continue to keep this place running smoothly ... for our futures."*

Adam opened the door and spotted Jena across the room near the filing cabinet. She was frozen, staring at a black speaker box that hung from the corner of the room. "What the hell? Years?"

Adam made his way to her. "You okay?"

"It's going to be years until that stuff clears out?" Her voice cracked. "Our kids will see it but not us?"

"Just because he said that doesn't mean anything." How did the person behind the announcements know anything about the future? Anything was possible, but Adam didn't believe in prophets. No matter if they called themselves prophets, psychics, or a fortune tellers, no one knew the future. No one.

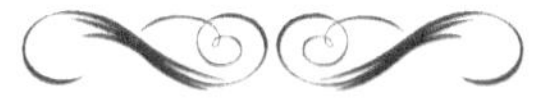

Elliot sat straight up in his bed, awakened from a nightmare where the little girl, Jess, and her dog, Charlie, were attacking him. The girl's hair was caked in dried blood while she tore and ripped at his clothes. He couldn't get away because the dog ripped at the flesh on his leg with its powerful jaws. All the while, the sound of Tami, Anita and even Adam booing him howled from a distance.

Sweat coated his forehead and had drenched the balled-up sheet he used as a pillow. Immediately upon waking he felt relieved, though his heart raced. After that kind of dream he knew he wouldn't be able to sleep.

He quickly threw on a clean shirt, the red R with the silver halo on his breast exhibited. He walked out into the pod where a few people roamed here and there, back and forth to the restrooms at the end of the pod or in and out of rooms. It seemed to be just as busy this time of day as it were earlier, nothing ever really seemed to slow down. He guessed people worked all times of the day and night. The lights never went out.

He walked casually down the hall and to the main room where the entrance to the staircase was located. Still a couple men guarded the door, but this time they were different men. Maybe they changed shifts just like everyone else.

Elliot went toward the guards.

"Stop!" one of them shouted. "No one's allowed to enter the staircase. Back away."

"Why can't we?"

"No one's allowed. That's all you need to know. Now back away."

"What's going on? Why can't you tell us what's going on? Where are all the pets, can you tell us that? Where's the guy who does the announcements, the prophet, does he know about the pets?"

A small crowd was beginning to form, people gathering from the halls to see what was going on.

"Sir, if you don't back away..."

"What? What would you do?" What would they do, pick him up and make him leave? They never had shown any violence toward anyone. They never even put their hands on anyone, except when Adam told him about the woman who tried to stab the prophet and her accomplice. Adam had said they took them to jail cells ... below.

Elliot hastily made his way down to Pod 6 to Adam's room. He tapped on the door and was greeted by the man he had seen earlier, the man who had told him he didn't see any animals come inside. Was this the new roommate Adam spoke of? The bitter former cop, Joe?

"I'm looking for Adam." Elliot looked past the man's shoulder at Adam who was lying in his own bed.

"You come to bother him about pets too?"

Adam opened his eyes and glanced toward the door. "It's okay, let him in."

The man grunted and backed away.

Elliot pushed the door opened slightly. "I need to talk to you." He glanced at the man who stared him down. "Privately."

"Alright, I'll come to your room." Adam stood and Elliot noticed the cast on his arm was gone.

"Your cast."

"Yeah, I got it removed today."

"How does your arm feel?"

"Great." Adam rubbed his arm. "Just great." They walked to Elliot's room silently. Once inside, Adam sat on one of the beds.

Elliot was too excited to sit. "I got a plan I need your help with."

"A plan?" Adam's eyebrows dipped over his sleepy green eyes.

"I need you to help get me downstairs."

"What's downstairs?"

"Answers. I need to know what's down there, if the animals are there and why they are keeping us on our own floors."

"I know why they won't let us on the other floors. I told you someone tried to stab the prophet, so they're on high alert right now for his safety. I can tell you what's down there too." Adam shrugged. "Trash disposal, waste disposal, pumps, generators, filters, drainage pipes, and everything else that's helping keep this place afloat."

"And jail cells?"

"Maybe, I never actually been but I've heard." He wiped at his eyes. "Why?"

"Get me down there and maybe I can explore the lower levels and see if the pets are there. And figure out why they're being so secretive about everything."

"The lower levels are just like this one." Adam shook his head. "They have rooms, a cafeteria, a medical station, everyone works, everyone contributes. It's all the same."

"I've never been down there. And as far as I know, neither have you. So how do you know what's down there, you heard that too?"

Adam nodded. "I had been thinking about the prophet's necklace, and wondering why there were certain people wearing regular clothes instead of scrubs like the rest of us."

"See?" Elliot could barely contain his excitement. He really wanted some answers.

Adam sighed. "Sorry, Elliot. I know you're trying so hard to right your wrongs and find Titan, I mean Charlie, but I don't think there is a vet or a place for pets here. I think the rumors are true. They never brought them in."

"Why would they do that?"

Adam shrugged. "Probably because they don't have enough supplies to take care of animals. Maybe they weren't equipped with room for animals. Maybe animals were the least of their problems. It sounds cruel but ... human survival or pets? What would you choose?"

Elliot squinted. "So you're telling me they have enough supplies to keep us alive for years but not even a place for a few pets? You did hear that announcement today, didn't you?"

"How could I miss it?"

"The person said it'll be years till it's safe to go outside. Have they prepared for that? Do we have enough food and stuff to make it for years? They sounded pretty confident. They built this place, they must've made it to last a long time. Why not tell us there was no room for animals to begin with rather than make us believe they would bring the pets inside?"

"I don't know, Elliot." Adam tucked his head between his legs and latched his fingers behind his head. He sighed. "I just don't know."

There was a long silent pause. Frustration and tension seemed to thicken the air.

"What's wrong?" He sat on the bed in front of Adam. "You look like something's bothering you. Am I bothering you?"

"No." He scoffed. "I've been trying to work on this honesty thing."

"Yeah?"

"Well, what I'm about to say you probably don't want to hear but I have to get it off my chest."

Elliot slowly nodded, bracing himself. "Okay?"

"You remember how I learned some basic first aid skills?"

"Um, because your fiancée dragged you to a class when she was going for a job as a medical assistant?"

"Yeah, and today I got my cast removed." Adam swallowed, gulping so loud Elliot heard. "Guess who removed it."

Elliot's eyes narrowed and he cocked his head. "Wha... what are you telling me?

"I ran into Jena. She's here."

Elliot stared at Adam. The way Adam wouldn't make eye contact with him spoke volumes. Memories of caressing and kissing Adam, and the intense intimate moment of having Adam inside of him flashed before his eyes. Hope of rekindling any sort of romance between them dwindled. There was a burning in his chest that made every beat of his heart feel like a slow buildup to an angry roaring fire.

Elliot knew Adam's feelings for Jena. But he also knew the only way he should feel a threat is if there was an actual chance they would get back together. If so, all was lost. "I thought she ran off to Denver."

Adam nodded. "Me too. I guess she didn't get too far."

He cleared his throat and gulped. "Does she want you back?"

Again, Adam nodded.

Elliot felt his breath escape him. He had no one, not his family, not his ex. No one knew he was alive, and no one knew what he had survived through out there. There was no one other than Adam, and soon he would be gone too. Taken away, this time by the fiancée that abandoned Adam but never left his mind since the moment they met. "What are you gonna do?"

"She's pregnant. With my kid."

Elliot couldn't speak. "Wow. I don't ... I can't ... This is crazy."

"Honestly, I feel so many things right now I don't know how to sort them out. I just—" Adam raised his head and stiffened his back. "Let's just figure out this plan of yours. The least I can do for you is help you get some answers."

Elliot took a deep breath then slowly, calmly let it out.

CHAPTER FIVE

The Plan

The cafeteria buzzed with people waiting to eat the infamous bologna soup. The soup always gave Elliot's an upset stomach after eating it but he didn't have much room to complain. Rather he hated it or not, he had to eat.

Dozens of people lined up, bowl on a tray with plastic utensils they moved down the line being served as they went. Anita was stationed to his left, scooping up ladles of rice and dropping them into the bowls as they passed by. She rarely made eye contact with the people, seeming to perform her duty with the least distraction.

An elderly woman placed her tray down on the counter in front of Elliot. He smiled and scooped a ladle of soup with bite sized chunks of meat and caramelized onions into the bowl.

"I enjoy the soup much more without all the spices." The lady smacked her lips together and made a sour face, the wrinkles around her lips and eyes grew deeper.

"Ma'am, there are no spices in the soup. Just salt and pepper."

"It's the pepper. It's too spicy."

"I'll tell you what, the next batch we make I will make sure I put away a portion just for you without the pepper." He smiled when she smiled, and she continued down the line.

Anita leaned in. "It's nice that you talk to everyone and stuff, but you know we could move faster if we keep the line moving steadily."

"I know." He huffed.

"And if you tell one person you'll make them a special order, everyone's gonna be looking for specials. I wouldn't get her hopes up either. She's really going to want that soup."

Elliot turned to Anita. "And I'm gonna give it to her. It's not a big deal. We're just holding the pepper."

Anita shrugged. "I'm just saying, one special is likely to turn into one hundred very quickly. So watch yourself."

"I know how to take care of myself, thanks."

"Is that so? If that was true you wouldn't have needed our help out there."

He sighed. "Can we please not bring up the past anymore? I already told you how I felt about it. If you and your friend don't want to forgive me, then could we at least move on?"

"Forgive you? How can we just forgive you? She was a little girl. Tami's only child. But you wouldn't understand because you don't have kids."

Elliot scooped some soup into a man's bowl. "I wasn't the one who let her run away. I never touched her. So stop treating me like what happened was my fault."

The man paused. "Something happened to a little girl?"

Elliot shook his head. "It's nothing. Sorry. Just continue down the line."

The man slid his tray down in front of Anita. "How old was she? The little girl?"

Anita bowed her head and was barely audible when she mumbled. "Eleven. But it's not a worry to you."

"Eleven?" The man scoffed. "That's not a little girl." He turned to the woman next to him. "When was the last time you called an eleven year old a little girl?" He chuckled to Elliot and Anita's amazement. "Eleven is when their buds are popping and their hips are curving, oh man."

"Okay, that's enough." Elliot pointed the ladle down the line. "Move on, huh? This conversation has nothing to do with you."

"Just tell me real quick, man. What did you do to her? Did you give them little buds a nice squeeze." The man slurped and licked his lips. "Ah, I bet you tasted what that little girl had marinating between her legs, now, didn't you?"

At that, most of the people in line gasped.

"Asshole!" Elliot dropped the ladle and quickly made his way around the counter. He nudged the man's shoulder. "Show some damn respect and move on."

"Keep your hands off me." The man pointed at Elliot's nose, a serious and somewhat frightened look on his face. "Now that's my one and only warning."

A woman beside him in the food line glared. "Get away from me, you pervert!"

"Why don't you do as the woman asks and take what you got and go sit down and eat it." Elliot nudged his shoulder again, gently pushing him out of the line.

"I told you to keep your hands off me." The man picked up his tray with the hot bowl of soup on it and threw it at Elliot.

A couple of panicked screams and gasps sounded throughout the cafeteria. People in the line scattered and others began to form a crowd. Elliot rushed forward and pushed the man against the counter, using his body weight and his shoulder to pin him there. Hot bologna and onion soup dripped down his shirt. "You're gonna apologize for disrespecting my friend. He glanced at Anita and the frightened look on her face as she stood behind the counter frozen.

"Kick the pervert's ass," someone called out from the crowd.

"Fuck you." The man lifted his knee and forcefully thrust it between Elliot's legs, connected it with his groin. Elliot grunted and fell to the floor. Almost instantly the man was on top of him, trying to pin him down as they scuffled.

In the distance a loud whistle screeched through the crowd's hollers and immediately the thump of heavy boots hastily making their way toward them grew louder.

"Stop!" A guard stood over them wearing a close-fitting black jumpsuit with cargo pockets on the legs and dark leather boots that stopped just below the knees. He wore some kind of heavy duty vest that melded with the top of his uniform near his chest and a helmet with the visor lifted. In his hand he carried a baton and the belt around his waist held a set of handcuffs and a small canister. Possibly pepper spray. "Get up right now and put your hands on your head."

The man stood. "I didn't do nothing. He put his hands on me first."

Elliot managed to stand. "I told him to move down the line and he wouldn't."

Another guard appeared from the crowd of hungry people gathering around. He wore the same thing as the first guard. Elliot made out the embroidered text on his left breast that read: *Enforcer*. "Alright, get back to your meals, people. Go on. There's nothing more to see here."

The crowd slowly started to disperse, while hungry people sat back down in front of their bowls at the table.

Two other guards, wearing the plain dark blue uniforms appeared. It took a minute for Elliot to realize that one of them was Adam.

"It's alright," the second guard flagged them away. "Everything's under control. Just a misunderstanding."

"No, sir." The man shook his hand. "Not a misunderstanding. This guy put his hands on me. He tried to kill me."

"What?" Elliot scoffed, chuckling. "That's bull. I wasn't trying to kill him." He looked to Adam. "He was saying things about Jess and I wanted him to apologize, but—"

"You can't put your hands on people," one of the guards interrupted.

Anita came from behind the counter. "That man was saying some pretty foul shit about my friend's little girl. Really nasty things."

"That's no reason to put your hands on someone." The enforcer looked to the guard beside him. "Should we cuff him?"

"No," Elliot interrupted, stepping forward.

"Yes." The man beside Elliot sneered at him. "He's a threat."

The man in the plain guard uniform looked to Adam. "What do you think?"

Adam stared at Elliot. "Well..."

Elliot glared. "What do you mean 'well'? Tell them *no*."

"With what happened a few days ago with the prophet we can't take risks." Adam rubbed his temple. "I'm sorry."

"Bastard." Elliot rushed forward and grabbed Adam by the collar. "How could you do this to me?" The other guards grabbed him and forced his hands behind his back. The clicks of the cuffs locking on his wrists and the pain from the pinch from them closing were simultaneous with the pain in his heart. As they led him out of the cafeteria, Elliot looked over his shoulder at Adam, realizing that would be the last time he'd see Adam for a long time.

They took him down the long, darkened stairwell. The lower they went the more it smelled dank and musty, like a load of dirty and damp laundry left in the hamper too long. The tiny lights that were embedded into each wall of the stairwell spiraled down all four floors and didn't do much to lighten the dim stairwell.

"Where are you taking me?" Elliot's voice echoed throughout the space, sending a distant feeling throughout.

"You're going to spend a few nights below until we determine if you're a threat." The guard tightened his grip on his forearm. "Now keep moving."

What would happen to him if they thought he was a threat? Would he stay there forever ... or something worse?

After twenty minutes or so of descending the stairs, they hit the fourth and final landing, they came to a metal door with a sign on it that read: Keep Out. Authorized Personnel Only. The guard dug in his pants pocket and pulled out a set of brass keys. He opened the door and shoved Elliot inside. "Keep moving."

It was dark and a loud mechanical humming bounced off the walls. As Elliot's eyes adjusted in the low lights, he could make out the large steel machines connected to pipes that ran along the ceiling. Some of the pipes were small and closely resembled those beneath a kitchen sink. Some were larger than his head. Even still, some dripped liquids from their joints that puddled in various spots on the uneven, stained concrete floor.

Farther in the back was a couple of what looked like large metal cages, huge squared off rooms sided with vertical metal bars.

"Alright." The guard pushed him forward. "Welcome to your new home." He pushed the bars and the door swung open, screeching on its hinges.

"How long do I gotta stay down here?"

The guard quickly took Elliot's cuffs off. "Until we say so. Now make yourself comfortable." He stepped out, closed the door and turned his key into three bolt locks that were equally placed vertically on the door frame. Then he turned and left the room.

Elliot looked around his cell only then realizing how cramped it truly was. He could stretch and touch the bars that served as his four walls. He looked directly up into a dim light bulb on the end of a cord that hung from the concrete ceiling. His fingers closed around the bars in front of him and he stared ahead into the darkness. His plan had worked. Instead of causing a scene with Anita, some strange man had invited himself into the fight and gave Elliot the perfect opportunity to cause a commotion. It all worked. What he didn't expect was the pain of betrayal to bubble to the surface when speaking to Adam.

After hearing about Adam finding Jena and they were expecting a child, he couldn't help but feel he'd soon be tossed aside and forgotten. Just thinking about losing Adam; his familiar presence, his deep gazes, his comforting touch, made it difficult to swallow. He relived the chills he felt just from looking at Adam, the shallow lines around his mouth when he smiled, his bright green eyes that Elliot swore looked deep within to his very soul, the magical way Adam comforted him with just a word or gentle touch. He missed that already. He smiled, letting it go, refusing to let his emotions get in the way of what was inevitable.

Anyway, he had to find a way out of the cell, the room and a way to get onto the other floors. They'd passed two landings on their way down the stairs, which meant there were four floors including the first where he'd come from, and the bottom where he was now. He had to find out where the pets were being held, on which floor, if they even came inside, and what exactly was on the other floors that made the guards so secretive.

On the way down, it had crossed his mind that they were just trying to keep an eye on everyone by closing off access to the stairwell. But then again, since they got here, no one but the guards had access to the stairwell anyway, to his knowledge. And Adam has only been told what was below. He never had a chance to explore it himself. So far what they had told Adam was correct. Still, something was just off and it nagged at him constantly.

Elliot looked beside him into the other cell. It was empty except for a man's Armani dress shoe and a dusty blue blazer. Elliot adjusted his eyes on the crevices and corners of the cell. The concrete floor was chipped in various places, looking jagged and not very well paved. In the room, the silhouettes of machinery casted distorted shadows along the floor and walls. Humming, swooshing and clinking sounds came from all around him.

Elliot gripped the cold, smooth metal bars and vigorously shook the door, looking for weaknesses in the structure. It seemed sturdy but he needed more force. He stepped back and then ran forward, ramming the door with the side of his body. He repeatedly threw himself against the door a couple more times before being interrupted by a laugh in the next cell.

"You're not going to knock that thing down." The voice and the chuckle came from a black form huddled in the corner of the darkened cell.

"Who's there?" Elliot strained his eyes to focus his vision on the heap in the corner.

The tired sounding voice came out slowly, lazily. "I'm the only person you're going to see until someone else gets locked up." He laughed manically.

Elliot narrowed his eyes. "What's so funny?"

"You." The shadowy figure rose and came forward. The light directly above Elliot reflected off the man's olive toned skin, and his voice creaked. "Every fool thinks they can open up a locked door just by beating themselves against it. It's quite funny to watch, really. You might dislocate your shoulder before you get that damn door opened. That might be funny to watch too." The man limped closer. His big toe peeked from a tear in the dirty black socks he wore. He held his right arm against his body with his other hand and moved slowly, grimacing with every step as if he were in pain.

Elliot pointed to the man's arm. "Are you hurt? What happened?"

"Who are you and why are they holding you here?"

Elliot stepped back. "You answer first. Why are *you* here?"

The man laughed quietly. "Because the world is shit, has always been shit, and will forever be shit. And has nothing to do with a damn asteroid." The man leaned against the door of his cell and twisted his face in pain. Never once did he let go of his arm that hung limply by his side.

Elliot snorted. "And that's why you're here?"

"I'm here because I stand up for myself and some people don't like that. It makes them uncomfortable. You, especially, should know that."

"What's that supposed to mean?" Elliot glared, crossing his arms over his chest.

"Come on, you know what people do with those they feel uncomfortable with. They try to separate them from the populace, get rid of them, or exterminate them. Look at what they did to the blacks and Jews. Fags too. They all make the world so uncomfortable. Let's just throw them at the bottom of the pit so we don't have to deal with them." He chuckled again.

"So you're one of those homophobic racists, huh?" Elliot rolled his eyes and took a closer look at the locks and bolts on his door. "This is definitely a punishment."

CHAPTER SIX

Moving Up

"They think I'm talking to you to get more information about what happened to figure out if Elliot's a threat." Adam lowered his voice to hide it among many others reverberating throughout the busy cafeteria. "So we can't be seen together later for any reason. Don't want anyone to get suspicious."

Anita had a worried look in her eyes. "They're not gonna come after me too, right?"

"No. Remember, we planned this to happen like this. Nothing is gonna happen unless we want it to."

"Well, what's gonna happened to Elliot? Do you know?"

"I'm giving Elliot a day or two to figure out everything while he's down there taking a look around. I don't want to get involved too soon—"

"Yeah, that would look suspicious." She nodded, crossing her arms over her soup stained top.

"Right." Adam saw the uncertainty written on her face. Is she truly worried for Elliot? Have they developed some sort of a bond or understanding in their short time working together? "He's doing this for you, you know?"

"Me?" Her dark, thin eyebrows dipped.

"Yes, you and your friend who lost her daughter."

"Tami? Why?"

In the distance a couple guards were approaching. "He's looking for the dog. I gotta go. Thanks, Anita." He turned to meet the two guards.

"Wait, why does it matter to him?" Anita whispered.

"He's trying to make it up to you and Tami," Adam said over his shoulder. "Everything that happened out there, he won't let it go. Gotta go." Adam met the men halfway, standing near the entrance of the cafeteria. "Looks like a simple misunderstanding. Don't think we have anything to worry about."

"Good." The guard threw his thumb back over his shoulder. "Prophet wants to speak with you."

"About what?"

The guard shrugged. "Come on. We'll take you to him."

Adam followed the men back to the staircase where he had met the prophet before. They all stood around the landing on guard. The prophet stepped forward, narrowing the space between them. He studied Adam's face, his clothes and shoes. Slowly he began a walk around him, seizing him up.

"Adam, we meet again."

Adam felt a hand brush his shoulder, sweeping something off of it. He turned and looked into the prophet's steel blue eyes. "You know my name, but what should I call *you?*"

"What would you like to call me, Adam?" The man tucked his arms behind his back and strengthened his posture. His chin ... high. His demeanor ... confident.

Creepy. "What's your name?"

"Ah, taking a cue from me and answering a question with a question." The man nodded, keeping his eyes fixed on Adam's. "Can I trust you with my name? Better yet, can I trust you at all? Seems a good way to find you is by looking for conflict."

"What are you saying?" Adam glared. "I'm doing my job."

"Indeed." He nodded again and looked to the guards. "Can you all excuse us, please?"

"Yes, sir," echoed through the stairwell as the men existed back into the hall.

The prophet extended his hand. "Eugene Edmond. Call me Eugene." Adam eyed his hand a moment before reaching out to shake it. "I should thank you for doing your job so passionately. I swear you're the only one who does so well without asking for anything in return. Why is that?"

Adam shrugged. "Because I don't want anything. I have everything I need. More than I could ask for really."

"Yes." Eugene hissed. "Ah, yes. If only everyone here felt that way."

"What did you want to see me for?"

"Well, to say thank you, of course. To show my gratitude for you being at the right place at the right time. You're probably not aware but a little birdie told me you were the one who decided to lock up that little brat from the cafeteria. Violence breaking out all over and you ... *You* are the only one who thinks to make sure that deviant doesn't hurt someone else. If I had a bottle of brandy right now I'll pour you a drink. Hell, I'd give you the whole damn bottle. You like brandy?"

"Well, uh, sure but—"

"That's sounds good right now. Unfortunately we're just going to have to make a toast without it. To the compound's safety!" He lifted his imaginary cup of brandy in the air. "Until next time, Adam."

Adam didn't quite know what to say to that. Instead of saying anything he nodded and exited the stairwell.

"So what'd you do?"

Elliot huffed. "I got into a fight with someone."

"Did you try to kill em?" He kept that uncomfortable grin on his face.

"Wha, no!" Elliot gripped the bars. "It was just a stupid scuffle."

The man nodded. "So, I guess they're trying to get rid of everyone who's showing signs of violence, huh? Hmm." He stepped forward, toward Elliot's cell. "Name's Mason." He slid his uninjured arm between the bars.

"Mason?" He ignored his hand. "Didn't I meet you on the top floor main room near the door? I was asking you about your suit and you got pissy with me."

Mason pulled his arm back. "Well, well, well. You win the prize for decent memory."

"What are you doing down here? You were 'violent' too?"

"I threw my eleven hundred dollar shoe at the fraud that's running this place, but it doesn't concern you."

"Well, what happened to you?" He gestured toward his injured am. "Did the guards do that to you?"

"Nah, I think I dislocated my shoulder." A soft chuckled crept out of him then erupted into a full-on laugh. "Oh, us tough guys can open any door just by throwing ourselves at it, right?"

Elliot shook his head. "Here, let me help you. Put your arm through and I'll pull it back into socket."

"I think it needs a quick push actually." Mason gently guided his arm through the bar.

Elliot took his elbow in one hand and held the upper arm with the other. "On the count of three push when I do. One..."

"Oh, this is gonna hurt—" He inhaled.

"Two..."

"Okay. Alright. Okay," he said to himself.

"Three." Elliot pushed and heard a *pop* as the joint went back into the shoulder socket.

"Fuck. Fuck. Fucking Christ." Mason held his arm to his body. "That was worse than getting kicked in the balls."

"Been there, done that." Elliot examined Mason's arm from the distance. "Did we do it?"

"Yeah, it feels like a success. I can move it now but it still hurts like a bitch." Mason sat down on the hard floor, resting back against the bars. "You don't have anything to eat, do you?"

"No."

Mason frowned. "They don't feed me much down here."

"How long you been here?"

"I don't know, a week. Almost a week. They took Patrice out four days ago." He shrugged. "I miss surf and turf. A slab of ribeye steak and steamed lobster tail. Mmm. Slathered with butter and ... oh, some nice merlot. Not that cheap shit either."

Patrice? Did he purposely just change the subject? "Yeah, that sounds good. I can easily settle for an ice cold beer right now."

"I got some. You drink regular or light. Got both actually."

Elliot chuckled. *What a nut.* "I don't have time to get drunk. I need to figure a way out."

"The only way you're getting out of here is when they let you out. Sorry, to burst your superman bubble. If you tried to kill a man you'll be lucky if you ever see your comfy little room again."

"I told you I didn't try to kill anybody. I'm not violent like you."

"You don't know me. So how can you say that definitively?"

Elliot sat near the door of his cell. "I just need to find a way out."

"If you did get out they'll just bring you right back in here." Mason stared out between the bars and into the darkened room. "Or you could just wait till they let you out."

"That's not part of my plan."

"Oh, you got a plan?" Mason laughed. "And what is your plan?"

Elliot glared, tired of hearing his cackling. "Why the hell should I tell you?"

"Come on. Amuse me. What am I gonna do, tattle tell on you?" He chuckled. Elliot crossed his arms and stayed silent. "Okay, how bout this? You tell me your plan and I'll tell you how to find whatever you're looking for. Cause I know you're looking for something."

"And how would you know anything about what I'm looking for?"

"Because I know as much about this place as the so-called prophet. Shoot, ask me something. What do you wanna know?" He grinned.

"I came here with a pet and now I'm trying to find—"

"There's no animals here." Mason interrupted. "They took them around back and left them for dead out there in that shit hole. There, does that answer your question?"

Elliot shook his head. "Wha ... How do you know?"

"Because I saw them do it. Stood there watching them gather up people's pets one by one. Slap a freaking collar on the cats or dogs with the last names of the owner written on it with a Sharpie." He scoffed. "With a damn Sharpie while everybody was getting settled inside, getting treated, looking for their sisters and mothers, nobody even realized the pets never came in. Never."

"So it's true." Elliot ran his hands through his hair. "You didn't say anything while they were doing this? You didn't do anything?"

"Wasn't my problem. Hey, at least I was safe."

Elliot was sure his glare was apparent enough to be seen from a mile away in the dark. "Selfish bastard."

"We're all selfish bastards. That was evident before impact and no different now. If anything, we're even more selfish."

"Speak for yourself."

Adam's thoughts were bouncing around in his head. He needed to talk to someone. Elliot was off limits. He couldn't be seen with Anita if he didn't want to raise suspicions. So that left Jena.

For some reason he couldn't quite put a finger on, he really didn't feel comfortable around Jena. The way she wanted to pretend that everything was perfect and start up immediately where they left off was awkward. Yet, he found himself in the medical station, watching her wrap gauze around a wound on some poor guy's shoulder, reminding him of the time he treated the gash on Elliot's leg.

"A nasty fall." She glanced up at Adam.

Adam waited to speak until the guy was all wrapped up and on his way with some pain killers. "How's your day?"

"Same ol'." She removed the blue latex gloves from her dainty hands and tossed them on the tray of used supplies beside her. "How about yours?"

"Getting by. How are you feeling?" He looked at her belly, trying to make out the hump beneath her scrubs.

She placed a hand on her stomach and smiled warmly. "We're feeling just fine." She approached and tangled her arms around his neck, standing on the tips of her toes as she always did when hugging him. She planted a kiss on his chin before laying her head on his chest.

Adam fingered the chain of her necklace. "Since they're not letting anyone use the stairwell, where are you staying until you can go back below with your uncle?"

"Staying with a friend in Pod 5. She had extra room so..." She stepped back and focused on his eyes. She slid a piece of hair behind her ear and cocked her head. "You're acting weird."

Adam dropped his head. "Me and you ... we have a lot we need to—"

"Everything's fine." She forced a smile. The horrified look in her eyes gave it away. "Let's not let anything fuck this up now, Babe.

Four years. Four whole years we loved each other. Let's not do this now. Okay?"

What was she scared of? That he would leave her? She seemed to be doing just fine when she left him. Why would she care now?

"Why now?" He looked back into her puppy dog eyes. "Why do you want me now?"

"I need you."

"But what about when I needed you? You left me, Jena. You were more than happy to leave me. From the looks of it you had no regrets."

"Sure. I regret it." She grabbed his chin when he looked away, forcing his gaze back on her. "I was upset! You upset me. You were talking to gay men."

Embarrassed that someone could be eavesdropping, Adam looked over his shoulder. "Sshh."

"Naked gay men. How was I supposed to react?"

"Okay. Okay." He placed his hands on her shoulders and took a deep breath. "Sorry for hurting you, but—"

"That's all that needs to be said." She caressed his stubbly cheeks. "It's over now. Me and your unborn son need you. Let's not waste any more time on the past. Okay?"

"I gotta go." Annoyed, adam pivoted and left Jena alone in the room.

There were so many things he wanted to say. He had contemplated just blurting them out but he didn't want to cause a scene or frustrate Jena and the baby. But it didn't take a prophet to see that things between him and Jena would never be the way it used to be. There were so many unsolved issues and a nagging feeling that she wasn't being one hundred percent truthful with him.

That Hello Kitty necklace had something to do with his uneasiness. Whoever gave that to her meant more to her than wealthy Uncle Tom ever did. She kept that necklace closer to her than he'd ever been. She never took it off even out of her uncle's site. And stranger yet, everyone had all their valuables and belongings taken from them when entering the compound. He'd only seen three people in the whole compound wearing personals; Jena, the prophet and the man in the suit who attacked the prophet.

Adam shuddered at the thought and continued down the hall to his room.

Pod 6 hummed with conversation from a few off duty guards. However, Adam's room was rather quiet. His roommate was gone but between the mattress and bedframe of Adam's bed was a package. He removed the square package and squeezed it. It was soft. Clothes maybe? The brown paper wrapped around it was held together with a long piece of twine.

He untied it and unraveled the paper around the contents. A small bottle of brandy fell out onto his bed, and in his arms he held the black fabric of a neatly folded enforcer uniform.

CHAPTER SEVEN

Stumbling Upon Truth

"People of the compound. Once again, thank you for your cooperation and for continuing to do your duties with our survival in mind. It comes to me that this falling substance beyond the compound walls is extremely toxic and deadly. The proof is in the fact that most of your beloved pets have become fatally ill or has perished due to the amount of the material found in their lungs. We extend our sympathies and condolences. Be grateful that you have found shelter and the necessities to live a comfortable life in the compound. Mourn your losses, but don't let it hinder your capability to fight for your survival. Again, thank you for your cooperation."

The new day was a brutal one. Adam already had a lot on his mind, now an announcement that all the pets were dead or dying. This wouldn't make for a good day. He wasn't in the medical station for a full twenty minutes before people started flooding it.

The few staff members that was there were continually on their feet. Jena looked overwhelmed. Strands of auburn hair fell from the messy bun atop her head as she moved about frantically, calming people and assessing their needs and concerns.

"I breathed that stuff in for a whole day before I found this place," one healthy looking woman complained. "What's gonna happen to me? Will I be alright?"

Hearing the same concern come from so many people made Adam question his own health. He and Elliot hadn't worn face masks while they were out there in the falling debris looking for the compound. He didn't think he had breathed any of that stuff in. At the time he had thought it was too thick and filmy to be breathed in. He could've been wrong. But if he was wrong, could it had affected him somehow? He took a deep breath, assessing his lungs. He felt fine. He could breathe without pain or any other issues.

More importantly, Elliot was down below and had been down there for a while. All for what? If he would've waited just a bit longer he would've gotten his answer. But then again, if there weren't rumors and concerns going around, including Elliot's questions, would they ever have been told about the pets? Poor Titan. Even if his real name wasn't Titan that's what Adam would forever know the dog as. Titan was as much of a hero for saving their lives as he and Elliot were to each other.

As more people flooded the medical station Adam had to keep some away. "If it's not an emergency you'll have to come back later. There're too many people in there already. Sorry, but they can't take any more people right now." He stayed at the entrance for hours until the crowd and chaos seemed to dissipate. One it was quiet and Jena seemed to relax again, he casually strolled the halls and the six pods.

"Hey, Adam?" The deep husky voice called from down Pod 6. He turned to see his roommate. "Why you not wearing your new uniform? You could've gave me a sip of that brandy too."

"Didn't drink it. Probably gonna send it back somehow. The uniform too."

"What? You deserved that uniform, man. Are you crazy?" Joe scoffed. "With that uniform you have weapons and major authority. You can boss us around." He laughed. "That means somebody trusts you. I'll wear the damned thing." He patted Adam's shoulder and left him with his thoughts.

Adam wasn't exactly sure what he did to gain Eugene's trust, but he couldn't help feeling uncomfortable, especially since the fight in the cafeteria he'd broken up. Sending Elliot below was all planned unbeknownst to everyone but Elliot, Anita and him. Plus, he really didn't do much but make the decision to send Elliot below. Was that really enough to earn a promotion of sorts? Maybe Eugene admired his decision making skills.

He hated lying, and it felt odd to wear the uniform and play along when he felt uneasy about everything related to Refuge Inc. Quickly he made his way to his room and gathered up the uniform, boots and helmet which was hidden under his bed and slipped the bottle of brandy inside one of the knee-high leather boots. He gathered them all in his arms and made his way to the two men guarding the staircase.

"I need these returned to ... uh, the prophet. Won't be needing these."

The guards looked confused. One spoke. "Uh, is that an order or do you want to go through to tell him yourself?"

These were now options? "Uh..."

The guard opened the door. "I'll take you."

Adam followed him inside, closing the door behind him. They stood on the landing of the stairwell, but the guard hovered his hand over one of the many recessed lights up high on the wall beside them. With four fingers he pressed the protective cover about two inches deeper into the wall until it clicked. Still glowing, the light popped back to its original place.

"Cool, huh? Rumor has it I'm next to get an enforcer uniform. Some of the enforcers just let me in on this little secret."

"What does it do?" Adam stared at the light. How didn't it burn the guy's fingers?

"Just watch." He waited with a huge grin on his face, nearly rocking on his toes from his poor attempt to contain his excitement.

Adam didn't know where to watch or what to watch for, but taking the guy's cue he stared at the concrete wall next to them. The guard stared, an amused grin still plastered on his face. And they waited no more than sixty seconds when a four-by-six-foot slab of concrete recessed into the wall by a couple inches, like a scene out of an Indiana Jones movie, and slide to the side revealing a small compartment that looked like an elevator. Upon entering the cramped room Adam noticed four buttons beside the door on the panel. They all had the Refuge Inc. logo stamped on top. The guard pressed the third button and the door quickly slid shut.

"What the hell is this?" Adam looked around the small compartment as he shifted the helmet and boots around in his arms.

"An elevator to the other floors. Crazy, huh? I didn't know about this till today."

The movement was subtle, but when the door opened they were on the third landing. Elliot must be confined on the floor below.

They exited the stairwell and entered a room that looked strangely like the top level's main room except the walls didn't looked as stressed and eroded, and different guards were standing at the door.

"We've come to see the prophet," the guard accompanying Adam said.

The two men eyed the pile of stuff in Adam's arms. "For what?" one of the men asked.

Adam cleared his throat. "To return the uniform. Name's Adam Weber."

One man looked to the other. "Check that stuff. I'll be back." He stepped around the corner, whistled and yelled, "Visitor. Adam Weber." And just as quick he was back beside his partner.

The partner took the clothes from Adam and patted it down. He tipped the boot upside down on top of the pile of clothes and the bottle of brandy plopped out. "Alright." The guard pointed down the hall around the corner, the hall that would've led to Pod 6 if they were on the top level. "Get your stuff and go on."

Adam gathered his stuff and continued down the hall.

"Not you." The guard gestured to the man that accompanied Adam. "Go back to your floor."

Adam nodded to the man as a thank you and continued down the hall, passing another guard who didn't acknowledge him at all. In the center of the hall on the clean, smooth concrete wall was the number six. And to Adam's surprise, the end of the hall didn't house several rooms in a pod but a lonely metal door. Three bolted locks were vertically positioned on the door near the handle. He knocked on it and listened to the solid sound of thick metal drum with each knock. Then the latch turned and the door slowly opened, creaking slightly from the weight on its hinges. There, standing on the other side was Eugene in a bright white, terry cloth robe with the notorious red R embroidered on the left breast.

"Ah, Adam. Come in." Eugene stepped aside and Adam's breath caught when he took a look at the room he was about to walk into.

The first things that seem to catch his attention were how white the walls were and how spacious the room was. Plush brown leather sofas that seated six sat on what looked like a Peruvian rug in the center of the carpeted room. A massive bookshelf lined one wall completely and framed awards and certificates lined another. Two matching brown leather recliners sat at an angle on the rug in front of the sofa. Beautiful floor lamps and end tables made the room look like a home. He was taken aback by the warm and comfy atmosphere. Even a curtain hung from a wall on brass rods, suggesting a window behind it which would have been impossible several feet below ground. However, it added to the aesthetics.

"You like?" Eugene smiled, gesturing to one of the leather recliners. "Here, I'll take those." He took Adam's uniform and sat them on the sofa. "Sit. Relax."

"Thank you." Adam sat in the chair and sighed. Comfortable was just one of the chairs great qualities. "How did you—"

"These are my personal possessions from my home in Flagstaff. Couldn't leave them there to possibly get destroyed. I'm sure you understand."

Adam nodded. "Sure." Maybe it made sense that the guy responsible for the compound lived comfortably. Would've been nice if they all could have a room like this. Yet, he was grateful to have a room at all. He wouldn't complain.

"So what brings you here?" Eugene glanced at the pile of clothes on the sofa. "Having second thoughts, hmm?"

"Sorry, but I like to stick with what I know. I never wanted authority over other guards or people, and I don't want to make big decisions. I can't be in the middle of chaos. Have too much on my mind." *And there seemed to be an eerie vibe lingering in the air, especially when it came to the compound's authority.*

Eugene sat in the other recliner beside him. He crossed his legs and rested his elbows on the arms of the chair. "Isn't that what you were trained to do out there, control chaos?"

"Well, yeah, sure. But I'd prefer to wear my old uniform and do what I've been doing."

"Despise change, huh?"

"Call it what you want." Adam stared at Eugene and he stared back. They watched each other in silence for a second, almost daring the other to cross the line and say or do something to add to the stress. The tension was so thick Adam could smell it; the faint stench of sweat, anger and a little bit of fear.

Then out of nowhere, Eugene chuckled. "See, this is the way I see it. Your new job is to continue doing what you do, but now you have the seniority to make even better decisions. You're an enforcer now, not just a guard. The more you put into the compound, the more you receive. You deserve the new uniform, Adam."

"Thanks for believing in me, but—"

"You are like me in regards to your stubbornness." Eugene dipped his fingers into his breast pocket and pulled out a thin rolled cigarette and lighter. He popped the cigarette in between his lips and lit the end.

"I just don't think—"

"That's right, you don't think." He tucked the lighter back into his pocket, took a puff of his cigarette, and blew the smoke in Adam's direction. At which point, Adam knew the thin rolled cigarette was something else entirely. The sweet smell of the herb quickly filled the air. "If you used you're head as you always had done, you'd realize I've given you a great opportunity. And you're being a stubborn jackass by not accepting. Are you not grateful for what I've done for you? Are you just like the other whiners and complainers in this place that refuse to see the gift that was given to them?"

Adam glared and gritted his teeth at the word *jackass.* He didn't hear the questions that followed, but he knew he had been asked a question because Eugene waited silently for an answer.

Eugene stood and walked to the wall of certificates and plaques. "You don't know what you've got until it's gone, right? Like air. You see. Come here, Adam."

Adam sat and scowled, demanding his body to calm down. "I'd rather sit."

Eugene grinned at him over his shoulder, then turned to the largest frame on the wall. "This is an award that launched my career. It's an award from NASA's Invention of the Year 2009. Me and a partner invented a light-weight thermal protection system for use on space vehicles during atmospheric entry at hypersonic speed. Which lead to me receiving this." He pointed to a framed gold metal as it hung from a blue and white striped ribbon. "The Exceptional Engineering Achievement Medal." Adam stood and went to the wall to take a closer look. The round metal had what appeared to be a hand holding up planet Earth with a ring around it. "Getting this award opened up doors for me and my partner to invent a solar powered air filtration system. We had to make adjustments to it several times, but you are breathing the crisp air of our invention." He took a puff of his joint and blew the smoke into Adam's face. "Of course, it's not entirely solar powered, but without this system you might as well be living out there."

Most of the awards looked prestigious. Awards from NASA. A doctorate in engineering from Stanford. Energy resources, civil and environmental engineering, philosophy in structural engineering awards, so many accolades and Eugene Edmund proudly stamped, written, signed or typed on them all.

Adam shrugged. "Accomplished a lot."

"And what have you accomplished? Surely you have some accomplishments with your background in law enforcement, hmm?" The cocky look in his eyes told Adam he suspected something. Did he know he wasn't really a police officer and never been? "Want some?" Eugene passed the joint.

"No, thanks." He pushed his hand away.

"Like the Oracle of Delphi, its toxins help me see future visions." He laughed so hard Adam wasn't sure if he should join him or ask if he was okay. Either way, Adam was on edge. Eugene knew more than he was admitting to at the moment. Could the weirdness and tension get any worse?

Adam grinned. "So are you admitting you really don't have visions of the future but instead hallucinations?"

"You don't believe I'm a prophet, is that it?"

"Kind of hard to believe when you're joking about it." Adam scoffed. "Plus, you're a scientist. I thought you'd believe in aliens on other planets before believing in divine messages of the future."

Eugene's grin dropped and he narrowed his eyes, glaring. "I knew the end was coming long before you knew what to do with yourself.

While you were living your pathetic life debating whether to buy single or double ply toilet paper to wipe your ass, I was trying to prevent the biggest worldwide catastrophe from becoming a reality." The veins in Eugene's neck seemed to pulsate. A few seconds later he chuckled and huffed. "You remind me of my old partner, always whining about morals and integrity, and how the truth shall set us free. Government isn't successful because of morals and integrity. If our government was honest we wouldn't have civility. You understand?"

"So lying about receiving divine messages is necessary because it's keeping us civil? That's crazy."

"My job is to lead a mass of people and the best way to successfully lead a massive group is to maintain their trust." He moved forward, placing his hand on Adam's shoulder. "We're not going to lose my trust are we, Adam? Don't make me regret making you an enforcer. Speaking of..." He went to the sofa and dug around in the front breast pocket of the enforcer shirt with one hand, the other held the smoking joint. "While you familiarize yourself with your new tasks I'll hold on to these in the meantime." He pulled out a keychain with three brass keys dangling from it. "Oh, and don't go blabbing about what you think you know. Trust, Adam. Trust. I think we're done here."

CHAPTER EIGHT

Revelations

Adam dunked his head in the washbasin. The cold water was nothing compared to the steamy, hot showers Eugene had been taking in his home within the compound. Adam hadn't took a real, satisfying shower in weeks. Reduced to washing himself down in the bathroom washbasins. He contemplated using the makeshift shower, which was nothing more than a small closet with a rusty pipe protruding from the ceiling and drizzling water, but he never had the nerves to actually go through with it. It seemed barbaric, especially now that he knew it was possible for Eugene to have the luxuries of a shower in the compound.

He dried his face with the sleeve of his shirt and left the bathroom, walking directly into the medical station. Jena flipped through files scribbling down notes here and there and subconsciously fingering the Hello Kitty necklace that dangled around her neck.

Adam watched her for a moment. The urge to open up and tell her everything he'd come to learn about the compound over the last few days was nagging at him. With Eugene's warning still fresh in his mind, he couldn't tell her about the elevator in the stairwell, the pot smoking prophet who was definitely more scientific than religious, or even about the house within the compound below with beautiful and comfy furniture, rugs and homey environment. What would

Eugene do if he had told? Anyway, there was one person he could trust with his secrets and that person he haven't seen in days.

He missed Elliot and not speaking to him or even seeing him for a couple days was enough to make him tense. Even if Elliot wasn't in the best of moods, seeing him and knowing he was okay helped Adam cope with their new underground home.

No matter how much Adam tried to forget about his time with Elliot and move on, the thought of touching Elliot's warm, bare skin seeped into his thoughts whenever he was alone. He would allow his mind to wander there, back to the time where they were scared and worried and believing that they might just be the only two people left alive. It wasn't the anxiety he focused on but his and Elliot's intimacy.

Their closeness had made them feel alive and took away all those bad feelings of doom, even if it were just for a little while. The powerful feelings that stirred Adam when they were together would last for eternity even if their intimacy was brief.

Being inside of Elliot and sharing a couple of blissful nights were more meaningful and significant than even an asteroid colliding with Earth. In his eyes, Elliot made him feel more alive back then than he felt now.

He would never forget cleansing himself under the falling water of that broken water main while Elliot's rapidly blinking eyes zeroed in on his exposed flesh. He'd always remember touching Elliot's muscular body, kissing the bruise on his plump lips, or stroking Elliot's impressive, hard cock in his fist. Those were all firsts for Adam and as memorable as living through a catastrophe.

Elliot's sex-drenched voice echoed in his fantasies, and the thought of feeling Elliot's warmness constrict around him while being buried deep inside—

"You okay?"

Adam focused on the confused, tilted smile on Jena's face as she moved closer. "Yeah. Yeah." He cleared his throat and his mind. "I'm fine."

"Whatcha thinking about?" She fingered her necklace and cocked her head. "I always know when you're daydreaming."

"Honestly, got a lot on my mind."

"Yeah, me too." She cleared her throat and stared at the floor nervously. "I've been thinking about how we haven't had a chance to... really spend some time together. You know? I mean, since staying on this floor I've been so busy and I never get any alone time with you. We both have roommates and—"

Was she hinting at sex? "What is this about, sex?" Adam hoped he didn't come off cocky.

"Well, I miss you and—"

"What about the baby?"

"What *about* the baby? We won't hurt the baby."

"Are you sure?" He sighed, rubbing his temple.

"Yes, I'm sure. The baby will be fine." She giggled. "Plenty of pregnant couples have sex, Adam."

"Not that. Are you sure we should even be thinking about sex? Honestly, sex is the last thing on my mind right now." He held a straight face. It wasn't a total lie. Sex with *her* never crossed his mind. He frowned. "I'm sorry."

"I'm just trying to bring us back to what we used to be." She touched his chin with her fingertips. "You're not the same anymore. In fact, you're totally different and it's scaring me."

"You're right. I am different. You have no idea what I've been through." Adam raked his fingers through his hair with both hands. "I've been through hell and back looking for you, holding on to the possibility that you were still alive. But I'd forgotten you left me. You left me to fend for myself. And for what?"

"Why are you doing this?" She crossed her arms under her small breasts.

"Because it's about time we talk about this. I can't just find you here safe and sound with no explanation other than wealthy Uncle Tom, find out you're pregnant with my kid, and just fuck you like nothing's happened. Let's continue on where our happy little life left off, right?"

"Why are you cursing at me?" She glared. "I'm trying to make this better."

"Then be honest with me. Where'd you get the necklace?"

"Uncle Tom."

"How did you find this place?"

"Uncle Tom took me here."

"Uncle Tom again. Was he the one that got you pregnant too?"

Jena's gasped and immediately her hand went across his face. Adam heard the slap before he felt the hot sting of it on his cheek. "What the hell is wrong *with* you?"

Adam gulped, refusing to make eye contact. "I loved you, Jena, but every time I look at you I see a liar."

"Liar? You want to talk about lying?" She lowered her voice into what resembled a growl. "You were the one talking dirty to men online while engaged to me and trying to make a family? You're the liar that's why I left you, Adam. You were a dirty liar."

"Then why do you want me now if I'm so dirty? I tried to tell you earlier, to come clean and be honest about what I've done out there. Me and Elliot—"

"I don't want to hear about you and some man. Are you serious, Adam? You think that's something I want to know?" She turned her back and walked away.

He followed her further into the large, empty room. "I'm trying to come clean, so you understand. I will always be there for you and the baby, but I don't think I can be with you. My heart's not in it. Not anymore."

Jena gasped, her hand went to her chest as she turned to face him. "Are you breaking up with me?"

"*You* left *me*!"

"You're breaking up with me because of some man you met out there, right?"

"I'd be lying to you and myself if we tried to make this work."

"Did you fuck him?" She nodded, tears in her eyes, her chest heaving rapidly. "Well? You did, didn't you? That's what you been trying to tell me?"

Adam slowly nodded. "And I liked it."

"Oh, my God!" She turned to run away but collided with a the corner of the desk in front of her. She grabbed her stomach and hit the floor, curling up in the fetal position.

Adam kneeled by her side. "Jena? You okay?"

"Don't touch me, you pervert." Jena rolled to her back, bloodshot eyes glaring at him. Her hands still clenching her stomach.

Adam was taken aback. She had never called him degrading names before, not before discovering his online activity. "Are you okay? Is the baby okay?"

"You disgusting bastard." She lifted the shirt of her scrubs to reveal her belly which was slightly bruised near her pelvis and flatter than a washboard. "There is no baby."

"What?" Adam stood staring at her trim belly.

"There's no baby," she repeated. "Never been. You understand. Now get out!"

"I don't believe this. Can't believe you lied to me." He was shocked and couldn't say anything else if he wanted to. Nothing else came to mind.

"Oh, really? Where do you think I got it from?" She slowly stood, her hand gripping her pelvic bone. "I thank God I'm not carrying your child. If I were pregnant by you I would probably just kill myself. Now get out and don't come back."

Adam instantly became numb. He walked out into the hall in a daze. His mind going over and over what she said and her big reveal. How dare she? After all she put him through after the impact and now decided to fake a pregnancy. Adam leaned back against the wall in the hall. He ran his hands through his hair and demanded himself to get a grip.

Jena had made him feel so low and dirty since finding out he'd been chatting online with men, and even now he felt the worse he's ever did. All those years denying who he really was had always been for her, for their family, and in the name of love. What a fool. However, knowing the truth made him appreciate what he had with Elliot even more. It made him realize where his heart truly was.

What if he never had the chance to tell Elliot what a mistake he'd made by going their separate ways? Elliot was all he had, the only one he fully trusted, and he was locked up somewhere down below, waiting for Adam to set him free.

There had to be someone he could confide in. Someone who hopefully could help him figure out a way to get Elliot back up top where he belonged.

Mason coughed. "Mr. Prophet has a problem with superiority. The problem is he insists on it to move any government, but he doesn't understand it. He doesn't understand that you can rule behind the curtain like some of the people he worked with understood. He needs a spotlight in order to function. And being in the spotlight nearly killed him." He grinned, still holding onto his arm. "To answer your question, I'm in here because I was an accomplice to that."

Elliot nodded. "So you tried to kill him."

"No, I said an accomplice. I threw my shoe and it happened to distract him and the guards while Patrice attempted and failed the dirty business. I never actually attempted anything other than a distraction."

Elliot rolled his eyes at Mason's effort to distance himself from any actual crime. "You mentioned that name earlier. Who's Patrice?"

"Does it matter?"

"Yeah, it does. Especially if you're trying to 'win my trust'. Tell me everything and then I'll tell you my plan, like we agreed."

"Patrice was a woman who needed some things and I'd provided them for a price."

"So you paid her to try to murder the prophet? You *are* sick."

"That never came out my mouth." Mason pointed a stern finger, a serious tone. "Okay?"

"Now how am I supposed to trust a person that can't admit he tried to kill someone? Why would I want to even talk to someone like you?"

"Because I can help you, and you can help me."

Elliot's eyes narrowed. "How am I supposed to help you?"

"We can help each other, but first we must trust each other. It's all about trust. That's the only way we will accomplish anything."

Trust? That was the last thing Elliot would give to a criminal, his trust. "Okay, I wanted to check out the other floors to see if and where they were keeping the pets, and also to explore a little since they locked us up on our floors."

"What are you expecting to find other than animals?"

"I don't know." He shrugged. "Answers."

"I told you the pets are not in here. What else do you want to know?"

"How much do you know and how do you know it?"

"I was a friend of the prophet. He needed me to help build some parts of this place, so I know a lot about it." The all-knowing grin on

Mason's face sent chills down Elliot's spine. It was something sinister about his facial expression when he made that statement. "I know things about this place and the so-called prophet that will make you cringe, but my information doesn't come free."

Elliot cocked his head. "What happened to trust?"

Mason showed a row of white teeth. "We're still working on it."

"Well, I just told you my plan. Now you gotta tell me something."

"How about this? All this time you thought a Texas-sized asteroid hit Earth. That's not true." He grinned and chuckled like a school girl with juicy gossip. "NASA discovered the asteroid two years ago. They watched it closely because it was on a collision course with Earth. Scientists all over the world scrambled to defend Earth from the big bad astral predator using every means necessary, but without disclosing findings to the public who would definitely panic, right?"

"Uh huh." Elliot listened attentively.

"They tried to veer it off course, was close but failed. They tried several other things until they came up with the bright idea to try to break it into fragments, in hopes the pieces would burn up into nothingness as it entered the atmosphere. Unfortunately, the pieces that broke off where bigger than they had anticipated and by then it was all too late. They finally grew some balls and broke the news to the public a couple days before all of the huge asteroid fragments impacted, but they never mentioned their failed attempts. They announced it as *one* large rock."

Elliot leaned forward, full of interest. "So you're saying there wasn't one impact but several?"

"Not only is that what I'm saying. I'm also saying that the asteroid was supposed to hit the west coast of the states but instead only the fragments did. I personally watched an asteroid fragment streak across the sky as a huge fireball. It was spectacular."

"I saw one too." Elliot's heart pitter pattered from the excitement of the sudden adrenaline rush. "I didn't know what it was but I saw it.

So if fragments hit the earth instead of one massive asteroid then the damage isn't as bad as we think it is."

"You're not as dumb as you look." Mason leaned back against the bars. "If an asteroid that big hit Earth we wouldn't be alive to talk about it."

"So the prophet must've had information about the asteroid and its course long ago and claimed he 'predicted' it?"

"Bingo!"

"I didn't think he was a real prophet."

"So you're not surprised?"

"Why is he pretending to be a prophet?"

"Desperate people are more susceptible to being misled and controlled. And desperate people tend to trust a religious, righteous leader in the name of all that's good and holy. A man of God can do no wrong. By the time you realized you've had the wool pulled over your eyes it's too late. It's all about trust, Elliot. That's what this place runs on. That's your currency." He cleared his throat. "And besides, how else was he supposed to tell them about the impact without everyone blaming him for knowing? He used God's message to get funds from these people, and later he could say 'I told you so' to those who didn't invest and didn't believe him."

Elliot thought to himself then narrowed his eyes. "So if he's not a real prophet then how did he get accurate information about the asteroid to claim predicting its impact?"

"Think about that for a minute."

Elliot slowly shook his head, thinking. "Someone told him?"

"Cold." Mason smacked his lips. "This was the best kept secret since Roswell. Come on, think."

"He had a friend that was a scientist? No, a family member. Someone he was close to."

"Warmer."

Elliot stared at Mason, reading his subliminal message in his eyes. "He's the scientist? He worked for NASA?"

"Ding, ding, ding!"

"Whoa, well why would he pretend? Why not just be honest? I would trust a NASA scientist about an asteroid before a prophet."

"Like I said, if he knew definitive information about an impact years in advance, a lot of people wouldn't take that lightly. Instead of seeing him as a savior they'd blame him, wouldn't respect him at all. That would defeat the whole purpose of trust, now wouldn't it?"

"You seem to know all the answers." Elliot narrowed his eyes suspiciously. "How do you know all this?"

"Told you I was close to the prophet."

"If you were so close to him to know so much, why would you try to kill him?"

"Now that's a good question. The one you should've asked long time ago."

CHAPTER NINE

The Truth

Adam sat on his bed with all kinds of thoughts running through his head. Primarily he had to see Elliot, just to know he was doing okay and also to ease his own guilt. Why did he go along with such a crazy plan? Now Elliot was locked below for a couple days and he had no way of getting him out.

Then it hit him. Adam possibly had the key to the bottom level all along in the breast pocket of his new uniform. The brass keys on the keychain that Eugene pulled from the shirt pocket. "Damn it."

"What's the matter?" Joe creaked the door opened and walked inside.

"Just worried about a friend."

"That boy that came looking for you that one night?"

"Yeah. His name's Elliot."

"Whatcha worried about?" Joe sat on his own bed opposite Adam's, hands on his knees.

"He's been locked below for a couple days and I'm worried. Wondering if he's okay."

"What's he below for? He wasn't the one fighting in the cafeteria days ago, was he?"

"That was him." Adam met Joe's eyes. "But no one knows he's my friend. And I want to keep it that way."

"Hey, that's your business." Joe raised both empty palms. "I won't go where I don't belong."

"Sorry."

"No, I get it. I'll give you some alone time." Joe stood to leave.

"Wait." Adam stood too. "You don't happen to have the keys to below so I can go see him, do you?"

Joe chuckled. "Man, you know only enforcers have keys. I haven't been lucky to get promoted yet. Check your uniform. You would probably know that if you wore it from time to time." He shook his head and left the room.

"Damn it." Adam sat and stared at the floor. Then he stood and paced between the two beds. Back and forth he walked. Finally, he decided to make a move and retrieved his black uniform, helmet, belt and boots. He tossed the bottle of brandy under his mattress and began to dress.

In full uniform including his handcuffs and the small silver key that went with it in his back pant pocket, the small canister of pepper spray, and his black baton on his belt, Adam stormed out of his room. Anger written on his face as shallow crease lines sketched on his forehead when he glared. He stepped into the pod where several guards and a couple enforcers were standing around talking. "Okay, who has it? Give it up." Some of the men laughed but the rest just stared dumbfounded. "Now, come on, guys. Stop fucking around. Who took my brandy?"

"Did somebody take the man's brandy?" one of the men asked.

"He has brandy?" another chimed in. "Where'd he get brandy from?"

"Nobody's got your brandy."

"I want some brandy."

Adam went to the nearest room. "I'll go get it back myself since no one wants to hand it over."

He rushed into the room and began throwing things around. Sheets and pillows plopped against the cold concrete walls as a couple guards and an enforcer entered. They grabbed him while most of the men tried getting in their opinions by yelling over each other. Among the noise and commotion, Adam fell and the enforcer fell beneath him. They struggled for what seemed like a minute.

"That's enough, Adam. Enough!" Joe's voice was louder than the rest. "Here's your damn brandy. You left it under your damn mattress." He tossed the bottle to Adam.

Adam caught it with both hands. "Shit. Sorry. I thought—"

"Yeah, well, you thought wrong." The enforcer stood and shook his head.

"Sorry." Adam stood and avoided eye contact. "Things didn't go well with my girl and I was looking for a drink, and I look like a total asshole right now. Sorry."

The enforcer patted his shoulder harder than a friendly pat. "Yeah, yeah. It's over now."

The men dispersed throughout the pod. Some went back to standing around doing nothing. Questions of where he got the brandy from were being asked as he walked down the hall with a set of brass keys in his pocket.

While smoothing the wrinkles out of his enforcer uniform, calming himself, and exiting the corridor, the presence of a woman with her ear on the main door caught Adam's attention. Even the two men guarding the stairwell were watching the woman move to various parts of the steel door with the side of her face pressed against it.

Adam went to her. "What's going on?"

The woman jumped back, startled. "There's something on the other side. I think someone's trying to get in."

Adam frowned and pressed his ear to the cold steel. A faint thud sounded deep within the door, ringing slightly from the echo. Again he heard the thud, and again, repeatedly and out of sync. He looked at the woman. "Maybe it's pipes behind the walls."

"What if it's people out there? What if they're trying to open the door?"

It was a possibility, after all. The way he and Elliot found he compound was by following the spray painted Refuge Inc. signs Anita and Tami placed over most of Phoenix. Maybe other survivors discovered and followed the signs as well. Either way, he knew deep down that that door wasn't going to open anytime soon.

One of the men guarding the stairwell came forward. "Alright, ma'am, step away from the door. Come on."

"But I hear something." Her eyes were wide and filled with concern.

"It's the pipes like he said." The man reassured her. "Now move on."

As the woman walked away she continually looked back over her shoulder at the door, worry in her eyes.

The guard turned to Adam. "Would you help Bill over there keep an eye on things while I go let the prophet know what's going on?"

"I can let him know." Adam started walking toward the stairwell. "I was on my way to see him anyway. I'll mention what happened here."

The guard scoffed. "And what happened down there?" He jerked his head toward Pod 6. "I heard a lot of racket."

Adam paused and chuckled. "A stupid misunderstanding that's all. I thought the guys were pulling a prank on me and took my stuff but it was nothing. Everything's cool."

"Everything's cool, huh?" The guard shook his head. "Go on."

Adam nodded and made his way through the doors and into the stairwell. Alone on the landing, he stared at the two recessed lights on the wall beside him and let his hand hover over one then the other. One of the lights radiated heat and the other didn't. With three fingers he press the cool bulb of the two inch round light until it clicked and wouldn't go any further into its socket. It popped back out, and seconds later the concrete slab on the wall beside him pulled into to itself and slid open to reveal the empty elevator.

He stepped in. Looking at the four buttons with only a Refuge Inc. symbol on them, and pressed the bottom one. The door closed and almost immediately he saw a key hole below the bottom button. It was there before but he wasn't alone then and didn't have time to examine it.

He dug in his pocket and pulled out the set of brass keys. He looked at the teeth of the keys, realizing they were all different. He chose the one that best matched the keyhole and slid it in. It fit perfectly, but what would happened if he turned the key? He was too impatient and slightly nervous to find out. Instead he removed the key, pressed the bottom button again and waited.

After a few seconds the door opened. It was rather eerie as he stepped out onto the landing beside ascending concrete stairs, and walked to the door opposite the elevator. The sign on the door warned to keep out: Authorized Personnel Only. He tried a key, ignoring the sign, suddenly anxious about Elliot's condition. The door unlocked with a clunk. When he opened the door and stepped inside, a loud humming and clinking of machinery filled his ears. He quickly closed and locked the door behind him using the same key.

Elliot sat in the back of the large, dark room inside a jail cell with a single dim lit light bulb dangling from a cord above him, illuminating his slouched form. Adam's heart sank and horrid thoughts raced through his head. Dirt caked Elliot's forehead and neck, and stains of bologna soup covered the front of his dingy, once white uniform.

Overwhelmed with an urge to touch Elliot's skin and kiss his lips, Adam brought his hand to his rapidly beating heart. As he maneuvered passed large drums containing swishing liquids, he knew exactly what would make the moment perfect. He yearned to see Elliot's bright and contagious smile. Then he'd know Elliot was okay.

Elliot stood, peeking through the bars. "Adam, is that you?"

Adam rushed forward, gripped the bars to his cell and smiled, relieved. "It's me."

"Oh, thank God." Elliot smiled.

For a moment his smile was Adam's only focus. He gazed into Elliot's brown eyes, his fluttering lashes stealing Adam's attention. Adam searched his face, staring, gazing. He gripped the pocket of his pants, preventing himself from reaching through the bars and sweeping his fingertips across Elliot's plump bottom lip.

Elliot looked him over. "What are you wearing?"

"An enforcer uniform. I've been promoted."

Elliot's eyes grew wide. "So I'm getting out of here, right?"

"I snuck down here to make sure you're okay." Adam ran his hand over his own damp forehead, doing something with it than making a move on Elliot too soon. "I'm not supposed to be in here."

"Wha... well, what about me?" Elliot dipped his eyebrows.

"And me." The guy in the other cell stood. "I'm Mason, by the way."

Elliot scoffed. "I need to get out of here, Adam. Mason told me the prophet is a fraud."

"He's not who he says he is," Mason interrupted. "And we're not being fed. I haven't eaten in—"

"The asteroid broke into several pieces before it impacted," Elliot continued, a look of worry in his eyes. "Remember that fireball we saw when we were out there?" When Adam nodded, Elliot continued. "That was just a fragment. They hit mostly in the west coast. You know what that means? That means the end probably didn't happen. Maybe my family in Georgia is alive and safe. Maybe it's only bad here on the west coast and—"

Adam reached a hand between the bars and guided Elliot toward him by the back of his neck. Their lips met through the small space, a chaste kiss at first but when Elliot moaned Adam slipped the tip of his tongue between his lips. A delicate whiff of bologna hit his nostrils but he didn't care. Elliot was in his arms again. He caressed Elliot's bottom lip with his own and sighed. Refusing to open his eyes and ruin the moment, he kept them closed and pressed his forehead to Elliot's. "I missed you."

Mason cleared his throat. "That much I can tell from over here."

Adam ignored him and finally looked into Elliot's eyes. "I let you believe you forced me to come out, that it was your fault we didn't become something more than friends. Can't let you think that. It's not true."

"This is clearly a private conversation." Mason walked to the other end of his cell and sat, humming the tune to *The Star Spangled Banner.*

"I helped you come down here looking for Titan because you felt responsible for him and that little girl. Her death wasn't your fault and everything that happened to us wasn't your fault. You don't have to try and make it right. You never did anything wrong. I shouldn't have gone along with that plan. I should've stopped you."

Elliot dropped his gaze, his hands visibly shaking. "So that kiss?"

"I meant it." Adam stepped back, giving Elliot space.

Elliot looked up. "What about Jena and the baby."

"There's no baby and there's definitely no more Jena. You're the only one in my life now."

"No baby?" Elliot frowned.

"She lied, but it's me and you now. I need it to be me and you. No more playing around. No more space. No more waiting. I know what I want."

"Me?" Elliot pointed to his own chest.

Adam nodded, stepped forward and pulled Elliot closer through the bars. He planted a series of soft, gentle kisses along his lips. Chest aching, Adam rested his forehead against Elliot's again. "I shouldn't have waited so long to tell you how much you mean to me and how much I need you."

"You told me now." Elliot clutched Adam's shirt, bringing them even closer. "I was never gonna give up on you and this only makes it easier. It feels so good to find out I mean everything to the person who means everything to me."

Mason stopped humming. "Oh, look, it's the end of the world and here we have a charming couple, wonderfully in love as if the sky's not literally falling on their heads."

"Shut your mouth." Adam didn't see the humor in their situation. He went to Mason's cell. "I know who you are."

"I was an accomplice to the prophet's attempted murder. I'm aware of my reputation, uh, Adam. I know who you are too. Thanks for stopping me from saving everyone's ass." Mason stood and crept closer. "But are you aware of the lie you've been told. Like your boyfriend said, there is no end of the world. A few pieces of a huge rock hit Earth, kicked up a bunch of dust and everybody's panicking. Exactly the right ingredients for the perfect scam."

With those words Adam thought of the old couple they left behind in Arrowhead hospital. Harold had said Refuge Inc. was a scam. He and Elliot themselves had questioned who in their sick mind would put together a scam in the days after a major catastrophe. Elliot had mentioned *isn't that the best time to run a scam?* He was right. He had heard of price gouging, ID theft and plenty other scams after natural disasters or terrorists attacks. But how would Refuge Inc. participate in a scam where money didn't matter?

Adam looked to Mason. "Tell me what you know."

"I'll tell you as soon as you let me out."

"They're gonna put me in here if I let you out. Where are you gonna go anyway? They'll catch you."

"I'm gonna get the hell outta this compound with your help."

"Not gonna happen."

"And here I thought you were smart men." Mason looked back and forth between Adam and Elliot. "Elliot, you should've told me you had a boyfriend with a key. I would've told you my plan long time ago."

"What's going on?" Elliot asked.

"I know an alternate exit instead of that main door. They won't even know we're gone until it's too late. We could be on the outside in less than thirty minutes."

Adam moved as close to the bars as he could. "Where's the exit?"

"It's somewhere outside of the compound. I remember exactly. I'm not gonna tell you until you let me out. Hell, I used to think one day I could flip a switch and open the main door anytime I wanted. Never thought I'd have to escape. But plans changed."

Adam frowned. "And why would we want to escape?"

"You boys are a couple of dumb fools." Mason chuckled. "Not only is your family in Georgia alive and well, Elliot, but the dust in the air has already settled to Earth by now. I don't know about you, but lately my biggest craving besides steak and beer has been sunshine."

CHAPTER TEN

Keycard

Adam glanced back at the door through the darkened room. "So you're saying there's sunlight out there?"

"True." Mason grinned. "So true."

"Well, why is he keeping us in the compound when we could be out there looking for our families and rebuilding?"

"Let me out and I'll tell you everything you want to know."

Adam exhaled, shaking his head. "You don't know anything. Who are you to know what's going on out there or in here or anywhere? You just want out and will say anything."

"How do I know about the prophet? You know who he really is, and if I was just saying anything then how did I get that one right? If you need proof I got the blueprints of this place. I'll tell you where the blueprints are, and while you're at it you can get the keycard we'll need. Then you'll let me out. Deal?"

"You're the last person I want to make a deal with."

"You're gonna have to trust me, Adam." Mason looked to Elliot. "Educate your boyfriend on trust, will you?"

Elliot grabbed the bars with both hands, pressing his face as much through the gap as possible. "He says trust is what this place runs on. It's our currency."

Adam looked over his shoulder at the door again, imagining guards and enforcers busting through. "I thought the more we give, the more we get back. I thought that was our currency. The right contribution?"

"You've got a lot to learn." Mason snorted. "Ten thirty-one. That's the code to my room on the second level. Pod 1."

"Halloween?"

"My birthdate." Mason went to the pile of clothes in the corner of his cell and retrieved his jacket. From the pocket he pulled out a wedding band. Here, put this on. In my room there's a light above my bed. Push the light in and a hidden door will open. Don't worry, it's an LED light it won't burn you. It's like the button for the elevator."

"Elevator?" Elliot looked confused.

"Long story, Elliot." Adam took the ring and slipped it on his left hand ring finger. "Why the ring?"

"It's your key. You'll see."

"I gotta be quick. So hang tight." Adam huffed.

Mason nodded. "Don't get caught. Hurry back. I trust you."

Adam went to Elliot. "While I think I still have some time, I'm gonna go check out his room." He unlocked one of the bolts, testing the key, and then took that brass key off the small ring and passed it to Elliot between the bars. "If I don't come back soon, within an hour, something's wrong. Either they caught me or for some reason I can't get back in. So give me enough time. If I'm not back, try your best to get outta here. If you guys get caught we're all fucked."

Elliot pulled Adam closer and left a peck on the corner of his mouth. "How will we know an hour passed?"

"Just guess. I shouldn't be gone all day." Adam left the room and quickly made his way back in the stairwell on the landing. He searched for the right light to push by letting his hand hover over each one and feeling for warmth. Once he found the correct light he pushed it in and the elevator door opened. He stepped inside and quickly pressed the second button from the top.

The door shut, and a moment later when it opened again he walked out onto the second floor landing. He composed himself, trying not to look flustered, in a rush, or suspicious, and pushed the doors open walking into the main room.

The two men guarding the door looked surprised. "Who are you?" one of them asked.

"I was sent from the third level to retrieve something private for the prophet." Adam paused briefly for a response. The men looked at each other speechless, while Adam nodded and continued walking. He assumed the level's layout was the same as the floors above and below so he went toward the hall that would have led to Pod 1.

Interesting how the main room resembled the top level minus the massive steel door. Interesting still was how the hall to Pod 1 seemed to magically transform from the corroded metal and concrete walls into a lavish hall with decorated oil paintings hanging on each side of the wall in even rows. Several people dressed in casual clothes moved about going on with their daily business, completely unaware that an intruder was gawking at their gold framed masterpieces. He didn't want to stare at the people or the art too long to become suspicious, so he continued down the hall which opened up to a pod like any other on the first or third levels. However, this pod resembled an indoor atrium of sorts. With greenery and flowers growing in the center of the room. The oval basin they were in was filled with potting soil and the entire pod smelled floral and alive like fragrant herbs. The ceiling had a brightly lit light between panels of glass. The heat from the light radiated throughout the pod, keeping it a warm but comfortable temperature.

Sitting on a wooden bench beside the garden was a woman reading a chapter book. As she turned a page of the book Adam notice a huge diamond on her finger. When she looked up at him he continued on into the first nook on the left that contained a door. He couldn't stop thinking about the crisp white dress pants the woman wore.

Beside the door was an electronic panel with rubber buttons on a numbered pad. He dialed the code Mason had told him. And the panel beeped three times. He tried the knob and it wouldn't turn. He dialed the number again, and again the three beeps followed. Did he have the wrong door? Was it the wrong code? He tried the knob again and still it wouldn't turn.

Suddenly his nerves kicked in. He glanced over his shoulder. The thought of someone stopping him and throwing him below with Elliot and Mason just wouldn't stop pestering him. He glanced at the woman who had briefly met his gaze and went back to her book. He dialed the number again, careful to press the correct buttons. Finally, there was one long beep and click from the door knob. He turned the knob, opened the door and quickly stepped inside. He closed the door behind him and locked it. His back rested against the door and he exhaled. He knew adrenaline was pumping ferociously throughout his body, he felt his hands shaking terribly.

Feeling a bit safer, he finally walked further inside the room, realizing Mason had more than a bed and a light. His room resembled the prophet's in that it looked like a replica of a homey house. The only difference was Mason's room looked like it had been ransacked. The bed was unkempt, sheets balled in the middle of the bed, pillows thrown on the floor near a pile of what looked like dirty clothes. Still, it was an amazing room.

The walls were painted in warm earth tones; browns, creams, and deep green as an accent. The chocolate brown carpet had a nice thick pad beneath it, making every step as light as air. He too had a window curtain hanging from a decorative wooden rod secured to the wall. The solid emerald green of the curtain matched the green of the accent wall. A nightstand with what looked like an empty bottle of beer sat next to a thick-spine paperback book. The wicker lampshade atop the lamp added to the earthy, homey atmosphere.

What was going on?

Seeing the room brought so many questions to the surface Adam's head began to ache trying to figure it out. To the right, through a door was a pristine bathroom with a beautiful porcelain tub, matching toilet and sink. The beige towels hanging from towel racks on the walls looked plush and extra clean, and the smell of a floral soap or cleaning agent filled the room.

Why was the top floor so different than the bottom two? Why couldn't the top floor have linoleum floors as beautiful and antique-looking mirrors as clean and clear as the ones he was looking at?

On the other side of the room was a personal sized refrigerator that contained small bottles of wines and beers. Adam felt his confusion suddenly switch to anger as he dug through the cold box. How fair was it to live on the top floor in their own filth, eating things like bologna soup and sharing a room that was no bigger than a walk-in closet, while below, certain people lived in bliss, drinking wine and beer? Or was everyone on the two lower floors living this way?

The shining light on the wall above the wooden headboard of the bed got his attention. Quickly, he jumped on the bed and pressed the light. A click sounded from the bathroom. When he peeked around the corner into the bathroom, one of the twelve-by-twelve linoleum tiles on the floor was raised at a ninety degree angle. He stood over it, looking down into the small compartment. Folded papers, mini CDs, and a CD player were among some other little gadgets and trinkets. Mason had been telling the truth about the light above his bed and the hidden compartment at least.

He kneeled beside the compartment and pulled out a thick folded paper. It was the largest paper in the compartment which captured his attention. When he unfolded it, what looked like a three dimensional print of the compound's architecture was on it. All three floors, and the room below where Elliot and Mason were being held, were included in the print. The stairwell was also included and connected to the stairwell was another room. Strangely a large area outside the compound connected to the stairwell resembled train tracks on the print. There weren't any text so he didn't know for sure, but the area was narrow like a tunnel and ran the length of the compound or more. He couldn't be precise because it trailed off the paper.

Adam scratched his head. What did train tracks have to do with the compound? Was that their way out, the alternate exit Mason spoke about?

He continued to study the print. He wasn't quite sure how to get to the long tunnel from where he was no matter how much he looked at it. It was somehow connected to the stairwell. The second and third floors of the place were much bigger and elaborate. Many of the rooms had several rooms within it, like small studios. Adam stood and hastily made his way back to the mini refrigerator, took out a cold beer and popped it open with the bottle opener hanging on the hook beside it. He took a long swig, downing most of the carbonated liquid. His nerves calmed almost immediately. "God, that's good." He sat the bottle on top of the fridge and went back to the compartment in the bathroom.

Adam reached for a CD, glancing at the ring on his finger. Mason had given him his ring, telling him it was a key of some sort. What would it unlock? Adam cleared his mind and examined the CDs.

The black ink of the handwritten label caught his attention. It read: Compound 6, Hollywood, CA. He shuffled through the others, reading the titles. Compound 2, Denver, CO. Compound 5, Salt Lake City, UT. Compound 1, Santa Fe, NM.

Adam took the mini CD player, popped the last disc into it, and pressed play. He listened.

"December 20... This is profess...Bernard logging in from compound one, Santa Fe, New..." Most of the recorded message was cut off by static,

making some parts indiscernible. "*Our crew did...study of the falling matter and has concluded that it is mostly pulverized rock...changed slightly in its molecular structure by the intense heat of impact, turning...crushed, light-weight glass-like material, making it slightly tacky. ...are too big to be inhaled into the lungs but can possibly cause serious harm if ingested.*"

Adam fast forwarded the recording, then played it again.

"*...going as planned and aids don't suspect.... We found a difference in the way they respond to messages. To make...aids stay obedient, it's best to begin a directive with compassion. I...thanking them for their corporation triggers a need for them to cooperate and make them feel as though they have contributed. ...recommend stating a brief thank you before every announcement no matter how trivial.*"

Adam pressed stop on the player. He ejected the disc and stared at it. What did he just hear? It sounded very manipulative. "Didn't like *that.*" Quickly, he dug around the compartment and found two other disc labeled: Compound 4, Las Vegas, NV and Compound 3, Phoenix, AZ. Quickly, knowing time was of the essence, he popped the Phoenix disc into the player and listened.

"*Eugene Edmund here, logging in from compound three, Phoenix, Arizona, first week of December.*" As Adam listened to the recording he realized the voice didn't break up like the others and he also noticed the person speaking was not Eugene. It's was the voice of a man who spoke slower, pronouncing his words clearly, and the voice itself was hefty and gravelly. Nothing like how Eugene sounded.

"*The compound's exits are to be sealed in approximately one week, we have acquired all the aids we need and will move forward. We have encountered our first miscalculation. We have a significant number of domestic animals accompanying our aids and realized we will not be able to accommodate them. Action has been taken and the problem should be completely resolved within a few weeks.*"

To hear the man refer to the compound residence as aids and mention their pets made Adam shudder. It was very weird to hear all those things and try to put it all together. Were he and the other residents the aids they referred to? And were they called that because they were contributing to the compound? And to keep them contributing they thanked them before each announcement? Were they part of some experiment on the human behavior of some sort? It all seemed pretty manipulative for a place that supposedly ran on trust.

He wanted to hear more but knew he needed to hurry. He randomly opened folded papers, skimming through them for anything that might be helpful. Most of them were important-looking letters from NASA specialists and engineers, some were signed by Eugene others looked like transcripts, but they all were too wordy and technical to make anything out of them in his haste. However, at the bottom of the compartment was a small, square plastic badge with a picture like some sort of identification card. The name typed on it was Eugene Byron Edmund but the picture beside the name was not Eugene's, it was of an older black man with deep wrinkles and rimless glasses on his nose.

Who was this man? Adam stared at the picture, thinking. What was going on? He closed his eyes, scratched his head, and still couldn't get to the bottom of it all. Then it settled in. Elliot's and Mason's words sounded in his ears.

Elliot's worried blinking eyes popped into mind just as Adam remembered them when Elliot said, *"Mason said he's a fraud."*

Mason agreeing with, *"He's not who he says he is."*

Adam felt like a fool. The whole time he was looking at, taking orders from, and believing in an imposter? That had to be the only explanation. If the guy wasn't a prophet, if he wasn't Eugene, then who was he and what was he up to? And more importantly, where was the real Eugene?

He turned the badge around, looking at a magnetic strip on the back that ran along the bottom. This must've been the keycard Mason was talking about. It obviously didn't belong to Mason. How did he get this stuff? Adam glanced around the bathroom. Did the apartment even belong to Mason? It could be since his security code was his birthday.

Adam put everything back into the compartment except the blueprint of the compound and the keycard. He stuck them both in the pocket inside of his shirt and left the bathroom. He had to make his way back to Elliot and tell him what he'd discovered. His mind was trying desperately to sort out everything that he almost forgot one critical thing he had heard on the recording. The part where Eugene stated they were sealing the exits. *Exits*...plural. There was definitely more than one exit. Could the tunnel with the railroad be one of them?

"People of the compound ..." Adam jumped, lunging himself back against the wall as the announcement broke through the grate on the wall in front of him. No static, no crackling, the voice just came out of nowhere. *"It has come to my attention that some of you on the first floor are hearing strange sounds near the compound door. Rest assured, the sound is coming from an electrical grid within the steel. It is a mechanism that is securing the door and preventing the failure of the lock. It is a backup safety and is completely normal. Thank you for your corporation, please continue to keep this place in tip top shape."*

Someone got to him before Adam could. "Damn it, Damn it, Damn." Adam went to the door and peaked out of the peephole. The only thing in his sight was the atrium. The woman who had been reading her book wasn't out there anymore. They knew he wasn't where he was supposed to be, because he was supposed to notify Eugene about the sounds coming from the door and he never did.

Adam felt a bead of sweat drip down the back of his neck. He took a calming deep breath and opened the door.

Quickly, without looking, he closed the door behind him and rushed around the corner, bumping into a woman who carried a box of laundry detergent that fell onto the floor from her arms.

Adam quickly kneeled, picking up the large box. "Sorry. Are you okay?" He stood and looked directly into familiar eyes. Tami's bright dangling earrings took his attention briefly.

"Wha—what are you doing here?" Tami snatched the detergent from him. "You're an enforcer? What are you doing on my level?"

Adam looked down the hall, sudden paranoia hit him in the chest. "Sshh. Okay? Sshh." He quickly made his way down the nicely decorated corridor to the main room where the two men were still guarding the entrance to the stairwell.

"Stop right there!" one of them called out." He whistled and two enforcers ran from around the corner of one of the halls and came to an abrupt stop.

Adam didn't move. "What's going on?"

An enforcer grabbed the black baton from his own belt. "What are you doing down here?"

"I was sent to ... find some information for Eugene."

"Where're you coming from? I know you're not from here."

"The third floor."

"Let me see your key?"

Adam cleared his throat. He had two keys since he'd given one to Elliot but ... then it hit him. Jena's Hello Kitty necklace and Tami's sparkling earrings came to mind. He lifted his hand with the ring on it. Jewelry was one of the ways the guards and enforcers knew you belonged on the lower levels. Jewelry was their key.

"Where'd you get that? Who gave it to you?"

"What do you mean? This is mine. I always had this." For a person who had lied most of his life, the skill seemed to elude him now. He couldn't even make his lie sound believable.

"Put your hands behind your back."

"Listen, guys—"

"No, you listen and do what I say. Put your fucking hands behind your back." The enforcer stepped forward, still gripping the baton. "I know you're not running errands for the prophet and I know you don't stay on the third floor because the prophet is on the third floor and he's looking for you himself."

Adam put his hands behind his back. "I didn't do anything—"

"Didn't I say listen?" The enforcer swung the baton and connected it to Adam's left knee. "I never said talk. So shut up."

Adam grimaced and dropped to the floor. He grunted in pain as the man cuffed his hands behind his back.

"Stand up and shut up or you're getting another one." He unclipped Adam's belt, taking away his handcuffs, pepper spray, and baton, his only defense. "Now come on."

CHAPTER ELEVEN

Confronting the Truth

Eugene opened his room door to him and the two enforcers behind him. "Well, well, well. Look who's finally decided to come and visit. On the sofa." He nodded his head toward the spacious living area. One of the guards pushed sharply at Adam's shoulder, causing him to stumble over his own feet as he entered the large room.

"Sit." The enforcer shoved him toward the sofa and Adam fell down onto the plush cushions.

Eugene paced in front of the large bookcase that took up the entire wall. "Where did you find him?"

The enforcer threw his thumb back. "On the second floor."

"Now what were you doing on the second floor?" Eugene paused, eyes fixed on Adam's as he waited for an answer.

"Exploring."

Eugene scoffed. "I assume you missed your childhood when your mommy let you go exploring the neighborhood with your magnifying glass? Exploring? What were you looking for, Adam?"

When Adam didn't respond the enforcer stepped forward. "He was coming out of Pod 1."

Eugene continued to pace with one arm tucked behind his back and the other rubbing his chin. "What's in Pod 1 that could be so interesting? Hmm." After a moment, he looked to the guards. "Send someone to look in on Mason and the other prisoner below, quickly.

Chain them both to the wall in their cell and report back to me. Go on."

He lifted a shelf on the bookcase and pulled out a black handgun. "You," he waved the handgun at the other enforcer, "stand guard outside of my room. I can take care of myself in the meantime."

As soon as the enforcer left the room, leaving Adam and Eugene alone, Adam situated himself on the sofa and sneered. "Who are you?"

"I was generous enough to save your ass. What are you and Mason up to?"

"I'm not answering any of your questions till you answer me." Adam sat back, hands cuffed behind his back, he relaxed letting his thighs fall apart. He glared. "I know you're not Eugene, the real Eugene Edmond. What'd you do to him and what are you up to? Is this some kind of social experiment or something? Determining how people react in certain situation after a catastrophe, right? You got rid of the real Eugene. Why?"

Eugene laughed. "Social experiment? Kid, you watch too many science fiction movies." He held the gun gingerly by his side with his finger lightly placed on the trigger. "Really, it's much simpler than that. I call it providing the right contribution for your secure future."

"Yeah, I know all about that."

"You know nothing."

"Don't tell me anything. I don't give a fuck. Just get me out of these cuffs and let me out of this place." Adam slid forward on the sofa to stand up when Eugene lifted the gun, pointing it directly at his face.

"You're going to sit down. It's not the first time I used this gun and it won't be the last." Adam sat back on the sofa, eyeing the gun. He'd never had a gun pointed at him before, and looking down the barrel made him realize how serious the situation was. "I liked you, Adam. I trusted you. You failed me. Just like Eugene, the real Eugene." He went to the trophy wall on the other side of the room. "You see this?" He pointed the gun to the NASA emblem on one of the plaques, with a white line encircling a red arrow-like symbol. "You know what this represents? The red wing represents aeronautics and then there's a spacecraft orbiting around the wing. Looks familiar? It was Eugene's idea to make the Refuge Inc. logo resemble that of his other great accomplishments, incorporating the NASA insignia. Wanting to represent humanity wrapped in refuge. Hell, he even came up with the name Refuge Inc. It was all about him. Except it wasn't. It was a team effort. He had forgotten that, so Mason took care of him."

"Mason killed him?"

Eugene shrugged. "So you *are* working with Mason. I should've known somehow he'd get what he wanted. Did he send you to kill me? Were you supposed to gain my trust and then slit my throat? What did he promise you, freedom and sunshine? Well, there isn't any sunshine."

"You're full of shit. The skies are clear out there, aren't they?"

He stepped forward raising the gun. "Where's your weapon?"

"Just let us out of here."

"Where's your weapon?!"

"I don't have a weapon. I'm not gonna kill anybody. That's not what I do. I just want out of here."

"You think I'm just going to open the door and let you out into the perfect world, sunshine and rainbows?" He shook his head. "Mason is lying to you. It's ridiculous that you believe a manipulative murderer. There's no sun out there. It's hiding behind the dark, dense clouds."

"Let me see for myself."

"You're not leaving. You have a contribution to fulfill." He paced back and forth in front of the trophy wall. "No, you're not here for a social experiment, Adam. You are here as part of a deal I made with my investors. Nine-eleven was a couple buildings and it changed everything. This cataclysm is the whole west coast of the US. The entire world is affected. The investors give me money, they get a replica of their home built here safely away from apocalyptic devastation. Give me millions and get your very own peace of mind in the days after a catastrophe. It's like nothing's ever happened. And as a bonus, we'll save a few outsiders, give them a standard room and eventually have them guard our homes, clean our toilets and run our errands after they're conditioned. So much simpler than mad science experiments."

"And it's all accomplished with a 'thank you for cooperating'." Adam shook his head, disgusted. "I guess I was being conditioned too, huh? Is my promotion part of the conditioning?"

He shrugged, a smug look plastered across his face. "Hmm."

"You're not the only one taking advantage of scared and desperate people. There's other places like this, with people like you all around the west coast, sending messages to each other, helping each other manipulate these poor people. This won't last. You all will be caught and put away for this."

"We're not doing anything illegal. Plus, it lasts for as long as it needs to. Until we're able to live life normally on the outside again. Not forever."

Adam scoffed. "You're holding people against their will. You're misleading people into thinking their lives are in danger when they're not. You—"

"Their lives are in danger from the toxins outside and everyone's here because they want to be. Everyone. You all walked in here, you all knew we were going to close the door, and you all stayed, watching it close. I saved you. All of you. How about a goddamned 'thank you' around here for once."

"How about a fuck you. Now get me out of these cuffs." Even though the enforcers took his belt with his pair of handcuffs, pepper spray and baton attached to it, they didn't search him. He still had his handcuff key in his back pocket. He changed positions, discretely digging his fingers as far into his back pocket as possible, not quite reaching the key.

Eugene continued to pace in front of his trophy wall. "If I let you go, you'll tell everyone what's going on and cause major problems for us. This project is too valuable for that to happen. I can't let you go, Adam. You understand."

Adam felt the hard metal on the tip of his finger. "So what are you gonna do?" His fingernail gripped an edge and he pulled the key higher. "Kill me?" The key was just at the lip of his pocket.

"Stand up," Eugene pointed the gun at him again. "Get over there." He waved the gun toward the bookcase. "I don't want to ruin my sofa with your blood."

Adam leaned forward to stand. The key flipped from his pocket and graze his hand as it fell beneath his bottom. "You can't do this."

"Move it!" Eugene shouted, taking Adam off guard. He quickly stood, hands behind his back, wrist hurting and probably bruised. He kept his eyes on Eugene's and watched in horror as Eugene's eyes moved to the seat cushion. "What's that? A key? You had a key. Step back." He growled.

Adam took a couple steps back. Quickly, Eugene moved forward to grab the handcuff key from the seat cushion, at the same time Adam rushed forward and kicked the gun from his hand. The gun went through the air hitting the back wall. Before Eugene could react, Adam rushed him using his body weight and his shoulder to knock him on the ground. Eugene squirmed, trying to catch his breath as Adam's shoulder connected with his gut. While on the floor, Eugene reached toward the gun that lay a couple feet away from him on the carpeted floor. Adam kicked the gun to the other side of the room where it bounced off the corner of an end table and disappeared under one of the plush chairs.

Adam quickly sat on the edge of the cushion and grabbed the key. He stood, desperately trying to find the lock by feeling for it with his fingertips. Eugene gasped and crawled on his hands and knees toward the door. He took one deep breath. "Guards!"

The key slipped in the lock of the handcuffs and clicked when he turned it. His hand slipped free and Adam dropped to the ground, quickly searching under the sofa for the handgun. From under the sofa he saw Eugene scramble to his feet. "Guards. Get in here," he coughed, "now."

Adam saw the dark mass near the leg of the sofa and grabbed it. He stood and pointed the hefty handgun at Eugene's back. "Don't move. I'll pull the trigger. I swear."

Eugene stopped in his tracks and the door in front of him swung open.

An enforcer stood on the other side of the door. The same one ordered to stand guard. His eyes bugged at the sight of the gun and his hands flew up in front of him. "Don't do it," he pleaded. "I have a daughter here. She has no one to take care of her."

"Get in and lock the door." Adam kept the gun pointed at them. The handcuffs dangled from his bruised wrist. He never held a gun before. It was heavier than he thought it would be, and the handle fit his hand perfectly. Power and nervousness surged through him at the same time. "Take your belt off and toss it over."

The enforcer unclipped his belt and tossed it, throwing it a few feet behind Eugene and directly in front of Adam. The baton, pepper spray and a pair of handcuffs were still attached. He quickly picked up the belt and the handcuff key from the floor.

"Where's your bedroom at in here?" Adam looked to Eugene. "I want you both in there. And don't do anything crazy. I *will* pull this trigger."

Eugene moved toward the bookcase, the enforcer and Adam followed at a comfortable distance. "You're making a big mistake trusting Mason." Eugene flipped a switch inside the bookcase and the entire wall shifted, revealing a narrow gap. Eugene pushed the bookcase and it moved easily, opening into a beautiful room with a massive bed and wooden headboard.

"Have a seat near the headboard." Adam took the cuff off of his own wrist and the set from the belt, watching the men sit on the bed next to the headboard as he instructed. "Tie yourselves to the headboard." He tossed each of them a set of handcuffs. "Give me your key for the cuffs, enforcer." He wasn't going to forget to get the enforcer's key like they forgot to take his.

"He's full of lies," Eugene warned as he clicked one cuff to his wrist and the other to the thick wooden bars on the headboard. "Whatever he's told you, don't believe it. He'd say and do anything to have me dead. I know that now."

"And why is that?" Adam kept the gun pointed at Eugene.

"We had made a monetary arrangement for him getting rid of Eugene. Yes. But after it was done things didn't go as smooth when he somehow found out about my dwindling financial situation. He, uh ... he started saying things, hinting at how he could do a better job than me at running this place. Little did I know, until it was almost too late, he was planning on taking me out and *forcing* people into doing what we needed done instead of letting them evolve to our liking."

"Evolve? You guys are sick. This is nothing short of kidnapping what you got going on here."

"We're not forcing people to do anything. They're making the decision themselves. They have free will."

"Influenced by your manipulation. That's not free will. We're getting out of here. I'm gonna expose what this place really is and then people will choose to leave. How bout that?"

"I'm not going to open that door. I'll die before I open it. I'm providing a service. People can't adapt to drastic change without changing themselves. They'll never make it out there. We need this place to continue living."

"You need this place to continue living *comfortably.* Admit it, it's all about you. That's what you're getting out of the deal. Wealthy people pay to help build this place, in return they get a spot here and you get to live like the world out there isn't going to shit, right? You, Mason, the real Eugene, and all the other leaders in the other compounds are nothing but selfish, greedy assholes."

"Call me whatever you like, Adam. I'm not going to open that door. I'm providing a service."

"We'll just leave using the other way out."

"Mason's lying to you. There's no other way out. If you think you can get out through the old mining tunnel you're wrong. We blew that tunnel to a pile of rubble a month ago while we were still gathering people. It was too risky leaving it exposed to invasion from the outside. There's only so much room in here."

"I don't trust either of you. I'd rather see for myself."

Eugene scoffed. "I should've had Mason taken out when I had the chance. Instead, I thought letting him starve was a better punishment, slow and painful. You can tell him I said that, by the way."

After obtaining the key from the enforcer and making sure he and Eugene were indeed locked to the bed securely, Adam turned to leave the room.

"Adam," Eugene called out. "I'm not a monster. Mason could rot in hell, but everyone else ... I'm doing them a favor. I've given them a chance to live. You hear me? I saved their lives."

Adam didn't respond, he said nothing as he stepped out of the room and pushed the switch on the bookcase till it closed, trapping the men inside.

CHAPTER TWELVE

Hide and Seek

Elliot fumbled with the key. "It has to have been more than an hour now, right?"

"I said that probably an hour ago." Mason slipped on his jacket. "Now let's get out of here."

"Wait. What's the plan?"

Mason frowned. "The plan?"

"Yeah, we need a plan." Elliot fingered the key. "We can't just go out there and demand someone to tell us where Adam is and take us to the exit."

"A plan. Okay. First, we're gonna get out of these cells. Then we're gonna go wait for Adam and the keycard in the storage room."

"A storage room? Let's just wait here. We're less likely to get caught."

"If they already caught Adam, they probably already know our plan. You think the guards are just sitting around, leaving us alone down here so we can escape? No. They're going to try and stop us before we get too far. That means we have to move now."

"How is hiding out in a storage room gonna help us?"

"It's not just any storage room. Where do you think they hold all the necessities, food and tools for everyone? You're going to have to start using your head if you want to get somewhere."

"So now you're calling me stupid?"

"See, now you're thinking. Yes, you *are* stupid if you think you can just sit here, wait for guards to come, and still believe you're getting out of this place."

"I'm just thinking about not worsening the situation by being caught outside of our cells. If the worse did happen and Adam got caught at least we weren't caught doing anything wrong."

"And they will just leave us here alone for who knows how long to allow us to escape? It's not going to work like that, Elliot. We have to leave now while we still have a chance, and hide out in the storage room."

"The only reason you're pushing for us to go to the storage room is because that's our way out, huh?"

"See what happens when you think?" Mason shook his head. "Yes, that's our way out. We can try to jimmy the lock until Adam comes. If he comes."

"And if he doesn't come?"

"Hopefully we can override the damn lock somehow, I don't know. We have to try something. Now open these damn doors."

Elliot reached through the bars and blindly searched for the keyholes to slip the key in. Adam unlocked the first lock. So when the key turned in the second lock and clicked he grew anxious. His hands shook as he unlocked the third lock and swung the door open. "Oh, my God. I did it."

Mason sighed. "Remind me to give you a gold star later. Open my door and hurry."

Elliot quickly unlocked the locks on Mason's door, and Mason bolted out toward the exit. "Wait. We have to be—"

"Stealthy, I know. Follow me." Mason opened the door to the stairwell, and quickly pressed in the small round light on the wall beside the door. Seconds later, the elevator door recessed and slid opened.

"Oh, shit. A secret elevator?"

"Give me the key." Mason stepped inside the elevator and held out his hand. Elliot dropped the key into Mason's palm and stepped inside the elevator too. Mason slipped the key inside the keyhole below the four round buttons with the red R and silver halo. He turned the key but nothing happened. "Fuck!"

"What? What's wrong?"

"This is the wrong key. Damn it."

"So what does that mean?"

Mason sighed. Visibly annoyed and using a mocking voice he said, "When I turn the key it's supposed to close the elevator door and take us to a really big room called the storage where exit number two is located."

"Okay, you don't have to treat me like some dummy. Alright? Is there another way to get there?"

Mason stared at him. "If there was another way why would I be so upset about this way not working?"

"Okay. Okay." Elliot huffed, putting up a dismissive hand.

"No, answer me. Please. You'd think ... well, not *you* particularly because you don't think, but *one* would think if there was another way to get to the storage I would've just gone that way instead of cursing in defeat, right?"

"You are such an asshole." Elliot sneered.

"Yeah, and to think we have someone like you running this place. Dumb as a box of nails."

"Asshole."

"You know what's funny. This place is a disaster waiting to happen but it hasn't happened yet. I'm dumbfounded. Security for this place is a joke, nothing was planned properly. Guards weren't trained, they don't even have weapons. They installed an elevator but no phones because they thought it'll somehow give away the technology this place had. There are so many flaws with this place. Frankly, I'm surprised we made it this long because the guy in charge knows nothing about leadership. He just wants everyone to worship him like some pompous god. That's all he's about, and that's what almost killed him too."

"So, you tried to kill him because he's arrogant—"

"He should've been dead long time ago. He's gonna run this place into the ground."

"If the dark clouds are gone and the sun is shining out there, why is he keeping us in here, lying about it taking years before the conditions out there clear up? What do you know?"

"You all are dumb sheep. That's what I know."

Elliot moved forward, stiffening his back and shoulders. "Tell me what you know."

Mason chuckled. "What are you gonna do, tough guy?"

Elliot grabbed Mason's wrist and twisted it until Mason turned. He pinned his wrist high on Mason back. "Tell me—"

"My shoulder, you asshole. That's my bad arm, you fuck." Mason struggled but Elliot pressed his body against him, using his weight to pin him against the wall of the elevator.

"Why is he keeping us locked in here? Why the lies?"

"He made promises to the investors, okay? Let me go."

"That's not good enough, Mason. Tell me what's going on!" He pushed Mason's wrist higher between his shoulder blades.

Mason grunted in pain. "You're their aids. You guys'll eventually do all the dirty work for them if you're not already."

"What? You mean like slaves?"

"Slaves, help, aids, whatever you want to call it."

"Aids for who? The prophet?"

"For the rich guys on the bottom floors. The investors of this place. They're still living their lives as if nothing ever happened." Mason grunted again and Elliot let him go. He grabbed his injured shoulder and grimaced. "They're making sure you guys live in conditions next to hell to keep you desperate so they can make you do whatever they want you to do without a fight. They're training you. They call it 'evolving'. Eugene and a few other scientists knew the asteroid fragments would hit the west coast, so they opened a firm targeting the wealthy, promising the investors peace of mind for their contributions. Refuge Inc. investors get peace-of-mind in return. But no one except the folks behind Refuge Inc. knows about the sunshine outside."

"Why stay in the west coast? Why not set up shop in a safer place away from the asteroid fragments?"

"The whole world isn't safe. Trade, food supply, gas, oil, everything's affected all over the world. Plus, they needed the guise of the apocalypse. Without the feel of Hell on Earth they had no urgency and definitely no desperate survivors looking for help wherever they can get it. They took a risk. For most of the compounds, it paid off."

"Huh?"

"This isn't the only compound. There're six up and down the west coast one in California, Texas, Utah ... the Nevada one didn't last too long but—"

"This is crazy." Elliot rubbed his temples, pacing inside the elevator. "We gotta tell everyone."

"You'd cause a riot and only make it worse. The less people who know the truth, the better chance we have of getting out of here."

"We can't just leave them without even telling them what's going on out there." He couldn't just leave Anita behind either. He owed her the truth, a chance to get out of there at least. That was all he could give her now to make up for his faults anyway. "Maybe we'd have a better chance if everyone was trying to get out of this place at the same time. Maybe if we demand they open the door they'll let us out to avoid riots."

"Maybe not—"

The elevator door suddenly slid closed.

"Shit. What's going on?" Elliot looked at the buttons on the panel. The third button was lit. "Someone from the third floor is calling the elevator."

"It has to be guards or enforcers. They're the only ones who know about the elevator."

"When the door opens let's take 'em." Elliot stared at the door, getting into position. Out of the corner of his eye he saw Mason readying himself too. Seconds later the elevator shifted slightly as it came to a stop. "Ready?"

The elevator door opened and the enforcer on the other side stood surprised. His eyes were wide as he took a step back and reached for the canister of pepper spray on his belt. Elliot grabbed him in a bear hug while Mason pulled the baton from the enforcer's belt and hit him over the head with it. His body became dead weight in Elliot's arms. He pulled him into the elevator before letting him slide to the floor. "What was that about?"

Mason shrugged, "Sorry?" and pushed the button for the bottom floor. "Get the handcuffs off of his belt before he wakes up." Mason grabbed the pepper spray and tucked it in his jacket pocket.

When the door opened on the bottom floor, Elliot unlocked the door that led into the room with the cells. He dragged the enforcer's body to the cell Mason had occupied. They lay him on the cement floor and locked his wrist to the bar with the handcuffs.

"Dig in his pocket for the keys," Mason ordered.

Elliot shook his head but searched anyway. He pulled the set of three brass keys out of his pants pocket and the little silver key for the cuffs. "Found them. Let's go."

Quickly, they locked the enforcer inside the cell and left the dark, loud room. The elevator opened as soon as they called for it and they rushed inside.

Elliot put one of the keys into the keyhole, turned it but nothing happened as before. "Fuck. Are these the right keys?" He fumbled with the keys, they jingled as he picked a second one and slid it in the keyhole. This time he turned the key and the elevator door closed. He laughed. "It worked."

"Good." Mason exhaled and nodded. It'll take us to the storage room."

"But what about everyone on the first floor?"

"We been through this."

"We can't just leave them. I have a friend up there. We gotta get her." Elliot pressed the top button on the panel and felt a sudden shift as the elevator stopped.

"What are you doing?" Mason reached for the set of keys that remained in the keyhole below the buttons, but Elliot grabbed them first. "We gotta go while we have the chance." The elevator shifted and began to move again, probably toward the top floor.

"I can't leave my friend." Elliot shoved Mason back. "I owe her."

"You're gonna get us fucking caught, Elliot. This will all be for nothing."

"We'll expose them and flip this place on its head. Everyone would rush the guards and enforcers and—"

Mason rushed forward, grabbing Elliot by the collar of his shirt. "You're fucking up our chance. Now give me the key."

The elevator door opened, revealing the top floor landing in the dim stairwell. "Stay on the elevator," Elliot said. "Keep it moving so no one can use it. Give me ten minutes, okay?"

Mason let him go. "I can't believe you're doing this." He reached into his pocket and pulled out the pepper spray. "Here take this. You're gonna need it."

Elliot grabbed it and placed it in his breast pocket. "Keep that baton, you're gonna need it too. He left the elevator. "Ten minutes."

Mason pressed a button and the elevator door closed. Elliot took a deep breath and pushed the door open, entering the main room. He was headed toward the cafeteria when the guards stopped him. "Hey, where you think you're going?"

Elliot didn't even look back as he ran down the hall toward the buzzing cafeteria. He went to the counter to look for Anita. With all eyes on him he quickly picked up a ladle to look busy.

Anita emerged from the kitchen and waved him into the dining area. "Hey. How's everything? They finally let you out?"

He kept a straight face. "That's what I came to talk to you about. We need to get out of here now. I don't have a lot of time."

Dirty pots and pans filled the sinks behind him, the smell of raw onion lingered in the air. She cocked her head. "We need to get out of here? What's going on?"

Elliot glanced over his shoulder and whispered, "This place is not what it seems. They're trying to make us slaves. They killed Titan. The prophet is not really a prophet and—"

"Wait. Hold on. Breathe, Elliot. What do you mean?"

Before Elliot could get another word out, commotion in the cafeteria caught him off guard. He turned to see a handful of enforcers and guards behind him. He put his hands in the air.

"You." An enforcer pointed to him with his baton. "Get down on the floor. Now."

The enforcers moved around him, some with batons in their fists, one holding a set of handcuffs and another with his hands on his pepper spray canister. The people in the cafeteria paused and all eyes were on him as if he was the lead of some bizarre performance.

"We have to get out of here." Elliot put his hands up to show he meant no harm, but he had to tell everyone the truth. He had to give them a chance. "They're locking us in here for no reason. There's no threat outside. There's no more toxic debris falling from the sky. The sun is shining. The world isn't shit out there anymore. We can go out now."

"Is that true?" Anita's eyes widen with hope as she brought her hand to her multicolored head wrap.

"It's true. They're only keeping us in here as aids for them. There're a lot of them downstairs, they're rich, they're happy, they don't have to live in these conditions eating bologna and onion soup. They're only making us eat it to condition us, to make us desperate so they can mold us into anything—"

"That's enough!" The enforcer stepped closer. "Get on the ground."

The enforcer beside him nodded. "This is the guy we locked away below for fighting, you remember that?"

"Well, son of a bitch. How'd you get out?"

Everyone watched Elliot. Low mumbles and sudden curiosity filled the cafeteria. He had no choice but to stick with his plans. "We can get out of here, guys. All of us. We don't have to live like this."

A tall, thin man stood from his table. "What's so wrong with this place? I like it here."

"Yeah." Another man at the same table lifted his hand. "I like it here too. Beats trying to find food and shelter out there."

A younger woman, standing near the food line stepped forward. "If there's really sunlight out there like you said, I'd rather try my luck out there." She looked around at the others. "The announcements are wrong. We can go out and get fresh air and feel the heat of the sun."

A woman stood from her meal. "Nobody's done anything bad to me. At least in here I know I'm safe and taken care of."

Elliot frowned. "But don't you have family out there? People looking for you?"

"My family's dead. There's nothing left out there for me. Not even sunshine will lift my spirits now."

A young man in the back of the room yelled, "I have family out there and I want to find them."

Almost immediately the cafeteria buzzed with outbursts directed toward him. In unison people called out, barely audible above one another.

"We like it here."

"Open the door!"

"This is the only family I have now."

"I want out of here."

He'd thought he heard enough, when rushing around the corner Mason and Adam appeared. They both were dressed in enforcer uniforms except Adam was missing his belt and Mason was missing handcuffs, pepper spray and a shoe.

"What's going on?" Adam said loud enough to be heard over the roaring crowd.

The enforcer pointed his baton at Elliot. "We think he's escaped from below. Now he's getting everybody all riled up talking about leaving."

Mason fidgeted with the baton, almost unsteady on his feet with nervousness. "Here, we'll take him back down."

"Wait, wait, wait." One of the guards stepped toward Adam. "Adam, what are you doing?"

Adam put his hand up, stopping him from getting any closer. "Joe, this isn't the time."

"This is the perfect time." Joe pointed to Elliot. "Isn't this the guy from below, your friend you been wanting to see? You were asking me if I had keys so you can go see him. What are you up to?"

He clenched his teeth. "Shut the fuck up, Joe."

Joe raised his voice. "You caused a bunch of shit earlier, blaming us for stealing your fucking brandy that you hid under your mattress. You knew damn well that bottle was there. You put it there."

Adam tried to interrupt. "Not now."

Joe continued. "He got into a fight with Joel and then later Joel noticed his keys were missing. You took his keys and let this criminal out, didn't you?"

"Damn it, Joe." Adam rushed forward, but Mason stopped him with a hand on his chest.

"Both of you," the enforcer looked to Adam and pointed to Elliot, "get on the ground now. Or I'll take you down with pepper spray then beat the bloody hell outta you." One hand held the baton but the other went for the canister on his belt.

Mason's eyes grew big and he shouted, "Elliot, your pocket."

Quickly, Elliot reached into his breast pocket, pulled out the canister, and pointed it in the enforcers' direction as he pressed the nozzle. A steady stream of clear liquid spewed from the canister hitting most of the men in the face. In no time, Mason swung his baton and connected it with Joe's temple, while Adam pushed an enforcer into two others who were stumbling over each other, coughing and rubbing their eyes from the burning spray.

"Go. Run." Adam made sure the enforcers were incapacitated before joining Elliot, Mason and Anita in their sprint down the hall. Mason led and Anita kept close, following Elliot.

"Is the door open?" she asked, still running behind Elliot. "Is that where we're going?"

"No." He glanced behind his shoulder at her. "But we know another way out."

"What about my friend Tami? I should tell her what's going on. She needs to come with us."

Adam's footsteps grew closer behind Elliot. "Your friend knows what's going on. She's an investor. Not sure if the investors know it cleared up outside though."

"Huh? What does that mean?" Anita paused at the end of the hall before entering the main room. "She'd never do anything wrong.

And she tells me everything. If she knew something crazy was happening here she'd tell me."

Adam placed a hand on her shoulder, catching his breath. "Everyone on the floors below live in beautiful, spacious apartment-like homes. Everyone. Isn't that where Tami stays?" Before Anita could answer, Adam continued. "I ran into her and she was carrying laundry soap with her. We don't even use laundry soap on the first floor. People down there are reading chapter books in an atrium full of live plants, herbs or something. They're wearing regular bright white clothes." He frowned. "I'm sorry but your friend knows what you're going through up here. Some people you just can't trust." He cut an eye to Mason then back to Anita.

A look of disappointment flashed across her face and she bowed her head. "I knew this place was no good. I knew it. I felt it. Didn't I say something was going on in this place?" She looked to Elliot.

Elliot looked around the corner into the main room and toward the stairwell. "Looks like we have another problem."

They entered the main room where more guards stood in front of the stairwell door about thirty feet away from where they stood, preventing them from going near it. As they stood in the main room, which connected all six corridors, Elliot saw a woman in light green scrubs standing in the middle of the hall watching them, the hall leading to the medical station.

CHAPTER THIRTEEN

On the Run

Adam looked down the hall where he saw her, nearly jogging, quickly moving closer. "Adam," she called. "What are you doing? What's going on?"

"I'm leaving, Jena. We're leaving."

Jena came closer, standing no more than a couple feet away from him. Looking at the guards who were in a combat stance, preparing for a fight. "You can't leave. Are you crazy?"

Elliot stepped closer. He looked intrigued by the woman who had captured Adam's heart for so many years. He glanced back and forth from her belly to where a baby was supposed to be but wasn't, to her face where her eyes were smeared with dark makeup that had run over her lower eyelids.

Adam had never noticed her eye makeup until now.

One of the guards shouted. "Get on the floor, all of you!"

Elliot looked to Adam, then to Jena. He gestured, waving a hand. "Come with us."

She scoffed. "I'm not going anywhere with any of you."

Elliot stepped back, frowning. "You don't have to be here. This place is a sham."

"She knows." Adam interrupted. Her Hello Kitty necklace was still visible around her neck. "She knows all about it. That necklace was your key to the floors below, right?"

"Get on the floor now. Right now." The guards slowly crept forward.

"Either you're coming with us or you're staying." Adam held out his hand for her to take it. "Last chance."

Mason raised his baton. "They're getting closer." He warned urgently.

Jena steeped back. A look of disgust swept her face as she looked back and forth between Adam and Elliot. "Go to hell. Both of you. Go to hell were you belong."

Elliot sneered at her remark. Adam just shook his head. "Good luck, Jena." He nodded at Mason and at Elliot who still had the canister of pepper spray in his hand. He looked to Anita. "Let's get outta here."

Adam reached down into the pocket on the side of his pants and pulled out the handgun he had taken from Eugene. He had no intention to use it, just to scare the guards into moving back. But instead of scaring them, the guards rushed them, foiling his plan. Mason, Elliot and Anita ran forward and bodies collided. Batons and fists flew through the air. Shouts and commands were ignored. Adam pushed and punched the guard who was trying to knock him to the ground. Suddenly the room grew louder as he heard the lurid cries and shouts from the swarm of people approaching from behind them from the cafeteria. Within seconds, his eyes were watery and burning and everyone struggling in the crowd was coughing, trying to catch their breaths.

The P.A. broke out, and Eugene's voice sounded over the shouts from the speakers in the room.

"People of the compound. It has come to our attention that certain individuals are threatening to further endanger our lives and attempt to force open the compound door. Seeing these people behave so treasonous saddens me. We've put so much into giving you a good life. But in spite of all of my trying, a handful of our own people insist on putting your lives in danger.

They must be stopped. Adam Weber, Mason Dresden, and Elliot Stewart are the perpetrators and must be stopped. I count on you, the residents of the compound, to put an end to this betrayal by any means necessary. And thank you all for your cooperation."

Eugene had escaped. Adam believed he had thought everything through. Now he had to fight not only to escape but to protect his and Elliot's life from the people of the compound.

"Adam!" Elliot called from ahead. Adam wiped at his eyes to clear his blurry vision when a fist connected with his nose, further interfering with his sight. He felt the weight of several bodies pushing him off balance like a hyped crowd at a concert.

Behind him he could barely make out the mass of people, most of them scrub-wearing residents with anger in their nature. "Get them. Stop them. Kill them," many of them shouted. "Let us go. We want out. Open the door," others called out.

Adam felt a tug on his forearm. "Get down. They're spraying that damn pepper spray," Elliot said in his ear. "Follow me." He pulled Adam by his arm and led him to the door of the stairwell where guards stood, arms linked, making a barrier. "The door's opened. We just gotta get past all the people and on the other side of it."

Adam tried to talk but the urge to cough prevented him every time he opened his mouth to speak. Once in the front of the pushing, swaying mass of people Adam realized how brutal it was. Many men had fallen down and were struggling to get up. The pushing crowd made it difficult to do much of anything but lie there and shield themselves with their arms.

A small woman next to Adam grabbed his shoulder and shouted in his ear above the commotion. "Please, take me with you. My husband is still out there. I have to go find him. I'm begging you."

Elliot coughed. "Okay," he told the woman. "Stick with us, alright?"

"Thank you." The woman said. "Oh, God. Thank you."

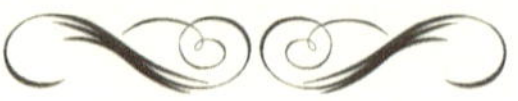

Elliot looked to his right. Mason swung his baton connecting it to one of the arm-linking guards gut, taking him down. Anita stayed behind Mason as the guard's barrier began to crumble. Mason gestured, fanning his wrist. "Let's go."

Elliot quickly followed Mason and Anita through the door, stepping over bodies and pulling Adam along. A handful of people broke through before them. They all ran down the long winding stairs toward the floor below, probably not aware of the elevator or even knowing where they were going, just trying to escape. Maybe they just wanted to get as far away from the chaos as they could. Maybe they wanted to see for themselves what lied below. Others tried to prevent them from fully entering the stairwell by pulling on their clothing and limbs, and pushing them back. Elliot and Adam pushed and shoved their way into the dim stairwell. Just as they crossed the fallen guards, a baton came out of nowhere and smashed the small, begging woman on her temple. She fell unconscious where she stood.

"Fuck!" Elliot yanked Adam toward the direction of the elevator and pressed the button to call the elevator while Mason and Anita fought to close the door and prevent any more people from entering the stairwell, including the guards. "Stay here since you can't see. I'll be back."

"Wait." Adam stopped him by pulling his shoulder. "Where are you going?"

"I need to get that woman. She's coming with us."

"No, it's too late." Adam rushed to the door, using his body weight to help it close. He rubbed his red, puffy eyes with his knuckles as he gripped the handle of the handgun. "You can't save her now."

Elliot shook his head vehemently. "She begged for our help. She wanted to leave."

Mason pushed the door with grunt. "Elliot, we tried. Okay? Shit. There's only so much we can do."

"He's right." Adam nodded.

Finally the elevator door opened. Surprisingly there was no one inside as he had expected. "Come on. Come on." Elliot stepped inside, and pulled the set of keys out of his pocket. Anita rushed inside and Mason followed. Elliot slid the key into the keyhole and turned it. The elevator door began to slide close. "Come on, Adam. Hurry."

Adam moved from the door and ran toward the elevator. Behind him, the stairwell door opened and a handful of bodies spewed forward, collapsing to the floor as the weight of the people behind them pushed them off balance.

Adam turned sideways and slid through the opening of the elevator door, crashing into Elliot right before it closed.

"You okay?" Elliot held onto to Adam's shoulders, looking into his red and irritated eyes.

"I'm alright." Adam nodded, leaning against the wall. "Damn pepper spray."

Elliot felt the subtle shift as the elevator began to move.

Mason took a deep breath and exhaled loudly. "Okay, it should take us to the second floor. Then it'll automatically connect to a separate track that'll take us across and up to the storage room." He looked over to Anita who was breathing heavy with wide eyes. "You must be a really good friend."

She shrugged. "What's that mean?"

"Me and Elliot were just about to get to the storage room and sneak right out of here unbeknownst to anyone when he had a change of heart."

"Alright, Mason." Elliot felt his cheeks heat up from embarrassment.

Mason grinned. "He just couldn't leave his friend in this place. He had to go rescue her from this hell hole."

Anita met Elliot's eyes. "Thank you."

"That's the least I can do." Elliot smiled. He turned to Adam. "Where did you come from? We thought they had caught you or something."

"They did but they couldn't keep me." The handgun dangled from his fingers at his side. "Took the gun from Eugene after he tried to shoot me with it. But I got the keycard and the blueprint of this place too."

Mason sniffed, wiping his nose with the back of his hand. "Yeah, as soon as you got off on the first floor, I went down to get our enforcer friend's clothes from the cell. On the way down, I ran into Adam trying to use the elevator to find us. After telling him everything, we went up to get you."

"I didn't trust you." Adam nodded toward Mason, pulling the wedding band from his finger and handing it back to Mason. "Eugene said not to trust you."

"I don't trust anyone." Mason shrugged and tucked the ring in his pocket. "Never have. But we're gonna have to trust each other if we're gonna get out of this place."

"True." Adam nodded.

"An elevator? What else do they have up their sleeve?" Anita crouched down, removing her head wrap that was nearly falling off on its own. "It's about time I get out of this place. I knew when I heard the announcement about the pets that this place was full of shit."

Elliot frowned. "Sorry about Charlie, by the way. I tried to find him for you or at least get some answers for you, but—"

"I understand why you lied to us, Elliot." Anita stood, folding her head wrap enough to stuff it in her pocket. "I probably would've done the same to save the person I loved." She met Adam's stare. "I don't blame you. I forgive you."

Elliot smiled. "You have no idea how much that means to me."

"Aw." Mason mocked. "Now hug each other like good friends do. Go on."

Elliot rolled his eyes at Mason, but opened his arms to Anita anyway.

"Why not?" Anita embraced Elliot in a friendly hug. With the hug her forgiveness felt more than sincere. Suddenly the elevator came to an abrupt stop. The overhead light and the panel lights went out, making it pitch black in the elevator. Anita gasped, backing out of Elliot's friendly embrace. "What happened?"

Mason rapidly pressed the panel buttons. "The damn electricity went out."

"They did it on purpose?" Elliot sighed. "To stop us, huh?"

"Maybe," Adam said. As soon as he said it the overhead light came back on, but it was red instead. "I don't know, maybe not."

"Maybe hell broke loose and everybody's going crazy." Mason continued to push the panel buttons. "Just like you wanted, Elliot."

"Yeah, but not like this." Elliot looked up at the red light above the wall where the panel was located. "I hope no one's claustrophobic."

"I'm not claustrophobic." Anita wiped sweat from her brow. "I just want to get the hell out of here."

"Me too. Look." Elliot pointed to the ceiling where a square metal sheet was located. "You think we could get out through there?"

"Here," Anita rubbed her palms together. "I'll open it. Give me a lift."

Mason and Elliot stepped forward to link their arms together by holding on to each other's elbows so Anita could sit on their forearms and they could lift her. They only needed to lift her a couple feet up for her to reach the metal sheet.

"Be good to my bummed arm, will you." Mason chuckled.

Adam placed the gun back inside of his pant pocket and pulled a thick folded paper from a pocket inside of his uniform. "On the blueprint, it shows ..."

Elliot and Mason lifted Anita to the metal sheet. She put her arms up and lifted the corner of the sheet slightly.

"It doesn't show the elevator going across." Adam smoothed out the paper. "Or a store room. It just shows a tunnel with railroad tracks."

"Not railroad tracks," Mason said, lifting Anita higher. "It a single rail track for mining carts. Not a train."

"Either way, it doesn't show me what's out there."

Anita pushed the sheet aside, and they all looked up into darkness. "I don't see nothing either except ... What's that red blinking light up there."

Elliot and Mason let her down and they all stared up into the dark elevator shaft.

Mason chuckled, a huge grin on his sweaty face. "That must be the storage room. We're almost there. Maybe a twenty, thirty foot climb."

"I don't know about climbing into an elevator shaft." Elliot shook his head. "I saw too many movies where they do that and end up dead."

"Well, this is not a movie." Mason jumped and grabbed the edge of the opening, grunting. "Now man up if you want to get out of here." He climbed up through the hole and disappeared in the darkness.

"I'll go next." Elliot jumped, grabbed the lid of the opening and pulled himself up through the hole. Once in the dark shaft, he looked up to see Mason's silhouette as he effortlessly climbed the siding of the small shaft.

Anita jumped, stealing Elliot's attention. She jumped again but couldn't reach the lid of the opening. Elliot kneeled beside the hole and put his arm out. "Grab my hand." He watched as Adam carefully hoisted her up by the waist, lifting her to the edge. Elliot grabbed her arm and pulled her through. Once through she immediately began to follow Mason, climbing up the siding of the elevator shaft.

Adam quickly hoisted himself through the opening and together he and Elliot avoided the two large cables that were connected to the elevator cart, and followed Anita and Mason toward the blinking red light.

CHAPTER FOURTEEN

Playing it Safe

Elliot emerged from the elevator shaft and climbed onto the landing. He stood, shivering from the cold and taking in the massive room and the many things that occupied it which took on a rich, red hue due to the steady blinking emergency lights. The room was larger than the cafeteria which could seat at least a hundred people.

"We made it," Mason said with a mouthful of peanuts that he followed with a swig from a bottle of beer.

"You couldn't wait until we got out of here before you decided to celebrate?"

"Not celebrating. Starving." He took another long drink and burped. "So good, but we have to be quick."

Elliot reached down into the shaft behind him to help Adam climb out.

"There's so much good food in here." Anita lifted a family sized bag of potato chips in her hand. "There's wine and cheeses. They even have huge frozen steaks, leg of lamb, seafood. It's ridiculous."

"And we were left eating plain rice with bologna and onion soup." Elliot grimaced. He stood in front of the single metal door directly across from the elevator. Above it in the center a single red light steadily blinked. It made no sound, just blinked on and off as it lit the room with an eerie red glow. Beside the door near the handle was a small chrome keycard reader. "Adam, where's the keycard?"

Adam shook his head, digging in his pocket at the same time. "Electricity's out. It's not gonna work."

"I wanna try anyway." Elliot held out his hand, where Adam placed the keycard in his palm. Elliot glanced at it to find the strip on the back of it and then slid the card through. Two quick beeps sounded from the device. He ran it through again and the same happened. "This is the right keycard, huh?" He looked at the picture of the old black man on it and the name beside it. "Who's this?"

"That's the prophet." Adam stepped beside him, looking down at the card. "The real prophet. The real Eugene Edmond at least." Adam looked to Mason. "He's dead, isn't he?"

Mason shrugged. "We should take as much of this food as we can. You know, we might need it once we get out there."

"Just admit it." Adam slowly made his way to Mason. "You might as well. We're almost out of here, nothing or no one can stop you. You told the truth about everything else so far. You killed the real Eugene and tried to kill that imposter too, right?"

"Okay, okay." Mason paced the area in front of the elevator shaft, subconsciously rubbing his shoulder. "Me and Petersen had a deal and he fucked the deal. Alright? Good enough?"

"Who's Petersen?" Adam cocked his head.

"The leader. The imposter. Okay?" Mason scoffed and left them, walking down to the end of the large room opposite the massive freezers.

Elliot looked down at the picture of the man on the card. "I already knew he tried to kill the prophet, the imposter or whoever he is, but he just won't admit it. And the woman who tried to stab the prophet was his accomplice."

"That's why they were sent below." Adam nodded. "They're both guilty."

Elliot looked up into Adam's worried face. "But where is she? The woman?"

Adam shook his head and sighed. "I don't know. All I know is that we need to open this door before they have a chance of catching up to us or putting a logical plan together to stop us. We still have to go down a long tunnel."

Anita came around the corner of a shelf, cradling packages of food in her arms. "We can wait for the power to come back on."

Mason appeared with a crowbar in hand. "No, we have to get out now before they gain on us. We need as much space between them and us as possible. I won't put it past them to have another secret passage somewhere leading to this place." He pushed the tapered end of the crow bar between the slit of the door between the handle and metal doorjamb.

Elliot watched him use his body weight to push the crowbar forward, causing the metal between the lever and the strike plate to warp. Maybe Mason could pop the whole thing off and just pull the door open. They all watched as Mason pushed, pulled and grunted, trying desperately to break and remove the metal around the bolt lock.

Anita shifted the weight of the small boxes of food in her arms. "Thank God this door isn't like the main door or we wouldn't be able to get out."

Mason pushed the crowbar and a piece of metal popped off. "That door in the main room is a blast door. Nothing could break in or out of it." He pulled the crowbar and another piece bent and peeled.

"You almost got it!" Elliot could barely contain his excitement.

Mason grunted with the pull of the crowbar. "I was one of the engineers for this place. Help build it with my own two hands, years ago. I didn't know what it was for at first. Thought it was some sort of military base or some crap. Then one day I overheard Eugene talking about an asteroid. I knew then, this place was serious." He pulled at the crowbar and groaned. "So I propositioned him. I'd work for free, for as long as I needed, if he saved me a spot here. A good spot.

We became close. He trusted me. He told me everything. Trusted me with important material."

Adam cleared his throat. "Like those CDs?"

"Yeah, transmissions to and from the other compounds."

Anita looked to Elliot. "There's other compounds?"

Adam rubbed the back of his neck. "Six. All on the west coast."

Mason broke another piece from the metal doorframe. It hit the floor with a *clunk*. "He used some device they had been working on to break through the dense atmosphere and transmit radio waves to satellites. It'll relay the message ... I don't know how it works, but they did it. I helped him out, kept all his secrets, little did he know a spot in this place wasn't no longer enough for my needs since I eventually learned the atmosphere would clear and life would return to damn near normal out there. So me and Petersen made a deal."

"Asshole," Elliot murmured.

Mason cut his eye at him. "Petersen was an acquaintance of Eugene's at NASA, his partner. He didn't like how Eugene was running the place so we decided to take over. I did the 'dirty work' for one hundred and sixty thousand dollars Petersen was supposed to give me once we were on the outside. He just forgot to mention how he put every penny he had into Refuge Inc. until after the deed was done. Can't trust a soul."

Adam cocked his head. "So if you have a great room on the second floor, why were you on our floor?"

"Petersen didn't have any idea what I was planning to do to him." Mason paused. "Hell, he didn't even know I saw some of his financial papers confirming he's broke. I had jewelry so I had free rein to go wherever I pleased. Hell, he trusted me. But I knew he would be showing off that damned bedazzled cross to the people up top. He's so power hungry I could've predicted it." He went back to prying open the door lock. "That was my chance to take him. Get rid of him and take over. Give him a taste of his own medicine."

"You know you're gonna pay for what you've done here." Elliot pointed a finger close enough to Mason's nose he stopped trying to pry the lock and stood back. "You all will pay for this. Just because we're getting out of here doesn't mean it's over."

Mason grinned. "Don't threaten me. You don't scare me, Elliot. Nothing scares me anymore."

Elliot glared. "It's not a threat it's the truth."

"I've been punished enough. Alright?" Mason dropped the crowbar sending sounds of ringing metal reverberating throughout the room. "They took Patrice. I think they killed her. In fact, I know they killed her. Probably buried her body with Eugene's.

He had mentioned Patrice before. Elliot frowned. "She's your accomplice, right?"

Adam nodded. "The woman who pulled the knife?"

"Yeah," Mason rubbed his forehead, staring down at the floor. "But she was more than that. So much more than that." He sniffed.

It just didn't make any sense to Elliot. "Why would they kill her but not you?"

"Because she had the knife. She had the intent. She tried to murder Petersen."

Elliot stepped closer. "But it was your idea. You planned it. You helped. You had her do it."

"All they know is that I threw a shoe."

"And you didn't admit fault, huh?" Elliot's eye twitched from the amount of disgust he harbored. "You didn't defend her. You let them take her. You let them kill her. Evil bastard."

"Look, I didn't have to tell you any of this—"

"It's all about trust, right?" Elliot shook his head and backed away.

"We're getting out of here." Mason massaged his temple. "Once we open this door. You can go your way and I will go mine. We don't have to see each other again."

"Damn right." Adam picked up the crowbar and took over prying the door open.

Elliot narrowed his eyes in disgust. "I'm glad you didn't get the chance to run this place because I would've killed you myself." In the middle of his next thought, suddenly the red light above the door turned a solid bright white, lighting up that area of the massive room. Other well-placed lights lit up the entire storage room and all the food on the many shelves.

Anita gasped. "The powers back on."

"Here, let me try the key." Elliot slid the keycard through the device. A long beep resonated from the keycard reader, but the door didn't unlock. "What's going on?"

Mason snatched the card from Elliot and ran it through the key reader himself. Again it beeped but the bolt didn't move. "Shit. We must've screwed something up."

Suddenly, the sound of the elevator in motion caught their attention.

"Shit." Adam dropped the crowbar, ran to the elevator shaft, and pressed the button on the wall with the Refuge Inc. emblem. He carefully looked down the dark shaft. "I think the elevators going back down."

Elliot watched the large metal cables in the shaft slightly tremble as the elevator cart moved lower. "They're gonna be up here in minutes. We gotta open this door."

Anita sat the boxes of food on the floor. "What should I do?"

Elliot pointed to the empty elevator shaft. "You watch for the elevator and let us know when you see it coming up."

Adam took the gun out of his pant pocket, preparing for confrontation. Elliot tried the keycard again to no avail. Mason picked up the crow bar and again tried to pry open the door.

"Shit." Elliot threw the keycard aside. "We don't have a lot of time." He watched Mason dig inside the slit with the crowbar and bend and warp the metal with force. "Wait. Wait. Look in there." He looked at the two inch length bolt that prevented the door from opening. The crow bar had impacted metal fragments into the lock keeping the bolt from recessing. "We have to get all that metal stuff out of there. Try to dig it out."

Mason angled the crow bar several different ways, trying to find the best way to scrap out the metal pieces. "I need something smaller and thinner. Check over there by the freezers."

Quickly, Elliot ran toward the freezers, passing aisle after aisle of non-perishable boxes of food , canned foods and drinks. There were twenty foot shelves of nothing but cooking oils, other shelves of nothing but grains, and more and more shelves of dried foods and food substitutes like powered milk and eggs.

Finally at the freezers, a small corner revealed many different kinds of tools. Various sized saws, hooks, hatchets, machetes and knives were hanging and neatly placed on the hanging wall rack. For the tools to be strategically placed beside the freezers he wondered if they had been used on frozen meats.

He grabbed a couple of the smaller knives and was headed back to Mason when it occurred to him that they probably would need protection if an enforcer or two did come up to prevent them from leaving. He went back and grabbed the large machete. On his way back he silently prayed that he would not have to use a weapon at all.

His way back was a bit slower than the sprint he did to the tool rack, but he was careful not to drop anything or hurt himself carrying such large and sharp knives.

He handed Mason the small knife with a pointed tip. "Here try this."

Mason sat the crowbar on the ground, took the knife from Elliot and began to dig out the metal fragments. "Yeah, this'll work."

Anita gasped. "I hear the elevator coming! Oh, my God. We need to hurry."

Adam pointed his gun to the shaft. "Step back, Anita."

She rushed over to his side, visibly shaken. "We're not getting out of here."

"Oh, we're getting outta here." Adam held the gun with both hands, a finger on the trigger. "We didn't come all this way to be stopped now."

"Hurry up, Mason." Elliot looked back and forth from the lock Mason was picking to the elevator shaft, impatiently waiting for something to happen. "Is the metal out?"

"Almost." Mason continued to pick. "There's just one thick piece that won't budge."

"We never should've messed with the damn door." Elliot couldn't help but feel stupid. He'd thought his days of making stupid decisions were long gone.

"Hell," Mason pried the knife inside the slit deeper, "we didn't know the power would come back on. We had to do something." The knife slipped and Mason cursed.

"You alright?" Elliot saw the bright red liquid drip from Mason's finger.

"I almost cut my damn finger off," Mason said, examining his finger.

The thick, braided cords inside the shaft began to rattle and the sound of the elevator cart approaching grew louder. Elliot sat the machete down and pushed Mason out of the way. "Where's the knife."

Anita rushed over and picked up the knife. "They're almost here." She handed Elliot the knife.

Elliot picked at the chunk of metal with the tip of the knife. "Get the keycard off the floor. I think I almost got it."

Anita picked up the keycard, careful to stay out of Adam's way as he pointed the gun, aiming it at the nearing elevator.

Elliot finally popped the metal fragment out from between the bolt along with some other small twisted metal scraps. He glanced at the shaft just in time to see the top of the elevator emerge. Anita ran the keycard through the key reader. It beeped twice, but did not open.

"Oh no." Anita shook her head, fumbling with the keycard. "It still won't work."

The elevator door came into full view as soon as the elevator cart came to a stop. Anita slid the keycard through again. It beeped twice and the bolt slid back into doorjamb just as the elevator door slid opened, revealing three enforcers and Petersen the imposter. Petersen's stance mimicked Adams; legs spread at shoulder length, arms extended, and two hands holding a gun.

"Get down!" Elliot ducked down just as Petersen's gun went off. The loud boom sent a ringing through the room.

Adam ducked down and blindly fired two shots toward the elevator. The men behind Eugene raised their arms as cover and hit the floor while one enforcer pressed a button on the panel to close the elevator door and send it back below.

Elliot thought he saw Eugene get hit and fall back against the enforcers, but he wasn't positive. However, there was one thing he was sure of. Anita had hit the ground hard and she still didn't get up. She didn't move at all.

CHAPTER FIFTEEN

Into the Night

Anita lay in the fetal position on the chipped and cracked concrete floor. Her long, curly hair obscured her face as she remained motionless.

"Anita?" Elliot knelt down beside her and rocked her hip slightly. "Anita, you okay?"

He felt the presence of Adam standing behind him. "Move her hair from her face."

Elliot tangled his fingertips in her thick, dark hair afraid of what he would see beneath it. He swept her hair from her face revealing a copious amount of blood coating the side of her face. The deep red liquid continued to pour from her temple, in front of her ear and down her neck.

"Oh no." Elliot couldn't believe what was happening. "Fuck, fuck, fuck." He stood and paced in a circle before kneeling beside Anita's body again.

"She was hit?" Mason asked, standing near the door with his hand on the handle.

"We were so fucking close." Elliot punched his knee, transforming the emotional pain he harbored to a physical one.

Mason turned the handle and pulled the door open. "We gotta go before they come back."

He glared at Mason. "Give me a minute, will you?"

Adam placed a comforting hand on Elliot's shoulder. "We don't have a minute. Sorry, Elliot."

Elliot tugged the end of her colorful headscarf from her pants pocket, pulling it out completely. "This wouldn't have happened if I never—"

"Don't blame yourself, Elliot." Adam knelt beside him. "Stop doing that to yourself. You don't deserve this and neither did she, but we have to keep moving."

Elliot swept her hair from her face and began to wrap her headscarf around her head, covering the gruesome wound while warm red liquid began to pool around her head, mixing with her hair. "You know they tried to take her scarf from her when she first came here." He wrapped the headscarf around her head a couple times and tucked the end inside the back like she used to do.

Mason didn't say anything. He just picked up the box of food Anita had collected and walked out the door disappearing around the corner.

"We have to go, Elliot." Adam tugged his shoulder and waited in the cracked door, hand on the handle.

"I'm not leaving her here." Elliot tucked his arms under her body and lifted her from the ground. "She's coming with us." Her body was heavy, dead weight. Her arm flopped down to her side, and her head fell back. Elliot could feel the wet stickiness on the underside of her, but it didn't distract him from the grueling pain of defeat. He had let her down for good. This was just another event to add to his major list of fuck-ups.

He carried her out the door into a long dark tunnel. A light bulb fixed in the center of the twenty foot wide arch lit the way. From first glance, it seemed like a mile long whichever way they decided to go. It was hard to see the end of it, but far ahead to the left Mason was hustling along on his way out into the world again.

Adam shut the door behind them. A click sounded as the thick bolt slid back into place, locking it. Elliot took a few steps in the direction Mason was headed, but Adam moved in front of him, stopping him.

"Elliot, I know this is crazy. I know you feel like you owe her, but you can't carry her all the way out of here." The sad look in Adam's eyes hurt more than anything Elliot felt before. Seeing Adam's discomfort reminded him of all his losses and failures. He had thought he'd grown, changed. He'd been trying to right his wrongs not create new ones. Adam outstretched his arms. "Here, we'll come back for her later."

Elliot stepped forward and together they laid Anita's body on the soft dirt. Her colorful headscarf was soaked as it slowly began to change from bright and cheery red, yellow, orange and green to a dark and gloomy rusty-brown. They placed her on her side. "Sorry, Anita." Elliot tried to swallow the huge lump in his throat but to no avail.

"We gotta go." Adam offered his hand. Elliot clasped his hand and together they jogged down the tracks far enough behind Mason where they could no longer see him. Elliot's feet became heavier and heavier with each step until he just stopped walking altogether.

"Elliot?" Adam tugged his arm. "You alright?"

He bowed his head and stood in the center of the track. He was overwhelmed with emotion he couldn't even speak to express it. But he knew Adam sensed his grief because Adam wrapped his arms around him and held him close. No words were exchanged just the comforting warmth and their mutual understanding. Elliot closed his eyes, resting his face in the crook of Adam's neck, feeling the strong pulse of his heartbeat against his cheek. A hazelnut-like aroma filled his nostril from Adam's hot skin, briefly took him to another place mentally. His body was numb.

Ever since they found the compound and Elliot had a chance to collect his thoughts and examine his previous actions he felt like a total prick. He had hope to erase those feelings by doing what he needed to do; give Adam his space and let him make his own decisions about who he wanted to love, find Titan for Anita and Tami and show them that he was more than remorseful for their losses, he even wanted to help the people of the compound and give them a chance to be free of lies and manipulation. Yet, he felt more like a failure now than he ever did. And the worse part, Anita was dead because of him.

He growled in anger. "It's all my fault. No wonder my family didn't want to have anything to do with me. I'm just a fucking waste."

Adam gripped both of Elliot's shoulders and looked directly into his eyes. "Don't ever say you're a waste again." The stern look in Adam's eyes gripped his attention. "If it wasn't for you I would still be trapped under that car, lying to myself about who I really was. I'd still be inside the compound believing every lie and living like a broken zombie if it weren't for you. You help make some of the best decisions to keep us alive. So don't ever say you're a fucking waste, yeah?"

Elliot nodded, bringing his hands to Adam's biceps. Their foreheads met and Elliot sniffed. "I still think I fucked up."

"We all fuck up, Elliot. I don't have to tell you that. I've made decisions I regret too. But no matter what you feel about yourself you have to know what I feel about you. You're the most important person to me and I'm not letting you out of my life over a couple mistakes. You hear me?" Adam pressed his lips to Elliot's, giving him soft and tender pecks on the lips. Elliot did the same, alternating between gentle licks and warm pecks, nearly melting from the overwhelming senses. He enjoyed being in Adam's arms. It reminded him of living in a magical bubble where only he and Adam existed and nothing else mattered but each other. Anytime Adam held him he felt important and ... special. Almost every time Adam was close to him it made dealing with everything outside of their little bubble that much easier.

Suddenly three loud bangs startled them, causing them to break their kiss. The noise came from down the tunnel near the door they exited from.

Adam pulled Elliot by the wrist. "Come on. We gotta run."

Running down the tracks was tiring. At times it felt as if they were on an incline, jogging up a hill. About every twenty feet another bulb would light up the tunnel, bringing attention to the large arched sides where metal pipes ran along lengthwise and wooden supports beams held up the loose rocks, preventing them from sliding into the tunnel. Large logs and plywood boards had been placed to keep the larger rocks from collapsing into the tunnel completely, but it still seemed very unstable.

He and Adam kept a steady pace, finally catching up to Mason who was hunched over with his hands on his knees trying to catch his breath. The box he was carrying was sitting atop the dirt beside him.

"It seems like it's just going on forever." He huffed. "Like we're running in circles or something."

"We're not running in circles." Adam reached into his pocket, taking out the blueprint. "This doesn't say anything about how long this tunnel is. It really doesn't say much." He handed it to Mason. "I thought you knew this place inside and out."

Mason nodded, standing straighter. "I hadn't spent too much time in the tunnel, but it can't be too much longer."

"Let's keep moving." Adam put his hand out to Elliot, he took it and they continued walking. Adam gently led Elliot's exhausted and emotionally overwhelmed body down the tunnel.

They passed an empty overturned rail cart. Deep and hollow with one of its two metal wheels broken and dangling from the body. Farther up ahead the nearest light blinked, threatening to go out completely, but even farther ahead was absolute darkness. Elliot squinted but couldn't make out anything beyond the darkness. As they got closer he understood why that was. A wall of rocks many different sizes had filled the tunnel from top to bottom. It looked as though the top of the tunnel had collapsed in on itself. What were once support beams and thick logs were now splinter wooden pieces mixed in with the dense rubble.

Elliot paused and stared at the massive wall of rock. "What do we do now?"

Mason dropped the box of food on the ground, ripped a hole into the fabric from of his shirt with his teeth, and tore a piece off with his hands. Then he wrapped and tied the small fabric around his finger where his wound was. "I'm climbing this and clearing the rocks so watch out." He began to climb the raggedy wall sending some of the smaller, loose rocks tumbling down and spewing up dirt and dust.

"You can't clear these rocks." Adam scoffed, scratching his temple.

"Just the upper ones so we can crawl through." Mason threw down larger rocks without looking, pulling some and allowing them to roll down the mound with help from gravity. "My damn shoulder better not give me too much trouble."

"We don't know how thick this pile is or how much damage was done to the tunnel." Adam's voice raised an octave probably from frustration. "Who knows. There might be rocks above that'll collapse, crushing you."

Mason paused and looked over his bummed shoulder at them. "Or we can just sit here and rot. Whatever sounds better to you. Hey, I know. I'll just wait here while you two deliberate."

Adam scoffed and sat down on the dirt floor, his back against the tunnel wall. "I don't know. I just don't know. I'm tired of running. I'm tired of thinking. Just want it all to be over."

"Let's clear the rocks." Elliot looked to Adam then to Mason. When they didn't say anything he went toward the mound of rocks.

His decision has been made. "We can't just sit here and rot, right?" He climbed the mound. Some of the rocks slid from under his weight and went tumbling down. He climbed to the top near Mason and settled in the best he could. Together they carefully plucked rocks from the top of the mound and threw them aside.

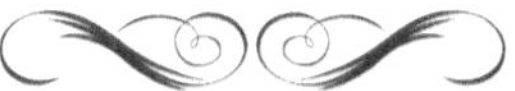

Adam couldn't help but think they were working so hard for nothing. However, he couldn't just sit by idly and watch Mason and Elliot do all the work. After all, they were right. They had to do *something*. Doing nothing was just like giving up and he would never give up. Not that easily.

They've been moving rocks for what seemed like hours. Every few minutes Adam had looked over his shoulder down the tunnel expecting to see a force of angry men and women being led by enforcers and the imposter Eugene himself. He's expected weapons and more bloodshed but was thankful they hadn't received any. Maybe they had given up on them. Maybe they're using their time to tend to the residents now or more important things. Maybe they understood it was too late.

Still moving aside rocks and crouching inside the ten feet tunnel they had dug, they were beginning to move slower, growing tired. Mason complained of hunger, their hands hurt and bled, but they were making progress.

Adam was about to call it quits, when he moved a large rock and a steady stream of dirt poured in on top of him. "Watch out," he warned, putting his hand up to stop the dirt from getting in his eyes and mouth. He soon realized the pouring stream was thinning. He coughed noticing a dank smell. "Get back some. This stuff is thick." It felt different than dirt. It was dry and tacky at the same time.

"That's not dirt," Mason said with excitement in his tone. "That's the stuff that fell from the sky. The heat of the asteroid changed the molecular structure or whatever nearly turning the sand into glass and this is the byproduct, which means we're almost to the outside of the tunnel."

"Don't breathe it in." Elliot warned.

Adam coughed again. "I think I already did." But he remembered what the man on the recorded CD had said about the dust not being harmful unless ingested and didn't worry.

They continued to move the rocks surrounding the jagged hole which allowed more of the sand to fall through. Beyond the hole was pitch black and they couldn't make out what was on the outside of it, but when enough rocks were removed a faint, cool breeze swept across Adam's face. "I feel air."

"I smell it," Elliot added.

"I think we've made it." Mason pushed Adam aside and began to crawl through the hole. "Yes, we're outside. We made it." He laughed hysterically. His loud chuckles seemed to float out into nothingness.

Elliot stood on the rocks, poking his head up through the hole. "Well, where is the sunlight? I thought there was sunlight." Elliot cautiously pulled himself through the hole.

Adam followed, carefully hoisting himself up to the rugged outside feeling the cool breeze hit his skin, smelling the musty air. "I think he was wrong about the sunlight, Elliot."

"I'm not wrong. I can't be wrong." Mason's tone turned serious, defensive. "The atmosphere was supposed to be cleared by now."

"Just admit it, Mason." Adam blindly reached out to rest a comforting hand on Elliot's shoulder. "You were wrong."

"Maybe it's night time," Mason said. "Maybe the sun hadn't come out yet."

Adam searched for a pin of light, disappointment overtaking him. He even looked for the red blinking light of the radio antenna. It was probably turned off somehow because he didn't see it or any light for that matter. "Then where's the moon and stars? If it's nighttime we would see the moon. You were wrong, Mason."

"There!" Mason shouted. "See there?"

Adam scanned the darkness with his eyes, looking for just a pin prick of light in his environment. To his surprise, far off in the distance a red color captured his eye. "What's that?"

Elliot grabbed his hand. "I see it but don't know what that is."

They watched it for a few minutes as the red light slowly turned into orange and yellow as it moved in the distance. He focused on the darkness surrounding the color. It had uneven edges that seemed to move and misshapen slightly. When he saw another hint of color in a separate area it occurred to him what he was seeing. "My God. That's the sun on the horizon peeking through the clouds."

"Yeah, look over there to the left." Elliot's voice was full of excitement and hope. "The light's breaking through!"

"I knew it." Mason laughed. "The sky's clearing up just like I told you it would. It'll probably take a few more weeks or months, but it's gonna go back to normal eventually."

They sat; resting their bodies and blistered fingers, and watching the sun rise up in the sky. It shined so bright through some of the clouds its beaming sunrays spotlighted sections of the crumbled valley.

It was strange to see the sky dotted with holes and the sunlight peeking through. It had been so long Adam almost forgot how beautiful it was. As strange as it was, it was even more amazing to know things were going to get better.

He looked down the gravel covered hill they were seated on, realizing the compound was in close proximity somewhere beneath them. He wasn't sure how near the compound was but they were obviously very close. Some parts of the environment were still cloaked in darkness, and a few hundred feet down the hill he spotted movement. The movements were quick then slow, diverse enough in behavior to not be some kind of debris blowing in the wind. Were those people of the compound who had managed to open the door and walk out to their freedom? Were they people who had followed the spray painted Refuge Inc. signs and were attempting to find the entrance? Or was his exhausted mind playing tricks on him?

"See those things moving over there." Adam pointed.

Elliot took notice. "What are those?"

Adam stood, balancing on the loose gravel that crunched beneath his feet. "It might be people."

Elliot looked up at him, eyebrows dipped. "From the compound?"

"Maybe." Adam dusted his bottom off. "Let's go have a look."

Mason sighed. "I'd rather stay here and figure out where I'm gonna go and what I'm gonna do now. That requires a lot of thinking. So—"

Adam nodded to Mason and headed down the rugged hill using the overcast light of the sky to guide his way.

Elliot followed closely behind. "We didn't bring any weapons. What if those people are savages and try to take our food or get into the compound through the tunnel? We're not prepared for that."

"What if they're in need of help like us?" Adam glanced at him. "Remember, two heads are better than one? Well, imagine how great four or five heads will be."

Once at the bottom of the hill and on more level ground they cautiously made their way toward the movement. Adam whistled to get their attention. The movement stopped, but it didn't take long for them to realize who they were targeting. The sporadic barks gave it away.

"A pack of dogs?" Elliot froze, balling his hands into fists at his sides. "What are we gonna do now?"

Instantly Adam was taken back to the first time they encountered Titan at the dental office where he and Elliot first met and took shelter. Titan was vicious then, defensive and hungry, but overtime he became a dear friend, especially to Elliot.

Before he could make a definitive decision about what they should do, the dog with a short, light brown coat trotted nearer. It didn't growl, snarl, or run over as if its intention was to attack. It approached them friendly, tongue hanging out the side of its gapped mouth. As the dog moved closer its tapered tale and boxy frame sent more than familiarity through Adam's mind.

Elliot gasped. "Titan?!" The thin dog scurried to Elliot, and as Elliot kneeled the dog jumped on his knee and licked his face with several short, friendly licks. "I can't believe it." Elliot ran his fingers over the short hair on the dog's leg where fur refused to grow over. "This is Titan. This is his scar on his leg. This is really you. And you remember us, don't you?" Elliot glanced up at Adam. "Are those the other dogs they left out here?"

The two dogs that accompanied Titan were sniffing around in the piles of rubble scattered about. Adam shrugged. "They could be. Probably hunted other small animals to stay alive. It's possible."

Elliot smiled, showing two rows of perfect teeth. "He stayed here this whole time almost like he's been waiting for us to come back. I know Anita would've liked to see this." He dipped his head and Titan licked his cheek, wagging his little tapered tail. Elliot laughed, scratching behind the canine's ear. "This is amazing. I got you, I got Titan, and we got our lives back. Now what do we do? What's the plan?"

Adam looked off in the distance at what he could make out of the mountains on the horizon. "I've been thinking about the old couple we left at Arrowhead hospital. You think they made it?"

"Only one way to find out." Elliot glanced up at him, then back to Titan. The dog turned his head and licked Elliot's petting hand. Elliot laughed, sitting down on the ground to play with him.

Adam smiled. He hadn't heard Elliot laugh in so long and to hear it again felt good. It felt right and brought hope to his heart. Sure, they had a lot to do, and a lot to strive for, but at least they had a future together that someone else didn't create. From now on they'd choose the direction their lives would take. The lives they fought for together.

The End

BEYOND THE

DARKNESS

REFUGE INC., BOOK 3

Leslie Lee Sanders

LLS BOOKS
QUEEN CREEK, ARIZONA

Prologue

The sour stench that came from the body of the old man lying in his own filth, snapped Adam back to reality. Another lifeless body didn't shock him the way it used to, but the putrid smell of decay never failed to remind him how much worse his situation could be.

There was no such thing as a better side of the coin. In this hellhole, one side of the coin meant living in hell, the other side meant *dying* in hell. Simple as that. He didn't have a choice on which side the coin landed either. He never did, and neither did Elliot, Anita, Jess or—he rubbed his temple and sighed—poor Harold.

From the way Elliot buried his face into the gruff of his beloved canine, Adam guessed he himself would have to be the one to deliver the dire news to the lonely old lady. He didn't mind appointing himself the task. Elliot had suffered enough loss.

He looked over his shoulder at Elliot's somber expression and diverted eyes. Images of him wrapping his strong arms around Elliot's narrow waist and resting Elliot's face against his chest filled his thoughts. He imagined such a therapeutic embrace would help heal Elliot's broken heart and do wonders for his own as well. Even for a little while. The need for physical affection cut him deeply, especially when he realized Edna would be alone now that poor Harold was gone. Also knowing Elliot wanted yards away from pity made Adam keep his distance.

Instead of a full-on embrace, he patted Elliot's shoulder and gave it a comforting squeeze as he walked by the slumped over beauty on the cold, linoleum hospital floor. Immediately, Elliot stood and followed. The sound of his mangled shoes sliding across the floor echoed through the hospital hall with each step.

Adam turned to see Titan follow closely behind. The dog's head hung low and his huge, brown eyes glanced up at him as if he were grieving too. Maybe the old mutt could sense their loss. Maybe Elliot's emotions were somehow rubbing off on the canine. Those two were closer than he and Elliot had been in days. Then again, the dog provided a special something Adam hadn't given Elliot in a while, the ability to just listen and not speak, especially about the past. It had been the only thing Elliot asked for that Adam couldn't deliver.

As much as Adam didn't want to speak about the horrors of the past, those things came up in every conversation. He couldn't open his mouth without mentioning how sorry he was for everything they'd been through—the abrupt changes and many deaths. And as much as he tried to prevent himself from instilling false hope, he couldn't help but to do that either. Except, he didn't think it false. He believed rescue was just days away, but he had stopped talking about that days ago to please Elliot. Elliot couldn't take getting his hopes up only to be let down.

Still, rescue was coming. If Mason had been right about the sky clearing, he could very well be right about the rest of the world not being affected. Someone had to be on their way to assist Arizona survivors and survivors in the surrounding states. There had to be someone thinking of them. Someone out there to help put an end to their suffering.

CHAPTER ONE

Expressions

As much as Adam tried, he couldn't keep himself from nervously running his hand through his light brown hair when facing Edna. He realized it was his body's way of trying to control stress and anxiety, so he didn't fight it. He sighed, looking into dark beady eyes. "It's not good news, Edna. I'm sorry."

"Now what the hell is he blabbing about?" Edna sat forward on the hospital bed, further tangling the sheets around her amputated leg. She looked to Elliot who sat on the floor with his back against the wall, but he didn't answer. She continued to stare at Adam, probably not expecting Elliot to speak. "You think it's ever good news to be stranded in a dusty old city that's crumbled to hell?" She coughed, and even in the poor light Adam could make out her pain on her wrinkled face.

"Something must have happened to him. I don't know ... a heart attack or stroke maybe." Adam dropped his gaze to the grimy floor. He huffed. "I'm sorry to have to tell you."

"That old bastard." Edna lay back, relaxing into the indentation her small frame made on the several not-so-fluffy pillows behind her. "Looks like the fool finally went and got himself killed." She waved a dismissive hand in the air. "It was bound to happen sooner or later. First, old Jerry," she pointed toward the dark room across from them where her husband died in his coma, "and now, old Harold seemed to get himself killed too." She crinkled her nose and smacked the air with her hand.

"You okay?" Adam stepped forward, narrowing the space between him and her twin-sized bed. "You need anything? Need some water or—"

"Got a cigarette?" She cocked her head.

Adam frowned. "You already know we don't smoke."

"Well, maybe you can't help me then. Now just leave me be." She shooed him off with a wave of her bony hand.

Adam nodded, pivoted and glanced at Elliot and Titan before leaving the room.

The dark and filthy hospital halls carried a stench that reminded him of the terrible bologna soup Elliot and the kitchen staff used to make back at the compound. Did Elliot recognize the odor permeating throughout the broken and battered facility? Did the sour aroma remind him of times in the compound and all the people, dead or alive, they had left behind? Was the smell contributing to the gloom Elliot harbored by reminding him of the poor little blonde girl, Jess? Or did it remind him of Anita, the friend he had made and lost back at the compound?

Adam wandered down the hall toward the main horseshoe shaped desk smack in the center of the Intensive Care Unit. He glanced at the chocolate brown sign that dangled from the center of the ceiling announcing his location, and took a seat behind the desk. Relaxing in the wheeled office chair, he stared at the drawer in front of him.

He had never used a gun before the incident at the compound. Hell, he had never even held one before then. But having one in his possession made him feel safe. From what? He didn't know, just knowing he had a gun with him made him feel a little better about the unknown. He opened the drawer to take a look at the dull, black metal. It had been fully loaded when he wrestled it from the so-called prophet who ran the compound. When he had fired the gun twice while trying to escape, it had occurred to him that he wasn't sure if the bullets had hit anyone. It had looked like Petersen grabbed his chest when closing the elevator door to protect himself, the guards and enforcers from Adam's bullets. However, he wasn't sure. What he was sure of was that firing twice left him with only four bullets in the chamber. Nothing would stop him from using those bullets to protect the people he cared about, especially Elliot.

"Get out of here, you nut!" Edna's angered voice echoed loudly through the empty halls. "Now, get!"

Adam took the gun from the drawer and ran down the hall toward the darkened room where Edna was. He held the gun low by his side as he rushed around the corner. "What's going on?" Elliot stood near the wall while Edna scowled at him.

She pointed a scrawny finger to Elliot. "I'm trying to ask this nut a question and he won't answer me."

"There's no more medicine." Elliot threw his hands up and shook his head. "There's no more insulin. There's no more aspirin. We barely have enough food. I don't know where else to look. I told you that."

"Thought something was wrong." Adam forced his heartbeat to slow by forcefully exhaling as he tucked the gun in the top drawer of the cold, metal desk next to him. "I thought something serious happened."

"This *is* serious." Edna smacked her thin lips. Her pale skin nearly glowed in the darkened, stuffy room. "I asked him a question and he ignores me. What kind of person ignores a lady?"

Elliot shook his head, his dark hair feathered across his eyebrow. "I answered you. You just didn't hear me. I said—"

"Never mind what you said." She sat forward, a light growl carried in her tone. "Next time speak up. Like a man. Where's your balls, hmm? If it's true what you say about being in that Refuge and using your head to come up with plans and ways to figure out the truth, and risking your life for this fool," she gestured to Adam, "and helping some people escape. Even lifting that car from on top of him. If all that is true, well what happened to ya? You don't look like the hero you two used to go on about."

Elliot didn't answer. He stared at the ground in front of him and slowly walked out of the room. Titan followed in close proximity.

As soon as Elliot's footsteps trailed off, Adam sighed, holding off the bit of anger that rose to his throat as heat. "He did great back there at the compound, you know. Even before the compound, he saved my ass so many times."

"Yes, yes, I know." She sat back against the pillows and rubbed her fingertips over her brow bone.

"He feels bad, he's hurt, and he's confused—"

"Welcome to the club." She fingered the sheets over her lap. Adam knew his explanation was thoughtless. They all were hurt and confused. Before he could apologize, Edna continued, "There's no more room for that now. If you're gonna make it out of this shithole you gotta stay strong, especially in here." She tapped her temple with a finger. "How do you think I made it in here for so long?" She chuckled and Adam smiled.

"Sorry, Edna." He patted her foot over the sheet. "We all been through a lot, but you ... you are the strongest." He waited for her snarky "Damn right," but instead she nodded with a crooked smile.

"We all have a breaking point." She looked at him as if she had broken away from her thoughts. "Now go on and see how Elliot's doing and put some sense back into his head, will ya?"

Adam nodded. "I'll be right back."

"Oh, I'm fine." She swiped the air. "I'm the strongest, remember? Now go on."

He left the room and headed in the same direction as Elliot, which led to the stairwell and down to the ground floor. He knew exactly where to find Elliot and the dog, in the main room ER with dozens of beds for triage. Elliot was near one of the beds when Adam turned the corner. The few lighted florescent bulbs made the white walls and grimy linoleum floors illuminate, brightening the large room.

Elliot ripped swatches from the sheet he held, making large, even sized pieces of fabric. "Come running after me like I'm some damsel in distress?" He didn't look up from his working hands, but Adam knew Elliot could see him out of the corner of his eye. "You know, since I lost my balls somewhere between helping that old woman and trying to stay alive?"

Adam chuckled at the half-hearted joke, attempting to lighten the mood. "I'm pretty sure you still got your balls." He remembered watching as Elliot washed sweat and dust from his body just a few hours ago. The water from the faucets seemed to slowly disappear since they returned to the old hospital. What used to come out with force now only drizzled and sometimes seeped. They had to be much more conscious of how much water they were using to wash up, even if that meant less time seeing Elliot undressed. "What's going on?" Adam nodded toward the torn sheet.

"I'm making some kind of satchel so we can carry what we can when we go out looking for more food and supplies. Something durable."

Adam wanted desperately to see the dark, chocolate irises in Elliot's rapidly blinking eyes, but Elliot wouldn't look up at him. He moved forward, inching closer to Elliot who had stopped fidgeting with the sheets and stared at the mussed bed instead. As Adam stood next to him, the heat from Elliot's body radiated from his exposed arms. Adam reached out, hooking Elliot's stubbly chin with his fingertips, gently turning Elliot to face him.

"You okay?" He narrowed his eyes, studying Elliot's full, moist lips and the freckles on his cheeks he grew to love. "You seem …"

"Worried, scared—"

"Tired." Adam rested his hand on Elliot's shoulder and allowed it to slowly slide down his arm, feeling, comforting. "Maybe if you let go of responsibility for a while." He grabbed Elliot's hand and held it. Callouses covered Elliot's palms. They had formed shortly after moving large rocks from the mining tunnel when escaping the compound. "Let me take care of things for a while until you feel better."

Elliot squeezed his hand briefly. "The thing is, I am feeling. That's the problem. I'm feeling weeks of abandonment by our government—"

Adam shook his head. "We're not sure what's out there beyond this city."

Elliot ignored him and continued, "I feel like a jackass. Anita was killed."

"That wasn't your fault. That could've been any one of us."

"I feel weak, sick, and powerless." Elliot stepped back, letting go of Adam's hand and bringing his own to his forehead. "I mean, look at me. I can't function properly. You want me to just let you do all the work because I'm not even capable of ripping a few sheets apparently."

"I didn't mean it like that—"

"I have to do *something* to feel like I'm still alive." Elliot threw his hands up. "At least I'm allowing myself to feel. Adam, you've been acting like nothing bothers you. Like you're too strong and powerful to let anything get to you. We're only human. We're not superheroes like we used to pretend to be."

Adam slowly nodded, letting Elliot's words seep in. He remembered being out in the darkness, pretending to be Midnight Man with Elliot his sidekick, Dark Lad. He smiled briefly from the memory. "You're right." He ran his hand through his own hair, bowed his head, and narrowed the space between them. "You're right, Elliot. We've been through so much and I won't let my feelings show. But that's because I'm in control." With a low, soft voice he continued, "I take pride in knowing that I'm still in control, and that's not anything against you. We all just handle things differently."

Elliot lifted his head, looking up into Adam's eyes. "I know I can't take anymore. That's one thing I—"

A loud *pop* sounded from upstairs, startling them and suddenly silencing Elliot. Even Titan barked, standing to face the stairwell.

"What the hell was that?" Adam looked back and forth between Elliot and the stairwell. Adrenaline shot through his veins and his heartbeat instantly doubled.

Elliot ran toward the stairwell before Adam registered his words. "Oh, my god. Edna!"

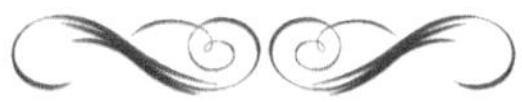

When Elliot turned the corner and entered the bedroom, his breath immediately caught in his throat. The sight before him shocked him to the core. *No. Not again.* He turned away and staggered back into the hall. His knees shook terribly, threatening to completely give out from under him. It took Adam a second to enter the hall from the stairway. His strong, large hands grabbed Elliot's shoulders as he searched Elliot's face. "What's wrong? What happened?"

Elliot couldn't answer. He tried speaking, but nothing came out. Even as his lips trembled they refused to form words. Instead of trying to read Elliot's mind, Adam entered the room behind him. "God damn it!" It was then Elliot knew Adam saw what he had seen.

Edna's delicate, brittle frame sprawled out on the floor in a wide crimson puddle. The handgun laid on the once white linoleum floor just a couple of feet from her body. Spatters of her deep red essence tainted the white sheets on her bed.

Elliot took a step toward the stairway and collapsed to his knees. His body shook uncontrollably. Adam's grunts and growls of anger filled the room behind him. Elliot's body wouldn't obey his command to stand and leave the vicinity, even as the metal bedframe slammed against the wall and the dresser crashed to the floor. The roars of destruction filled the room behind him, along with Adam's deafening grunts and swearing, paralyzing Elliot.

Finally, Adam had allowed himself to feel.

A minute later, all sounds in the room ceased. Adam walked by Elliot in the hall, holding the gun at his side. Deep anger lines creased Adam's brows as he disappeared toward the stairs.

There was no desire to look in the room. From the sound of it, Adam had wrecked it worse than Phoenix had been after several earthquakes. Elliot dug his fists into the cold, dingy floor and rose to his feet. Without much strength in his knees, he made it downstairs to Adam, who stood where Elliot had been standing before the loud shot of the gun interrupted them. Adam stood with his back toward him, but it was apparent that Adam was in his zone, cleaning the red stains off of the gun with some of the torn parts of the bed linen.

Without saying a word, Elliot slid his hand along the wall to anchor himself before pressing his back against it and sliding down to sit near Titan. The dog licked Elliot's chin before snuggling beside him and resting his head on his light brown paws.

"Guess Harold's death really *did* get to her." Adam kept his eyes on the gun as he carefully cleaned it with torn pieces of linen. "All that talk about staying strong mentally... she was bluffing."

Elliot cleared his throat. "Well..." He paused, thinking of what to say next while Adam continued to clean the red spatters from the gun. "Well," he began again, noting his inability to verbalize his thoughts. "Well, there are three bullets left..." Adam paused and listened. "One for each of us," Elliot finally finished.

Adam turned, anger written on his face in scowl lines. His eyebrows dipped so low they twisted his face in what looked like disgust. "You fucking kidding me? You're thinking about doing what she just did?"

Elliot shook his head and brought his knees to his chest. "No, I don't know what I'm thinking."

"Damn right." Adam stuffed the clean gun into his pants pocket. "We're not gonna go out like she did. You hear me?"

"Yeah." Elliot nodded, looking into angry green eyes. "I'm sorry. I shouldn't have said that."

Adam's face relaxed as he knelt beside Elliot and the dog. "She wants us to be strong. She said it herself. We've made it too far to start thinking about giving up now."

"Sorry, Adam." Elliot grabbed Adam's forearm. "She was fucking right. I lost it. I'm going crazy or something. This is too much."

"We're getting out of here, Elliot." Adam stood. "We're getting far away from this hospital. We've been here long enough. We're out of food and water, and there's no other reason to stay here. We're going to have to find better shelter somewhere away from all this."

Elliot knew what he meant by "all this." Adam meant the bodies, the death. He also knew where plenty of food, water and decent shelter was. Adam knew too, but they would die before going back to the compound. The way he saw it, returning to the compound was no different than signing his identity, his soul, and his body over to a madman who called himself a prophet, who wanted to control or "evolve" desperate survivors. He and Adam weren't that desperate. They had found food, water and shelter while being away from the compound. They could find more without going back. His last memory of the compound, before escaping it, was the angry mob of people trying to capture and possibly kill him, Adam and Mason.

Mason.

Elliot glared at the floor. The thought of Mason heated his blood. Mason was as dirty, manipulative and untrustworthy as the so-called prophet, Petersen. He had helped build the compound and even helped them escape it. Nonetheless, Mason and Petersen were responsible for the helpless people on the top floor of the compound, who lived in next-to-hell conditions, being trained to slave for Refuge Inc.'s rich investors. Investors who lived in the lavish quarters directly below the survivors. How sick were Petersen and Mason to know the sky had cleared but continued to scare the hell out of everyone for their own benefit? Still, those poor people had no idea the world thrived beyond the compound.

Adam descended the stairs and entered the large room. He carried an arms-full of supplies; plastic water bottles, medical dressings and ointments, and what little packaged food they had left. Elliot hadn't realized Adam had left the room. He had been too immersed in his own thoughts to notice.

"We're getting out of here before it gets too dark outside." Adam dropped the supplies on the bed, turned, and headed back toward the stairwell.

Elliot stood beside the bed. He wanted to finish making the satchels out of the torn linen from the bed sheets, but the rust colored swatches made him pause. How many more death and destruction would he witness? How much until he finally snapped?

Adam appeared with a folded sheet and a couple of bottles of personal sized shampoo. "Maybe we can go by another convenience store and look for food. We'll have to camp out until we find more permanent shelter too."

Elliot snorted. "Any place but here."

CHAPTER TWO

On the Road Again

The overcast sky took on an ominous appearance, even as the setting sun and its rays shone through gaps of dense clouds. Parting clouds allowed light to illuminate the valley's surrounding mountains and other landmarks. A thick layer of tacky dust coated the earth like a heavy, dirty quilt, including vehicles, trees, rooftops of standing structures, even the dead power lines. The material was so thick, with every step, a trail of distinctive shoe prints trailed them. Without much wind or rain, the footprints seemed to hold forever like a personal stamp on hell itself.

Adam and Elliot walked for the last hour with Titan trotting closely behind. The handmade cloth packs were strapped to their backs with a wide band of braided bed sheet that went across their chests.

The small, collapsed shops and vacant businesses they investigated didn't contain much of anything valuable, and rummaging through them slowed them down.

"There's canned food, but carrying too much will just make our packs heavy." Adam wanted to take every bit of food they found, but knew to be wise about what they carried.

"It's all vegetables anyway." Elliot shrugged. "At least we know where to look when we're in need of canned green peas."

Adam scoffed. "Hey, it's better than nothing."

Elliot nodded. "I'm not complaining. But ..."

Adam knew Elliot was about to mention the food at the compound. Adam waited for him to continue his statement but he never did. Maybe he knew going back to that hellhole was foolish. The last time they were there it was as if an angry mob with pitch forks and torches ran them out, banishing them. Elliot had tried to explain to them the world outside was better, that they could leave the compound if they wished.

Was that the truth? Was the world outside really better? Sure, the sunlight beamed through the blackened clouds, but they weren't sure what was outside the city or the state. Was the world beyond Arizona really untouched by the fragmented asteroid as Mason had said? If so, where were the rescue units to come to their aid?

Titan barked and stared ahead at the building that used to be Payday Loans but was now a once shaken shell. The windows were without glass, and what was left of the tall billboard that had once announced its presence was now toppled over and shattered into a nearly unrecognizable pile of clutter.

First, Adam considered the decent shelter the space would make, but then it registered that Titan had been barking at something in particular.

"What is it?" Adam asked, as if the dog could answer.

Titan stood at attention. His tapered tail stiff, neck muscles taut. He stepped forward, barked at the building, and then stood silent again.

Adam shot an uneasy look to Elliot. Elliot shrugged and they continued to watch the building for movement. After a few seconds and no movement, Adam called out, "Anyone there?"

Nothing.

Adam lifted a brow. "Want to check it out?"

Elliot shrugged and headed for the building.

Every step made indentations in the tacky dirt. Even Titan left a trail of paw prints leading toward the building. Elliot entered first. Adam followed, slipping through the unlocked door. The room appeared smaller on the inside than it did from the outside. It was mainly a shell with small animal tracks scattered around the dust. Maybe a lizard or some other desert creature had been rummaging around the area.

"It's getting dark." Adam glanced at Elliot over his shoulder. "We need to find a place to rest for the night."

"Why not here?" Elliot stared at a pile of flattened cardboard boxes.

Elliot lay asleep on the thin, and slightly hard, improvised mattress of cardboard boxes. Adam lay beside him, thoughts of their morning trek kept him awake. That, and the cool breeze that flowed through the broken windows, making it difficult to keep warm. A couple of sheets didn't do much to ward off the cold. Every now and then, the blackened sky would glimmer with the light of the moon or the brightest star. Titan, too, seemed to be fascinated with the shifting of the dense clouds.

Elliot whimpered, breaking the silence. Adam glanced over. Elliot's bare shoulder seemed to tremble in the barely-there moonlight. Adam gently pulled the sheet up and over Elliot's arm. Still, Elliot trembled and groaned, "No, no, no."

Was he dreaming? A nightmare?

Adam rolled over, pressing his chest to Elliot's back. He placed a comforting hand on Elliot's shoulder and he shrugged and jumped as if startled. He turned to look into Adam's eyes. "What? What happened?"

Adam shook his head. "Were you dreaming? You sounded … scared."

Elliot turned away, keeping his back to Adam. "I might've been dreaming but I'm not scared."

"It's okay if you're..."

"I'm not scared," Elliot repeated, talking away from him. "I'm a big boy, Adam."

He knew Elliot couldn't see him, but he nodded anyway. He rubbed Elliot's shoulder to remind Elliot that he was there if needed. He gingerly glided his fingertips along the curve of Elliot's shoulder and toward the dip of his neck. They traveled along the slope of Elliot's long neck and up behind his ear, softly grazing the skin, then back down again.

Adam panted. He tried to control his breathing and his racing heartbeat but couldn't. Elliot was bliss on his fingertips, and Adam's body was involuntarily reacting. Heat radiated from Elliot's skin and lingered on his palm as he caressed Elliot's arm. Did his touch tell Elliot all he wished to say but couldn't verbalize?

Without warning, Elliot quickly rolled to face Adam and grabbed the collar of his shirt, pulling Adam against him and crushing their lips together. He closed his eyes and savored the sweet taste of Elliot's tongue as the wet muscle slithered between his lips.

"I can't stand not touching you," Elliot whispered in the kiss. With one hand, he caressed Adam's waist,. his abdominal muscles, and then glided his palm over Adam's erection which strained against his pants. "I dream about it. Touching you." Elliot's breath caught when Adam's did as Elliot's palm slid over his hardened length. "I remember it." Elliot gently nipped Adam's bottom lip with his teeth, taking the lead. "I can't forget it. I don't want to forget." Adam sighed and willfully surrendered control.

Out of nowhere, commotion in the distance startled them. Adam broke their kiss and sat straight up, his gaze fixed on nothing in particular beyond the broken window. "Hear that?"

"Yeah, I heard it," Elliot whispered. "What do you think it is?"

"Don't know." Adam crawled off of their temporary mattress and to his satchel to retrieve the handgun. "Listen."

A few seconds went by when commotion cut through the silence again, reminding Adam of rummaging. Was it coming from the nearby structures?

Titan stood and barked.

"Titan!" Elliot whispered. He sat on the cardboard mattress with the sheets tangled around his legs. "Quiet. Sit."

Titan briefly whined but sat.

Adam opened the satchel and fingered the gun. He lifted it from the sack and crouched as he snuck to the window. Although faint, the rummaging continued. He searched for movement beyond the opening, but the darkness made it difficult for him to make out anything beyond the distorted shadows and silhouettes of buildings and debris.

"Anything?" Elliot whispered.

"Don't know." Adam waited a few minutes before returning to the mattress. "Could be a dog or cat or something."

"People?" Elliot's eyes widened.

Adam shrugged. "Maybe."

CHAPTER THREE

Encounters

Adam awakened to a bright light which blinded him instantly upon opening his eyes. "What the hell?"

"I got your gun," warned a deep, muffled voice that came from the figure who stood before him. "And I know how to pull a trigger."

Elliot remained fast asleep under the thin sheets on their cardboard pallet. "Elliot—" Adam said, only to be interrupted by the dark figure before him who swept the light from Adam's face and replaced it with the gun.

"Shut the fuck up or I'll do it."

Adam sat silently. Once again in a predicament where he stared down the barrel of a gun. The exact gun as before. With his eyes, he searched the darkened room for Titan but the old mutt was nowhere to be seen. However, the silhouette of a second person nearly hidden in the corner shadows caught his eye.

The person directly in front of Adam continued to point the gun inches from his nose, while ordering his accomplice to, "Check that bag over there for anything good."

Adam waited for the perfect opportunity to knock the gun from the intruder's hand. In the meantime, he allowed the second person to search Elliot's bag. Both intruders wore dark clothes, gloves and a helmet or some sort of protective headgear which concealed their faces.

"Anything good?" The intruder glanced over his shoulder at his partner and lowered the gun a bit. Quickly, Adam stood, grabbed the man's wrist with one hand and the barrel of the gun with the other. Surely, he had taken the intruder off guard. Removing the gun would be easy. However, Adam was wrong. Even with Adam's strong grip, the man managed to twist his arm free as easily as simply pulling.

"Drop it!" Adam panicked, surprised by the intruder's wrist move.

Surprisingly, Elliot flung the sheets aside, rolled over, and rammed the heel of his foot against the side of the intruder's knee. The man fell, growling and writhing in pain. The flashlight hit the ground, barely lighting the scene as Adam straddled the screeching intruder. He wrestle with the man, trying to take control of the gun.

Elliot stood and quickly approached the shorter thinner partner who had huddled back into the darkened corner.

Adam used a combination of his body weight and strength to put pressure on the intruder's arms, forcing his wrists high over his head and toward the floor. Adam repeatedly slammed the intruder's wrist against the dusty floor until the gun left his grip. He continued to pin the man's wrists to the floor, while Elliot struggled with the second person. Elliot pinned the partner to the wall and held one wrist between the partner's shoulder blades until the struggling ceased.

Muffled pleading came from behind the intruder's mask. "Please, let me go."

Adam glared. "What are you doing here?"

The intruder shook his head. "We weren't gonna hurt you. I swear."

Adam's teeth clenched. "Then why the gun in my face?"

"We're just looking for medicine. Food and medicine. That's all."

Elliot continued to pin the whimpering intruder to the wall. He looked back, as if waiting for Adam's next move. Adam sneered at the man he straddled. "I'm gonna let you go and you're gonna take that damn helmet off."

Beneath him, he nodded. "Right. Okay."

"No stupid shit," Adam warned.

"Right, no stupid shit. Right."

Adam released him and lunged for the gun. In the uneven light, Adam pointed the gun to him and the man's hands slowly raised. "Now take that shit off your face."

The intruder lifted his hands to his head, about to remove his helmet, when a fist came out of nowhere and connected with Adam's jaw. Out of his peripheral appeared a third person who must have emerged from outside and interfered at what he thought was an opportune time.

Commotion broke out around them. Adam swung the butt of the gun toward the head of the third person. Only after his hit landed he realize the person wore protective headgear too. The same intruder swung again. His hit landed on Adam's cheek, making him lose grip of the gun. Without much effort, the masked man took control of the firearm.

Adam kneeled, pain radiated along his cheekbone.

The man lifted the gun, pointing it at Elliot. "Let her go."

Elliot's eyes widened, probably from being threatened with a deadly weapon and the revelation that the person he had pinned was female. Adam was just as surprised. Elliot released her and retreated, glancing back and forth between the intruders and Adam. "You alright, Adam?"

Adam nodded, and Titan barked from a distance. "Where's my dog?" He looked toward the man who held the gun. The man took advantage of the shadows, using them to remain unseen. Adam sneered.

The man pointed the firearm at Elliot but faced Adam. "Come on, you guys. We got work to do. Get those bags and let's go."

Elliot scoffed. "That's our stuff. We need that."

"We need it more." The nearly inaudible words escaped the headgear like an angry demon from the depths of Satan's bowels. "Now, back down."

Elliot stepped forward. "You can't just take our food and leave us with nothing."

"Watch me." The man continued to point the gun.

Adam imagined a sinister grin curling the man's lip from under the helmet.

"We need everything we got," Elliot went on. "There's three mouths we need to feed and we've been looking for food for days. It's not that easy to find. You're just gonna let us starve?"

"We're starving too, man." The intruder glanced to the female who remained hidden under her dark headgear like her partners. "You alright? Did he hurt you?"

She shook her head. "I'm fine, but we can't leave them without *something*."

The man on the floor stood and inched his way toward the door. "Let 'em keep whatever medicine they have as a bargain. We take the food."

"You want food?" Elliot shot Adam a look. "I know where you can get food. Drop the gun, leave our stuff, let our dog go, and I'll tell you where to get food."

The man lowered the gun and chuckled. "You know where food is but you haven't went for it yourself? You think we're crazy or some shit?"

Adam cleared his throat. "There's an underground compound near South Mountain. There're a bunch of survivors there. Hundreds maybe. They have food, medicine, shelter ... everything you'll ever need."

Everything you'll ever need. Adam remembered the compound's claim, and although it was close to the truth, the price was steep.

"Right. Right." The man chuckled again. The sarcasm in his muffled laugh was apparent.

"It's true." Elliot shrugged. "The compound's run by Refuge Inc."

The female nodded excitedly. "The R's?"

"Right." Elliot nodded too, mimicking her. "The R with the halo. You saw the spray paintings?"

The man swung the gun, gesturing subconsciously. "You guys painted that shit?"

"No." Adam shook his head. "But we know who did. Anyway, who painted it doesn't matter. What matters is the food they have. Go try your luck at getting some real food and leave us alone with ours."

"Wait." The guy rubbed his broad chest. "Why would we need luck if this place is for survivors?"

"Honestly," Adam said. "It's a piece of shit place and—"

"If they want food they're gonna have to go there to get it," Elliot interrupted. "That's it. Simple as that. Now leave our stuff. The gun too."

The man laughed, chest heaving. "You guys know a lot about Refuge Inc." The man lifted the gun to Adam's face. "What's up? What the hell are you hiding?"

"Dylan, let's just go." The female tapped his shoulder. "Let's just figure it out ourselves."

"They're talking about food, Mira." He shook his head and steadied the firearm.

Adam looked past the dark metal to the man behind it. "We escaped from there a couple weeks ago."

"Escaped?"

"They locked everyone inside. Made us live like shit, telling us it'll take years for everything to be normal again out here." Adam glared. Remnants of anger boiled to the surface. "They were planning to use us as slaves while rich investors lived in replicas of their nice, cozy homes within the compound."

"You're shitting me." He lowered the gun again. "What kind of refuge are you trying to send us to?"

Elliot scoffed. "Look, you want food. We're telling you where to find it. Just let us do our thing and you go on and do yours. We've done you a favor."

The man shook his head. "You're gonna show us where this place is."

"What?!" the girl shouted. "We are not going there, especially with *them*."

"You want to starve out here?"

"That place sounds pretty fucked up," she added.

"We're not going back." Elliot carefully made his way over debris and stood next to Adam. "We're staying put. Waiting for rescue."

"Rescue?" The intruder snorted. "Nobody's coming for you. For none of us. They're too busy trying to defend the country from North Korea."

"North Korea?" Adam cocked an eyebrow. "What are you talking about?"

"We've been left for dead. That's what I'm talking about. Ain't nobody coming for us."

"Why not?" Adam's eyebrows dipped from confusion.

"I'll let you figure that out."

Elliot huffed. "Come on. We're trying to end this peacefully. We're all starving. None of us wants to get hurt. Let's just move on like this never happened."

The guy shook his head. "But it's happening and we need food and medicine."

Adam straightened his back and ignored his throbbing cheekbone. "Tell us what's going on out there. We've been wandering this city for weeks, lost friends and family, doing what we can while waiting for rescue. If no one's coming for us, at least tell us why."

Seconds of silence passed as if no one wanted to speak the truth. Mira finally spoke. "America's at war."

"What?!" Elliot nearly gasped. "With North Korea?"

"That's what it sounded like." Mira shrugged. "There was an abandoned car on the road with the keys still in the ignition. We turned it on and searched the radio for news."

"Radio works?" Surprise and excitement rushed through Adam all at once.

Mira nodded. "It wasn't great but enough to get some pieces in about North Korea and a couple other shit countries taking advantage of the asteroid impact and threatening the United States. It's crazy."

Adam could barely contain his anxiety. "So everyone outside of the impact area is fine. They weren't affected by the asteroid fragments." Just as Mason had said.

Dylan shrugged, his finger still on the trigger. "Fragments?"

Mira continued, "No, everyone's not fine. From the sound of it, they're reporting 'no impact survivors' and their attention is now on North Korea. They have no reason to send help if they believe we're all dead. Apparently, the priority is protecting the country from war rather than finding survivors."

As crazy as it seemed, it explained why they had been abandoned. "What else did you hear?" Adam asked.

"Don't tell them anything else until they take us to that compound," Dylan ordered. His voice like thunder underneath his headgear.

Adam nodded. His mind going a mile a minute. "We'll take you to the compound."

Elliot glared. "What?! I'm not going back there."

"Even if we can get word out that we're alive and need help? That there are plenty of survivors in need?" A grin cleft Adam's lip. Hope had returned.

Elliot shook his head, confused. "How would we do that?"

"Remember the compound's radio antennae with the blinking red light?" Adam grinned. "That's how."

CHAPTER FOUR

On a Quest

Elliot hoisted the makeshift sack on his back as they walked. The night sky silhouetted every object in the vicinity. Thankfully the two flashlights they had with them helped light their way. Elliot held one and the invaders had the other.

Titan trotted beside them as they climbed over broken concrete walls that had once separated homes and business. Their imprinted footprints in the thick layer of fallen ash resembled the prints on the moon.

"Why don't you guys take those helmets off?" Elliot said. "It's gotta be dangerous to walk in those things. I bet you can't even see as good. Or breathe."

The three intruders kept a comfortable distance between them. Dylan held the gun, but had yet to point it at either of them since beginning their trek. Mira popped off her helmet, revealing her olive-toned complexion and mussed strands of a dark cropped haircut. The other guy pulled off his helmet too, exposing his pale skin, slender neck and high cheekbones. Elliot peered over his shoulder, waiting for Dylan to remove his helmet. He didn't.

Mira cleared her throat. "Tell us more about that compound and its radio."

Adam stepped onto the cracked and littered sidewalk to avoid a large pothole in the road. "I don't know much about the radio, but I know they have one. The prophet, I mean, the leader kept correspondences to the other compounds through the same radio."

"Whoa. Whoa. Whoa. A prophet? Other compounds?" Finally, Dylan pulled off the helmet, revealing his dark mocha-colored skin, cornrow braided hair and a sharp chiseled jawline. "There's more than one of these twisted compounds?" His voice was less like the thunderous pits of hell now that he wasn't speaking through the headgear, which he strapped to his backpack.

Adam nodded, calculating every step. "Yes, there're six, apparently."

Elliot chimed in. "And he's not a prophet. He's not even the guy he claimed to be. We think he had the real Eugene Edmond killed so he could take his place and run the compound."

"Right," Adam continued. "Apparently him and his partner were some NASA scientists who designed the radio to somehow cut through the dense clouds to monitor the other compounds. To keep the leaders of the other compounds up to date on the process of 'evolving' people, and probably to keep tabs on what's going on throughout the rest of the world too. Who knows? But if the radio is capable of transmitting communications from one compound to another, it's probably capable of tapping into states where they can send some help."

Dylan scratched his head and sighed. "This compound sounds like the real deal."

Elliot scoffed. "Yeah, it's not some simple camp they put up overnight. And the only reason we're telling you this is so we all can get what we want with as little complication as possible. You got it?"

Dylan shot an angry glare at Elliot. "There's no need to get all macho with me, pretty boy." He teetered on the edge of the sidewalk as he strode. "We're not out here to hurt anybody."

"Could've fooled me." Elliot shot a glare back.

"Listen." Dylan pointed a finger directly at Elliot. "We need food. If that compound has as much food as you say it does, then we'll co-operate so we can get to it as quickly and as safely as we can. That means we need to trust you and you need to trust us. Right?"

"Trust?" Elliot chuckled. "Trust. I don't trust anyone … ever. Especially big *tough* guys with guns."

Adam sighed. "Trust nearly got us killed."

Dylan stopped next to an abandoned car. "How do we know we can trust *you* then?"

Elliot cocked his head and gripped the strap of the pack that hugged his chest. "Why wouldn't you trust us? You had that gun pointed at us demanding us to take you to this place. Why wouldn't we just bow down and do what you want? Besides, we need the radio. So what are we gonna do, lie about where this place is?"

Dylan smirked. "Okay, I got you."

"But how can we trust *you* guys?" Elliot lifted an eyebrow. "Waking us up to rob us? After leading you to the compound, how do we know you won't thank us with a bullet to the face?"

Mira smacked her lips. "We don't do that. We don't kill people."

Elliot's eyebrows dipped and he crossed his arms over his chest. "You just hold guns to their faces for the hell of it?"

"Listen, we don't know you." Dylan's voiced rose as he took a step toward Elliot. "How do we know you wouldn't do the same to us if you were in our position? How do *you* know you wouldn't? Me and you aren't the only ones out here scraping for food. Just the other day, another group stormed us and held Mira at knifepoint, trying to—"

"That's enough!" Mira cried out. While holding the helmet in one hand she covered her face with the other. "That's … enough, Dylan."

"Sorry, Mira." Dylan softened his gaze. He looked to Elliot. "You gotta be tougher than the tough guys to make it out here. That's all I'm saying." Mira sniffed and turned, hiding her discomfort from the group. "Let's keep moving. All right, Mira?"

She nodded and continued walking.

They were silent for the next hour while they hiked through the littered desert. Thinking seemed to make time go by quickly for Elliot. Had Mira been assaulted by the group they referred to? Was that their reason for being cautious and threatening? Elliot was determined to get inside their heads. If they were to make it to the compound, they were going to have to figure out a way to work with each other in order for everyone to get what they wanted.

"What are your names?" Elliot looked to the men first. "Your full name."

Adam rested a hand on Elliot's shoulder. "It's not important."

"It is." Elliot squeezed Adam's arm. He wanted to instill a physical connection and remind Adam to have confidence in him without verbally saying it. "We're gonna have to work together. As much as we don't like it and as much as we don't trust each other, we're gonna have to know each other's names, especially if we're gonna make any progress."

"Dylan McKinley." He grinned. "But don't expect us to become drinking buddies when we're through."

"Was that a joke or your ego talking?" Elliot rolled his eyes. "I don't drink much anyway. So, no worries."

Adam grinned. What had amused him? Elliot didn't know, but he ignored it and looked to the other man.

"Oh, me?" He pointed to his own chest. "I'm Tyler Dalton."

"And I'm Mira Stapley."

Elliot nodded, satisfied. "I'm Elliot Stewart and he's Adam Weber." Adam's handsome lips still held a grin, inappropriately sending butterflies to the pit of Elliot's stomach, which he desperately tried to ignore. He cleared his throat. "Anybody have any special skills?"

Mira shrugged. "I can hold my breath for three minutes." She seemed proud of that achievement, but Elliot hoped for special training that would help them survive harsh environments.

"Anyone have medical training or knows how to filter stagnant water, that kind of thing?" He watched and waited.

Dylan snorted, dangling the gun from his fingertips. "I fix cars. A mechanic."

"Okay." Elliot nodded. "We're not driving anywhere. Driving wouldn't get us too far anyway because of all the crap in the streets, but we might need handy work on the radio in the compound."

Dylan smirked. "I don't do radios. Only cars. I said 'mechanic' not 'radio tech—" Adam snatched the gun from Dylan so fast, he looked at his hand as if trying to remember what he had been holding. "What the fuck, man?!"

Everyone but Elliot took a step back.

"You won't be needing it." Adam held the gun at his side, pointing toward the ground. He glanced to Elliot. "Told you names weren't important."

"So you gonna kill us?" Dylan glared, eyebrows pinched together. "You need us!"

"Not gonna kill anybody." Adam tucked the gun inside his belt at the small of his back. "If we want to get help we're gonna have to work together, and we're gonna have to trust each other."

Elliot snorted. "I don't know about trusting them. They had a gun pointed at your face, Adam."

Mira scoffed, throwing her hands up. "We had to."

"You could've just walked by." Elliot looked to her, making direct eye contact. "Or you could've just asked us for whatever you needed instead of threatening us."

"How could we have known that you wouldn't have pointed the gun at us demanding *our* stuff?" Mira's arms crossed under her nearly nonexistent breasts. "Everyone's looking for something you got. Asking nicely doesn't work when you're dying and desperate."

She had made her point, so Elliot remained silent.

"I haven't aimed a gun at you and I'd like it to stay that way." Adam shrugged. "You in or out? We gotta keep moving." He waited for their responses. Tyler continued walking in the direction of the compound and Mira followed. Anger was written in the scowl lines on Dylan's face, but he followed the other two silently.

CHAPTER FIVE

A Helping Hand

The sun had yet to rise over the horizon and light up the morning with its sporadic glow. Darkness casted black shadows beyond the reach of the flashlight beam. Adam directed the light feet ahead as he walked with Elliot and Titan beside him. Dylan, Mira and Tyler stayed a few yards away but closer to each other, subconsciously, or maybe purposely, forming two distinct groups.

"I remember doing this weeks ago." Adam eyes briefly met Elliot's. "I couldn't wait to get to Refuge Inc. and get medicine and food. I just knew the compound was our dream come true."

"Not so much, right?" Elliot frowned. "With all the fighting we did to get out of that place I'm surprised we're actually going back."

"We gotta do what we gotta do, Elliot, whether we like it or not. We can't keep living like this, waiting around for rescue that isn't coming."

"Exactly." Elliot scoffed. "Deep down you knew rescue wasn't coming, huh?"

Adam shrugged. "I don't know what I was thinking. Maybe I was hoping more than actually thinking. Wishful thinking. That's what they call it, right?" The others formed their tight group, directing the beam of their flashlight to a pile of mangled cars that blocked the road ahead. He lowered his voice. "What do you think of them?"

Elliot looked to the group, watching them with a suspicious glint in his eye. He didn't have to say anything for Adam to know exactly what he thought. "I think we should watch them," Elliot muttered. "Closely."

Adam nodded. "Dylan especially."

"Nah." Elliot gestured to the other man. "That one, the quiet one?"

"Tyler?"

"Yeah, he reminds me of Jeff."

Adam narrowed his eyes and scrunched his nose. "Your ex-boyfriend? Really?"

Elliot fumble for words, fidgeting and gesturing awkwardly. Adam's chest cavity heated. He realized he had been holding his breath in anticipation.

"He looks and acts a little like him." Elliot stared at his own feet as he walked, keeping his eyes from gazing at Tyler or from meeting Adam's as well. "Those quiet types are usually the ones with the most shit up their sleeve."

Titan trotted beside Elliot, tongue hanging out of his gaping canine mouth. The mutt's presence removed the uneasiness that had come over Adam, if only briefly. Elliot was physically attracted to Tyler, the man who had surprised them with a gun to his face upon wakening. Adam wasn't the jealous type, especially when there was no threat. Tyler, Dylan and Mira were the outsiders. They'd have to earn Adam and Elliot's trust before they'd even be considered partners in this dangerous mission. They would have a hard time winning Elliot over especially. Adam knew that. So, there was no risk of Elliot forming some sort of bond with the kid.

Not yet, at least.

A row of empty, collided vehicles blocked the road ahead. Adam moved onward and squeezed through two of the cars, pushing one of the doors closed as he shimmied between. As soon as he lay his hand where the passenger side window had been, his wrist clipped a jagged piece of the mangled side view mirror.

"Shit." He grabbed his wrist and continued through the cars, Elliot and Titan following.

"What happened?" Elliot gently pulled Adam's shoulder until Adam turned to face him. "Did you get hurt?"

"It got me good." Adam eased the satchel off of his shoulder, and the others stopped to watch from a distance. "I need the bandages from my pack."

Elliot had begun digging through the supplies before Adam could finish his sentence. He retrieved the needed materials, and opened a pack of sterile gauze. He then applied the gauze and pressure to the injury. "Does it hurt? Need some aspirin?"

"No, I can bear it." Adam stared into Elliot's dark eyes, witnessing a few locks of his hair sweep over his long, moth-like eyelashes. "Aspirin doesn't allow blood to clot and I'll just keep bleeding."

"Yeah." Elliot wrapped a roll of fresh gauze around Adam's wrist, moving carefully but efficiently.

Adam watched as Elliot worked. The way he moved fast but gingerly warmed Adam's heart and drowned out any pain. He lowered his voice to a mere whisper. "I can stare at you forever."

Elliot paused and looked to Adam, finally making eye contact. "Where did that come from?" Amusement lit up his gaze.

"Watching how you handled that back there..." Adam held back the warm smile that threatened to curl his lips. "I liked that."

Elliot shook his head. "I'm just doing what I gotta do."

"I know. Like taking care of me. You've changed so much. I was worried that you weren't ever gonna talk to me again after what happened back at the hospi— Well, you know."

"You can say it, Adam," Elliot's hushed voice intimately drew Adam in as he continued to wrap the wound. "After what happened at the hospital you thought I was gonna turn into a big, whiny crybaby and give up. How I was when we first met. It crossed my mind, I'm not gonna lie. For a moment, huddling in a corner was tempting, but ... where would that have gotten us? I'm thinking ahead, imagining what our lives together would be like once we're free from this hell and allowed to live and let go. You know? Really let go of our pain and finally enjoy each other ... you and me."

"I know." Adam's smile broke through. "I'm proud of you for staying strong."

Elliot tied the ends of the bandage and looked up into Adam's eyes. Heat hit Adam deep in the chest, the warmth slowly traveled to his extremities, and the urge to pull Elliot against him and deliver the most meaningful kiss struck him. However, he realized he was being watched and swept his thumb across the light stubble on Elliot's chin instead.

Adam turned, looking in the group's direction. They all looked away. "Come on. Let's keep moving."

Another hour went by. They stopped once for a rest and to reenergize with a food and water break. They had made sure everyone was well fed, including Titan. During the trek, little supplies were found from vacant houses and standing structures. Adam had to remind himself that plenty of food and outside help was near. He didn't have a plan to get back inside the compound or to the storage where the food was kept. He had no idea how they were going to get through the blast door. The entrance through the mining tunnel was locked too, and they probably needed a keycard to open it.

Thinking back, he wasn't sure if the mining tunnel provided keycard access from the outside. Even so, they had left the only keycard they knew existed in the storage room when they escaped. They would have to put their heads together for solutions when they got there. Getting there was half the battle.

Tyler rested next to a warped and mangled chain-link fence near one of the buildings they had rummaged through. Barbed wire tangled around the top of the fence where some of the metal links were damaged or missing altogether. Adam made himself comfortable next to Tyler. "Speaking of special skills, what was that move you did with your wrist earlier?"

Tyler shrugged, barely making eye contact. "What do you mean?"

Everyone grew quiet and listened. It was apparent they were curious of the conversation, especially as they repeatedly glanced at Adam and Tyler.

"Back at that building, when we were sleeping," Adam explained. "I grabbed your wrist and you twisted it and did some weird move that made me lose my grip. I mean, I thought I had you, but you just pulled away as if it was nothing."

"Oh, that." Tyler sheepishly smiled. "I learned that in some self-defense classes."

Elliot scoffed, nearly blinding Tyler with the flashlight beam. "So you *do* have special training."

Tyler frowned. "Not really. I learned that years ago, when I was fifteen or sixteen. That's all I really remember from the whole thing."

Adam grabbed his own wrist. "Show me how to do it."

"Okay." Tyler put his arm out and grabbed his wrist with the other hand. "It's simple really. You see this part where your thumb meets the rest of your fingers?"

Adam nodded. "So?"

"So, that's the weakest part of the grip. All you do is twist, yank, and pull your wrist through that weak part of the person's grip. Make sure it's through the weakest part though. You'd get free every time."

Adam tried it on himself. "Every time?"

"Every time." Tyler nodded. "You'd want to do it quickly, before whoever grabbed you has a chance to grab with both hands. If they grab with both hands, you're just fucked. Here, I'll grab your wrist and you just twist, yank and pull your wrist toward you."

Adam held out his uninjured wrist and Tyler grabbed it with one hand. Adam did as instructed. "Twist, yank, pull." His arm was free almost instantly.

"See?" Tyler grinned. "No matter how tight the grip, you'll be able to get out of it. Every time."

"Twist, yank, pull." Adam grinned. The kid had skills.

Rays of light had yet to brighten up the blackened sky. Darkness enveloped them along with the scarcely falling ash. Guided by the beam of Elliot's flashlight, Titan followed obediently. The others strolled along but kept their distance.

Suddenly, out of the silence, a panicked cry came from far in the darkness. Without hesitation, Mira and Tyler darted off into the blackness.

Mira's breaths were hasty as she called out, "Dylan, what happened? Where are you?"

"Down here!" Dylan called back from far in the distance. "Pull me out."

Adam and Elliot looked at each other wide-eyed. A brief moment of awareness hit them as they realized they were needed.

Elliot dashed toward the commotion first, Adam and Titan on his heels. "What happened?"

Mira and Tyler were kneeling, and it took a second for Adam to realize what he was looking at. Elliot quickly swept the light over the wide, gaping hole in front of them. The hole swallowed the light in its massive pitch black abyss. A pair of hands held the rim of the broken asphalt that hung over the mouth of the crater.

"He fell down." Mira slapped Tyler's shoulder. "Do something, stupid."

"What do you want me to do?" Tyler reached down to Dylan, but before he could grab onto him Adam had already taken hold of Dylan's wrist.

"Can you climb?" Adam tugged, noting the heft of the man. "Use your feet."

"The dirt is too loose." Dylan attempted to climb and hoist himself up to no avail. "You need to pull me up before I lose my grip, man."

"Alright, Elliot." Adam glanced over his shoulder to Elliot and held Dylan's wrist in both hands. He anchored himself by digging his feet into the gravel. "Grab my pack so we don't go over."

Before Adam finished talking, Elliot had clutched his pack. "I got you."

"Tyler?" Adam called out. "Come grab his other wrist. Mira, hold Tyler like Elliot's holding me."

Once in place, they inched Dylan over the edge. However, the sound of shoes sliding in the dirt stole Adam's attention. Mira screamed and fell to the floor after losing her balance.

Tyler grunted and jerked forward, letting go of Dylan's hand to brace himself on the broken asphalt at the lip of the hole.

The momentum of Dylan dropping, along with his weight, yanked Adam forward, causing Elliot to lose his grip on Adam's pack. "Oh no." Elliot stumbled and quickly caught onto the waistband of Adam's pants, right alongside the gun, preventing them from falling into the abyss.

Adam was angled in such a way that he peered directly over the heavy, dangling man, and into the dark pit below. One false move and they both would be swallowed up.

"Pull me out of this fucking hole." The bass in Dylan's voice came from anger rather than fear.

Elliot's struggle was apparent. His feet slipped and slid against the gravel while he desperately tried to anchor both men.

Adam's grip on Dylan's wrist weakened. "Stop kicking. You're too damn heavy and you're slipping!"

Mira gasped and rose to her feet. "No! Please don't let him go. Please." She moved behind Elliot and Elliot's pull suddenly became stronger.

Elliot's fingers dug into the waist of Adam's pants. "If I slip again we're all going over."

Adam pulled. "No, we're not. Now come on, Dylan."

With his free hand, Dylan clutched the overhanging asphalt, attempting to hoist himself up and over the cliff. His teeth gritted and he groaned as he used his strength. Most of his upper body was over the rim when the screeching sound of shoes over loose gravel filled the air.

Titan barked. Adam's biceps ached. Elliot pulled and grunted.

Mira screamed, "Tyler, come on. I'm slipping."

Suddenly, Dylan's strength gave way and he let go of the asphalt, nearly dropping into the darkness, but by then Tyler had completed the chain. With one good tug, Dylan slid up and over the ledge. The jagged edge of the asphalt scraped and scratched his chest and belly, but in no time he was sprawled out next to everyone completely safe.

As he attempted to catch his breath, he looked up at Tyler and angrily sneered.

A few moments later, after relaxing and catching their breath, Elliot shined the light down into the massive crater. "What do you think happened?"

Adam shrugged, squeezing and rubbing the tips of his aching fingers. "Maybe a piece of the asteroid did this. It's too big to be a sinkhole."

"How long has this been here?" Tyler asked.

"Probably since the quakes." Elliot stared down thirty or forty feet, as far as the light could reach. "We probably walked near this before and never even knew." He glanced at Adam.

Adam only nodded, his eyes on Dylan, who was drinking the last of a bottle of water. "You okay?"

"Peachy." Dylan shot Tyler a menacing glare, turned away, and walked off into the darkness.

"You might not want to wander off," Elliot said as he lit up Dylan's broad back with the flashlight.

Dylan paused, and then turned to face Elliot. "How about not telling me what I might not wanna do?"

"Look," Elliot stepped forward, "we just saved your ass from plummeting off a cliff because you wanted to wander off."

"Thank you." Dylan shrugged. "Is that what you want, hmm? Thank you, man, for saving my ass. Now if I want to wander off I can do that. You gonna stop me?" He outstretched his arms and puffed out his chest, welcoming a confrontation.

"If you fall down another hole I'm not gonna risk my life to pull you out." Elliot turned back around and stared down into the crater and at its steep, slightly curved sides.

"That's cool." Dylan's voice rose. "I don't expect you to. Hell, my own partner didn't even want to lend a hand."

"I tried!" Tyler crossed his arms over his chest. "You know I lost my glasses. I'm dam near blind. I tried my best. It wasn't like I was just sitting there."

"Might as well," Dylan growled. "That's what you ended up doing."

"I can't fucking see, Dylan. What do you want me to do?" Tyler threw his hands in the air. "You wanted us both to fall to our deaths?"

"It's great to know you'll just let my ass dangle there next time." The sarcasm was obvious in Dylan's voice.

Mira kicked some dirt with the toe of her shoe. "Stop it already, guys. Jeez. Now's not the time. Can we just keep moving?"

CHAPTER SIX

Upon Approach

The sun had finally peeked over the horizon, illuminating the dense eastern clouds in fiery reds, oranges and yellows. The collapsed homes and rugged landscape made the morning feel somber rather than cheery as sunrises used to do.

Adam sensed the gloominess in the air only because he knew in a few minutes he would confront the unwelcoming compound again. Even though he was not excited about it, he reminded himself that the only way they would have a chance at making it out of the gloom was with help from the radio.

As they approached the giant mountain, Adam realized there was no blinking red light from the radio antenna. The large mountain and its many peaks casted menacing shadows that cloaked most of the rocky terrain in complete darkness, including the arched main entrance.

Dylan's heavy boots crushed the fallen dust and molded his shoe prints nearly perfectly in the tacky ash. "So we're just gonna walk through the archway, knock on the door and they'll let us in?"

Adam shook his head. "There's another way in. It'll lead us right into the storage room where they keep the food." Adam stopped and everyone paused too. "I don't know if this is gonna work, but we're gonna have to do this together—"

Dylan lifted his hand, cutting off Adam midsentence. "Me and my crew are *not* gonna just grab the food and leave. Alright? We wanna get the hell out of this city too, you know."

"Right." Adam narrowed his eyes. Was Dylan reading his mind or his body language? Did Dylan notice how Adam kept his back turned away from them at all times, to make sure there were no more surprises with the gun? "We have to get down to the third floor where the prophet, um, Petersen's room is. He has so many secret compartments in that room, I'm sure that's where the radio controls are."

"Okay," Elliot nodded. "It makes sense to have the controls to the important stuff, like the radio and the blast door, in his room."

"Blast door?" Mira shrugged. "Like underground military bunkers? We can't break into blast doors. I mean, that's what they're all about."

Adam cleared his throat. "That's why we're going in another way, but it might not be easy. We'll need some kind of tools to try to break the lock. We already weakened the lock from the inside, but I don't think it'll be that easy getting back in."

"And if we get in," Mira moved forward, worry wrinkled her eyebrows, "how exactly are we gonna get to the radio and food without someone trying to stop us?" It was silent. For a few seconds Adam stared at them without making a sound. They stared back. "Is the plan to kill them?"

Mira had said it. She had said the words Adam was thinking but couldn't verbalize. He didn't want to kill anyone. That was the first time he even thought about it.

Elliot snorted and shook his head. "We're not killing anybody." He looked directly to Mira and used the same words she had spoken earlier. "We don't kill people."

Tyler scratched the short hairs near his temple that had collected an ample amount of dust flakes. "We'll have to prepare ourselves for that. You know, we might have to defend ourselves by any means necessary."

Silence swamped them while contemplating Tyler's words. Adam remembered firing the gun at the elevator when it opened to Petersen and a few enforcers inside. He had pulled the trigger twice. He couldn't even keep his eyes open to see where his bullets had hit, but he had to shoot in defense. It was either pull the trigger or be killed, because Petersen had already shot at them. That time, Anita had been the one to meet Petersen's bullet. Adam wasn't sure he had it in him to aim a firearm and shoot someone point blank.

"We need weapons," Dylan said, interrupting Adam's thoughts. "Let's search those buildings for anything we can use as a weapon; metal pipes, heavy sticks."

Everyone dispersed. Elliot shot Adam a look, shrugged and left to find a weapon too. Adam stayed with Titan, keeping the mutt company. He massaged his aching fingers while kicking around the loose gravel underneath the thick layer of dust. Pulling Dylan from that crater really did a number on his fingers. When everyone returned, Elliot held a long, thin metal rod. It reminded him of the rod that had failed him when hanging from the crumbled overpass bridge weeks ago. Mira held the neck of a broken wine bottle and Tyler had a thick piece of wood with several twisted, rusty nails protruding from it.

Dylan twisted a pieces of dense, sharp metal into a long knife-like weapon. "I'm ready. Let's do this." He headed toward the mammoth mountain and his crew followed.

Adam turned toward the mountain, when Elliot brushed his lips across his tingling earlobe. "Watch them." Elliot shot him a wary glance and then followed behind the crew, heading toward the mountain. He knew Elliot didn't trust them. They knew that too. Adam wasn't even sure if he trusted them either. More reason to make the moment more awkward.

Knowing the blast door would be impenetrable and there was absolutely no way for them to breach it, Elliot led them to the opening near the topside of the mountain—the place they had escaped from weeks ago. He imagined what the inside of the tunnel looked like since his memory escaped him.

He directed the flashlight over the dimly morning-lit landscape, to get an idea of where he stood in proximity to the hole. Everyone searched the gravel and dust covered mountainside for an indication of the hole, the one he, Adam and Mason dug out with their bare hands.

He took a step and tapped the thick dirt with his foot, feeling for anything out of place. With another step, the ground instantly gave way beneath him. A grunt rattled his throat as his foot and leg twisted into the hole he'd been looking for. He slumped forward, arms outstretched to break his fall, but still managed to slam his chest against the ground. "Fuck." He lifted himself to the sitting position and slipped his leg out. "I found the hole," he said dryly.

Adam put out a helping hand. He took it, allowing Adam to pull him to his feet.

"I'll go first." Adam kicked away more of the tacky dust and some of the gravel it clung to. He climbed down into the dark hole, barely squeezing through the jagged opening. Elliot passed him the flashlight and Adam disappeared deeper inside. Everyone followed, including Elliot who chose to go last. Cautiously, Elliot kneeled down into the hole, careful to descend the large hill of rock fragments like everyone before him. No matter how careful, he dangerously skidded down the wall of loose rocks—the remnants of what had been blown from the tunnels to conceal the exit. Titan too skidded down the wall but stayed close.

Once inside, the familiar arched tunnel grew bright with a red hue as round lights secured to the top railing lit the way. Elliot remembered the lights being bright white when they had exited the tunnel. The red gave the tunnel an ominous and aura. The dirt beside the twin mining rails still had his, Adam and Mason's footprints coming from deep within the tunnel. Also present were the large paw prints that trailed around the dust too. The paw prints resembled those of a large dog with teardrop shaped toe pad indentations.

Elliot called out in a loud whisper, "Careful of dogs or coyotes. Big ones."

Quietly and cautiously, they jogged down the tunnel toward the storage room door, passing light after light, which were spaced twenty feet or so apart. The red light illuminated the curved walls and the many wooden logs and boards that had been placed to hold back large loose stones and to keep them from falling into the tunnel, or to reinforce the tunnel and keep it from collapsing in on itself.

The lights also lit up the slumped pile in the dirt beside the door.

Everyone who passed Anita's body looked down at her and grimaced or covered their nose due to the putrid smell of decay.

Even Tyler gagged and dried heaved when passing her body. "Jesus. What happened?"

Adam continued to the door. "Petersen shot at us. He missed us but hit her."

"I don't know if I really want to do this." Mira hastily moved passed the body. "Where I come from, we don't break into places, especially if they're known to inhabit killers."

"What if breaking in was our only way out?" Adam looked down at the metal door where the doorknob should have been. It was as smooth as glass and not even a keycard reader present. Adam hit the door with his palm. "Damn it."

"What's plan B?" Elliot looked at the others, waiting for them to come up with some ideas. Anything.

"There is no plan B." Dylan kicked the loose dirt at his feet.

"Can't hurt to try the main entrance." Adam shrugged.

Everyone headed back to the hole they had entered, except for Elliot. He paused by Anita's body. The colorful headscarf was still wrapped around her long, thick hair, and she looked as peaceful as she did when he last said goodbye. She was no longer lying on her side the way he remembered, but he assumed the dog or whatever animal that had been in the tunnel had been sniffing around her. His heart grew heavy. "Sorry, Anita. I promise, when we get help I will make sure you're properly buried."

No matter the situation, he always felt like he owed her. That feeling would probably never go away as long as her death weighed on his conscience.

Going through the main entrance turned out to be just as ominous as the mining tunnel, especially when lighting was concerned. The lights which used to line the archway were off or no longer working. Dylan reached for his flashlight.

"Keep it off," Adam warned. "Don't wanna use up the batteries."

The main blast door ahead towered eight or nine feet tall, with solid metal density, rusted bolts and oily dirt in the crevices. Out of instinct, Adam placed both hands on the door and gave it a push. To his surprise, the door creaked open.

Adam glanced over his shoulder at all the wide-eyed expressions. Again, he pushed the door until it opened wider than a couple of inches. Elliot and the others took their cue and helped push. Slowly, inch by inch, the door slid open, moving rather fluidly as chunks of rusted metal fragments chipped from its hinges. The door made no sound other than a brief crack and creak. Adam placed his index finger to his lips. "Sshh."

Stepping inside, a sudden sense of familiarity struck him. The last time he was in the main room, it was dimly lit, cold, and several people roamed the corridors or sat on the two wooden benches that lined the walls. Now, the wooden benches were broken into pieces beside the door. No one was seen or heard, and a deep red hue lit up the darkened space.

Where was everyone? And why was the door open?

He looked up to where one of the white lights had been embedded into the metal beam above. The light now shown red, creating a haunting and menacing atmosphere. An odd sensation crept over him, one he couldn't shake.

The silence was loud. A hollow and empty echo originated from the hall where the medical station was located. Suddenly, images of his ex-fiancée, Jena, in her bright green scrubs flashed in his mind. Adam turned to Elliot. Elliot glanced down the same hall and nodded, probably hearing the noise too. Probably understand Adam's need. Adam slowly approached the hall. He grabbed the gun from the small of his back and held it perched at his side. Elliot and Titan followed closely behind.

"Wait." Mira stopped Adam by placing her hand on his shoulder.

He turned, looking into worried eyes. "We have to be quiet."

She nodded, quickly bobbing her head, and then whispered, "Can't we just get some food and go to the radio? We don't have to investigate noises."

Adam looked to each person, and in a low, clear voice, he said, "Stay here. I need to see if someone's back there." *Mainly Jena.*

"We're wasting time." Mira threw her hands up. "We could be in and out without running—"

Adam silenced her by raising one index finger between them. "I need to do this. Okay? Please. Stay here." He turned, slowly continuing down the hall. He glanced back over his shoulder once. Elliot waited with the others and they all watched Adam. Titan watched and waited too as if understanding Adam's intentions.

The sound of shuffling came from the room at the end of the hall and bounced off the cold metal walls of the arched hallway. Adam took one step before the sound of sniffing replaced the shuffling. Was someone wounded and in pain? He continued down the long hall until he was near the medical station. He flattened himself against the wall in order to peek around the corner and into the room undetected. Could it be her? Could she still be there healing people's injuries, or tending to her own and waiting for rescue too? He waited for the sounds to quiet down before he looked around the corner. He swooped around the curve and stared directly into the bloodshot eyes of the hungriest, meanest looking animal.

A massive mountain lion.

"Shit." Adam stiffened his spine, standing tall, as he slowly backed away from the large two-hundred-pound looking beast. She had to weigh as much as he did, give or take. Her muscle and mass was the first thing that registered in his mind.

Her fair coat shown red from the red lights that illuminated the space, the lighter patch under her belly shown brighter. Rounded ears perked above her head as she stared with dark, bloodshot eyes and glided forward, matching Adam's speed as he moved away. The muscles under her coat were clearly visible as they flexed around her sharp shoulders when she slinked along, moving closer, head down, round eyes locked onto Adam's.

He clutched the gun more firmly in his palm and thought pointing the gun at her would cause her to pounce, as if she understood the threat of the weapon and would act in self-defense. So instead of lifting the gun, he watched her movements, gauging if and when to aim and shoot. One foot behind the other, he slowly backed down the hall. He couldn't take his eyes off of the wild cat, afraid that she was clever enough to seize the moment and make him her snack.

From down the hall behind him, Mira's gasp was followed by the low grumble of indiscernible whispers. With every step backward, one foot carefully behind the other, Titan barked. Adam paused and the cat paused too. She was definitely as smart as he had feared.

A guttural purr bellowed from the feline and she crouched even lower, her chest inches above the uneven, chipped concrete floor. She crept closer, her eyes still locked onto Adam's as if waiting for an opportune moment. If he broke eye contact she'd take him by surprise and attack. Because of that concern, he kept his eyes locked onto hers.

Their breathing matched as he watched her belly rapidly rise and fall with every hastened breath. She, too, must have had adrenaline surging throughout her body, triggering that flight or fight reaction. As much as Adam wanted to run, he could sense she wanted a fight. Before he could think too much into it, Titan barked again and again, louder, closer, threatening, viciously.

A breathy whisper broke through the barks. "Adam, run. Run."

Running would surely trigger her. "*You* guys run," Adam said, between Titan's barks. The cat growled again, the deep rumbling purr came from deep within like a menacing beast. She continued to slowly move closer. Her large paws tapped the floor lightly with every step, like a light-weight dancer, except her tapping and mass was related to her skill as a predator.

"Titan!" Elliot shouted.

Adam desperately wanted to turn to see what was happening but he knew better than to take his eyes off of the cat. Then something brushed the side of his leg and he looked down just as Titan ran by, rushing toward the cat and stopping a meager foot away to bark, growl and snap his teeth at the much larger feline.

"Adam!" Elliot called out. "Titan!"

Adam moved quicker, nearly jogging backwards, watching in horror as the cat swiped her paw at their beloved canine and sent the dog tumbling down the hall. Adam backed into the wall and quickly looked behind him toward the large main room where only Elliot stood, waving for him and pointing toward the stairwell. Quickly, Adam turned back around. The cat stood over their wounded dog and gapped her mouth, revealing sharp teeth that looked as if they were coated in blood due to the overhead lights.

She lowered her opened jaws to Titan's neck and Adam lifted the gun, aimed and pulled the trigger.

The roar that escaped the cat drummed down the hall and reverberated through Adam's every nerve. She backed away from Titan and quickly turned to escape into the medical station.

Elliot was suddenly beside him, startling him. "Let's go. Now."

CHAPTER SEVEN

Breaking and Entering

"Everybody's waiting in there for the elevator." Elliot pointed toward the stairwell door. "I'm getting Titan." He lifted his rusted iron rod in his hand.

"That cat's gonna kill you." Adam grabbed Elliot's other hand and tugged him back.

Elliot pulled his hand free. "Cover me." He met Adam's eyes, the look of utter horror transferred between them. "I can't leave him, Adam." Just the thought of allowing that cat to do what it pleased to Titan didn't sit well with Elliot and fueled him even more. Not only was Titan one of them, he was a symbol of strength, perseverance and hope. The dog had been outside the compound for weeks almost intuitively waiting for his and Adam's return. How could he just abandon the poor mutt now?

"Be quick." Adam pointed the gun down the darkened hall, inching toward the injured dog. The red light casted shadows down the arched corridor that could easily conceal a big cat. Adam took note.

Elliot moved fast. He ran the few feet to Titan who lay on the concrete floor. Blood seeped from the dog's ear. He tried to hoist Titan into his arms, but the rod in his hand prevented him from getting a good grip. He dropped the weapon. The clinking of the metal against concrete rang in his ear. He squatted and tried to lift the dog again but the weight of the dog and his haste unbalanced him.

"He's too heavy—"

The large cat suddenly appeared from around the corner. It purred and the sound sent rumbling chills throughout Elliot's every nerve and along his arm hairs. He fell back on his bottom, eyes locked on the larger, intimidating cat as it snaked closer.

"Shoot it," Elliot yelled. "Adam, shoot."

"I will if I have to. Get Titan and move."

Elliot's legs didn't lift him to run as he had demanded, they slid him back along the floor instead. "Adam. Shoot it."

"Get Titan!"

"Kill it."

"I only have two bullets. Now move."

Elliot didn't think, he just stood, grabbed Titan's forearms and pulled, dragging the unconscious mutt down the cold, narrow hallway and back toward the main room.

Adam continued to aim the gun at the cat, one hand held the butt of the gun, one finger placed on the trigger, the other hand supported his wrist. "You need to run, Elliot. I'm gonna shoot and it might not stop her."

Elliot dragged the dog back through the door to the stairwell landing. Mira held the door for him while gripping the neck of the broken bottle. Adam quickly followed, backing onto the landing and helping to close the door.

The darkness was more apparent in the stairwell than it was in the hall. The round, embedded lights lined the concrete walls, spiraling down the squared staircase and glowed red and dim. Dylan took out his flashlight to help light the space.

Elliot had expected the elevator door to have been opened, waiting for them to enter. It wasn't. He pressed the bulb of the embedded LED light beside the door. It clicked but nothing else happened.

Elliot looked to each person, who all held their respective weapons at their side. He wondered if they would have intervened if the cat had attacked him. Trusting someone depended on their actions, after all. "Did you call the elevator like I told you?" He huffed, trying to catch his breath.

"There was nothing, man." Dylan threw his hands up. "Let's just take the stairs."

"We're gonna have to move now." Elliot kneeled next to Titan whose belly rose and fell rapidly. He was still alive but the dog's eyes were closed and he lay motionless, bleeding from his ear. "Damn it, Titan." The sadness in Elliot's voice carried through even though he tried to prevent it. He lifted the sixty pound dog and took a few steps down the concrete staircase.

Adam stopped him by placing a hand on his shoulder. "I'll carry him. You lead the way."

Elliot turned and stared into the worried eyes of his best friend. He tried to smile. "Thanks." He placed Titan into Adam's strong arms and received the gun in exchange.

"There're only two bullets left," Adam reminded him.

Elliot took the gun in his palm. It was warm from Adam's body heat and heavier than it looked. Holding a firearm gave him some sort of boost. He felt more in control with the gun in his hand than he did without it. Strange. "Come on, guys." He slipped his fingers around the handle and dropped the gun to his side like Adam had done, being conscious of where he pointed it. "If anybody's here they might be on the bottom floors. So be prepared."

Dylan cleared his throat. "Is that where the food is?"

"No, the way to the storage was through the elevator." Elliot nodded toward the concrete wall across from him where he remembered the slab once recessing and opening to a secret elevator. "I think the power's down or something. Whatever happened here is stopping the elevator from working. To get to the storage room we need an enforcer key to access it from the elevator. We'll need power to use the elevator."

Mira moved forward, hands rung together from apparent nervousness. "So what's down there then? The radio?"

Adam stepped forward. "Probably. The controls anyway. But there's somewhere we can go to get settled, prepare, and plan our next move. If we're able to get to it."

"Where?" Mira asked, her dark eyes wide.

"Mason's room." Adam looked to Elliot. "If we can get to the second floor and get inside to the pods without a problem, then I can get us into—"

A loud bang rang the landing door, startling everyone. Then another bang followed by immediate scratching.

"Is that the cat?" Mira's voice quivered as she took a few steps down the stairs, keeping an eye on the door.

"I think it is." Adam descended the concrete stairs too, carrying Titan's in his arms like an injured and sleeping child. "We need to move before it gets in here."

They rushed down the stairs as the banging continued. The noise faded and eventually ceased the further they descended. The stairs hooked right in a square pattern that seemed to go on forever. Finally, Elliot reached the second floor landing.

Elliot glanced over his shoulder at Adam, lifted the gun, held it up shoulder-level as he once saw Adam do, and reached for the door with his other hand. The door opened almost effortlessly until it snagged on debris. He soon realized broken furniture and twin sized mattresses were placed by the door as a barricade. Beyond the obstruction, an empty space replicated the first floor exactly, except the walls weren't rusty, and the floors weren't uneven and chipped.

Quietly, Elliot stepped over the threshold, maneuvering past the debris and entering the main room. Dylan's flashlight lit the darkened areas, while an odd silence rattled Elliot's nerves. Where had everyone gone? He nearly tiptoed as he walked farther into the large room. Six halls connected to the main room and fanned out like fingers. Only a soft red glow shined from the overhead, recessed lights of every darkened hall.

"Turn the flashlight off, Dylan. Conserve the batteries." Adam adjusted Titan in his arms. "Let's check out Mason's room but be quiet. We're probably not alone down here."

From the look of it, Elliot thought otherwise.

"Who exactly is Mason?" Dylan loosely held the makeshift blade at his side near his thigh.

Elliot eyeballed Dylan's weapon, remembering waking up to a gun pointed in Adam's face. "He's the guy who helped us get out of here. Well, we helped each other."

Adam took a few steps toward the hall to Pod 1. "He was one of the people who helped build this place, and he had a room down here. I know how to get in."

"This is crazy." Mira shook her head and ran her palms over her face. "This place is freaking creepy. I just wanna do what we came to do and get the hell outta here."

"Wasn't always creepy." Adam looked down the Pod 1 hall. "Last time I saw this floor it was beautiful." He continued down the hall, eyes focused on the darkness ahead.

Elliot allowed Tyler and the others to go before him as he kept an eye on Dylan and his knife, which Dylan nervously tapped against his thigh. Tempted to say something, to voice some sort of warning about the weapon, Elliot cleared his throat and ... He paused.

The sound of footsteps came from the main room behind him.

He quickly turned, aiming the handgun at ... nothing. Again, it was quiet. He searched with his eyes, remaining motionless and holding his breath. The compound definitely had a creepy vibe to it when empty and surrounded in a blood red hue usually seen in horror movies. He turned again and continued to follow the others farther into the hall. On the floor beside him, propped against the wall, lay an oil painting of some sort of abstract art, protected by what could have been a golden frame. Farther down the hall hung another painting. It looked similar to the piece of art beside him, but crookedly dangled on the wall instead. And further down the hall, nearly hidden in the shadows, was what looked like wilting plants in a raised flower bed positioned in the middle of the hall. Plants? Underground? Above the plants, on the ceiling, was a large piece of glass and—

A thud sounded from behind him. He turned and raised the gun again, wishing he had his flashlight instead. Keeping his voice low but loud enough for the crew to hear, he whispered, "Guys? Something's down here."

"What are you talking about?" Tyler's soft voice echoed.

"Something's here." Elliot swallowed, gulping. "Listen."

The hall was deathly quiet while everyone remained motionless, listening. A cold chill swept over Elliot as he waited for the sound again.

Finally, Adam exhaled. "Come on. The room's right up here."

Elliot shook his head. "I know I heard something. It sounded like—" A loud bang sounded from one of the other halls.

Mira gasped. "What the hell was that?"

Then uneven booted stomps followed the bang and grew increasingly louder. Closer?

Elliot rushed down the hall to Adam who had placed Titan on the floor beside the door and had disappeared into a shallow entryway in front of the door. Adam pressed numbers on the keypad anchored on the wall next to the door, causing three loud beeps to follow after every fourth dial.

They all huddled together. Dylan, Mira and Tyler gripped their weapons and stared down the hall toward the noises, waiting the door to open or for a challenge. Whichever came first.

Elliot tried the doorknob. "I thought you knew the code."

"Halloween. Remember?" Adam pressed in the date again. "His birthday."

The sound of the heavy boots stomping the solid concrete grew louder, faster and closer.

"Well, what's the problem?" Elliot's heart raced at the thought of confronting unpredictable strangers.

Adam growled. "It's not working." He reached out, testing the doorknob after another series of beeps.

"Fuck." Elliot looked down the hall at the dark humanoid shadows creeping along the floor of the main room.

"Guys?" Tyler whispered nervously.

"Maybe because the power's weird." Adam punched in the numbers again, carefully and a bit slower. "One, zero, three, one." It beeped once and a *click* came from the lock.

A deep male voice called from the main room, "Who's there?"

CHAPTER EIGHT

Cleansing

As everyone quickly rushed inside the brightly lit room, Adam scooped Titan up in his arms and hustled inside. Once inside, Adam quietly closed and locked the door behind him. He stood by the door, looking out of the small peephole, waiting and listening. The heavy disembodied footsteps didn't follow them down the hall as he had expected. He didn't hear or see anyone at all. Where was everyone anyway? Especially the people on the top floor? The ones who really needed rescuing.

"What the hell is this?" Dylan walked by the massive, unkempt bed and into the open, large and cozy living area. Adam followed them deeper into the room, watching the confused expression on Dylan's face as Dylan wondered aloud, "Am I seeing this right?"

The lights were soft, giving the room a comfy, cozy feeling. No red lights to exude underground dungeon vibes.

A curtain hung on the wall as if drawn closed over a large window. Elliot scoffed. "So this is how great they were living down here. Never thought life was *this* nice for everyone on the lower floors." He pulled the curtain back to reveal cream colored drywall on the other side.

Mira snorted. "For a second, I really thought there was a window back there."

Tyler sat on the corner of the bed and placed his weapon on the floor beside him. The rusted nails of his wooden club dug into the cream colored carpet. "Perfect for the aesthetics."

Elliot looked over his shoulder to Tyler. "Huh?"

"You know." Tyler shrugged. "Perfect way to make it look like a real home and not an underground bunker."

Elliot's gaze lingered on Tyler's a beat too long. Adam caught the look as he lay Titan in the center of the plush bed. Adam ran his palm along Titan's furry back, realizing the mutt was awake, blinking and looking at him with dark, sorrowful eyes. The dog remained nearly motionless, languidly licking tiny, dried blood drops from his snout.

Elliot sat next to Titan. "You think he'll be alright?" He took his pack off and retrieved a bottle of water from inside.

Adam patted the dog's head. "Sure. He'll be fine. Probably needs a rest."

Elliot huffed. "We need to figure out what we're gonna do if those people come back. Who were they anyway? Guards?" He poured some of the water into a small cup and allowed Titan to drink from it.

Adam nodded. "From the sound of their boots, they were probably enforcers."

"This place seems empty." Elliot shook his head. "Everyone disappeared. Why are enforcers still here?"

"I don't know." Adam walked to the corner near the bathroom. "Maybe they have nowhere else to go. I don't know. But they didn't follow us. So maybe they don't want trouble, and as long as we stay out of their way they'll leave us alone."

Dylan scoffed. "Sounds like wishful thinking to me."

Adam dropped his pack to the floor and scanned the room with his eyes, ignoring Dylan's comment. The room looked the exact same way he had left it the last time he was there. A pile of dirty laundry on the floor, a messy bed, pillows thrown about. The empty beer bottle was still on the nightstand next to the thick-spine hardcover book and the wicker shaded lamp. Everything looked the same, which surprisingly made him relax. "There's booze in the fridge, by the way."

Mira opened the mini refrigerator. "Oh, my god. There is!" She grabbed some of the bottles by the neck. "Shit, they're warm. The fridge is fried."

"Or the power's out," Elliot suggested.

"Why would the lights be on if the power is out?" Mira asked.

Elliot shrugged. "Maybe only certain things work. Like, some of the lights and the keypads. I don't know."

Dylan reached out to Mira. "I don't care if they're warm. I'll take one."

Entering the bathroom, Adam looked to the floor for the lifted twelve-by-twelve linoleum tile where he had found the compound blueprint, along with several mini CDs that contained recordings from the other compounds, and the real Eugene's keycard. The image of the older black man with the rimless glasses was forever burned into his memory. Petersen was no prophet. He was a fraud in every sense of the word.

Adam stood before the sink and studied his reflection in the antique mirror. The image revealed a filthy and much thinner version of himself than he was used to. Survival was surely kicking his ass. He turned on the faucet. To his amazement, clear water sprouted from the nozzle. He grinned as he dipped his face into the basin and splashed warm water onto his forehead with his palms. He even took a few gulps.

From the room, Tyler called out, "There's clothes in the closets and drawers too. Maybe we have enough time to relax and freshen up a little."

"Are you crazy?" Dylan chuckled. "We don't have time to freshen up. We need to do what we came to do."

Adam emerged from the bathroom. "Let's stay alert and prepared no matter what. That's number one. But we can still wash up a little bit. Breathe and recoup for a second. Grab a bite, a drink, tend to our wounds." He looked to Titan who now lay alert on the bed with his paws under his chin.

Elliot immediately pulled first aid supplies from his pack. "Sounds like the water's running in the bathroom. I vote clean up. Take turns, but make it quick." He glanced over his shoulder. "Ladies first."

Mira looked to Dylan, her eyes widened as her neck muscles flexed from tension. "Dylan, can you—"

"Sure." Dylan nodded. A haunting sadness took over his expression. "I'll be right here keeping an eye on everything."

Mira glanced to each man as if gauging their intentions. "I'll be really quick. Okay, Dylan?"

Dylan smiled warmly. "I'll be right here. Promise."

She entered the bathroom, closed and locked the door behind her. A few seconds later the shower started.

Dylan paced in front of the bathroom door. "That woman's been to Hell and back." He shook his head, not making eye contact with anyone.

Elliot cleaned the deep scratch near Titan's ear and wiped away the dried blood from his fur. As soon as he finished, the shower shut off and Mira walked out of the bathroom fully clothed. Her face and hands were clean, but Adam could tell she never stepped foot in the shower. She must've rushed because her hair was still dry and contained traces of ash.

Dylan put his hand on her shoulder as she emerged. "Everything alright?"

She nodded. "Next."

"Do you mind if I go?" he asked her.

She shook her head and bashfully glanced at Adam.

Dylan patted her shoulder and stepped into the bathroom, closing the door behind him.

Elliot opened another package of sterile gauze. He cut his eye to Tyler and cleared his throat. "Uh, you got a scratch by your eye. You want me to look at it?"

Tyler turned from the closet, where he had been eyeing the clothes. "Who? Me?" He pointed to his own chest.

"Yeah." Elliot stood with the gauze in hand. "I mean, I can clean it for you if you want."

Tyler looked back and forth between Adam and Elliot as if he was unsure. "Well, uh, okay."

Elliot moved forward and stopped millimeters from Tyler. He lifted the gauze to Tyler's brow bone, and Tyler hissed and flinched. Elliot chuckled. "It'll burn for just a second."

Adam folded his arms over his chest, exhaled and chewed his bottom lip. He focused on the way Elliot tipped and angled Tyler's chin with his fingertips, lifted the gauze, and blew on the tiny cut. Anger rose to Adam's throat in the form of a lump that wouldn't budge, especially when Elliot's lips vaguely puckered as he blew.

Mira sniffed, taking Adam out of his thoughts and making him more aware of his searing body heat. He looked away, but the urge to watch, the fear of missing something important—a touch, a look, a well-timed smile—made him look up again.

Elliot placed the gauze into Tyler's palm and lifted Tyler's hand to the cut. "There. You'll be fine." Elliot finally looked to Adam. "How's your wrist? Want me to take a look at it?"

"It's ... fine." He crossed his arms tighter over his chest. Even his breathing was affected— shallow and quickened. Or was that an odd feeling of disloyalty that grew under his skin?

"I can take a quick look at it." Elliot moved closer, his bicep flexed when he reached out toward Adam. "Just tending to everybody's needs."

Had Tyler noticed Elliot's muscular arms? Adam glared at Tyler while images of his thin, dry lips on Elliot's full, moist lips flashed before his eyes. He couldn't stop that damned what-if scenario from entering his thoughts. Elliot had practically shoved the thought in his mind after revealing that Tyler reminded him of his ex-boyfriend.

Before Elliot got any closer, Dylan came out of the bathroom, interrupting the moment. He had scars on his naked shoulders and chest, fresh scratches near his navel, and his braided hair held onto tiny droplets of water.

"That water's nice and hot." Dylan grinned. Just the look of satisfaction on his face made it obvious that he had enjoyed his cleansing.

"My turn." Tyler slid past Dylan to lock himself inside the bathroom. Elliot handed Dylan gauze and tape for his cuts, but Dylan refused. A few minutes later, Tyler emerged from the bathroom, looking just as satisfied as Dylan.

"Well," Elliot dropped his hands to his sides. "I guess I'll go next." He flashed Adam a worried look, did the same to Titan, and disappeared inside the bathroom.

Adam paced in front of the messy bed, arms still crossed. Strangely, it felt better that way, to cross his arms. It seemed like he had more control of his emotions because of it. But then again, with him seeing red literally and figuratively, he didn't quite trust his emotions.

Mira sat on the carpeted floor with her back anchored against the bed. Tyler held the gauze near his eye and stood before the closet. Dylan went to the mini fridge and grabbed another bottle of beer.

Every time Adam looked to Tyler, curse words came to mind, but he bit his bottom lip to keep them from escaping his mouth. It was then he realized why he had been keeping his arms crossed, to prevent his hands from gripping Tyler's neck and strangling the pretty bastard. He really didn't have it in him to hurt someone because of his own insecurities. Instead of envisioning his hands around the guy's throat, he leaned closer to the bathroom door and listened to the spray of water that came from the shower. He tapped the door with his knuckle and waited for Elliot to crack it open. Once open, he squeezed through the crack, entering the decent sized bathroom.

Sticky humidity hit him instantly. The mirror which hung on the wall fogged over as he attempted to look at his reflection.

"What's going on?" Elliot narrowed his eyes as he stood near the shower wearing nothing but his nearly-too-large boxer-briefs that hung from his narrow hips.

Adam swiped his hand over the cold glass of the mirror to clear the foggy mist and to get a better view of Elliot in the reflection. "I need to brush my teeth."

"What about them?" Elliot gestured to the door and lowered his voice. "You trust them out there alone?"

"I'm not worried about them." A quiet stillness overpowered the roaring of the shower. A few seconds went by and Adam looked up in the mirror to see Elliot nod behind him. Then Elliot hooked his thumbs into the loose rim of his underpants and pushed them down over his shapely thighs and off completely. His ass muscles flexed perfectly as he stepped into the tub and under the spewing water droplets. Adam cleared his throat and opened the mirror. The sound of textured glass rattled as the shower door close.

In the underground home of a fortunate man like Mason, Adam expected to find sealed toothbrushes behind the mirror but only saw a half used tube of toothpaste, a box of Band-Aids, and other hygienic items. He squeezed a pea size of the mint-scented paste onto his finger. Sensing a strange numbness near his fingernail, he paused to examine it. Seeing nothing out of the ordinary, he then continued to use his finger as a toothbrush to clean his teeth and mouth.

The squishing sound of soap lathering as Elliot washed himself came from the shower. "After this, we're gonna make our way down to the third level or should we try to get to the storage for food first?"

Adam didn't answer, he removed his clothes instead, peeling off layer after layer of grimy clothing from his tense body, taking off the bandage around his wrist too, which he quickly replaced with a Band-Aid. The cut wasn't as bad as it initially seemed and the bleeding had stopped. Elliot eyes widened when Adam stepped into the shower with him, but neither said anything. Elliot only moved back from the stream to allow the warm water run down over Adam's body.

"Elliot." The name whispered past Adam's moist lips. He reached out, touching Elliot's slender abdomen, trailing his fingers down along one of the two deep creases that led below to his hairline. "I might..." The water trickled down over Adam's hair and face, hot and refreshing at the same time. Memories of cleansing under the broken water main when they had first met flooded his thoughts. The lump in Adam's throat ached. "I'm ..." He huffed, struggling to let the words through. "I'm afraid I might lose you."

"You might lose me?" Elliot scoffed. "I'm not going anywhere, Adam." He stepped forward, blatantly allowing Adam's fingertips to further explore his torso. Elliot's voice came out low and seductive. "You got me, if you want me or not. I'm not going anywhere. Ever." Elliot glided his own fingertips along Adam's sharp jawline, forcing him to make eye contact. "You never seem to be afraid of anything. So why are you afraid now?"

"You're all I've got." Adam's fingers glided up over Elliot's wet shoulders. He gripped them and pulled Elliot closer until their soaked foreheads rested against one another's. It was true, Adam didn't have anyone else. "I need you to—" He paused. "Be mine ... always."

Elliot narrowed his eyes in what looked like confusion. "I'm all yours." He lifted his head and kissed Adam's bottom lip as waves of water and heat coated their bodies. "Forever."

"Promise me." Adam pulled Elliot's against him, chest to chest. The small patch of coarse hair on Elliot's chest scratched Adam's nipple as he slid his hands down to the small of Elliot's back, holding their bodies against one another's while he searched Elliot's beautiful, rapidly blinking brown eyes.

"I swear, Adam. I'm all yours." The worried look in Elliot's eyes dissipated when he grazed the stubble on Adam's chin with his teeth. "No one or nothing can come between us. I'm all yours. Forever. I promise." He smiled briefly. "Now touch me." He nipped the heated flesh on Adam's neck with his teeth. Adam moaned, closed his eyes and allowed his head fall back, further exposing his neck. Sharp electric prickles shot down his body and straight to his groin.

"Elliot." He lifted his head and looked back into Elliot's eyes before tangling his fingers into the dark loose curls at the nape of Elliot's neck. He loved the way Elliot had taken control out there under the clouded darkness, the same way he took the lead now. Warmth crept to Adam's loins as he replayed Elliot's orders in his mind. *Touch me.* Both hands cradled Elliot's head and Adam dropped his mouth to those amazingly full, moist lips. Instead of closing his eyes he lowered them, keeping them slightly open as not to miss the sex-starved look on Elliot's face.

Elliot spoke into the kiss, "I missed you."

He had never left Elliot's side to be missed, but he knew exactly what Elliot meant. "I missed *you.*" And he had. Elliot—the once lonely beauty, the passionate fighter, the heroic companion, the real Elliot—was back. "Missed this too. Touching you, tasting you ..." He sighed as Elliot reached down between them to cup Adam's heavy balls. "... Fucking you."

"Mm, yeah." Elliot's teeth grazed Adam's bottom lip while he gently fondled Adam in his wet palm. "Touch me," Elliot reminded him.

Adam fingers met Elliot's hardened shaft. Elliot's hot, thick erection pressed up against his own belly, right under his navel and between the deep grooves on each side of his lower abdomen. Adam watched his working hand through the stream of water that ran down his face while he rhythmically caressed the tip of Elliot's cock with his fingertips.

He glanced up just in time to see Elliot's eyes flutter in pleasure and a moan escape his parted lips. Using the natural lubricant that collected at the tip, Adam easily glided his fingers up and down, focusing directly on and under the flared head. His own cock hardened and lengthened between their bodies as Elliot continue to fondle him.

Suddenly, he caught sight of the tip of Elliot's tongue as it slid out from between his plump lips, moistening them and making them even more desirable. Adam leaned forward and captured Elliot's lips in a kiss. This time, the kiss was fast and rough, fueled by a need to have a part of his body inside of Elliot. In this case, his tongue attempted to satisfy the urge. Alternating between pecks, licks and an occasional suck, he wrapped his fingers around Elliot's cock and began a slow glide up to the tip and down to the base, feeling it throb in his fist.

"God, Adam," Elliot whispered. "You're gonna make me come already." He panted heavily as if he had been struggling to hold back.

"You want me to?" Adam continued to lay soft kisses on Elliot's lips. "You want me to make you come?"

"Uh-huh." Elliot nodded. "Only if *you* want me to."

"I do." Adam spotted a bottle of body oil in the corner of the tub, standing next to a collection of shampoo and other hair products. After squeezing a tiny amount into his palm, he dipped his head, lowering his mouth to Elliot's nipple as he gently squeezed his oiled grip around Elliot's cock. "Tell me how you like it."

Elliot groaned. "You can do whatever you want to me. As long as you're doing it, I'm gonna love it."

Adam licked and gently sucked Elliot's hardened nipple, and then stood to meet his gaze. "You wanna watch? I like to watch as it shoots."

Elliot's breathing grew heavy. His eyes widened, he nodded and bit his bottom lip. Was he surprised by Adam's admission, aroused by it, or both?

Adam ran his palm along the length of Elliot's cock, distributing the oil evenly along Elliot's shaft. His own heart seemed to beat out of his chest as he witnessed pleasure sweep across Elliot's face. His palm glided up toward the head of Elliot's cock and up over the tip, causing the darkened cock to slip from his grip. Elliot moaned in pleasure and rested against the cold shower door, hips pushed forward, eyes fluttering, chest heaving.

Again, Adam gripped the head with his thumb and the tips of his fingers, and ran his slick fingertips up over the sensitive flared skin and back down again. He paused just under the ridge of the flare to tease the thick vein, and then continued up, over and back down repeatedly. He moved slowly, teasingly, milking the pent-up pleasure. He watched as his thumb swept along the tip, smearing the beads of pre-come equally around the head.

"God!" Elliot's eyes squeezed shut and he cupped his own balls in his palm, gently massaging. The other palm caressed his lower abdomen just above his hairline, as if making use of both hands in an attempt to stifle the urge to grab his own cock and finish himself. Adam controlled Elliot's cock and when, and if, Elliot would finish. Knowing that made his own hard-on throb in excitement.

Adam's thumb slid over the slit at the tip, over and over, slower and slower. He felt the drumming of Elliot's rapid heartbeat on his flesh as it pulsed through Elliot's cock. Elliot's moan caused Adam to hold his own hardened flesh in his free hand, squeezing it to satisfy its urge to be touched. He watched as more and more pre-come coated the tip of Elliot's hard-on. As bead after bead formed, Adam swept it away with the pad of his thumb.

He finally tore his eyes away from the impressive cock to look into Elliot's flushed face. "Open your eyes," Adam whispered. "You gotta watch."

When Elliot opened his eyes they were low, and his once rapid blinking slowed. Elliot continued to bite his bottom lip, letting the plump, wet flesh pull through his teeth just to remoisten them with a lick and bite it again. Elliot's hand glided over his navel, then his nipples, then down further near the base of his shaft. Elliot was close to orgasm, but was desperately trying to prolong it, to hold back, to control the urge.

Adam began a gentle tug and pull of Elliot's hardness, flicking his wrist near the tip the way he did when working his own. He moved closer, just enough to allow his wrist to graze his own stiff cock while he fisted Elliot's. His gaze lifted to Elliot's eyes again. Satisfaction swirled through him as he confirmed Elliot was watching. "You like it?" Adam whispered.

"Oh, yeah." Elliot panted, briefly closing his eyes. "It so good."

"I can do this forever if you let me." Adam grinned, remembering similar words Elliot had said to him during their second sexual encounter surrounding a campfire out in the darkness. However, it wasn't just the moment that compelled him to make such promises, he meant every single word including *forever.*

"Adam..." Elliot squirmed and panted. "I'm ... I'm..." He shut his eyes and a deep groan escaped his lips.

"Open your eyes and look," Adam insisted, anticipating the moment.

Elliot looked down at his stiff cock in Adam's pumping fist, and together they watched as a long, thick rope of semen suddenly spurted from the slit. "God—" Followed by another rope, and another, landing on Adam's torso. "Fuck ..." Elliot groaned through clenched teeth. The last bit of milky semen drizzled down Adam's knuckles and disappeared into the water below. Elliot breathed heavily, relaxing against the shower door.

"Love that." Adam pressed his lips to Elliot's and gripped his own throbbing cock. "That was so good."

Elliot pulled Adam against him and returned the kiss, tongues glided alongside one another's, and they sucked and nibbled each other's lips. Their noses pressed together, so they turned their heads to the side, alternating sides as their hands moved over each other's body as frantically as their kiss.

Adam dropped to his knees before Elliot, smelling the vanilla scented soap on his skin. He pressed a kiss to the flesh over Elliot's pelvic bone and licked the skin over the exact spot.

Elliot pushed him back and shook his head. "No. Enough of me. Now, it's your turn." He pushed Adam's shoulder until he lay back against the sloped end of the tub. The water trickled down over Elliot's body as he towered over him, handing Adam the bottle of body oil. The water wasn't as hot as it once was but Adam didn't care. He took the bottle, poured a liberal amount of the oil in is palm, and handed it back. With his eyes on Elliot and Elliot's eyes on Adam's cock, he rubbed the oil onto his own erection, making sure to smear it from tip to base, with the excess he massaged his balls. Adam worked his own harden flesh, stifling a groan that threatened to escape his lips.

Watching the water sheath down Elliot's fit body and run off of his semi-hard cock and empty balls, made Adam more excited than watching Elliot orgasm. God, the anticipation.

Elliot moved forward, one leg on each side of Adam's body. He cupped his own balls in his hand as he kneeled over Adam's cock, straddling him. Adam's heart skipped a beat when he realized what was about to happen. He aimed his cock toward Elliot's tightness and Elliot lowered himself onto it.

Adam groaned and sat forward until he and Elliot were nearly chest to chest. "Ride it," he ordered, moaning and flexing his hips in anticipation. "Mm, Elliot. Ride my cock." Elliot's grinded his hips and they both moaned. Adam's slick cock nearly slid completely from Elliot's warm, tight body, but quickly glided back inside. "Ah, that's it."

Elliot rocked, holding his own cock in one hand and pulling Adam forward by his shoulder with the other. "It's your turn to come," he whispered. "I want to feel it inside me."

"Yeah," Adam breathed, looking up into brown eyes. He wanted the same.

Elliot lifted himself until Adam's cock nearly slid out of his tightness, then he lowered himself again. "Mm, you like that?"

"I do."

"You want more?"

Adam nodded, nearly out of breath.

Elliot lifted and lowered himself onto Adam again and again, impaling himself on Adam's thick, ridged length. "Feels good."

"Yes," Adam agreed. "More. I'm almost there."

Elliot bit his own lip and braced the wall. Using his legs, he lifted himself again, but instead of slowly lowering himself onto Adam's hardness he bounced, sliding it in and out with a quick, even rhythm. Adam's senses were overwhelmed. The thought of being connected by the few inches of his cock, plunging in and gliding out of Elliot's body, sent him over the edge.

Then it happened, Adam's legs stiffened, his head dropped back, and a violent orgasm tore through him, making him shudder. "Oh, god," he groaned. His toes curled and he gripped Elliot's hips, ending his seductive ride. A few seconds past and Elliot stood. A copious mount of semen trickled down his cock, balls and thighs.

Adam tried to catch his breath as he watched Elliot continue to bathe, washing off all evidence of their intimacy.

"Water's cold now," Elliot said from under the spray of the shower head.

"Good thing we went last, huh?" Adam stood. He moved carefully to prevent his weak knees from buckling. "That was amazing."

"It was, huh?" Elliot brought his lips to Adam's. "You know why?"

"Why?"

"Because you didn't question yourself this time." Elliot kissed his lips, a quick peck. "You didn't worry, you didn't hold back, you did what you always wanted to do, the way you always wanted to do it. You fulfilled your fantasy and you don't have any guilt or regret. It's like you're really free now, and it feels damn good. Doesn't it?"

Adam returned the kiss, only his was passionate and thorough. He tasted and savored Elliot's tongue and lips. Kissing a man—Elliot—the way he had always wanted to do. Elliot was right. It felt amazing and there was absolutely no guilt.

Adam emerged shirtless from the steamy bathroom to a room full of stares. "What?"

Everyone dropped their gazes, going back to what they were doing before he emerged. Everyone except Dylan.

"This?" Dylan pointed to the bathroom. "We don't have time for this. We took our little break, now it's time to get back to business, man."

Tyler interrupted. "I fed your dog, by the way. Hope you guys don't mind."

Adam nodded, glancing at a shirtless Elliot as he exited the bathroom with strands of his damp hair stuck to his forehead, lips dark red, nearly bruised but attractive from the rough kisses. Elliot went to the bed where Titan stirred, and petted the injured dog's head.

"I fed him a little," Tyler went on. "He kinda ... snapped at me like—"

The sound of a person clearing his throat came from the speakers near the door, cutting Tyler off mid-sentence.

The male voice demanded, "*Stand. For it's time for our daily dose of the Star Spangled Banner. Honor our country by singing along ...*" then the male voice broke out into song. "*Oh, say can you see ... by the dawn's early light, what so proudly we hailed at the twilight's last gleaming ...*" The voice paused and a maniacal laugh followed. Seemingly uncontrollable laughter eerily filled the room.

Adam looked to Elliot, wide-eyed and nearly speechless. Elliot looked back, probably realizing the same thing. The mysterious voice wasn't from a stranger. It wasn't from Petersen, the prophet imposter, either. The voice belonged to the man who helped build the compound and who had helped them escape the very same place ... Mason Dresden.

CHAPTER NINE

Down Below

"Mason?" Dylan shook his head. "The guy that led you out of this place? What the hell is he doing on the P.A. system?"

Adam nervously ran his hands through his damp hair. "Don't know." Mason had mentioned wanting to do a better job running the compound than the leader. Had he finally got his chance? If so, was the compound's vacancies part of his leadership?

Mira slid to the edge of the bed. Her hands visibly shook. "So what does this mean?"

"This means we're fucked," Dylan said with a growl in his voice.

"No, not really." Elliot went to the closet and took a couple of white tank T-shirts that were hanging on wooden clothes hangers. "If Mason is in control, or at least able to access the P.A. system, then maybe he can help us get to the radio."

"What makes you think he would want to help us?" Adam took one of the clean T-shirts from Elliot.

"Well, why wouldn't he?" Elliot looked into Adam's eyes.

"The last we know of Mason, he was trying to take over and replace the prophet." Adam pulled the tight shirt over his head and down over his torso. "Looks like he's got his wish."

"Yeah, but he knows us." Elliot mimicked Adam and slid the T-shirt on. "He helped us once. Maybe he'll help us again."

Dylan scoffed. "Don't always assume it will be that easy, man."

Mira cleared her throat. "Well, what if it is? Maybe he will understand."

Silence stilled the room.

Finally, Tyler stepped forward. He looked confident, as if acting as the deciding factor. His thin arms crossed his chest. "I say we give Mason a chance."

Dylan shook his head. "If Mason was bent on getting help wouldn't he have done it already?"

"The main door is open. Maybe he opened it, right?" Tyler shrugged. "Maybe he let everyone go."

"We don't know that for sure," Adam said. "We don't know anything. There may not be people on the top floor but there sure are people down here. And the red lights?"

"Right." Elliot nodded. "So what do we do?" He looked at each blank face.

"I guess the only thing we *can* do is make our way down." Adam glanced at the slight grin on Tyler's face. "Stay armed and alert, but approach him like old friends."

"We're not friends." Elliot cocked an eyebrow. "That's one thing I know for sure."

"We'll approach him that way though." Adam picked up his pack.

Mira stood. "Well, what about the Eugene or Petersen guy? The prophet or whoever? Where is he?"

"His name's Petersen," Adam said.

Elliot gasped. "What if they're working together? No, Mason tried to kill him."

Adam shook his head. "What if he's dead?" Everyone paused and watched him, probably waiting for his explanation. "Remember, I blindly shot at him? I could've hit him. I don't know."

"What?" Mira backed away. "Whoa. You shot somebody? And you say *we're* untrustworthy?"

"It was either us or them." Adam bowed his head, unable making eye contact. "Not sure if it hit or missed, but..." He adjusted the pack's strap on his shoulder. What if he *had* killed Petersen? He never thought he would take someone's life. Even if it was in self-defense, it'll never escape his conscience.

Elliot rubbed Adam's shoulder and sighed. "We'll stay armed and alert, and approach him like we're old friends. There's no reason he shouldn't trust us. We're just looking for help. He's gotta understand."

Adam nodded and walked away.

"Uh," Mira started. "What about the dog?"

Elliot slapped his own thigh. "Come on, Titan. Let's go." The dog stood and huffed out a quiet bark, then hopped off the bed and ran to Elliot. "He's coming with us."

"Alright." Dylan picked up his makeshift blade of rusted and twisted steel. "You ready?"

Everyone in the room quickly prepared and quietly followed Adam out of the room.

Resembling the silence, darkness crept through the hall like its own entity, occupying every nook and cranny the red light couldn't reach. Together, they snuck down the long hall with their eyes locked onto the red hue emitting from the main room.

Elliot listened for the sounds of heavy footsteps, voices or any noise that warned of others in the vicinity, but heard nothing. Quietly, they headed toward the stairwell, following each other in single file. Everyone gripped and raised their individual weapons, prepared to fight if need be.

Titan followed alongside Elliot just as quietly.

Finally, entering the main room, Adam looked back over his shoulder and pressed his forefinger to his lips, reminding them to be quiet. He then put a hand up, and with his best sign language, he pointed to his eyes and then toward Pod 6. Elliot guessed he meant for them to stay put while he took a peek down that hall. It would make sense to assume the guards of the second floor resided in Pod 6, because that's where guards and enforcers had stayed on the top floor. Adam would know all about it, being one of them once.

Everyone waited as Adam cautiously placed one foot before the other, creeping by the hallway of Pod 2, 3 and 4, and on past Pod 5. As he crossed each hall, he looked down them like a paranoid animal trying to escape its hunter. Just before making it to Pod 6, he flattened himself against the smooth wall and sidestepped closer toward the opening. He turned his head to look down the sixth corridor and sighed, visibly relaxing. He came away from the wall and waved them on.

Elliot nodded and gestured for Mira, Dylan and Tyler to go ahead. He watched them as they all tiptoed and glided along toward the staircase. Titan followed. Each one looked down each hall as they went by, just as Adam had done, probably out of instinct.

Elliot followed. He watched Adam stand awkwardly close to the debris near the stairwell door, holding it open wide enough for everyone to squeeze through quickly and effortlessly.

Elliot continued beyond Pod 5, when a metallic *click* from down the hall stopped him in his tracks. His head quickly jerked to look at the silhouette in his peripheral. A small, dark-haired lady stood in the center of the hall, wearing what could have been a white gown that appeared red due to the well-spaced red lights. The lady stood frozen. Her stillness reminded him of something supernatural, paranormal or otherwise unearthly. Thoughts of popular campfire stories and old urban legends went through his mind. He shuddered. For a few seconds they watched each other.

"Elliot?" Adam whispered.

Elliot turned to acknowledge Adam and quickly spun back to face the woman. She took a step back, pivoted, and disappeared into the impression in the wall where the door to a room was located. A split second later, the sound of her slamming her door echoed throughout the floor. Finally, Elliot moved. He ran to the door of the stairwell and slipped inside. Adam quickly followed, and they joined the others in their descent.

Fifteen minutes went by before they approached the third floor landing. Their cautious and quiet tactic cost them most of their time but provided them safety from detection during their descent. The metal door was the only thing that separated them from whatever roamed the third level main room.

Adam peered over his shoulder at the group. "Ready? When they all lifted their weapons, Adam opened the door. A loud metallic whine sounded throughout the stairwell and main room, and beyond the door resembled the top two floors, minus rust and corrode. Nothing in the red lit room startled him as he had imagined, so Adam led the group down the Pod 6 hall where Petersen's room was located. The large, dull metal door to the room was feet ahead.

Finally, Adam stood in front of the barrier that prevented him from simply stepping into Petersen's homey room; the metal door. He lifted his hand to the door handle and Dylan batted it away.

"What are you doing?" Dylan whispered, anger carried in his tone. "What if he's not alone? What if he has enforcers or whoever with him?"

"What do you want me to do, knock?" Adam allowed his sarcasm to match Dylan's tone.

"Yeah." Dylan nodded, voice low. "We're approaching him as friends not trespassers, remember?"

"If only you and your crew had done the same when meeting us." Adam smirked and turned the door handle anyway. "It's locked. Looks like we're doing it your way after all." He knocked softly on the metal, and glanced back over his shoulder at Elliot who had the gun hidden in the back of his pants under his shirt.

Elliot nodded, understanding Adam's subliminal message. *Stay alert.*

"Who's there?" a low panicked voice came from the other side of the door.

Was that Mason or Petersen?

"We need help," Adam answered through the barrier.

"No help here. Keep moving."

"Mason? Mason, you gotta help us." Adam tried the door handle again. "We walked for hours to get here. Don't turn us away."

Dylan slowly lifted his weapon, readying himself. The rusty, jagged edge of the blade rose between them. Adam pushed the weapon back down and shook his head.

"Am I speaking to Adam?" Intrigued carried in Mason's voice.

Adam grinned. "It's me."

"Who's with you?" There was a pause.

Adam cleared his throat, stalling while determining how much he should reveal. "Elliot's here and a few of our ... friends. We need help."

Mason snorted. "Why'd you come back? You wanted out, you got out, and now you're back. What sort of help are you looking for, anyway?"

Elliot stepped forward. "We ran out of food and medicine." It was silent for a second, while they waited for a response. Then Elliot continued, "Why did *you* come back?"

"Ah, personal reasons." Mason chuckled. His laugh resembled a mix between a sly fox and a drunken hyena. "If you need food and meds you know where to find them. What do you need me for?"

Adam pressed his palms to the cold steel and bowed his head. "We can't get to the food. The elevator's not working. Is the power down or something?"

"Something like that," Mason said.

"Can we come in so we can figure out what to do next?" Elliot asked.

"Who do you think I am?" Mason snickered. "The guy who was in this room before me made the stupid mistake of opening the door. *Stupid* is not one of my traits."

"Come on, Mason," Elliot pleaded. "We're out of food and meds, and we just want to get the hell out of here. There're some guards or somebody following us. We need to call for rescue and get some help out here."

"Ah, Elliot," Mason sighed. "I missed you, buddy."

Adam curiously looked to Elliot.

"Yeah?" The awkward look on Elliot's face probably mimicked the look on Adam's. "I—I missed you too?"

"Oh, come on." Mason chuckled. "I was being sarcastic. And I know you all too well. You don't miss me."

"You helped us get out of here, Mason." Elliot hit the door out of anger and probably a bit of embarrassment. "Now enough with the games. Help us again."

"How is opening this door gonna help you, Elliot? How is opening the door going to bring help?"

Elliot sighed. "The radio. We want to try to send out an SOS or something."

"SOS?" Mason snorted. "Look at you, trying to sound all smart and stuff. Good for you, finding your way back inside and all, but I'm not opening this door."

"Mason, please. We need your help," Adam pleaded. "We only want to reach outside help through the radio. Please."

Silence filled the hall.

A few seconds later, the doorknob jiggled. "Well ... since you asked nicely," Mason said. Adam grinned at Elliot and backed away from the door. Dylan lifted the blade again, preparing for anything. Then the fox-hyena chuckle came through the door again. "Are you really waiting for me to open this door? You guys really *do* think I'm stupid."

Adam growled in frustration. "We're gonna have to find another way."

Mason tapped the door, demanding attention. "I'll help you make a wise decision and warn you that accompanying me in this lavish room is my best bud. A gun. So don't do anything you'll regret."

Elliot stepped toward the door, mouth inches from the steel. "Mason, you gotta help us. There's a huge cat up on the first level that attacked us, we're hungry—"

"Not my problem," Mason interrupted. "Hungry? Everybody's so hungry." He snickered. "You sound like Petersen. And I don't care if goddamned Sasquatch is upstairs, you're not coming in, Elliot. So just give up."

Elliot scoffed. "You know, I knew you were as much of an asshole as you are a murderer. I don't know why I thought you'd help us."

"I've given you guys enough help." A loud bang came from Mason's side of the door, the sound vibrated the door as much as his angry voice would have if it could. "I helped you both get out of here. It's not my fault you came back. Not my problem either. Now leave me alone."

Adam walked away from the door and farther down the hall. What else could he do? There was no way to get to the food storage or the radio, and nowhere else to go but sit around in Mason's old room and wait for those enforcers, or whoever they were, to find them and do who knows what to them. Then it hit him. "Elliot?" he called out, excitement in his tone.

Elliot appeared by his side along with the rest of the crew. "What is it?" Titan, too, stood in the semicircle they formed.

Adam lowered his voice so only those near him could hear. "You catch what Mason said? When you mentioned being hungry, he mentioned Petersen."

"Yeah." Elliot narrowed his eyes. "So?"

"So Petersen isn't dead." Adam looked down the hall toward the stairwell. "Mason's starving him. Revenge for when Petersen tried to starve Mason by locking him up."

Elliot's eyes widened in sudden realization. "Petersen's in the jail cells."

Dylan rubbed his temple. "Wait. What? Where're the jail cells?"

Adam headed toward the stairwell. "The bottom floor."

Elliot jogged to catch up. "Wait, wait, wait. We can't get inside without a key."

Adam paused. "Well, then we're gonna have to go get one."

CHAPTER TEN

Surprises

Elliot pushed open the door to the second floor. He lifted the gun as he shimmied through the mattresses and broken bedframes that slumped against it as a barricade. Silently, he walked through the main room toward Pod 6. The darkness still lingered, the eerie red glow still casted creepy shadows in every corner, and the chill in the atmosphere was much more apparent.

While the group went ahead, Mira and Titan waited by the stairwell entrance as planned, keeping a watchful eye on any perceived threat, and simultaneously staying out of direct danger. Adam moved ahead, carefully leading them down the quiet hall. Elliot followed closely behind, keeping his ears open and his eyes peeled for anything out of the ordinary, like footsteps, moving shadows, or the peculiar apparition.

Doors lined the hall every few feet or so in their recessed areas in the wall, resembling the front porch of a home.

"Where did the people with the boots go?" Elliot whispered to Adam.

"Don't know. Probably in these rooms."

"I guess we can knock on the doors," Elliot suggested. "Explain who we are and get a key. Or tell them we're from below on to third level and need a key."

Dylan shook his head. "Sounds good and all, but what if these people just want to be left alone? Then what?"

Suddenly, a scream and a bark startled them.

Elliot's grip tightened on the gun as he ran back down the hall toward Mira and Titan, fully aware that the firearm only contained two bullets. He turned the corner and came to an abrupt halt. Before him stood the woman in the white dress. This time, she appeared about ten feet away, holding a shotgun with both hands, aiming it directly at Mira and Titan.

"Whoa, whoa, wait!" Elliot put his gun down on the floor before him and raised his hands. "No one's gotta get hurt."

The woman nervously pointed the gun at him. "That's right. Now get outta here."

Adam, Dylan and Tyler approached from behind him with their weapons in hand, but lowered to their sides. The woman fumbled to properly handle the shotgun, managed and lifted it higher, aiming at their heads. Elliot dropped his hands to his sides, nearly giving up until Adam stepped beside him, grabbed his hand, and squeezed gently before letting go.

"You're not gonna hurt us," Adam said softly. "And we're not here to hurt you. We're just looking for some help."

"Find it somewhere else." The woman's voice shook as she spoke, as did her shotgun. "Please, just leave."

"We need food." Elliot raised his open palms before him, silently assuring her that he meant no harm. "We're trying to get to the food and call for help from the radio."

"There's no more food and it sounds like some nut job already got to the radio." She grunted and lifted the gun slightly. "Now get outta here."

"We'll go." Adam took one step forward. "Just tell us where the enforcers are. They can probably help us."

Her eyes widened. "You know about enforcers? Do you stay here in the compound?"

"We used to, but we got out of here," Elliot said. "This place isn't safe, especially now. You can come with us."

"I may look crazy but I'm not," she said. "Just leave me alone. Please?"

"Okay, alright." Adam nodded. "We'll find another way to use the eleva—"

Titan barked viciously and growled, interrupting him. However, it wasn't the woman who he growled at. He snarled and bared his teeth at Adam.

"Titan?" Elliot slapped his own thigh. "Calm down, Titan."

The dog rushed forward, stopping just a couple of feet in front of Adam, who backed up a bit, bracing himself for an attack.

"Titan, stop!" Elliot demanded, but the mutt continued to growl at Adam.

"What the hell is wrong with him?" Adam moved closer to Elliot and Titan leapt forward. All sixty pounds jumped up onto Adam, making him stumble backward. Titan's jaw clamped around Adam's forearm, and his canine teeth sunk into his flesh. "Fuck."

Mira gasped as commotion ensued.

"Titan, no." Elliot wrapped his arms around the dog's ribs. "Stop. Let go, Titan." However, the dog flailed his head, trying to rip flesh from Adam's arm. Adam yanked his arm, dragging Titan along the floor as he struggled to pull his arm from the dog's powerful jaws.

Dylan took a stance and lifted his blade. "Move, Elliot."

"No," Elliot kneeled behind the dog as Adam bent forward. He struggled to hold the dog around the belly with one arm and around the neck with the other. Elliot squeezed Titan's neck between his forearm and bicep, adding pressure until the dog went limp.

Adam pulled his arm from Titan's relaxed jaw and placed his hand over wounds to stop the bleeding. "He's never attacked like that before."

"Something's wrong with him." Elliot put his ear to the dog's chest, listening for a heartbeat. Titan's heartbeat quickened. Satisfied,

Elliot stood, picked up his handgun, placed it in the back of his waistband, and rushed to Adam's side. "Let me see."

Adam removed his palm to reveal several small but deep puncture wounds where Titan's teeth sank in, and a few small defensive wounds on the fingers of his good hand. The wounds bled but not as much as he had expected. Elliot took off his pack and searched for gauze anyway.

Adam examined his own hand. "Didn't know my fingers were cut."

Elliot scoffed. "I'm surprised you still have fingers or arms left, the way your luck's been going."

"Someone must be looking out for you." Adam looked at Elliot.

"Looking out for *me?*"

Adam dipped his head. "Instead of putting you through more than you can handle, they're throwing me the challenges. I'd die before I let anything happen to you. So I wouldn't change a thing." He winked.

Elliot forced a brief smile. "Thank you, Adam, but I don't want you to die for me. I don't want you to die at all."

Adam nodded. "Titan's been through as much hell as the rest of us."

Dylan moved in to take a look at the wound. "Maybe that fight with the cat messed your dog's head up."

Elliot wrapped Adam's arm in a gauze bandage. "We're almost out of supplies." Suddenly he remembered the woman with the shotgun. He looked toward her but she was gone. "Hey, where'd that woman go?"

"She ran down that hall," Mira said, pointing down the hall to Pod 6.

"Shit." Dylan glanced down the hall. "She's going to get those enforcer guys." He went to Mira's side. "You okay?"

She bobbed her head. "I'm fine."

"We need to go, guys." Dylan went to the barricaded door. "Now."

"I'm getting Titan," Elliot said, and swooped Titan into his arms.

Dylan glared. "That dog is messed up. You want to bring it even after it tried to bite Tyler earlier and just attacked your boy?"

"Whatever's wrong with him, I'm not leaving him here to rot." Elliot balanced the limp dog in his arms. "I don't leave behind those I love." He quickly glanced to Adam then dropped his gaze sheepishly.

The woman appeared from around the corner, holding the shotgun in both hands and angling it at Adam. "Don't do anything stupid, okay?"

Adam nodded.

Suddenly, the sound of heavy booted footsteps from Pod 6 took their attention. From the hall appeared four men in enforcer uniforms—dark blue coveralls with the word enforcer embroidered over the left breast; a belt with handcuffs, pepper spray and a baton attached to it; and black knee high combat boots—the complete ensemble.

One of the enforcers came forward. "We don't want any trouble. Okay?"

"Neither do we." Adam shrugged. "We're trying to get rescue out here for us and some food. That's all."

"Rescue? The enforcer chuckled. "The rest of us have already given up on that, but we'll help you. What do you need?"

Adam looked to Elliot, hope in his eyes. Excitedly he said, "We need access to the elevator, the storage room, and the control room for the radio."

"The power's been funky lately so the elevator has been out," the enforcer said. "We stocked up on food weeks ago when all hell broke loose. So we haven't been able to use the elevators since then. We don't know where the radio controls are, we don't even know who's taken over the damned P.A. system. All we know is that we need to stay here and keep safe. That's been our only mission lately." He handed Adam a set of three brass keys. "You take these and get the hell off of our floor and don't come back. You here? That's all we ask."

Adam took the keys and nodded. "Thanks."

Elliot smirked, remembering when Dylan had mentioned things wouldn't be so easy.

CHAPTER ELEVEN

Answers

In bold black letters, the sign on the door ordered: Keep Out. Authorized Personnel Only. Adam inserted the key into the lock anyway. Upon opening the door, a horrible stench hit his nostrils, nearly gagging him. A loud *whoosh* reverberated off the concrete walls. Compared to what it used to sound like when Elliot had been held inside, it was much quieter. His eyes immediately focused on the back of the room to two large barred cells. A lone light bulb shined above one of the cells while it hung from the electrical cord it was attached to. Had he taken a glimpse into a serial killer's dungeon?

A man lay sprawled out on the dusty floor of the second cell.

"Hey," Adam called out, entering the room and inching closer to the cell. Everyone followed him closely. A chill crept down his spine due to the cold and eerie atmosphere, however, he kept most of his attention and gaze on the occupied cell. "Hey? You okay?"

The man rolled over to his side and grunted. A layer of greasy dirt caked his face, hair and clothes, but from what Adam could make out through the grime, the man resembled Petersen. He spoke but his words were muffled. The closer Adam got, the more he could see the man's features. His short, salt and pepper hair, the tight clusters of wrinkles around his mouth and eyes, the oversized tunic draping his frame, all helped confirm his identity.

"Petersen?" Adam gripped the bars, peering through them.

Petersen lifted a hand toward him. "Water," he whispered. His eyes were low, his movements slow and weakly. "Drink."

Adam looked to Elliot and nodded. Elliot then placed Titan into Dylan's arms and took his bottle of water from his pack. He handed Petersen the bottle through the bars.

Petersen gripped a bar and pulled himself up to a sitting position. As soon as he did, a strong whiff of ammoniated urine took Adam off guard. Petersen drank the contents of the bottle fast, gulping and spilling some of the water down his lightly bearded chin.

Dylan looked down at Titan in his arms. "What do you want me to do with this dog?"

"You can lay him down," Elliot said, keeping his eyes on Petersen.

Once Petersen emptied the bottle, he passed it to Adam through the bars. "I needed that."

Adam stared, watching closely, barely blinking and not showing much emotion. Petersen's condition brought thoughts of an unkempt child to mind. Except unlike an innocent child, Adam felt no sympathy. "Did Mason do this to you?"

"Yes." Petersen coughed, clearing his throat of phlegm. "Can't remember how long—" he suddenly clenched his extended stomach and spewed forth most of the water he'd just consumed. A puddle of the rancid liquid spread out before him and pooled underneath him where he sat on the uneven concrete. "Let me out."

"Can't do that." Adam crossed his arms over his broad chest. "You killed our friend and tried to kill us. Remember that?"

Petersen looked to Elliot. "I was doing what I had to do in order to protect—"

"Don't wanna hear it." Adam knelt to Petersen's eyelevel. "In fact, the only thing I *wanna* hear from you right now is how to get to the radio controls."

"Power's in emergency mode." He backed into the corner and rested against the bars. "Only certain generators are running. I did that to keep unauthorized people, like you, from accessing unauthorized places."

"Well, how do we get the power back up?" Adam took his pack off and sat it beside him. Still, the detached expression on his face. "And how do we send out a distress signal?"

"It's radio, not Morse code. You just ask for help." Petersen eyed the pack. "No one's going to hear you though. It won't matter."

Adam kept the no-nonsense look. "Answers."

"You want answers?" Petersen sighed, grabbing his shoulder where blood had collected and dried. "Answers."

Tyler's feet slid along the floor as he moved closer to the bars. "You locked people in this underground bunker? Why? And where are they now?"

Petersen coughed, again clearing his throat. "There was chaos, I had to shut down some of the generators to keep people from—"

Adam huffed impatiently. "—to keep people from accessing unauthorized places. We know."

"Shutting down generators compromised my award winning air filtration system," Petersen continued between languid breaths and multiple sighs. "People were having trouble breathing or were afraid that the toxic air from outside was going to somehow enter and cause more problems, so they wanted out. They panicked. Circulated airflow had to be better than stifled toxic air, at least that's what they believed. It was utter chaos, thanks to you two, but they got what they wanted."

Elliot scoffed after the sarcastic comment. "They're all probably still alive because of us. The stuff falling from the sky can't harm you unless you ingest it. They might believe your lies about the toxins killing the animals and pets, but we know the truth." He glanced to Titan.

"The truth?" Petersen flashed a crooked grin.

"We already heard the recordings," Adam said. "The recordings on the mini CDs? A scientist from one of the other compounds said the ash is not harmful."

"That scientist then reported his original findings were wrong." Petersen held the lopsided grin on his oily, dirt caked face. "In fact, the toxins are so potent, it damages the nerves in your extremities first..."

Adam frowned and briefly glanced down at his own fingertips. "Then what?"

"Then," Petersen continued. "Then the brain has trouble recognizing danger, then the person has bouts of sudden violent outbursts, then *permanent* nerve damage to the tips of extremities like ears, fingertips, toes, lips ..." He paused and stared at Adam, a slight grin on his bruised lips. "Someone affected?"

Tyler looked to Titan who still lay on the chipped concrete floor. "Can all that happen to dogs too?"

Petersen chuckled, grabbing his chest. "But you all claimed I didn't know the future."

Titan had been left outside during Adam and Elliot's stay in the compound. He was exposed to the material more than Adam or Elliot. Weeks more. Poor dog. Adam was first to manage the fallen substance when investigating it during their first stay at Arrowhead hospital. He went out into the stuff looking for spray painted R's when Elliot's leg infection prevented them from walking long distances.

Was he next to act out violently like Titan had?

Petersen coughed. "Proper medical treatment can heal the dog. But it'll need medical attention sooner than later."

"That's what we're trying to do." Adam gripped the bars. "We just need to know how."

A moment went by where no one said a thing, and only waited, watching Petersen improve his posture while he sat in the corner of his cell. The brief silence in the darkened room made the mechanical noises that surrounded them grow louder. Or so it seemed. "Do you understand humans are the most valuable resource we waste?" Petersen looked to Tyler and his stunned expression. Tyler shrugged and Petersen continued, "We're not utilizing our full potential because of our emotions, greed, and arrogance."

Adam sneered. "What does that have to do with us and getting help?"

"Imagine how many young scientists, mathematicians, and scholars this country could have if higher education was available for free," Petersen said. "Instead of making higher education readily available, we'd rather charge ridiculous fees, keeping most of this country from quickly advancing.

"Telsa and Edison were just two of the geniuses on this planet who could've worked together to change this world forever, to turn this world on its head with inventions and breakthroughs, but instead, one of them was set on sabotaging the other. Arrogance, greed, a waste. An absolute waste."

Elliot shook his head, a look of disgust on his face. "So what are you trying to tell us, that you are one of those geniuses who tried to save the world? By luring helpless people here to make them your slaves? You're a sick, egotistical monster. That's not genius."

Petersen coughed up a dry, wheezy chuckle. "The North Korean leaders are evil, oppressing their people, raging war on a country at their weakest hour. The leaders of the child armies of Uganda are evil, all those innocent children forced to kill. That's evil. Not me. I'm a man with honest intentions." When Elliot snorted he continued, "The only way to get funding and save all those lives was to come up with a way to give the wealthy something in return for their money. We provided their replicated homes, comfort and service. The only way to save everyone else, the non-privileged, was to provide them a place to live for a contribution ... their service. That's what kept the compound functioning, that's what keeps the world functioning. Without contributing, the world might as well stop spinning. Everyone wants something in return. Everyone. And in a time where money is insignificant, service becomes the most valuable. Now that's effectively utilizing human resources."

"You made us think we had to live in filth," Adam said through clenched teeth. "You were making us eat slop while everyone below had steak and beer."

"I thought you understood, Adam." Petersen slouched lower, eyes blinking slowly. "We needed to instill that illusion in order for everything to run smoothly. No phones, no luxury, even the brass keys gave in to the illusion. If you ran around with keycards instead of brass keys, people would naturally start expecting things."

Elliot shook his head. "Expecting things to be easier, right? Like wondering why there were no elevators to get up and down all those stairs, or easier ways to communicate between floors. Or even questioning if what you said about the sun always being hidden behind black clouds, or everyone's pets dying from the falling toxic flakes, was true."

"Call me what you want." Petersen looked to Tyler, Mira and Dylan when he spoke. "I'm not evil."

Adam pulled his bag closer, stealing the attention. "How do we get help to us?" He stuck his hand in his pack and pulled out a bottle half filled with water.

"Help's not coming, Adam." Petersen reached between the bars, holding out his hand. "I need another drink."

Adam stared at him. Again the serious unemotional expression on his face. "How do we get help to us?"

"America's too busy fighting a war and protecting those who really need help and protection." Petersen looked to Elliot. "You were forgotten. You all were forgotten at the bottom of the government's to-do list. Even the American Red Cross says 'screw you.' I'm the only one who can help you now."

Dylan crossed his brawny arms over his chest. "Not much help being locked up down here."

Adam lifted the bottle of water. "You can help by telling us how to call for rescue."

"I told you, Adam. Help is not coming." Petersen stared at him without blinking.

"Because of the U.S. war with North Korea?" Tyler asked, eyes narrow with curiosity.

"That's right." Petersen grinned. "Now, all we have is each other."

Adam looked over his shoulder at Elliot, who had anger written all over his face from his dipped eyebrows and the deep wrinkles in between them. "Elliot, we need to talk." Adam stood and went to the corner of the room where it was more private. Elliot followed. Using the roaring sound coming from the oversized pipes to conceal his voice from the crew, Adam cleared his throat and lifted his palms.

Elliot confusingly stared at Adam's hands. "What's wrong?"

Further in the room, Tyler immediately claimed attention by talking about Nikola Tesla's life and inventions. Adam seized the moment. He stared into Elliot's eyes and Elliot ominously stared back, waiting. Adam sighed. "I can barely feel my fingertips."

"What?" Elliot placed his own hands onto Adam's, touching his palms and running his fingers down Adam's narrow digits. "Are you sure? I mean, he has to be lying about the toxins, right?"

Adam shook his head. "My fingers have been numb for a while. I noticed it a little after meeting *those* guys." Adam glanced to the crew who were still listening to Tyler's enthusiastic speech.

"Shit, Adam." Elliot moved closer, but held Adam's hands tighter. "First, Titan. Now, you? You think it's gonna get worse like he said? You going to turn crazy violent and have permanent damage? You think it's gonna happen to all of us?"

"I don't know." Adam dropped his gaze to the floor. "I hope not. All I know is that we need to get help and medical attention. Real medical attention. Fast."

"What if he's right about the war?" Elliot bit his bottom lip nervously. "I mean, what if we're fucked?"

"It's weird, really." Adam shrugged. "He knows about what's going on outside the compound, the state?"

"The radio, right? He was getting information from out there, so that means we can send information back, like we had hoped."

"One thing I've learned through this whole crazy experience is that nothing is impossible." Adam looked down at their interlaced fingers. "Nothing keeps us down, no matter what's thrown at us. You know?" Tyler's voice grew louder as he became more excited. Adam cleared his throat. "You still think he looks like your ex-boyfriend?"

Elliot's eyes cut to Tyler. "I guess. But who cares about *him?* I'm worried about you and Titan. What if we don't get help in time or at all?" Elliot gulped. His jaw tensed and his Adam's apple shifted. "I can't lose you, Adam. I can't."

Adam smiled, relieved. "I'm not going anywhere. Just as you promised me you weren't ever leaving my side, I'm promising you. I won't give up on you, on us. You're too special."

Elliot sighed "You know, I believe you. I really do, but if we don't get you and Titan treated soon ..."

"We're gonna get help. Okay? Don't let it cross your mind that something bad might happen to us. You're strong and smart. Remember that. Never forget that. You know not to let those doubts slow us down."

Elliot sheepishly looked at their clamped hands. "If I didn't know any better I would think you have some serious feelings for me. You know, with all that you're talking about."

Adam wasn't good at expressing his feelings, or at least that's how he used to be. He used to blatantly refuse to acknowledge them, believing that if he didn't think about his feelings and how uncomfortable they made him, then they didn't exist. It felt simpler then, to just put his feelings aside, especially the negative ones. But now...

Adam cleared his throat. "You remember earlier, after our shower, when I told you how amazing it was being with you like that again? You thought it was because I didn't hold back, because I did what I always wanted to do?"

"Yeah." Elliot nodded.

"That was partly true." Adam cleared his throat again. "The other reason why it felt amazing was because ... Well, I think it was love I was feeling." That wasn't as difficult to say as it would've been for the old Adam. A sense of relief flooded his chest and he felt a weight lift.

Small dimples on Elliot's cheek formed as he smiled. He leaned forward until their foreheads met. Neither spoke for a few seconds, and for those seconds it felt like they were the only ones in the room. Never mind the dark, smelly, eerie environment. Elliot squeezed his hand and nodded against his forehead. "Okay, what's the plan?"

CHAPTER TWELVE

A Losing Battle

Adam dangled the set of three brass keys from his fingers.

Petersen's eyes lit up. "Getting me out of here will be the best thing you've ever done."

Adam tucked the keys back into his pocket. "I don't want to hear anything about Tesla, Edison, or North Korea. All I need is for you to tell me where the radio controls are and how to call out for help. That's it."

"I'll take you to them." Petersen nodded, excitement making him more energetic than before as he attempted to stand.

"No." Adam lifted his pack from the floor, slung it over his shoulder, and pulled the strap across his chest to secure it. "Tell us what we need to know, we'll go check it out. If I'm satisfied, we'll let you go. That simple."

"Okay." Petersen sat.

"But, if I'm not satisfied," Adam continued. "You stay down here and rot." The look on everyone's face told him he might've been too cruel with his threat, but even so, no one questioned him. If anything, Adam was being very generous with his offer.

"You want me to believe you will return to let me out once you have what you want?" Petersen sneered, doubt in his eyes.

Dylan wore a face littered with anger lines. Tyler bit his bottom lip and rocked on his toes. Mira stood with her arms crossed over her chest, mimicking Dylan. "Tyler and Mira will stay with you," Adam said. "And we *will* be back for them."

"Whoa, whoa, whoa." Dylan shook his head and stepped forward. "What's this? Were you gonna run this by us?"

"No one worry." Adam pointed to the door of the room. "That door will be locked. Tyler and Mira will have their weapons."

"It's alright," Mira said. "Whatever we have to do to get out of this city I'll do it. Anyway, Tyler will be with me."

Tyler nodded, agreeing. "Like Mira said, whatever we have to do."

"The electrical power panels are in my room on the third floor. You know where my room is, Adam." Petersen grunted and gripped his injured shoulder. "But you don't need the electricity on in order to operate the radio. It has its own power supply near the broadcast transmitter. It's located in the storage room, inside the freezer. But you will need the electricity in full power mode to use the elevator."

Adam wondered if Petersen knew that Mason had taken over his room. Trying to get inside the room with Mason occupying it would be damn near impossible. What other options did they have? There had to be another way. "How do we get to the storage without power?"

Petersen sighed. "No clue."

Adam's voice rose and carried a menacing tone. "Do you want out of this piss-smelling cell? Remember, I have no problem letting you rot down here."

Petersen threw his hands up in a lazy shrug. "What do you want me to—?"

"Getting the full electricity to come back on is not gonna happen," Adam said, interrupting. "So how do we get—?"

"Through the elevator," Petersen said, also interrupting. Anger carried in his voice as well. "That's the only way to the storage. The only way from inside, at least."

Adam was already aware of the second entrance through the mining tunnel, which hadn't been much help. He pointed to Mira and

Tyler. "Stay here. Be safe. Look out for Titan. We should be back soon." When they nodded, he gestured to Elliot and Dylan and he left the room.

Out on the landing, Adam locked the door to the room, appreciating the quietness of the stairwell. He sighed, eyes on Elliot's. Elliot, although quiet and ready to follow Adam into Hell if that's what they needed to do, looked more worried than determined. He could barely stand still as if he was anxious to get going. The way Elliot kept glancing at Adam's hands gave away his intensions. His fear that Adam would suffer permanent nerve damage or turn into something similar to a vicious wild animal ready to attack, fueled him.

Adam gingerly caressed the nape of Elliot's neck and pulled him forward. He rested his forehead against Elliot's, and for a split second, they both were at peace. It was as if Elliot's breaths began to match his, and their heartbeats synchronized.

Adam closed his eyes, foreheads still connected. "You ready?"

"I'm ready," Elliot whispered.

"Come on." Adam stepped back, separating their bodies. "Let's go." He shot Elliot a reassuring smile, looked to Dylan who had been patiently waiting, and began a steady paced jog up the concrete stairs.

Every couple of minutes, Adam would glance behind him to make sure Elliot and Dylan were keeping up. After passing the third floor, their ascent slowed bit by bit. They continued to make progress, but their legs were tiring rather quickly. Each step became harder and harder to take, every breath became more and more labored, but eventually they were at the second floor landing.

Out of breath and tired, Adam sat on the top step. "It feels like we've been up and down these stairs a dozen times."

"We have." Elliot chuckled. "If only the damned elevator worked."

Dylan rested against the wall and scoffed. "If only we had enough food in our system to fuel us. We look like a bunch of unhealthy old men right now."

Adam stood and went to the wall where the elevator door would have recessed into the wall had the power been on. He pushed the red glowing LED light to call the elevator, and like he imagined, nothing happened. He knocked on the wall, listening to the hollow sounds behind the thin concrete.

Dylan appeared beside him, makeshift blade still in hand. "What's going on?"

Adam held his palm out, gesturing for Dylan's blade. "It's about time we use these damn things, huh?" Dylan handed over the large metal weapon and stepped back. Adam swung the blade, hitting the wall and chipping off a piece of concrete. He swung again, but again only small chips of the hard material broke off.

"Here, watch out," Dylan warned. He stepped back a few feet and ran forward, kicking the wall next to the chipped marks. When the area produced a long thin crack across it, Adam and Elliot looked at each other, surprised.

Adam took his cue from Dylan and handed the blade to Elliot. Together, they continued to kick the wall, alternating their kicks. Elliot stayed out of the way, keeping to the stairwell, looking out for any surprise interruptions or dangers.

Finally, Adam's foot broke through the cracked concrete, pushing a huge chunk back to the emptiness behind the wall.

Dylan looked in the dark hole. "What the fuck?" He scrambled to get his flashlight from his pack and shine the light through the wall into the darkness. Elliot sat the blade down and helped Adam remove pieces of the broken concrete from the wall, until it was large enough to allow their bodies to slip through. But before entering, they all examined the dark shaft. Two thick, braided cables stretched the length of the shaft, probably connecting to the lift somewhere below or above. What was most interesting, was how a second, separate shaft continued to the left.

Dylan shined the light down the sideways shaft and lit up the walls of the empty channel. Far at the end were railings, cylindrical pipes and other ridged parts that led up the second shaft.

"That's our way to the storage," Elliot said, looking toward the second vertical shaft. "Looks like we're gonna have to get in there and climb." He reached behind him to make sure the gun was still nicely tucked in his waistband.

Dylan's eyebrows raised. "How far up is it?"

"Don't know." Adam shrugged. The last time they had to climb up to the storage room, the elevator cart had took them most of the way before the power shut down.

Adam climbed in first, careful to hold on to some of the ridges on the side of the darkened space. He cautiously shifted his body and weight toward the landing to the left. With one foot on the metal works connected to the shaft wall, and the other foot pointed toward the landing, he jumped and landed successfully. The momentum of his body threw him forward, but he balanced nicely.

Dylan's flashlight lit up most of the area, making their attempt to safely breech the shaft much easier.

Elliot went next. He mimicked Adam almost precisely with every action. Even landing the jump nearly perfectly. Adam pulled Elliot toward him with one hand, giving him a brief hug that translated to a job well done.

Before Dylan climbed through, he tossed the flashlight to Elliot, and then copied their exact moves to land safely.

Elliot shined the light down the cramped space, following what looked like a pair of rail tracks as they led to the barrier at the end, where it went straight up. What interested Adam the most about the shaft was the elaborate setup. Directly above them, connected to two steal, braided cords was some sort of device. At close examination, the device looked like a metal sheath attachment that would somehow connect to the cart as soon as the cart made the sideways transition and appeared underneath the sheath, helping it lift smoothly and effortlessly. The technology the compound had hidden within and behind its façade fascinated Adam.

Farther up the shaft, about twenty feet, a red light glowed from the storage room and blinked on and off steadily.

"Is that it up there?" Dylan pointed, his burly arm erect and his lightly stubble covered neck exposed as he looked up.

"That's it." Adam gripped the side of the shaft, testing the strength of the metal cylinders and ridges with his weight.

"We're climbing up there?" Dylan scoffed. "I don't do heights, man."

Elliot pulled Dylan's shoulder, turning Dylan to face him. "I don't go back into places where I'm not wanted alongside the man who pointed a gun at our face, but—"

Dylan smacked his lips. "Are you really bringing that up again?"

"But," Elliot continued. "I want to get the hell out of here. So I do what I have to. Without complaints."

Dylan sighed, running his palm over his face. "Okay, look. We're gonna have to bury the hatchet once and for all. I'm sorry for pointing a gun in you guys' face and trying to rob you. No excuses. It wasn't right. It won't happen again. Cool?"

When Elliot glanced to Adam, Adam nodded. "Fine," Elliot said and held out his hand.

Dylan shook firmly. "Alright. Let's do this."

Adam started the climb. Elliot placed the flashlight as securely as possible in his pocket and he and Dylan followed.

"This seems like a long way up," Dylan said as he climbed. "And down."

"It's not as bad as it looks." Adam knew the more one thought about the height, the more it seemed to increase. "It's all in your head."

Dylan scoffed. "You're seriously trying to tell me that this isn't a far climb?"

Adam paused and looked down into the darkness at Dylan's silhouette. "You climbed the equivalent of a refrigerator. We have about six refrigerators to go." He continued to climb using his leg muscles to push him up while his arm muscles kept him balanced.

Dylan chuckled. "I don't know what kind of mind game you're trying to play with me, but this is a far climb. Period."

It took a while to reach the top. Mostly because it acquired a lot of energy, coordination and balance to ascent a ninety-degree climb which wasn't meant to be scaled. It reminded Adam of those rock climbing walls people ascent for fun, however, minus the fun.

Once at the top, Adam pulled himself over the ledge and into the large storage room. The red blinking light placed over the lone metal door poorly lighted the immediate area, while the momentary darkness bathed the room in that familiar eeriness. He kneeled to help Elliot and Dylan over the edge.

One glance at the metal door and its mangled strike plate, Dylan asked, "Is that the door from outside in the tunnel?"

"Yeah." Elliot nodded while retrieving the flashlight from his pocket. He shined it at the door, lighting up the door handle in a bright white beam.

That door had originally led to their freedom. Adam would never forget it. He quickly replayed the vivid scene in his head. He envisioned the elevator door opening and Petersen standing there, pointing the gun at them. Because of Petersen, Anita's body still lay just outside the door, waiting for a proper burial and justice.

"Let's keep moving." Adam headed for the large, walk-in freezer at the end of the oversized room. He was all too familiar with the storage room and thought he knew where to look and what to expect.

However, as they went by shelf after shelf and dozens of aisles, there was there was no longer any food, drinks or supplies stocked. Most of the shelves were empty or not far from it. Some canned and dried foods were still on some shelves. Some had been toppled over and spilled in the aisle. Passing more empty shelves, Adam continued toward the freezer.

Dylan paused to put some of the food into his pack. He knelt to open his pack. "I imagined there was more food, huh?"

Adam ignored him and kept moving. Every few seconds, the well-placed red lights went out, bathing them in what would be utter darkness if it wasn't for Elliot's flashlight, which gave them the sufficient light they needed.

Beside the walk-in freezer hung a metal shelf where a few large meat hooks and other tools were stored. Still, it looked like many of the tools were missing or out of place. Whoever ransacked the storage room nearly took everything. The enforcers they had encountered on the second level mentioned stocking up on food. Were they responsible?

Adam turned the large handle on the solid steel door, which required a quick pull to open. The heavy door moved slowly on its hinges. The worst part of the freezer was that it wasn't cold inside, and the odor upon opening it nearly gagged him.

"What's that smell?" Elliot grimaced, and shined the light into the large room.

To Adam's surprise, there were large slabs of beef and lamb meat hanging from hooks. The meat lined the walls and hung in rows in the center of the large freezer. Most of it was rotten and dripping putrid liquid, as none of it was frozen and might not have been frozen for a long time. The horrendous smell would be forever burned into his memory.

Adam pressed his lips tightly together, afraid of opening them and tasting the foulness in the air. That's when he realized the sensation in his lips were gone. He put his fingers just below his bottom lip to test how far the numbness traveled.

"What's wrong?" Elliot stared at Adam's lips and fingers with a strange look in his eye.

Adam quickly dropped his hand to his side, but it didn't keep Elliot from staring. "I'm fine. Let's go." He gestured for Elliot to enter first, since he had the light source. Elliot turned his body to the side to better maneuver between the foul smelling pieces of hanging meat. Adam did the same, slowly making their way to the back where the radio transmitter was supposed to be. Hopefully, Elliot wouldn't question him about the lack of sensation in his fingertips or lips. He didn't have it in him to reassure Elliot when he himself wasn't sure of the fate of his own health. Curiously, he pinched his earlobe—

"Oh, my God!" Elliot yelled out from a few feet ahead. "Oh, my... I can't do this. I can't." He quickly turned around, nearly slamming into Adam.

Adam stopped him from fleeing by grabbing his shoulders. "What is it?"

"There's a body up there." The look of horror in Elliot's eyes told Adam that Elliot had not mistaken.

"Dead?" Adam paused, impatiently reading Elliot's body language.

"That's probably half of what we're smelling." Elliot grabbed his stomach and dry heaved.

"Give me the flashlight." Adam took it in hand. "You go out there with Dylan. Keep watch."

As if on cue, Dylan called out, "What smells like that?"

Elliot left Adam alone in the freezer, but before he could investigate the body, static broke out from speakers located somewhere in the storage room.

The sound of Mason's nervous laugh echoed throughout the room, demanding their attention.

"Elliot..." Mason sang, holding out the note in a mocking tone. *"Adam... I had hoped you two wouldn't cause any trouble. But my experience, and the facts, tell me that it's too late for hoping. You two lovebirds have really pissed me off."* He sighed, exhaling loudly. *"It's a shame too. We could've just ended this as fellow toughies. You know, friends. Now I*

gotta clean up your fucking mess." Silence followed and then the static ceased.

Adam peered behind him through the hanging carcasses to Elliot.

"Damn it!" Elliot ran his palm through his hair and paced in front of the open freezer. "He knows what we're up to."

"So?" Dylan shrugged.

"He's gonna try to stop us."

Dylan shook his head, anger lines formed on his forehead. "We'll just kick his ass."

Elliot sighed. "Weren't you the one who said not to expect things to be so easy?"

"It's one guy," Dylan reminded them. "We can take one guy."

Elliot continued pacing. "Mason is not stupid. He doesn't do stupid things. He's not just gonna roam the compound by himself, waiting for someone to kick his ass."

Adam shined the light between rows of rotted animal meat. "Then we better hurry." He pointed the beam to the back of the room, as he squeezed through wet, dripping slabs. The smell and the humidity seemed to get more intense the farther back he went, and he soon saw why.

Lying on the floor underneath a sopping slab of meat was the body of what looked like a woman. If it wasn't for her large breasts and long dark hair he wouldn't have been able to determine her gender. It seemed obvious to Adam that her death wasn't an accident. He wasn't sure how she died just from looking at her, but the way she lay tucked near a corner, behind dozens of hanging carcasses, must've meant someone tried to conceal her body.

As much as he wanted answers to the many questions that suddenly popped into his mind, he knew he had to hurry. He shined the light at a second metal door farther back to his right. The air entering his lungs felt heavy with humidity, laboring his breathing. He swallowed hard, suppressing the sudden sensation to vomit.

Once at the door, he turned the handle. It was locked, but when he pulled it hard enough, he realized how flimsy it was and how easily it would open if he had a tool or ... the key. He reached into his pocket and pulled out the set of brass keys. The first and second key wouldn't budge the lock, but the third key turned the lock effortlessly. He had always wondered what the third key of the set was for. One opened the jail cells, another allowed for elevator access to the storage room, and the third key, apparently, was for access to the radio transmitter. Why would Petersen give enforcers the key to the radio transmitter? Would controlling radio broadcasts eventually be a part of their "evolving"?

Adam's mind searched for possible answers while he opened the door to the small walk-in closet. It was nearly the size of a standard linen closet. But lining the walls were panels with buttons, switches, levers and dials, and a couple of meters with immobile needles.

What the hell?

He had no idea where to start, what to push, what not to push, or what to do at all. For a few long seconds he just stared at the controls. Then it came to him. Power. He needed to power on. How would he know if or when the power was on?

"Adam?" Elliot called. "Everything alright? We gotta hurry."

"Don't know what the hell I'm doing." Adam clicked the largest switch and a thin metal plate popped open like the mirror over the bathroom sink. Glued behind it was a paper with instructions and labels on it, showing exactly what each button and dial was for.

The first thing he had to do was turn on the power. The words power control caught his attention but there were two buttons under the label, one read: *main.* The other read: *auto.* Something labeled the *AC Voltmeter* grabbed his attention. The little needle didn't move, but after pressing several buttons the needle jumped.

He had no idea what he was doing, but unexpectedly a female voice spewed from small speakers embedded in the front panel near the controls. Hearing the voice told him that something had worked.

Listening to the stranger made Adam's heart skip a beat with excitement, but the panic in the woman's voice quickly made him wary.

"Hello? Anybody hear me? We need help. Can you hear me?"

CHAPTER THIRTEEN

Separation

Elliot continued to pace near the freezer door. "We have to do something. Now. Mason's gonna do something to fuck this up. I can feel it."

Dylan hoisted his pack on his back more securely. "Mason's really bad news, huh?"

"He killed the real Eugene for Petersen." Elliot nodded.

"A murderer too. Nice." Sarcasm carried on Dylan's tongue. "Well, what would he want with you guys? I mean, how is calling for help 'causing trouble'?"

"It's throwing a wrench in whatever plans he had, that's for sure."

"Maybe he knows you guys were talking to that Petersen guy."

"Shit!" Elliot stopped in his tracks.

"I mean, the guy did say Mason locked him down there. Maybe because we talked to Petersen we're fucking up Mason's plans or something."

"You're right." Elliot impatiently looked inside the dark freezer and back toward the glow of white light. "He's probably gonna go down there to the cells and see Mira and Tyler. Or he might come up here. Shit, he's probably already in route. Damn it."

"He better not touch Mira," Dylan threatened with a stern look on his face. "That girl is special. I'd die before I let another man put his hands on her."

Elliot looked into the freezer toward the direction of the decomposing body. It sickened him knowing he had to face yet another death. His stomach couldn't handle it and neither could his heart.

Too much loss.

"You know," Dylan continued. "I met her just a couple weeks after the earthquakes. I knew she was, you know, damaged. She wanted to give up, but I promised her I would take care of her. Her father is a mechanic down in Texas, and she loves that man. You know, a daddy's girl. Talking about her dad was all she used to do. I told her I was a mechanic too, thinking it would help her open up to me."

"You're not?" It had never crossed Elliot's mind to question what a person said they did for a living. After thinking more about it, he felt a little dumb. He and Adam had done exactly that when finding the compound. Adam had done the exact same thing when meeting him. Even Petersen had lied about who he was. It was almost as if everyone despised being who they really were. As if being their true selves was like confronting a nasty demon that they would rather hide from.

"I worked at a call center." Dylan sighed. "But I couldn't tell her that. She needed someone she could relate to, someone strong, smart, someone who could protect her. Someone like her dad."

Elliot nodded. He understood, all too well, how someone could lie about their occupation. Especially the reasons Adam had for lying about once being an exotic dancer. Shame? Guilt? Dissatisfaction? All the above? "So, you know nothing about radio transmitters?"

Dylan slowly shook his head. "I tried to tell you."

"Elliot?" Adam called out from the back of the freezer. "Hey. You guys gotta come see this."

As much as Elliot tried to ignore the harsh smell in the room, he couldn't stand to see any more dead bodies. "I don't think I can."

"I'm getting a message," Adam said excitedly. "Come listen."

Elliot entered the freezer first, and Dylan trailed. He followed the glow from Adam's flashlight and the sound of voices. The volume was low but the message was clear.

"We need help," the woman's voice started. *"We've been trapped down here for weeks and we need help. Um, I don't know ... My name is Adriana Belle. And we're in the Refuge Inc. complex in Vegas, and— Is anybody out there?"*

Then a mysterious male voice sounded through the radio speakers. *"Maybe you have to push* this *first."* Sounds of random clicking filled the atmosphere. *"I don't know. Hopefully, we did it. Here, try again."*

"Hello?" The woman's panicked voice returned. *"This is Adriana Belle. We need help. Everybody's gone crazy. There's fighting and, and ... killing, and we need help. Please. Anybody?"*

"What's happening?" Elliot had chosen to breathe through his mouth to prevent getting nauseous from the smell. "They need help. What do we do?"

Adam shook his head and pointed the flashlight to the counting timer. "It's a recording." He pressed a button on the panel and a mini CD ejected. Was the mini CD like the one Adam mentioned he had found under the bathroom tile in Mason's room? "This was recorded. Don't know when or if they ever got help, but—"

"Did you send any messages out?" Elliot asked.

"Don't know how." Adam shrugged. "And from the sound of it, those people didn't know how either. They probably just got lucky. Probably never even knew they actually sent out a message."

"They needed to give more information," Dylan said. "Where exactly are they? What do they look like? How long have they been trapped? I mean, that kind of information helps to find their exact location."

"Exactly." The excitement in Adam's eyes stole Elliot's attention more than the putrid smell, for only a brief moment. Adam pressed a couple of buttons and then spoke into a tiny grate on the side of the panel that Elliot assumed housed the microphone. "This is Adam Weber. I'm an Arizona survivor here in Refuge Inc.'s underground compound. I am one of many survivors here in the South Mountain compound of Phoenix, Arizona, located near Seventh Avenue and Roosevelt Rd..."

Elliot smiled, excited and confident at the same time. Maybe they will get a response.

"Now *that's* helpful information." Dylan looked to Elliot. "You guys really know this compound, huh?"

"It's been a long journey for us," Elliot said.

Adam continued speaking into the grate, "We're just one of six compounds. We've been out here for many weeks, waiting for rescue. If anyone is out there, please send help. There are hundreds of survivors in need of food, water, and medical assistance. Please. People are dying out here."

Elliot gripped Adam's shoulder. "That was good. Did you send it?"

"I don't know." Adam shrugged. "I followed the instructions on the back of that panel, so I think it broadcasted the message. But..."

"But what?" Elliot cocked his head.

"But listen to this." Adam pressed a couple of buttons on the control board and a male voice spoke.

"I regret to inform the U.S. citizens that we are currently under attack by North Korean militants and their allies—"

Dylan nearly gasped. "That's the message we heard on the car radio. The one we were telling you guys about."

"—those countries have taken advantage of the asteroid that impacted the west coast of the United States more than two months ago, and have forced the U.S. government to postpone any survivor retrieval efforts until the rest of the country is safe and secure."

"This doesn't sound right." Adam scratched his head. "It just doesn't make any sense. Survivor retrieval efforts? So they know there're survivors?"

"Maybe he meant, efforts to see *if* there are survivors." Elliot shrugged.

"Look," Dylan swallowed and grimaced, "I can't stay in here anymore. I'll pass out. Plus, I need to get back to Mira."

Elliot nodded. "We need to hurry. Is there anything I can do?"

Adam pressed another button, a look of curiosity on flashed across his face when another Mini CD ejected from the slot beneath the previous one. "That message was also a recording." He looked to Elliot.

"Yeah? And?" Elliot wasn't quite sure why Adam had that worried look on his face, but he knew it wasn't good news that would follow.

"That message is a recording that was being broadcasted." Adam flipped the panel, revealing a sheet of paper glued behind it. He tapped the words labeling the slot as: Outgoing Transmission. The slot above it, where they had found the recording of the woman, Adriana Belle, was an Incoming Transmission Recorder. "This compound was sending out that message."

"How would they know what the government was doing?" Elliot asked.

"My point exactly." Adam shined the light at the panel controls.

"You think they got that info from one of the other compounds, or an unaffected city?"

"Probably." Adam stared at the panel blankly. "Didn't the voice sound a little like Petersen?"

Before Elliot could answer, commotion broke out behind them in the storage room. They all heard the noise, because they each looked at one another and then behind them simultaneously. Elliot quickly made his way back through the slabs of meat and out of the freezer.

He took a sigh of relief when he saw Mira helping Tyler crawl out of the elevator shaft and into the room. The smell of decaying flesh didn't bother him as much as watching Tyler kneel and reach down into the elevator shaft. The red lights poorly lit glimpses of the scene, as every few seconds the lights would go out, leaving them in utter darkness. When they came on again, they illuminated a different part of the unbelievable scene that unfolded before him.

As far as he was from the elevator, Elliot still knew what Tyler was reaching down for. Or rather, *who.*

Petersen emerged from the shaft. He flopped over the edge without Tyler's assistance, and sprawled out on the concrete landing, arms outstretched.

Elliot yelled into the freezer to Adam, "They let Petersen out. They're all here." *How the hell did they get him out of his cell without a key and why?* His heartbeat suddenly raced as fast as his mind searched for answers, trying to make sense of what was happening and, at the same time, orchestrating his next move. Adam and Dylan quickly appeared by his side.

"Mira?" Dylan called out.

Mira's head turned in their direction. The lights went out for a few seconds. They came back on in the midst of her walking the vast space toward them. She peered back over her shoulder at the elevator where another pair of hands suddenly gripped the edge of the hole. The lights went out again. When they came back on, Mason had nearly pulled himself up over the edge and into the room. Then the lights blinked off, blanketing them in seconds of intense anxiety.

"Mira!" Dylan shouted, terror in his voice.

The lights brought Mira back into view just as she started to run toward them. Seeing the panic in her body language made Elliot apprehensive. He knew what they were about to encounter wasn't good. He looked past her to Mason, who struggled to stand and balance while his arm rose, gun in hand.

The lights went off and a loud *pop* rattled throughout the room. Elliot ducked out of instinct and two sparks lit up the darkness, nearly simultaneous with the *pop*. One spark lit up the area near Mason, and the other by a shelf near Mira. She screamed and the lights came on. She stopped running—momentum causing her to take a few more lazy steps—and she lifted her hands above her head, surrendering. She was much closer. Adam shined the flashlight at her, and Elliot made out the fear in her eyes.

Elliot reached behind him to grab the handgun he had tucked in his waistband, but Adam's arm snaked around his back, stopping him.

In his ear, Adam whispered, "Stay nonthreatening. Don't give him a reason to shoot."

Mason had just tried to shoot Mira, but Elliot took Adam's advice and stood motionless, attempting to look as nonthreatening as possible.

It wasn't until Elliot saw Dylan grab Mira around her waist, that he realized Dylan had been making his way to her the whole time. They quickly embraced as Dylan pulled her into one of the aisles and disappeared behind a shelf.

Mason kept the gun pointed at Elliot and Adam. "Why are you making me do this?" He looked to Tyler and gestured for him to walk toward them, then briefly looked down at Petersen and gave him a swift kick between his legs. Petersen grunted loudly then groaned, rolling over on the floor with both hands shielding his groin. "Get up, you bastard," Mason ordered, and kicked Petersen again, this time in his back. Petersen struggled to stand, and instead, crawled down the long walkway behind Tyler. He didn't speak a word, the only sound he made were loud grunts.

Tyler lifted his hands over his head, palms up, as he slowly walked a couple of feet ahead of Mason and Petersen in the direction of the freezer. Adam shined the flashlight beam on Mason, the light glimmered off of the silver cross encrusted in sparkling diamonds that hung around his neck.

"Mason, put the gun down," Adam warned. He switched off the flashlight and grabbed Elliot's hand.

"I really don't want to do this." Mason groaned and sighed, pouting. "I really didn't think I'll see you two again, and now look what you went and done. You fucked everything up."

Adam's gently tugged Elliot's hand as he slowly pulled Elliot toward the nearest aisle. "We're done. We're out of your way. Just let us leave."

"Done?" Mason frowned. "What do you mean, *done?* What did you do?" He looked beyond them and into the freezer, moving closer. "What's that smell, huh?"

"It's rotten meat," Adam said.

"And a body," Elliot added, in defense of his and Adam's innocence. "But we don't have nothing to do with that. All we wanted was to call for help and get the hell outta here."

Petersen collapsed on the ground near the aisle where Mira and Dylan had disappeared. He was visibly exhausted and weak, probably tired from climbing the elevator shaft without the proper fuel. "We need everyone to come back," he said.

Mason yelled to Tyler, "Stop walking." He kicked Petersen again. "Shut up, old prophet. *I* need them back. This has nothing to do with you anymore. Give up and die already."

"I told you," Petersen took a breath, "We can do this together. Like partners. Real partners."

Mason laughed maniacally. "Us? Partners? I'll just end up like your last 'real' partner. Anyway, no one will ever take orders from you again. It's time to pass the torch, old prophet."

Petersen coughed. "What makes you think they'll take orders from *you*, asshole?"

Mason narrowed his eyes and the vein in his neck twitched. "I have a shitload of guys that take orders from me because I supply what they need. "They're on their way as we speak, by the way, so don't try anything stupid. You guys won't get away with it."

Petersen grabbed Mason's ankle. "People will come back. They will." Mason kicked his hand away, but Petersen continued, "I made sure they will come back. We just gotta work together—"

"Touch me again and I'll make you crawl all over this damn compound without kneecaps." Mason sneered. "I promise you." The malicious grin disappeared from his face and now all that displayed on Mason's face was pure evil.

Petersen continued, "I put out a scheduled broadcast, telling people we're their only hope for survival. I made it convincing. They will be back, Mason. They'll come back to us. This doesn't have to be the end all."

Mason looked down into Petersen's pleading eyes. His hollow gaze grew more empty, unconnected, and distant. He placed the gun to Petersen's knee and a brief grin twitched his lips as he pulled the trigger.

CHAPTER FOURTEEN

Letting Go

Petersen's blood-curdling screams filled the entire storage room. Tyler covered his ears with his palms and fell to the concrete floor, eyes wide as he watched Petersen writhe in pain.

Mason exhaled, content sweeping over him through his relaxed facial muscles. "God, that felt good." Adam pulled Elliot by the hand as they attempted to walk around the men toward the elevator. "Where are you lovebirds going? We're not finished."

Elliot's heart thumped so hard he felt it in his throat. He paused, causing Adam to halt as well. Speaking over Petersen's screams of agony, he said, "We're leaving." As much as he tried to pretend he wasn't horrified with Mason's unexpected actions, he knew his fear was probably showing through. He squeezed from every nerve in his body to prevent his terror from exposing him. Even by refusing to react to Petersen's screams, or not acknowledging the crimson liquid which spewed from his knee.

No emotion.

Mason sneered. He had the same look in his eye that he had just seconds ago when pulling the trigger. "I'm not done with you guys yet."

Petersen grunted, loud enough to demand all the attention in the room. "Let them go."

"Let them—?" Mason scoffed. "Just like you begged me to let you go? Just like you let me go when you had me locked up down there in that shit for a cell?" The sarcasm was obvious. "I will always remember when you let Patrice go too. The only person who I ever really trusted. How can I forget?"

With that, Elliot knew exactly what was going on. The entire confrontation was about Mason and Petersen. Whatever Mason's plan was—either to starve Petersen to death for locking him up and killing his beloved accomplice, or to kill Petersen in order to take over the compound, or both—he knew that deep down it had nothing to do with him, Adam or anyone else. And the mention of Patrice reminded him of something else.

"Patrice?" The last time Elliot had heard her name, Mason had told them how Petersen killed her and probably buried her body the way Mason had buried Eugene's. But what if they had tucked her body in the back of the freezer?

"Don't talk about her like you know her," Mason threatened.

Elliot raised his hands, showing he meant no harm, trying desperately not to let his emotions or sudden actions provoke Mason. But he did have a plan. "The body in the freezer? Someone tried to hide a woman's body in there. That's what we're smelling." It could have been Mason who had hid the body in there, Petersen or someone else for that matter. Either way, he had to test out the outcome. And by the looks on their faces, he knew he had said the magic words.

"Did you do it, old prophet?" Mason kicked Petersen again, his entire shoe stomped his ribs. "Did you stow her body in the freezer. I bet you did. You were too busy predicting the future to have anybody dig a hole out there to bury her in, huh? And you were too lazy to do it yourself. Did you offer to pay someone a hundred and sixty thousand dollars, that you don't have, to get rid of her too, huh?"

Petersen growled. "Fuck you, Mason. Fuck you." He laughed. His laugh was soft and throaty and sounded very close to a cry. "She's in there. Right alongside the old, fat, rotted cows where she belongs. Her weapon, the steak knife, is with her too. In her fucking back."

Mason's eyes widened and he pushed past Elliot and Adam and ran toward the freezer, gun still in hand. Elliot looked to Adam and to Tyler who was still sitting on the floor. "Let's go."

Tyler stood and together they ran down the long walkway toward the elevator, Dylan and Mira emerged from an aisle and joined them. They stopped near the elevator shaft when Mason appeared from the freezer. Mason shouted something indiscernible.

Petersen spoke over him, crying out, "Kill me. Just do it. Do it." Their voices combined like a vocal pair of wild animals fighting over a piece of meat.

Then Mason pointed the gun to Petersen's face. For a split second it was silent. As the red light continued to blink on and off, they listened as Petersen's demands suddenly turn to pleading. Then two shots followed and two bright sparks lit the area near Mason and Petersen.

Again it was silent.

"Fuck," Dylan yelled, breaking the silence. "We gotta get the hell outta here." He kneeled near the empty elevator shaft.

"No!' Mason screamed. He drug his feet as he walked closer, aiming the gun in their direction.

Elliot knew now was his only chance. He reached behind him to retrieve the handgun from his pants but it wasn't there. "The gun. It's gone."

"Huh?" Adam looked behind him, then they both looked to Tyler who pointed the gun directly at Elliot. "What the hell are you doing, Tyler?" Adam moved in front of Elliot, shielding him with his own body.

"I wanna stay." Tyler's eyes were big and his hands shook. "Mason, please. I want to stay. I can help you."

Dylan moved forward. "What the hell are you doing, man?"

"I'm surviving." Tyler backed up a bit, keeping space between him and everyone else. "I can't do it out there anymore. I can't keep robbing people for food and—"

Mason chuckled. "But you can rob *my* compound? Storm in here like a savage, like some stray animal, and take *my* food?"

Adam held Elliot's hand even as he continued to shield Elliot. It was comforting to know that Adam would give his life for him, but now that Mason and Tyler had guns, knowing that didn't do much to settle Elliot's nerves. In fact, it hurt his heart. Could he just stand there and allow the death of his best friend to save his own life? No.

Elliot gently pushed Adam aside. "Tyler, don't do this."

Tyler sighed. "I will do anything to stay here. There's food, perfect shelter, hot showers. Did you see the rooms?"

"You'll do anything?" Mason grinned.

Tyler nodded. "Anything."

While the lights continued to blink, creating moments of utter darkness, Mason snorted. "Prove it."

Tyler lifted the gun quickly, with unsteady and fidgety aim.

Elliot put his hands up. "Tyler, please." He looked into the unsure eyes of the man before him. "We all can get out of here and still be safe."

"I don't want to leave," Tyler cried out. "Didn't you hear me?"

Elliot sighed. "Don't you have family? They're probably still out there, waiting for you to come home. Isn't there things you always wanted to do? You still have a chance to do them."

"Shut up, Elliot." Tyler sighed.

Adam took a small step forward. "Tyler, just—"

Dylan quickly launched forward and tackled Mason to the ground, creating an opportunity for them to take Tyler.

"Shit." Tyler rushed forward, pushing Elliot down and out of the way with one hand, and simultaneously hitting Adam in his chest with the butt of the gun in the other hand. The force caused Adam to stumble back several steps toward the elevator shaft until there were no more steps to take.

Adam teetered over the edge of the open elevator shaft, reaching out for something to grip and keep him from falling back into the hole. Just in time, he grabbed ahold of Tyler's arm, stopping him from falling backward into the deep, hollow opening. Tyler used his free hand to grip the wall next to him, to keep them from going over. Elliot grabbed Tyler by the waist, suddenly feeling Adam's weight and struggle. Mira grabbed the back of Elliot's pants, and just as they did before, while helping Dylan out of the crater, they pulled.

But Tyler struggled too, not doing much to assist in Adam's rescue. Elliot looked up into Adam's wide, round eyes. And in what felt like slow motion, Adam's other hand came up to grip Tyler's arm as well. The lights continued to blink on and off. Suddenly, before Adam had a chance to grabbed Tyler's arm with both hands, Tyler twisted his wrist, tugged and jerked it out of Adam's grip almost effortlessly. And just as fast, Adam dropped back into the shaft, arms outstretched as if in one last attempt to grab ahold of Elliot. Then the lights went off.

Due to the weightless pull, Elliot, Mira and Tyler dropped back onto the cold concrete floor. Elliot, stunned by what he just witnessed, pressed his fist into his ribcage as if his heart had just been ripped out and dropped into the pit along with Adam. He lay on the floor which was no longer cold or hard, or anything at all but a part of the growing mass of emptiness around him. Seeing Dylan struggle with Mason, and Tyler take a pounding from Mira's fists, was like viewing a movie on a screen in which he had no urge to watch. He looked up into the blinking red light, nearly numb and unwilling—unable—to move, think, or breathe. All that played through his mind was Adam's arms reaching out to him before disappearing into the darkness.

The commotion around him grew louder and more frantic, snapping him out of his dreamlike state and back to reality. Then an ache in his heart suddenly seized him, the pounding of every beat sent pain like shards of glass through his body. Images of Jess, Anita, Howard and Edna in their final state of being overpowered his thoughts. And now Adam... He let out a guttural yowl in an attempt to stop the agony, and punched the floor beside him in an attempt to feel something other than the fierce grip on his heart. The pain in his fist reassured him that the cold, hard concrete remained beneath him. The bright red liquid that oozed from his knuckles reminded him that he was still alive and still had his own life to defend.

Giving up wasn't an option anymore.

He stood and immediately kicked the gun out of Tyler's hand as he sat, allowing Mira to scream at him, slap him and push him around. Tyler kept his eyes on the elevator shaft all the while, as if waiting for Adam's hands to appear on the edge.

An urge to drop down next to the shaft and peer over the edge gnawed at him, but Elliot knew better. Quickly, he fetched the gun and aimed it at Mason, who still struggled with Dylan over control of the gun. "Mason, let go of the gun or I'll do to you what you did to Petersen."

Mason allowed Dylan to take the gun. "Elliot, it's over." He glanced at the elevator shaft. "It's done."

Elliot couldn't help but to glance at the darkened abyss too. He caught Tyler's sorrowful eyes. And pointed the gun to Tyler instead. "I should've never trusted you. Adam should have never trusted you either." Elliot's voice caught when he said Adam's name but he swallowed and loosened the lump in his throat. He sniffed and wiped away a watery tickle from his chin with his shoulder. "I should toss your ass down there too."

Dylan shook his head. "Elliot, don't."

"I begged you not to hurt us." Elliot cleared his aching throat. "I begged and you still—" His chest burned again. Having the gun in his hand reminded him how easily it was to end his pain, to have it go away instantly as if it never existed. But then he remembered Adam's words: *"We've made it too far to start thinking about giving up now."* However, he couldn't keep himself from envisioning Tyler and Mason's death. Who the hell were they to come into his life and royally fuck it up? He looked to Mason. "We're getting the hell outta here?"

Mason reached into his pocket and pulled out Eugene's keycard. Elliot snatched it from him and examined it. The picture of the old black guy with the rimless glasses was plastered on it near the magnetic strip. Mason sighed. "I picked it up before we escaped. I thought it'll be my way back in."

"So you had this planned the whole time," Elliot said in a matter of fact tone. "I always knew you were a no-good murderer."

"Just leave," Mason said. "It's over, Elliot. This never had anything to do with you guys. You should've never came back. You should've stayed out of my business and none of this would've happen. You would've still had your lover boy and life would've been less shitty. Now look at us?"

Elliot gritted his teeth. "You should shut up now," he warned, and placed the keycard in his pocket. "You already know we can't go through that door. The power's all fucked up." He pointed to the door with the single red light above it and the mangled strike plate, the door they had corrupted trying to break out the first time. "But you're gonna get us out."

"What?" Mason looked to the door.

"Get up," Elliot ordered. "Go find some tools and get started on the door. Hurry. I have enough bullets in this gun to take care of you *and* Tyler." He looked to Tyler. "Go help."

Mason stood. "You really—"

Elliot stepped forward and pressed the barrel of the gun into Mason's temple. "I will do this. If only as a public service."

Tyler quickly began walking, probably not even aware of where he was going but willing to cooperate. Mason turned and headed down the long walkway, passing Petersen—who lay motionless in a crimson puddle that slowly continue to spread under his body—and onward toward the freezer where the tools were located.

Elliot kept the gun on them the entire time while they picked out suitable tools, and even on the way back to the door. When passing Petersen, he didn't focus on the body. He didn't even look at it except out of his peripheral. "Keep moving," he said. "Now get that door open. I'll stand here until I decide to go ahead and pull the trigger."

Tyler sat the tools beside the door and kneeled. "I never killed anybody before." His voice was cracked and low.

"Neither have I but I will if I have to." Elliot stood and waited, watching them pick and prod at the lock. "You didn't have to though."

Tyler looked back over his shoulder. "It just happened so fast—"

Dylan moved forward, pointing his gun. "Don't go there, Tyler. Just open the damn door. I don't know why I let your ass tag along with us. We should have dumped your ass back there at the crater."

With pressure on them, they moved fast, sliding tool after tool in between the latch and the strike plate. Half of the work was already done since the last time they tried to escape through the door. So after a few minutes focused on the lock, finally it popped.

Looks of surprise colored everyone's face when the familiar *clink* sounded throughout the room. Mason pulled the door open. The dark tunnel with a double rail track was there on the other side.

The darkness rushed him like the lonely presence of Death. By now it must have been midday, and the sun would have been shining brighter through the dense clouds. The bright light ahead confirmed it. His chest ached, the pain gripped him deeply and grew more intense as he thought of his companion, his lover, his best friend.

It's not everyday people find someone as special. Hell, it took the end of the world to happen before he felt anything as close to the intense and emotional relationship they had. His heart skipped a beat at the very thought of not seeing, connecting or touching the most important man in his life ever again.

The red light became something he grew used to. It had become part of his experience and struggle. The red light had become part of his existence just as the compound was. Everything he had seen and been through would forever be with him. Forever, meaning the rest of his life.

And thank God, for he had a life to live.

Adam limped through the first floor main room, wondering how long he had been unconscious, and if the large cat still roamed the space. Waking up on top of a stranger in an enforcer uniform wasn't what he had expected when opening his eyes. That must have been what, or who, he had hit on the way down, what had broken his fall and lessened the blow. His labored breathing caused his chest to spasm uncontrollably. His sprained ankle slowed him down considerably. Climbing—or rather, crawling—up the stairs to the first level had tired him out. But nothing was going to keep him from seeing Elliot again.

Not one thing.

Not a broken rib or a twisted ankle. Nothing.

Adam followed a trail of dark rusty-colored paw prints that went toward the large blast door and led to the outside. He must have hit the big cat when he fired at it, and the tracks he followed were from her blood. He didn't hear the feline or see her anywhere as he hobbled through the empty main room. The large paw prints resembled the ones from inside the mining tunnel. Elliot had been wrong about what species the paw prints belonged to, but Elliot was rarely wrong about anything. In fact, Elliot had been right about almost everything.

Elliot was right about Adam's sexuality insecurities, about him using his ex-fiancée as a cover, and he was right about allowing Titan to live. Poor dog. He wished he had the strength to descend all those stairs and rescue the old mutt from the bottom floor, assuming that's where Mason had left him. Elliot and Titan were his family now. The thought of losing that was unbearable, more painful than his injuries.

Adam took another languid step and his foot slid from under him. He crashed to the floor, landing in a puddle of the cat's viscous blood. For a second, it felt good to just lie there on the floor and do nothing but breathe, even if he was in a pool of blood. Doing anything else took too much effort. He sighed and relief swamped him almost euphorically.

He could lie there forever, just let it end, but not before seeing Elliot again. The urge to look into those beautiful, moth-like brown eyes gave him the strength he needed to push himself up and continue. Limping and dragging his aching foot, he forced his body through the large metal door. Looking out through the tunnel archway, and the light at the end of it, already felt victorious. But he kept on, forcing himself to keep moving through the length of the rugged archway and out into the dry desert.

Ash fell as steadily as the northern snow on a cold winter afternoon. Knowing it was toxic didn't stop him from taking a deep breath. Even as sharp pains ravaged his throbbing ribcage, he had to live it. Even if it was his last breath, he had to breathe it.

A sound came from the mountain slope beside him. He turned to see the bright blinking red light of the radio antenna. Its bright light blinked on and off steadily just as the lights in the storage room had. He couldn't help but think of the first time he and Elliot had spotted the antenna light after trekking Phoenix and following the spray painted Rs. They had thought they were saved, that Refuge Inc. and the compound was the start of their relief, of not having to struggle to survive. Boy, were they wrong.

"Adam?" Someone called his name from the dusty mountainside. Excitement filled his heart and emotions took over his body when he recognized the voice.

"Elliot?"

From where the exit to the tunnel was located, Elliot nearly ran down the slope, kicking up dry ash. Mira and Dylan followed closely behind.

In no time at all, Elliot rushed him. He ran up to Adam with a huge, bright smile and arms outstretched. Elliot hugged him as if he were hugging a dear friend. And the feeling wasn't off. His relief resembled that of seeing a good old buddy again after so many years, and just in the nick of time. At the exact moment he needed him.

Adam grunted from the pain in his chest, but he didn't break the embrace.

"Shit, Adam." Elliot separated their bodies. "Is it really you?"

Adam nodded, a grin twitched his lips. "It's me."

"It's been hours and I thought you were dead. I thought that was it." Elliot's voice was filled with so much pain that his words were barely audible.

Adam looked into his eyes, finally seeing the brown beauties he'd been longing for. "I love you, Elliot. I'm never gonna give up on you. Not that easily. But I *am* gonna stay away from heights from now on."

"Damn it, Adam." Elliot's voice hitched and he chuckled, then immediately he pressed his forehead to Adam's and they both held each other, mirroring Dylan and Mira.

Adam sighed. "I told you someone's looking out for you."

Far in the distance the sound of thunder breaking through the clouds took their attention. They all looked in the direction of the noise.

Mira was the first to notice. "Oh, my god. Look!" She pointed and jumped up and down excitedly. "It's a helicopter. It's a freaking helicopter."

Elliot's eyes widened. "We did it? Did we do it?"

Adam knew Elliot was asking if their broadcast had went out. He wasn't sure how a helicopter made it to Phoenix, if they had gotten their message requesting help, or if rescue had already been in motion. He wasn't sure of a lot of things. But there was one thing he was sure of.

"No matter what," Adam whispered into Elliot's ear. "We got each other. That's more than I can ask for."

Epilogue

The greenery surrounding Two Independence Square still took Adam's breath away. It was the complete opposite of Phoenix. The air was more humid, the vegetation greener, the sky clearer. The sun lit up the cluster of manufactured structures beautifully, while he and Elliot looked out of the window of the low rise building.

Elliot rested his head on Adam's shoulder while they gazed beyond the clear glass. "I decided to take Dylan up on his offer. He's proposing beer."

Adam smirked. "I thought you weren't a huge beer drinker?"

Elliot shrugged. "Well..."

Adam chuckled and held Elliot's hands, interlocking their fingers. "I think it's a good idea."

"Luckily there was not really a war, huh?" Elliot scoffed. "Damn Petersen could make people believe anything. Damn fraud."

"One thing I can't believe is how being in the valley, surrounded by mountains was what kept those toxic clouds overhead." Adam shook his head. "Why does Arizona have to be the most mountainous state with the least rainfall?"

"Don't know if that's true." Elliot laughed. "But it's great to know we can joke about it, huh?"

The room door opened and Thelma—a well-dressed woman with auburn hair and dark roots—entered the room. She held the familiar container by its handle. "How was your showers? Food filling you all right?" Her government badge read: Dr. Thelma Rodriguez.

Adam nodded. "Yeah, yeah. Everything was great. We feel great. Right, Elliot?"

Elliot nodded.

She fingered her pen and sat the container onto the wooden table in the middle of the room. "Can I take a look at your fingers, Mr. Weber?"

"Sure." Adam smiled to Elliot and sat in the chair at the table. He slid his chair closer and fanned his fingers out onto the wooden tabletop. "I think the meds are working."

"Well, it will take time, Mr. Weber." The darkened roots near her scalp of wavy red hair reminded him of his ex-fiancée, Jena. Then thoughts of the other Phoenix survivors entered his mind. "We're still waiting on results of several tests, but I think you, Mr. Stewart, and your dog, will be just fine." She smiled, but the smile looked routine, planned. "Speaking of your dog—"

"Titan." Elliot reminded her, mimicking her smile.

She cleared her throat and lengthened her spine. "Speaking of Titan," she continued. "He just received his meds and his meal."

Adam smiled too, briefly. "Good. Now, will Elliot get to see his family soon?"

She ran the blunt end of the pen along Adam's index finger. "Yes, his family is on their way as we speak. You can join them as soon as they arrive, Mr. Stewart. How's this feel?"

"Much better than yesterday." Adam nodded and eyed the container. "Bring anything good in there?"

"Your meds." She set the pen down on top of the table and took the lid off of the plastic container. "I'm sorry for all you and your friends have been through. It must've been absolutely horrific."

Every time he had seen her she had apologized. It was beginning to sound scripted. "You guys found everyone we talked about, right?" He glanced at his hands which were still splayed out on the table. "Mason Dresden? Tyler Dalton? Petersen? All the other people out there."

"Right." She nodded reassuringly. "Mr. Dresden is being held and treated at the criminal facility, we've started the process of charging him for his crimes."

"Good." Adam glanced to Elliot and back to Thelma. "What now?"

"I'm sorry?" She cocked her head.

"What's gonna happen now?"

She smiled again. "Now, let us straighten out this whole mess and you two get some rest, visit your friends and family, eat, or do whatever you want to do." She patted his hand and shot Elliot a smile. "Just remember, we want to get all the facts straight before we go public with any of this."

"Right." Adam nodded. It had become habit to not take everything said and offered at face value. He would've been suspicious of the meds if he initially had the choice to take them. So far, everything seemed legit. However, was his anxiety his intuition, telling him something was wrong, or was it proof that living around untrustworthy people for weeks had heightened his suspicion of strangers?

"Here, I brought you two some water." She lifted the bottles out of her container along with Adam's regular medications and the supplies needed to administer it.

The look in her eye, the fake smile, the small talk, all started to get to him. Maybe it was his gut speaking to him all along.

Elliot stared at her, unblinking. "You're giving off weird vibes."

Her mouth dropped open and she sat back as if he had just insulted her.

Adam looked from her to Elliot, and back to her. Elliot felt the uneasiness too? The more Adam thought about her reaction, the more he realized how offensive Elliot's comment had been. "I'm sorry," he said, "I think he means to ask if you're holding back something. Some information?"

She sat forward and crossed her arms under her breasts. "I was thinking of a way to prepare you two for what you're gonna hear out there in the public."

Elliot narrowed his eyes. "What do you mean?"

Adam frowned. "You came to deliver bad news?" He stood. Disappointment turning to rage in his system. "After what we've been through. There's more?"

"It's over, Mr. Weber." She remained seated, calm. "I promise you, it's over."

"Then what is it?" Adam couldn't contain his anger, the feeling of betrayal, the feeling of being duped. "Say it? Is it Elliot? Is it our health? Is Mason not ever gonna see a courtroom? What is it?"

"Nothing like that." Her voice was low and reassuring. "Believe me, you two have nothing to worry about. But there's a lot of conspiracy theorists rallying out in public, making people believe that our U.S. government allowed the asteroid impact."

"Mason had said you guys tried to destroy it but instead it broke into smaller pieces," Adam said. "Some of you—"

"Not us," she corrected.

"Some NASA scientists knew about the impact and took advantage by building underground compounds, setting up Refuge Inc. to fund the whole thing. All so they could have peace of mind and boss people around. Allowing an impact to happen for greedy reasons, or trying to stop the impact, failing, and then using it for greedy reasons ... It's all conspiracy, right?"

Thelma stood. "How would you feel about this whole conspiracy if you knew what you suffered through was all for the benefit of your children's children or maybe even the future of mankind?"

The what-if game. "Is that a hypothetical scenario?" Adam sneered.

"According to these conspiracy theorists, it's the truth." Thelma repacked the container with all the supplies.

Adam looked to Elliot confused, then back to Thelma. "What about the treatment?"

"We can do this later." She picked up her things and headed for the door. "In the meantime, enjoy your family, each other, and the sunshine." She opened the door, not even looking back.

But Adam was curious. Why would she seem so bothered by the sudden shift in small talk? "Hypothetically speaking, how would what we've been through benefit mankind?"

"I told you, Mr. Weber. You, Mr. Stewart, and everyone you know are safe and will be safe for the rest of your lives. But to answer your question..." Finally, she looked back over her shoulder at them. "Maybe we—they—needed real life post-disaster conditions to learn how to get it right in preparation for the big one in the future. Hypothetically speaking." And she left the room.

The End

COMING SOON

Darkness Eternal

A Refuge Inc. Story

It had been predicted, the catastrophe that would change the world and mankind forever. Surviving what came after was the challenge.

Connor Nichols had been training for the position for years, preparing for an important role as a contra in the Refuge facility, formally known as Refuge Inc. He'd heard strange tales linking the facility to mysterious compounds that had been home to terrible government controversies over a century ago. Tales of botched research efforts that most assumed were urban legends.

Fascinated with the legend, a leader of the facility begins some terrifying experiments of his own, a form of behavioral modification known as evolving.

Connor unknowingly makes himself a target when he gets a little too close to Vince Moore, another contra. Their days of keeping the facility safe and developing a close bond, turns into a battle for survival.

What is Connor to do when the man who dangerously tries to alter his behavior is his partner's father and a trusted leader of the Refuge facility?

ABOUT THE AUTHOR

The author of several books of fiction and fiction with spice, I reside in Queen Creek, Arizona, with my husband, three daughters, and a wild beast I call my imagination.

I'm known for writing erotic romance, mostly in the gay and ménage categories, and recently plunged into writing deep, dark romantic sci-fi with my post-apocalyptic and dystopian series, Refuge Inc.

I love to hear from readers and fellow authors! You can reach me at the addresses below.

LESLIE@LESLIELEESANDERS.COM

WWW.LESLIELEESANDERS.COM

www.ingramcontent.com/pod-product-compliance
Lightning Source LLC
LaVergne TN
LVHW050913080826
845145LV00001B/74

* 9 7 8 0 6 1 5 8 7 3 9 6 1 *